The
MX Book
of
New
Sherlock
Holmes
Stories

Part XL – Further Untold Cases
(1879-1886)

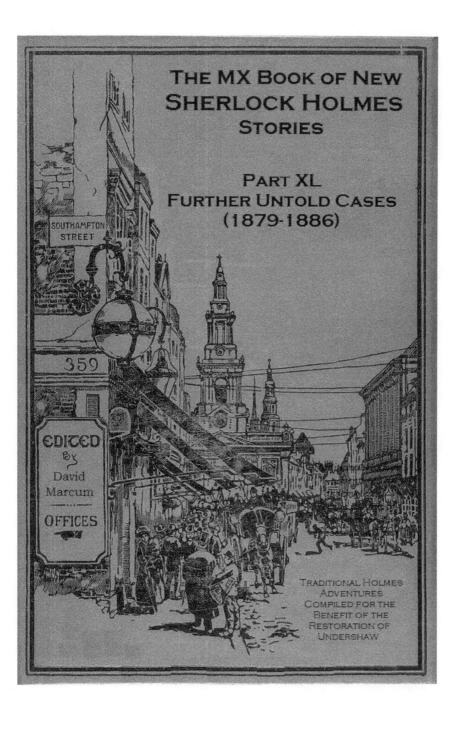

THE MX BOOK OF NEW SHERLOCK HOLMES STORIES

PART XL
FURTHER UNTOLD CASES
(1879-1886)

SOUTHAMPTON STREET

359

EDITED
By
David
Marcum

OFFICES

TRADITIONAL HOLMES
ADVENTURES
COMPILED FOR THE
BENEFIT OF THE
RESTORATION OF
UNDERSHAW

ISBN Hardback 978-1-80424-357-2
ISBN Paperback 978-1-80424-358-9
AUK ePub ISBN 978-1-80424-359-6
AUK PDF ISBN 978-1-80424-360-2

Published in the UK by
MX Publishing
335 Princess Park Manor, Royal Drive,
London, N11 3GX
www.mxpublishing.co.uk

David Marcum can be reached at:
thepapersofsherlockholmes@gmail.com

Cover design by Brian Belanger
www.belangerbooks.com and *www.redbubble.com/people/zhahadun*

Internal Illustrations by Sidney Paget

CONTENTS

Forewords

Adventures

(Continued on the next page . . . .)

(Continued on the next page . . . .)

These additional adventures are contained in

Part XLI: Further Untold Cases
(1877-1892)

Part XLII: Further Untold Cases
(1894-1922)

(Continued on the next page . . . .)

These additional Sherlock Holmes adventures
can be found in the previous volumes of
The MX Book of New Sherlock Holmes Stories

(Continued on the next page . . . .)

(Continued on the next page . . . .)

PART V – Christmas Adventures

(Continued on the next page . . . .)

PART VI – 2017 Annual

(Continued on the next page . . . .)

The Unwelcome Client – Keith Hann
The Tempest of Lyme – David Ruffle
The Problem of the Holy Oil – David Marcum
A Scandal in Serbia – Thomas A. Turley
The Curious Case of Mr. Marconi – Jan Edwards
Mr. Holmes and Dr. Watson Learn to Fly – C. Edward Davis
Die Weisse Frau – Tim Symonds
A Case of Mistaken Identity – Daniel D. Victor

PART VII – Eliminate the Impossible: 1880-1891
Foreword – Lee Child
Foreword – Rand B. Lee
Foreword – Michael Cox
Foreword – Roger Johnson
Foreword – Melissa Farnham
Foreword – David Marcum
No Ghosts Need Apply (A Poem) – Jacquelynn Morris
The Melancholy Methodist – Mark Mower
The Curious Case of the Sweated Horse – Jan Edwards
The Adventure of the Second William Wilson – Daniel D. Victor
The Adventure of the Marchindale Stiletto – James Lovegrove
The Case of the Cursed Clock – Gayle Lange Puhl
The Tranquility of the Morning – Mike Hogan
A Ghost from Christmas Past – Thomas A. Turley
The Blank Photograph – James Moffett
The Adventure of A Rat. – Adrian Middleton
The Adventure of Vanaprastha – Hugh Ashton
The Ghost of Lincoln – Geri Schear
The Manor House Ghost – S. Subramanian
The Case of the Unquiet Grave – John Hall
The Adventure of the Mortal Combat – Jayantika Ganguly
The Last Encore of Quentin Carol – S.F. Bennett
The Case of the Petty Curses – Steven Philip Jones
The Tuttman Gallery – Jim French
The Second Life of Jabez Salt – John Linwood Grant
The Mystery of the Scarab Earrings – Thomas Fortenberry
The Adventure of the Haunted Room – Mike Chinn
The Pharaoh's Curse – Robert V. Stapleton
The Vampire of the Lyceum – Charles Veley and Anna Elliott
The Adventure of the Mind's Eye – Shane Simmons

PART VIII – Eliminate the Impossible: 1892-1905
Foreword – Lee Child
Foreword – Rand B. Lee
Foreword – Michael Cox
Foreword – Roger Johnson
Foreword – Melissa Farnham

(Continued on the next page . . . .)

Part IX – 2018 Annual (1879-1895)

(Continued on the next page . . . .)

(Continued on the next page . . . .)

(Continued on the next page . . . .)

PART XIV: 2019 Annual (1891 -1897)

(Continued on the next page . . . .)

(Continued on the next page . . . .)

(Continued on the next page . . . .)

Part XIX: 2020 Annual (1882-1890)

(Continued on the next page . . . .)

The Adventure of the Matched Set – Peter Coe Verbica
When the Prince First Dined at the Diogenes Club – Sean M. Wright
The Sweetenbury Safe Affair – Tim Gambrell

Part XX: 2020 Annual (1891-1897)
Foreword – John Lescroart
Foreword – Roger Johnson
Foreword – Lizzy Butler
Foreword – Steve Emecz
Foreword – David Marcum
The Sibling (*A Poem*) – Jacquelynn Morris
Blood and Gunpowder – Thomas A. Burns, Jr.
The Atelier of Death – Harry DeMaio
The Adventure of the Beauty Trap – Tracy Revels
A Case of Unfinished Business – Steven Philip Jones
The Case of the S.S. Bokhara – Mark Mower
The Adventure of the American Opera Singer – Deanna Baran
The Keadby Cross – David Marcum
The Adventure at Dead Man's Hole – Stephen Herczeg
The Elusive Mr. Chester – Arthur Hall
The Adventure of Old Black Duffel – Will Murray
The Blood-Spattered Bridge – Gayle Lange Puhl
The Tomorrow Man – S.F. Bennett
The Sweet Science of Bruising – Kevin P. Thornton
The Mystery of Sherlock Holmes – Christopher Todd
The Elusive Mr. Phillimore – Matthew J. Elliott
The Murders in the Maharajah's Railway Carriage – Charles Veley and Anna Elliott
The Ransomed Miracle – I.A. Watson
The Adventure of the Unkind Turn – Robert Perret
The Perplexing X'ing – Sonia Fetherston
The Case of the Short-Sighted Clown – Susan Knight

Part XXI: 2020 Annual (1898-1923)
Foreword – John Lescroart
Foreword – Roger Johnson
Foreword – Lizzy Butler
Foreword – Steve Emecz
Foreword – David Marcum
The Case of the Missing Rhyme (*A Poem*) – Joseph W. Svec III
The Problem of the St. Francis Parish Robbery – R.K. Radek
The Adventure of the Grand Vizier – Arthur Hall
The Mummy's Curse – DJ Tyrer
The Fractured Freemason of Fitzrovia – David L. Leal
The Bleeding Heart – Paula Hammond
The Secret Admirer – Jayantika Ganguly

(Continued on the next page . . . .)

Part XXII: Some More Untold Cases (1877-1887)

(Continued on the next page . . . .)

Part XXIII: Some More Untold Cases (1888-1894)

Part XXIV: Some More Untold Cases (1895-1903)

(Continued on the next page . . . .)

Part XXV: 2021 Annual (1881-1888)

(Continued on the next page . . . .)

(Continued on the next page . . . .)

Part XXVIII: More Christmas Adventures (1869-1888)

(Continued on the next page . . . .)

Part XXIX: More Christmas Adventures (1889-1896)

Part XXX: More Christmas Adventures (1897-1928)

(Continued on the next page . . . .)

The Adventure of the Chained Phantom – J.S. Rowlinson
Santa's Little Elves – Kevin Thornton
The Case of the Holly-Sprig Pudding – Naching T. Kassa
The Canterbury Manifesto – David Marcum
The Case of the Disappearing Beaune – J. Lawrence Matthews
A Price Above Rubies – Jane Rubino
The Intrigue of the Red Christmas – Shane Simmons
The Bitter Gravestones – Chris Chan
The Midnight Mass Murder – Paul Hiscock

Part XXXI: 2022 Annual (1875-1887)
Foreword – Jeffrey Hatcher
Foreword – Roger Johnson
Foreword – Steve Emecz
Foreword – Emma West
Foreword – David Marcum
The Nemesis of Sherlock Holmes (A Poem) – Kelvin I. Jones
The Unsettling Incident of the History Professor's Wife – Sean M. Wright
The Princess Alice Tragedy – John Lawrence
The Adventure of the Amorous Balloonist – I.A. Watson
The Pilkington Case – Kevin Patrick McCann
The Adventure of the Disappointed Lover – Arthur Hall
The Case of the Impressionist Painting – Tim Symonds
The Adventure of the Old Explorer – Tracy J. Revels
Dr. Watson's Dilemma – Susan Knight
The Colonial Exhibition – Hal Glatzer
The Adventure of the Drunken Teetotaler – Thomas A. Burns, Jr.
The Curse of Hollyhock House – Geri Schear
The Sethian Messiah – David Marcum
Dead Man's Hand – Robert Stapleton
The Case of the Wary Maid – Gordon Linzner
The Adventure of the Alexandrian Scroll – David MacGregor
The Case of the Woman at Margate – Terry Golledge
A Question of Innocence – DJ Tyrer
The Grosvenor Square Furniture Van – Terry Golledge
The Adventure of the Veiled Man – Tracy J. Revels
The Disappearance of Dr. Markey – Stephen Herczeg
The Case of the Irish Demonstration – Dan Rowley

Part XXXII: 2022 Annual (1888-1895)
Foreword – Jeffrey Hatcher
Foreword – Roger Johnson
Foreword – Steve Emecz

(Continued on the next page . . . .)

Part XXXIII: 2022 Annual (1896-1919)

(Continued on the next page . . . .)

(Continued on the next page . . . .)

Part XXXVI: "However Improbable . . . ." (1897-1919)

(Continued on the next page . . . .)

(Continued on the next page . . . .)

Part XXXIX: 2023 Annual (1897-1923)

*The following contributors appear
in the companion volumes:*
The MX Book of New Sherlock Holmes Stories
Part XLI – Further Untold Cases (1887-1892)
Part XLII – Further Untold Cases (1894-1922)

The MX Book of New Sherlock Holmes Stories
Further Untold Cases – Parts XL, XLI, and XLII

are dedicated to

Kelvin I. Jones

I first became aware of Kelvin in the early 1980's, when I managed to obtain a number of his expert Holmesian monographs. Little did I know that one day I'd be able to be friends with him (even if we haven't met in person) and that he would continue to contribute so ably. The world – Sherlockian and otherwise – is a richer place because of him.

Editor's Foreword:
Untold Infinite Possibilities
by David Marcum

In 1932, Edith Meiser did an amazing thing: By way of her Sherlock Holmes radio show starring Richard Gordon and Leigh Lovell as Holmes and Watson respectively, she related one of Holmes's *Untold Cases*. I may be wrong – I claim no expertise in Sherlock Holmes radio and film history, other than having a lot of reference books – but I think that this was the first time that anyone had done this – told an *Untold Case* – in any format.

For those who don't know what an *Untold Case* is, or believe that any post-Canonical Holmes adventure is an *Untold Case*, the term refers specifically to those *other* cases that Holmes solved (or some with which he was at least involved) that are mentioned in passing in The Canon. There are around 130 of them, some more famous than others, and – as seen with a few stories in this collection – other Untold Cases are being identified and related all the time. (More about that in a minute.)

I've been collecting and reading and studying Holmes's adventures since 1975, both those known as *The Canon* – those pitifully few sixty tales that came to us by way of the First Literary Agent's desk – and all the others that have been pulled from Watson's Tin Dispatch Box since then. And I'm pretty sure that "The Giant Rat of Sumatra", possibly the most famous of the Untold Cases, was the first one of those that were shared with the public. It was transcribed by Meiser from Watson's notes and broadcast on April 20th (although some sources say June 9th), 1932, and again on July 18th, 1936; and then on March 1st, 1942 (this time with Basil Rathbone as Holmes). Sadly, all of these versions are apparently lost, although I'd dearly love to hear – and read – them! (According to one source shared with me, Meiser's script for "The Giant Rat of Sumatra" is held within the Sherlockian collections at the University of Minnesota, but my attempts to see this – or any of her scripts that are kept there – have been unsuccessful.)

Meiser's "Giant Rat", though the first related Untold Case, wasn't her first post-Canonical tale. After numerous Canonical broadcasts, she approached the Doyle Heirs, who were in a non-litigious mood that week, about doing something different, and she was then allowed to present other Tin Dispatch Box-sourced adventures. The first of these was "The Hindoo in the Wicker Basket", broadcast on January 7th, 1932 (although one source I've seen shows some sort of Holmes *Christmas Carol* on

1

December 23rd, 1931.) During early 1932, there were a few more Canonical broadcasts – "The Yellow Face", "The *Gloria Scott*", and a six-part version of *The Hound*, but there were also a few others that people hadn't heard of before, such as "Murder in the Waxworks", "The Adventure of the Ace of Spades", "The Missing Leonardo da Vinci" – and then "The Giant Rat".

I would give much to hear (or read) some of these lost adventures (although some of the scripts aren't "lost", just hidden away). And of course there are many other cases from the Tin Box out there, also lost, would be just as interesting to read, see, or hear. Meiser wasn't the first to pull non-Canonical adventures from the Tin Box. For instance, not counting parodies, Kowo Films, a German concern, might have been the first, producing nine post-Canonical Holmes films between 1917 and 1919. (Apparently being on the losing side in an ongoing World War couldn't prevent the production of Holmes films by a German company about one of their enemy's greatest heroes.) These were fascinating titles like *The Earthquake Motor*, *The Indian Spider*, and *The Fate of Renate Yongh*. One of them, *The Cardinal's Snuff Box*, might possibly maybe could-have-been the actual first portrayal of an Untold Case – *The Sudden Death of Cardinal Tosca* – but as of now, we cannot know.

Now, assuming that one gives Meiser due credit for being the first to relate an Untold Case (as far as I can tell) with her version of "The Giant Rat of Sumatra", some might be inclined to think that she had staked that one as her own claim, and that there would be no need for someone else to find and publish an alternate version of "The Giant Rat". After all, Meiser had brought it forward first, and there's no reason to suppose that what she presented wasn't perfectly fine. But in truth, there have been lots of versions – all very different indeed – of this particular Untold Case. Over two-dozen of them, in fact, not counting irrelevant parodies, science fiction and fantasy attempts, and versions where the true Holmes is not present.

"The Giant Rat" is mentioned Canonically in "The Sussex Vampire":

> "Matilda Briggs *was not the name of a young woman, Watson,*" *said Holmes in a reminiscent voice.* "*It was a ship which is associated with the giant rat of Sumatra, a story for which the world is not yet prepared.*

That, and the fact that Morrison, Morrison, and Dodd said that Holmes's action in the case of the *Matilda Briggs* was successful, are all we officially know about the Giant Rat. We can speculate a few other things: Morrison, Morrison, and Dodd specialized in the assessment of machinery – and yet they were somehow involved in the matter of the Giant Rat enough to know of Holmes's successful action. The fact that Holmes has to explain that the *Matilda Briggs* was a ship and not a young woman implies that Watson doesn't know about it – and that possibly this case occurred during some period when Watson wasn't involved in Holmes's cases – perhaps before they moved to Baker Street in January 1881, or during a period when Watson was married and living elsewhere. And we know that it was especially serious, and of a nature that might cause panic or with a solution that might stretch credulity. The world is not yet prepared. *The whole world? Not prepared?* That implies something that's seriously disturbing.

Or perhaps someone else might read this short description from "The Sussex Vampire" and interpret it an entirely different way. In fact, many have. Many of the different versions of "The Giant Rat" never even mention involvement of any sort by Morrison, Morrison, and Dodd. Instead of Watson being ignorant of details, all versions involve Watson right alongside Holmes. And he knows about the *Matilda Briggs* – except in some iterations, where the *Matilda Briggs* isn't mentioned at all.

The fact that there are so many versions of "The Giant Rat" might be a source of consternation for some, who think there can only be one, and that all others are simulacrums and distractions of greater or lesser quality. Just as some might think that because Edith Meiser was the first to describe Holmes's connection with the Giant Rat, and therefore no other descriptions are valid, others might prefer a different version. My personal favorite is the late Rick Boyer's *The Giant Rat of Sumatra*, published in 1976, one of those first post-Canonical adventures to ride the initial wave propagated by Nicholas Meyer's *The Seven-Per-Cent Solution* in 1974, beginning a Sherlockian Golden Age that has never faded since.

If I were to decide that my favorite "Giant Rat" by Boyer was the *only* "Giant Rat", I would have cheated myself of over two-dozen other versions, equally good in their own ways, and also any others that have yet to be revealed.

I play *The Game*, wherein Holmes and Watson are recognized as historical figures who lived and died – Yes, they're dead now, and have been for a long time. When doing that, one might be a bit wobbly when trying to figure out how one charmed and famous lifetime and notable career could have included over two-dozen encounters with a Giant Rat. Nearly everyone who has ever lived has never met a single Giant Rat. The easy answer is that these are all different encounters, and there just happened to be a lot of Giant Rat crimes across the decades between when Holmes commenced his career and when he and Watson discussed the Giant Rat in "The Sussex Vampire. It isn't as if Holmes solved the case

3

with a specific set of individuals, places, and circumstances, and then the deck was somehow cosmically reshuffled and the game replayed with the same individuals, places, and circumstances proceeding along different lines, (as were the characters in two Stephen King back-to-back companion novels, *The Regulators* and *Desperation*, both published on the same day in 1996.) The Giant Rat adventure related by Boyer is vastly different than the ones rescued from the Tin Dispatch Box by Paul Gilbert, Hugh Ashton, Amanda Knight, Alan Vanneman, David Stuart Davies, and many others.

And the Giant Rat is just an example, used because it is the Untold Case that has been related in the most versions. There are so many others that have also been told in multiple ways. The peculiar persecution of John Vincent Harden in 1895? Just keep in mind that there were a *lot* of tobacco millionaires in London during that time, all being peculiarly persecuted – but in very different ways – and Watson lumped them in his notes under the catch-all name of *John Vincent Harden*. Huret the Boulevard Assassin? There have been a number of different narratives telling how Holmes caught Huret – all completely different from one another, and all accurate and true and part of *The Great Holmes Tapestry*, that amazing mix of Canonical adventures, serving as the main cables, and the thousands of post-Canonical tales that make up fibers in between that fill in the details and provide all the color and nuance. The explanation for so many Huret narratives? There was a whole nest of Hurets to be rooted out in 1894, and each separate story relates how Holmes did it is just part of the bigger tapestry.

Since Meiser brought us the first Untold Case, there have been many others – far too many to list here. In *The MX Book of New Sherlock Holmes Stories*, we've had several volumes of them. In 2018, we presented Parts XI and XII – *Some Untold Cases*, and then in 2020, Parts XXII, XXIII, and XXIV returned to that theme with *Some More Untold Cases*. In the initial 2018 set, I required contributors to let me know beforehand which Untold Case they were going to choose, so that no one would provide more than one of them, and there would be no duplication. I only made one exception: Nick Cardillo had already signed up to bring us his version of "The Giant Rat" when Ian Dickerson made available the 1944 "Giant Rat" radio script written by Leslie Charteris and Denis Green – Rathbone and Bruce's *second* time telling that story, in a completely different script and investigation from the one by Edith Meiser which had been broadcast two years before. This worked out okay, because the 1944 script was set in the 1880's and included in Part XI, and Nick's story occurred in the 1890's and was in Part XII.

4

For the 2020 set, I had no requirement that anyone had to sign up and reserve an Untold Case. I was happy for people to send whatever Watson recorded, as long as it was traditional and Canonical. This was fortunate, because every story was excellent, even if there were some duplications of Untold Cases. For example, the matter of the Two Coptic Patriarchs occurs on a specific date in July 1898. Three contributors – John Davis, DJ Tyrer, and Harry DeMaio – all told versions of the Two Coptic Patriarchs, and since these books are arranged chronologically, these three stories were all presented side by side. There was no contradiction – they all told about different cases with Two Coptic Patriarchs that came to a head in that moment. (And of course, there have been a number of other narratives about these same Patriarchs in other books. Two, as a matter of fact, were by John Linwood Grant and Séamus Duffy and included in other parts of the MX Anthologies.)

In these new volumes, there are several versions of old intriguing favorites – *The Addleton Tragedy. The Sudden Death of Cardinal Tosca. The Most Repulsive Man. The Paradol Chamber. The Grosvenor Square Furniture Van* – all different, and all wonderful. Strangely, for all that I've mentioned it here, this time no one chose to provide any new revelations about one of the Giant Rats that Holmes faced during his career. But there are a few of Untold Cases described in these volumes by Alan Dimes and Chris Chan (and me) that no one had previously thought to add to the list. (My friend, the late Phil Jones, had a special passion for Untold Cases, and he would have been thrilled to see these.)

If you read Holmes adventures for very long – novels, themed or un-themed collections by one author or many, single magazine stories – chances are that someone will soon be telling you an Untold Case. And with so many of them, and with their mysteriously intriguing but often vague descriptions, one never knows what in what directions they'll jump.

In *The Valley of Fear* and "The Norwood Builder", Holmes used the phrase *"infinite possibilities."* In "Wisteria Lodge" he also used the phrase *"a perfect jungle of possibilities"*, and in "The Six Napoleons" he mentioned that *"There are no limits to the possibilities . . . ."*

Possibilities are what to expect when beginning any new Holmes adventure – reading one or writing one. As I've stated before, these can leap in any direction. One might find a comedy or a tragedy. A police procedural or gothic horror. The story might be set early in Holmes's career, or very late. It could be a city adventure or a country tale. Watson might be the narrator, or it could be Holmes, or someone else, or it might even be related in third person. And it might be long or short, taking just what it takes to tell what happened.

You may have read other versions of some of these Untold Cases before, and you may have favorites, but keep in mind that just because one version occurred in Holmes and Watson's life doesn't mean that it was the *only one* and that another didn't. They're *all* true, and they fit together like a most-intricate and complex puzzle, and in a vastly entertaining way.

In "The Sussex Vampire", Holmes states that Watson has *"unexplored possibilities"*. This, as well as *"infinite possibilities"*, is a good description of what one can expect when finding new adventures within Watson's Tin Dispatch Box – and also in the case of these volumes of *Further Untold Cases*.

* * * * *

> *"Of course, I could only stammer out my thanks."*
> – *The unhappy John Hector McFarlane,* "The Norwood Builder"

As always when one of these collections is finished, I want to thank with all my heart my incredible, patient, brilliant, kind, and beautiful wife of thirty-five years, Rebecca – Every day I count my blessings and realize how lucky I am! – and our amazing, funny, creative, and wonderful son, and my friend, Dan. I love you both, and you are everything to me!

With each new set of the MX anthologies, some things get easier, and there are also new challenges. For several years, the stresses of real life have been much greater than when this series started. Through all of this, the amazing contributors have once again pulled some amazing works from the Tin Dispatch Box. I'm more grateful than I can express to every contributor who has donated both time and royalties to this ongoing project. It's amazing what we've accomplished – over 860 stories in 42 volumes (so far), and over $116,000 raised for the Undershaw school for special needs children!

I also want to give special recognition to the multiple contributors of this set: Arthur Hall, Tracy Revels, Dan Rowley, Susan Knight, Alan Dimes, Brenda Seabrooke, Barry Clay, Ember Pepper, and Tim Newton Anderson. Finally, I cannot express how thankful I am to all of those who keep buying these books and making them the largest and most popular Sherlockian anthology ever.

I'm so glad to have gotten to know so many of you through this process – both contributors and readers. It's an undeniable fact that Sherlock Holmes people are the *best* people!

I wish especially thank the following:

- *Tom Mead* – Tom has burst on the scene as the new face of locked room mysteries in the best Golden Age style. We are all very fortunate that he's writing these type of stories, and also that we live in an age where social media, for all of its evil problems, also allows us to be in contact with authors in real time. When preparing these books, I realized that I wanted very much for Tom to be part of them. I'm still trying to recruit him to write a Holmes story – and what a Holmes story that would be! He's interested, but he's also very busy! – but in the meantime, he immediately agreed to provide a foreword to these latest books. I'm very grateful for that, and also the opportunity to have "met" him (though not yet in person) at the start of what promises to be his long and wonderful career. Thanks Tom!

- *Steve Emecz* – From my first association with MX in 2013, I observed that MX (under Steve Emecz's leadership) was *the* fast-rising superstar of the Sherlockian publishing world – and ten years later, that has not changed. Connecting with MX and Steve Emecz was personally an amazing life-changing event for me, as it has been for countless other Sherlockian authors. It has led me to write many more stories, and then to edit books, along with unexpected additional Holmes Pilgrimages to England – none of which might have happened otherwise. By way of my first email with Steve, I've had the chance to make some incredible Sherlockian friends and play in the Holmesian Sandbox in ways that I would have never dreamed possible.

    Through it all, Steve has been one of the most positive and supportive people that I've ever known.

    From the beginning, Steve has let me explore various Sherlockian projects and open up my own personal possibilities in ways that otherwise would have never happened. Thank you, Steve, for every opportunity!

- *Roger Johnson* – From his immediate support at the time of the first volumes in this series to the present, I can't imagine Roger not being part of these books. His Sherlockian knowledge is exceptional, as is the work that he does to further the cause of The Master. But even more than that, both Roger and his wife, Jean Upton, are simply the finest and best of

7

people, and I'm very lucky to know both of them – even though I don't get to see them nearly as often as I'd like. I look forward to getting back over to the Holmesland sooner rather than later and visiting with them again, but in the meantime, many thanks for being part of this.

- *Brian Belanger* –I initially became acquainted with Brian when he took over the duties of creating the covers for MX Books, and I found him to be a great collaborator, and wonderfully creative too. I've worked with him on many projects with MX and Belanger Books, which he co-founded with his brother Derrick Belanger, also a good friend. Along with MX Publishing, Derrick and Brian have absolutely locked up the Sherlockian publishing field with a vast amount of amazing material. The old dinosaurs must be trembling to see every new and worthy Sherlockian project, one after another after another, that these two companies create. Luckily MX and Belanger Books work closely with one another, and I'm thrilled to be associated with both of them. Many thanks to Brian for all he does for both publishers, and for all he's done for me personally.

And finally, last but certainly *not* least, thanks to **Sir Arthur Conan Doyle**: Author, doctor, adventurer, and the Founder of the Sherlockian Feast. Honored, and present in spirit.

As I always note when putting together an anthology of Holmes stories, the effort has been a labor of love. These adventures are just more tiny threads woven into the ongoing Great Holmes Tapestry, continuing to grow and grow, for there can *never* be enough stories about the man whom Watson described as *"the best and wisest . . . whom I have ever known."*

David Marcum
October 4th, 2023
The 123rd Anniversary of
the first day of
"The Problem of Thor Bridge"

Questions, comments, or story submissions
may be addressed to David Marcum at
thepapersofsherlockholmes@gmail.com

Foreword
by Tom Mead

It is perhaps notable that I'm writing this on Arthur Conan Doyle's birthday, and so I am thinking now about Conan Doyle as a man – as a human being, rather than a mere name embossed on leather spines. My image of him will always be the one conjured by John Dickson Carr in his excellently readable biography. Carr was a fervent Sherlockian, not to mention a *pasticheur* – his *The Exploits of Sherlock Holmes* collection, co-authored with Adrian Conan Doyle, is such a fascinating curio. So it's through the lens of Carr's admiration that I have recently revisited the Holmes stories.

My very first experience of Sherlock Holmes came courtesy of Basil Rathbone. They used to show those movies on Channel 5 here in the UK, padded out with commercials for a ninety-minute runtime. This was in the mid-to-late '90s, and I'd get my mum to record them on VHS while I was at school, to watch repeatedly at my leisure. To begin with, Holmes signified *adventure* rather than mystery: Espionage, the *Pursuit to Algiers*, the hunt for *The Scarlet Claw*, Gale Sondergaard as *The Spider Woman*.

Thus, when I actually sat down and *read* my first Holmes tale, it was certainly an eye-opener. It was the fabled "Adventure of the Speckled Band", not only a great mystery but a great *locked-room* mystery, a subgenre which has had a profound influence on my own writing – and which fascinates me still.

It was a slim illustrated edition with a colourful painted cover that completely gave away the solution to the mystery. But even that could not impair my enjoyment. The book was somewhat out of place on the shelf in my primary school's library – it was bigger than the other books (not thicker, but taller), and of course it had that weird title. What was a *speckled band*? The first image in my head was a marching band.

And the next Holmes I read was *The Hound of the Baskervilles*. Perhaps unsurprisingly, I was more interested in the hound when it was an entity of uncanny origin. And yet I remained enthralled by Holmes's unorthodox detection – his elaborate chains of deduction, his disguises which fooled Watson every single time.

I did not *devour* the Holmes stories the way I did those of other authors – Agatha Christie, for example. Rather, I eked them out over the years, and as I matured so did my appreciation of Conan Doyle's momentous accomplishment.

I read "The Man With the Twisted Lip" at university and found it to be a vivid, gothic portrait of psychological schism akin to Poe's "William Wilson". I read "The Red-Headed League" and found it to be a marvellous logic puzzle. And when I reread *Baskervilles*, I was surprised to find it was folk horror masquerading as detective fiction – a tale of rationality clashing with superstition in an uncertain world.

Now more than ever I see what a glorious sparkling gem each tale is, and what a towering figure Conan Doyle has always been. To have redefined a genre, but also to have gifted so many talented writers with so much scope to develop, to reimagine. I suppose you could say it took me a while to fully immerse myself in Conan Doyle's literary world – the world of the stories, which transcend the countless cliches they have spawned. I had to "find my way in", so to speak. But now I'm here, I have no intention of leaving any time soon.

Tom Mead
May 22nd, 2023

"What Is It That We Love in Sherlock Holmes?"
by Roger Johnson

Edgar W. Smith asked that question back in April 1946. It's the first line of his editorial in the second issue of *The Baker Street Journal*. The founder of the Baker Street Irregulars was, of course, Christopher Morley, but it was Smith who ensured the BSI's stability and viability. He was one of the great Holmesian scholars and commentators, so his creation and editorship of the *Journal* was surely natural.

I don't intend to discuss Edgar Smith's answers to his own question, except to say that they are intelligent and wise. (The two don't always go together.) [1]

However, it seems to me that the Great Detective is, on a superficial level, much easier to respect than to love. He can be remarkably churlish to those whose intellects are, by his standards, inferior to his own – particularly his professional rivals in the police, and on occasion he is more than waspish to the man he considers his only friend. Read "The Disappearance of Lady Francis Carfax" again, and note the words exchanged after Holmes has rescued Watson from his attacker:

> *"I cannot at the moment recall any possible blunder which you have omitted. The total effect of your proceeding has been to give the alarm everywhere and yet to discover nothing."*
> *"Perhaps you would have done no better,"* I answered bitterly.
> *"There is no 'perhaps' about it. I have done better."*

Watson has every right to be bitter. In his admirable book *The Curious Case of 221B: The Secret Notebooks of John H Watson, MD*, Partha Basu imagines his unspoken response:

> *"It was I who tracked Lady Frances; it was I who discovered the Shlessingers, and their hold on her and the fact that they spirited her away to London. I did not raise any alarm with the Shlessingers or with Lady Frances because they had already left the Continent when I happened onto their trail. You, on the other hand, ignored my accurate deduction that*

*the three were in London and not in Montpellier where you
landed up in your ludicrous disguise . . . ."*

Nowhere in the Canonical sixty records, fortunately, is Holmes's
asperity as bluntly expressed as in one of the movies starring Basil
Rathbone and Nigel Bruce. The exact context escapes me, but I remember
the line exactly: *"No, no, Watson! D'you have to be so stupid?"*

Holmes's lack of manners and of friends does not inspire our
affection, though it may amuse us. And, after all, that isn't the complete
picture.

In "The Dying Detective", we learn that the faithful Mrs Hudson *"was
fond of him . . . for he had a remarkable gentleness and courtesy in his
dealings with women. He disliked and distrusted the sex, but he was
always a chivalrous opponent."*

There are numerous instances throughout the Good Doctor's
chronicles of Holmes's respect for women – or, more accurately, for those
women who deserve his respect, from Mary Morstan to the tragic Eugenia
Ronder. He even, most unexpectedly, refers to the wife of the missing Mr
Neville St Clair as *"this dear little woman"*, and he treats Irene Adler with
great respect, even while working against her. He is polite but cold towards
Mary, niece of the unfortunate banker Alexander Holder, and he is
necessarily harsh in dealing with Susan Stockdale and her employer
Isadora Klein – though his manner towards both is naturally different.

After their first meeting with Mary Morstan, Watson exclaims, *"What
a very attractive woman!"* To his surprise, Holmes languidly replies, *"Is
she? I did not observe."* His friend's response is, I suspect, largely
responsible for the image of the Great Detective as a man devoid of human
emotions:

> *"You really are an automaton – a calculating-machine!" I
> cried. "There is something positively inhuman in you at
> times."*

In fact, however he might appear to the average person, Sherlock
Holmes is one for whom Walt Whitman's famous words might have been
written:

> *Do I contradict myself?
> Very well then I contradict myself,
> (I am large, I contain multitudes.)* [2]

Holmes is not a superhero. He is more intelligent than most, and he has developed his talents to an unusually high degree, but they are human talents, and he is a human being, who makes the occasional mistake. If we were to dedicate an immense amount of time and concentrated effort, a select few of us might actually be able to be something very like him. Would we really want to, though? Most of us, I suspect, would rather be a Watson – and in reading the accounts of Holmes's adventures, whether for the first time or the hundredth, we can effectively place ourselves in the Good Doctor's rôle, accompanying the Great Detective in his investigations, sharing the danger and the excitement, marvelling at his perspicacity and the almost magical moment when he reveals the truth, and perhaps relaxing with him afterwards, discussing the case over a glass of brandy and a cigar.

That is what we love in Sherlock Holmes!

Roger Johnson, BSI, ASH
Editor: *The Sherlock Holmes Journal*
September 2023

NOTES

1. If you don't have a copy, you can read the editorial online at: *https://www.blackgate.com/2015/11/16/the-public-life-of-sherlock-holmes-edgar-smiths-the-implicit-holmes/*.
2. "Song of Myself", Section 51, from *Leaves of Grass*, first published in 1855.

An Ongoing Legacy
for Sherlock Holmes
by Steve Emecz

Undershaw
Circa 1900

With over five hundred Sherlock Holmes books, it's been a fantastic fifteen years publishing novels, short story collections, graphic novels and more. *The MX Book of New Sherlock Holmes Stories* remains our greatest program and achievement – made possible by the authors, the editor, and the fans who support the series. The total raised for Undershaw school for children with learning disabilities has now passed $116,000.

In 2023, every book bought on our website means we donate a meal to a family in need through ShareTheMeal from The World Food Programme (WFP). I am proud to have been a member of the external advisory council and a mentor with the WFP for several years, and part of the team in 2020 that was awarded the Nobel Peace Prize.

You can find links to all our projects on our website:

https://mxpublishing.com/pages/about-us

As long as the fans want more Sherlock, we'll be here to publish it.

Steve Emecz
September 2023

The Doyle Room at Undershaw
Partially funded through royalties from
The MX Book of New Sherlock Holmes Stories

A Word from Undershaw
by Emma West

Undershaw
September 9, 2016
Grand Opening of the Stepping Stones School
(Now *Undershaw*)
(Photograph courtesy of Roger Johnson)

"Find a voice in a whisper."
– Martin Luther King, Jr.

Why is it so important to us that our students have a "voice" at Undershaw?

It seems like an obvious question, but all too often the very people for whom a school exists are not heard when it comes to decision-making. A healthy, inclusive, and inspirational seat of learning should have a whole-school approach to listening to the voices of everyone in the school community, including our children.

Our students offer us a unique insight into what it is like to be a learner at Undershaw and thus, involving them in the decision-making process makes perfect sense. We have made significant improvements to the curriculum, the pastoral care, and the learning environment over the last academic year. These evolutions often come about by listening to our

16

children. We are here to ensure they have meaningful opportunities to share their views and their input features in every corner of our school life.

Our school vision clearly puts the child are at the heart of everything that we do, so what better way to achieve this then through listening to their voice.

> *Undershaw is an inclusive school where the best interests of the child are at the heart of everything that we do.*
> *Undershaw is a school where we empower students to aspire and achieve.*
> *Undershaw is a caring and safe environment which allows students to thrive and flourish, and prepares them to be socially and economically engaged in the future.*

If we are ever in doubt of our ethical centre, it is this. Our vision guides us, shapes us, and holds us to account. It is our conscience and our true North. Undershaw is a thriving centre of learning, friendships, noise, and bustle . . . and we will always strive to find a voice in a whisper.

As ever and on behalf of all our voices, my heartfelt thanks for being by our side during all of our evolutions. We have such a vibrant community here and we are very fortunate to have such a committed band of friends and supporters. Undershaw and MX Publishing have a friendship that spans a decade, and for that we are all incredibly grateful.

Until next time . . . .

Emma West
Headteacher, Undershaw
October 2023

"Undershaw", Hindhead, Conan Doyle's House.

Editor's *Caveats*

When these anthologies first began back in 2015, I noted that the authors were from all over the world – and thus, there would be British spelling and American spelling. As I explained then, I didn't want to take the responsibility of changing American spelling to British and vice-versa. I would undoubtedly miss something, leading to inconsistencies, or I'd change something incorrectly.

Some readers are bothered by this, made nervous and irate when encountering American spelling as written by Watson, and in stories set in England. However, here in America, the versions of The Canon that we read have long-ago has their spelling Americanized, so it isn't quite as shocking for us.

Additionally, I offer my apologies up front for any typographical errors that have slipped through. As a print-on-demand publisher, MX does not have squadrons of editors as some readers believe. The business consists of three part-time people who also have busy lives elsewhere – Steve Emecz, Sharon Emecz, and Timi Emecz – so the editing effort largely falls on the contributors. Some readers and consumers out there in the world are unhappy with this – apparently forgetting about all of those self-produced Holmes stories and volumes from decades ago (typed and Xeroxed) with awkward self-published formatting and loads of errors that are now prized as very expensive collector's items.

I'm personally mortified when errors slip through – ironically, there will probably be errors in these *caveats* – and I apologize now, but without a regiment of professional full-time editors looking over my shoulder, this is as good as it gets. Real life is more important than writing and editing – even in such a good cause as promoting the True and Traditional Canonical Holmes – and only so much time can be spent preparing these books before they're released into the wild. I hope that you can look past any errors, small or huge, and simply enjoy these stories, and appreciate the efforts of everyone involved, and the sincere desire to add to The Great Holmes Tapestry.

And in spite of any errors here, there are more Sherlock Holmes stories in the world than there were before, and that's a good thing.

David Marcum
Editor

Editor's Note:
Duplicate Untold Cases

In some instances, there are multiple versions of certain Untold Cases contained within this volume. Each of these are very different stories and do not contradict one another, in spite of their common jumping-off place. As explained in the Editor's Foreword, no traditional and Canonical versions of the Untold Cases are the definitive versions to the exclusion of the others. They simply require a bit of additional pondering and rationalization to consider what was going on in Watson's thinking, and why he chose to present them in this way.

In this volume, the reader will encounter several versions of The Old Russian Woman, The Grosvenor Square Furniture Van, The Amateur Mendicants, The Paradol Chamber, The Most Repulsive Man, the Blackmail Case (from *The Hound of the Baskervilles*), The Addleton Tragedy and the British Barrow, The Sudden Death of Cardinal Tosca, The Service for Sir James Saunders, and the interesting cases brought to Holmes by his brother Mycroft and Stanley Hopkins.

Enjoy!

23

Sherlock Holmes (1854-1957) was born in Yorkshire, England, on 6 January, 1854. In the mid-1870's, he moved to 24 Montague Street, London, where he established himself as the world's first Consulting Detective. After meeting Dr. John H. Watson in early 1881, he and Watson moved to rooms at 221b Baker Street, where his reputation as the world's greatest detective grew for several decades. He was presumed to have died battling noted criminal Professor James Moriarty on 4 May, 1891, but he returned to London on 5 April, 1894, resuming his consulting practice in Baker Street. Retiring to the Sussex coast near Beachy Head in October 1903, he continued to be associated in various private and government investigations while giving the impression of being a reclusive apiarist. He was very involved in the events encompassing World War I, and to a lesser degree those of World War II. He passed away peacefully upon the cliffs above his Sussex home on his 103rd birthday, 6 January, 1957.

Dr. John Hamish Watson (1852-1929) was born in Stranraer, Scotland on 7 August, 1852. In 1878, he took his Doctor of Medicine Degree from the University of London, and later joined the army as a surgeon. Wounded at the Battle of Maiwand in Afghanistan (27 July, 1880), he returned to London late that same year. On New Year's Day, 1881, he was introduced to Sherlock Holmes in the chemical laboratory at Barts. Agreeing to share rooms with Holmes in Baker Street, Watson became invaluable to Holmes's consulting detective practice. Watson was married and widowed three times, and from the late 1880's onward, in addition to his participation in Holmes's investigations and his medical practice, he chronicled Holmes's adventures, with the assistance of his literary agent, Sir Arthur Conan Doyle, in a series of popular narratives, most of which were first published in *The Strand* magazine. Watson's later years were spent preparing a vast number of his notes of Holmes's cases for future publication. Following a final important investigation with Holmes, Watson contracted pneumonia and passed away on 24 July, 1929.

Photos of Sherlock Holmes and Dr. John H. Watson courtesy of Roger Johnson

The
MX Book
of
New
Sherlock
Holmes
Stories

Part XL – Further Untold Cases
(1879-1886)

The Untold Cases
of Sherlock Holmes
by Joseph W. Svec III

There are stories of Sherlock Holmes untold,
their clues mysterious, ancient, and old.
For reasons, one may never share,
the secrets, Watson will not dare

reveal more than just a word,
a hint, a whisper, how absurd!
Yet, if you look within the story,
they are there in all their glory.

The time that Holmes was summoned to
Odessa for a murder new,
Trepoff was the name they say
untold even to this day.

And the singular tragedy,
of the Atkinson brothers at Trincomalee.
If known, the bards would surely sing
of the remarkably brilliant ring

that Holmes received for his success.
What he did, who can guess?
T'was a delicate case you see,
for Holland's reigning family.

The Darlington substitution scandal,
Holmes did magnificently handle.
The Arnsworth castle fire trick
provided answers very quick.

(He's used this ruse more than one time
to solve a mystery or a crime.)
And if a secret no one knows
can be famous, the one I chose

is the ship Matilda Briggs,
(not for her mast, or sails, or rigs)
but for a giant Sumatran rat.
Can you even imagine that?

Yet, the world can never know,
so untold this case will go.
But, there are those who digging deep
Into imagination steep,

have uncovered cases strange
and before your eyes arrange
stories lost to ages past
that grab your imagination fast.

They'll astound, and feast your senses
when the reading, it commences.
Yes, they sure will rattle your bones,
the untold cases of Sherlock Holmes.

The Case of the
Cases of Vamberry Bergundy
by Roger Riccard

Prologue

"*They are not all successes, Watson," Sherlock Holmes had said, "but there are some pretty little problems among them. Here's the record of the Tarleton murders, and the case of Vamberry, the wine merchant . . . ." The consulting detective, Sherlock Holmes, had made that statement to me as part of the introduction to his narrative of the Musgrave Ritual. We were discussing cases he had worked before he and I began sharing rooms at 221b Baker Street.*

After his recollections regarding his old classmate, Reginald Musgrave, I put his story into proper form for publication. But I did not forget the others he had mentioned and eventually convinced him to relate this episode of his earlier work during a stormy evening in September as we sat before a cozy fire smoking our pipes and enjoying after-dinner brandies.

"It was late October 1879," said my friend, swirling his snifter in the palm of his hand, "when Peter Vamberry came knocking at my door at 24 Montague Street. A warm autumn evening, as I recall. Vamberry was a middle-aged gentleman. Five-foot-eight inches tall, and a bit stout at two-hundred pounds.

"He had a receding, brown hairline with no sign of grey as of yet, and a thick moustache curling around thin lips. He was stylishly dressed, with a burgundy cravat instead of a necktie. As it turned out, the color was a common one in his wardrobe accessories, as it reflected his particular specialty of imported wines. When I opened the door to his knock, he introduced himself and said he was referred to me by a certain Duke, who was a former client of mine, as well as his, but whose name I must withhold, even now, due to the sensitivity of his case.

"I invited him to come and sit on the settee, which was my particular interview spot for potential clients due to the lighting arrangements in the room. I offered him a cigarette – cigars were a bit pricey for me in those days – but he declined, stating, 'I do not indulge in tobacco, Mr. Holmes. It spoils the palette, and my tasting skills are essential to my work.'

"'I perceive you are an importer of fine delicacies as well as wines, Mr. Vamberry. What is your particular issue?'

"'You've heard of me?'

"'I have not.'

"'Then how did you guess my occupation?'

"'I deduced your occupation, sir. You are giving off odors of multiple kinds of cheese, your breath smells of caviar, and there is just a drop of wine spilled upon your cravat which, despite its near match in colour, is just distinct enough to show against the fabric. I have also been working on an exact knowledge of London's streets, and am currently an expert on those businesses near the docks where there is a building with signage proclaiming Vamberry Imports. Putting those facts together, it was elementary to presume your occupation. Now, pray tell, how may I help you?'

"The merchant nodded in satisfaction at this explanation and replied, 'My business is under attack, Mr. Holmes. I don't know who, for I am unaware of any enemies, but my last two shipments of burgundy from France have each had one crate's worth of spoiled and sour wine. Our mutual friend received several bottles from one of those crates and brought it to my attention.'

"'How many crates of bottles were in each shipment?'

"'Two-dozen in the first, and thirty in the second.'

"'Did you happen to note if they came over on the same ship each time?'

"The wine merchant paused, trying to remember, then answered, 'No. They were both French ships, but of different names.'

"'Were they sailing vessels or steamers?'

"'Both were streamers.'

"I tapped out my cigarette and folded my hands across my waist, 'I should like to examine your warehouse, Mr. Vamberry. Would now be convenient?'

"'By all means, young man. I should value your opinion as quickly as possible so as to prepare whatever steps may be necessary to stop any recurrence.'

"I stood and moved toward the coat rack where I put on an overcoat, for I didn't know how long I might be, and darkness would fall soon after we reached the docks. As I did so, Vamberry preceded me to the door and together we exited my home and boarded a hansom for the Canary Wharf and the gentleman's warehouse . . . ."

Chapter I

(Note to The Reader: I find it somewhat cumbersome to maintain the style of this story as though quoting from my friend's perspective, and shall therefore continue writing from this point as a third-person narrative.)

The six-mile journey took nearly an hour due to heavy traffic from citizens returning home after a day's work. The city's lamplighters were busily plying their trade, and that section of the warehouse district was well-illuminated as Holmes and his client disembarked directly in front of Vamberry's business. The smell of the Thames was heavy in the evening air and a fog was rising. One could hear ships' horns and boat whistles close by as they navigated around each other, hurrying to their home destinations in the waning sunlight.

Vamberry's warehouse was attractive from the outside. Its paint was bright and bold against the punishing clime of the mist off the river. Buildings on either side were weather-beaten and faded in sharp contrast. There was a pedestrian entrance off to the side of the great loading bay where wagons pulled right in and dropped their cargo out of the weather. Holmes and Vamberry entered through this smaller door used similarly by businessmen visiting Vamberry in his office to buy and sell merchandise, or by the public conducting their shopping excursions.

At Holmes's request, Vamberry led him to the underground cellar where the wine was stored at a suitable temperature. The detective asked his client to remain in the doorway while he examined the room for any signs of trespass or tampering. The block walls radiated the cooler underground temperatures, and the room itself was a suitable cool temperature for the storage of the types of foodstuffs and wines which were the majority of Vamberry's imports. There was a series of mechanical fans that circulated the air to assist in the deterrent of molds and mildew. As he traversed the room, Holmes lit a series of lamps to their full illumination. He checked the floor for any signs of footprints and made note of their size and shape to check against Vamberry and his employees.

He called out to his client. "Where were the contaminated crates? Were they each in the same place?"

"Over against that wall, Mr. Holmes," replied Vamberry. "I don't know if the contaminated crates were stored in the same position, since we didn't discover the problem until after they were delivered."

There were several crates still piled against the wall, which kept Holmes from examining it immediately. However, he did climb atop the stack so he could examine the upper portion and feel the blocks to note their temperature. He turned toward the entrance and asked another question. "Do you know what is on the other side of this wall? Does the business next door also have a cellar?"

"Chastain's Furniture? I am not aware if they have a cellar or not. Do you suspect some sort of contamination leeching through the walls?"

Holmes continued to feel the blocks along the row of crates as he replied. "There are no contaminants of which I am aware which could leech through stone blocks, wooden crates, and glass bottles, Mr. Vamberry. It is merely a habit of mine to have complete knowledge of the geography of any potential location where a crime might occur. One never knows what minor bit of information may hold the key to solving the problem."

Holmes hopped down from his perch atop the crates and brushed his hands while returning to the doorway where Vamberry stood. "In addition to your friend, what other customers have complained about these particular batches of wine?"

"The larger crate went to the Hotel Metropole – also a long-time customer with never a complaint before."

Holmes pondered that momentarily, then asked, "May I see your shipping records regarding these particular bottles?"

Vamberry led the detective back up to his office. It was a spacious room and well-decorated for entertaining potential clients. Red leather chairs and an overstuffed sofa patterned with maroon-and-gold afforded plenty of seating, while mahogany bookcases and shelves held various items on display. At a cherry-coloured French provincial side table, Holmes pored over the books noting dates, delivery vans, and other shipping information. He asked his client, "I see your supplier is Chateau Coquillade in the Rhone Valley. Have you contacted them regarding this issue?"

"I have, Mr. Holmes. They are just as puzzled as I. They assure me they have inspected their procedures and cannot determine any manner wherein just one crate could have an issue. The winemaking process could possibly affect one particular vat or even just one barrel. But were that the case, affected bottles would be spread over several crates, and not just one per shipment."

"Yes," said Holmes a bit testily. "It's obvious the problem had to occur after the wine was bottled. The question is, did someone in France deliberately sabotage the bottles going into a particular crate? If so, why? They couldn't possibly know to whom you would sell the contents of that crate, so no specific customers are the target. This narrows the situation to two possibilities.

"One, the perpetrator wanted the sour wine traced back to the vineyard to ruin their reputation. But if that were the case, why just the bottles in one crate and not a whole barrel which would spread over several crates? To investigate that would require me to travel to France. For now, I prefer to remain here and explore option two, which I believe is more likely. That would be that someone is out to cause you harm by somehow arranging for the bottles in these particular crates to become adversely affected. That could be one of your employees, or someone at the delivery company."

"That is what I fear, Mr. Holmes!" cried the merchant, his voice rising in excitement as he raised his fists in the air. "I believe some competitor or someone with a grudge is out to ruin me!"

"Interesting for you to say so," responded Holmes. "Did you have a suspect in mind?"

Vamberry paced the room, his head shaking to and fro. Suddenly he stopped and slammed his fist onto his grand mahogany desk. "Peabody!" he cried. "Aloysius Peabody! He and I have competed for years over various restaurant and hotel accounts. I have beaten him out more often than he has beaten me. The Hotel Metropole account was one in particular where the bidding was fierce. I had to reduce my profit considerably, but the reputation gained by having my wines featured there was worth it. Peabody couldn't afford to cut his prices so drastically. He only deals in wine and doesn't have other products to sell where he could make up some of the lost profits."

Holmes tilted his head and enquired, "Do you believe his character to be so devious as to undertake this attempt to sabotage you?"

Vamberry fell into a red leather chair and slumped. Sighing, he replied, "Actually, no. We have had some public arguments at a club to which we both belong, but even in the heat of the moment, his tone was more of bitter disappointment than threatening. He only comes to mind because he is my main competitor."

"What about employees, or former employees?" asked the detective. "Or perhaps a relative who may have a grudge against you?"

The merchant shook his head. "I've never had to give anyone the sack. My men are fairly paid and don't complain. There are no family feuds. I have no son, just a daughter, so I'm training my nephew to take over the business someday."

"Is he the ambitious sort? Does he believe he shouldn't have to wait until you retire?"

Vamberry shook his head again. "No, sir. We get along very well. I don't always take his suggestions, but I do so enough that he seems content and understands my reasoning when we don't always agree. I pay him a salary that allows a comfortable life and he is soon to be married, at which point I shall give him a suitable raise for a wedding present."

Holmes nodded thoughtfully, then asked, "What about your daughter, sir? Does she have any ambitions regarding the business?"

Vamberry smirked and waved his hand dismissively. "She is a woman of but nineteen years of age. Her only ambition is to obtain a good match in marriage, not run a business. Don't be preposterous!"

Holmes folded his arms and stared at his client. "I shouldn't need to remind you, sir, that Victoria became queen at the age of eighteen, despite the opposition of her uncles and others. Women can be just as ambitious as men, depending on their personalities."

His client pursed his lips and slowly shook his head once more. "Hester has no such ambition, I assure you. Her main interests are fashion and romantic books. She is attractive in that she takes after her mother's fine and fair features and not mine. Her only problem is her determination to marry someone who is like the heroes of the books she reads, rather than make a practical match with any of the potential suitors I have introduced her to, who are all fine young men with excellent prospects."

Holmes rested his hands over his waistcoat and bowed his head in thought. Then he spoke one more time. "Is it possible that any of these 'fine young men' may hold a grudge against you for their rejection by your daughter?"

Chapter II

Vamberry blanched at the suggestion, then shook his head vehemently. "No, no, Mr. Holmes. These men are all from society families with successful positions or excellent prospects. None of them are desperate to get their hands on my business or my daughter's dowry."

Holmes stood and replied, "Nevertheless, I should be grateful for a list of names, just so I may eliminate them for my own satisfaction."

The merchant's bushy eyebrows rose in surprise. "I can't have you investigating these lads! Their families would never speak to me again if they think I've accused them of some crime!"

"I have my methods, Mr. Vamberry. I can find out what I need without them being aware of your involvement at all. In all likelihood, they won't even know that I'm looking into them."

Reluctantly, the wine merchant took up a pencil and wrote out a list. It contained three names and some pertinent information about each. He handed it over with the plea, "You promise to be discreet?"

Holmes took the paper and inserted it into his inner breast pocket. "You have my word, sir. In the meantime, could you have your employees move the remaining crates away from the wall so that I can examine it further? We still need to determine how those particular crates were affected. I shall return tomorrow morning and see what may be learned. By the way, were you able to retrieve the crates that contained the contaminated wine?"

"The contamination wasn't discovered until long after the crates had been discarded by the client. We were unable to examine them for any damage."

The next day, Holmes sent out some telegrams to gain information on the three former suitors of Miss Vamberry, as well as Mr. Peabody, then proceeded on to the merchant's warehouse. Per his request, his client had removed the remaining crates a fair distance from the wall. The first thing the detective noted was a floor drain. He stooped to examine it. "What is the purpose of this drain at this location?" he asked his client.

Vamberry came and peered over Holmes's shoulder. "That is a flood drain. Should this room ever become flooded, the water would flow under the pallets to this area and the drain would take it out to the Thames through an old Roman aqueduct."

"Has that ever happened?" asked Holmes.

"One time many years ago. There was a particularly stormy winter when the roads overflowed and water seeped down into this area. Fortunately, this drain acted to minimize water damage."

"It has never backed up and flooded this cellar?"

Vamberry looked puzzled, raised his hand to the back of his head, shook it, and replied, "No, Mr. Holmes. The tides of the Thames have never risen high enough to cause that. It would take a flood of Biblical proportions to overcome the difference in elevation between here and the river."

Holmes observed the drain cover, felt it with his fingers, and then smelled his hand. Finally, he nodded and moved on to examine the lower section of the block wall which had been inaccessible the previous day. There was a roughly semicircular discolouration about three feet high and four feet wide along the bottom. He questioned his client again as to the cause. This time, Vamberry had no answer. "I've never noticed that before, but then, there are usually crates piled up against this wall."

"At any rate, I need to question your employees. Would there be anyone in particular who may be aware when this occurred?"

The merchant raised a pudgy hand with an upraised index finger and quickly responded, "Hodgkins, the foreman. He would be the most likely to have taken note of it."

41

Finished with his physical examination, Holmes obtained permission to use Vamberry's office to conduct interviews with his four employees. He began with the foreman. Hodgkins was a short but thickly built man in his forties. Curly black hair covered his head, ears, and collar, and his rolled-up sleeves revealed hairy arms thick with muscle and an occasional scar. His hands were calloused from hard work, and the knuckle on his left ring finger was swollen as if it had been broken at one time and not healed properly. Holmes noted he also had a pair of eyeglasses in his shirt pocket.

The detective sat behind Vamberry's desk with his hands folded and leaning forward. Even in this stance, his eyes were above those of the shorter man. He opened the conversation casually. "Mr. Hodgkins, how long have you been employed by Mr. Vamberry?"

"Sixteen years," he answered in his Limehouse accent. "Right out of the Navy. Worked my way up to foreman seven years ago."

"I presume your continued employment and advancement have left you satisfied as an employee here?"

"Aye, sir. Mr. Vamberry's a right fair employer and I've no complaints. Nor do any of my crew."

"Do you have any idea how the bottles of wine in those particular crates could have become spoiled?"

The foreman leaned forward conspiratorily. "I've no proof, Mr. Holmes, but I can only assume someone at the customer's site must have stored them crates improper like. They were never opened all the time we had 'em, and they spent the whole time here in the cool of the cellar."

Holmes nodded. Then he stood and asked, "Would you please come with me, Mr. Hodgkins? I've something to show you."

Together they went down into the cellar and the detective pointed out the discoloured wall. "Do you know why the wall is stained in that particular place, and when it happened?"

The foreman walked over to it and felt the wall in that spot. "I first noticed it a couple months ago. It wasn't this big. But now, this is near twice the size it was then. It never felt wet so I wasn't concerned. Could it be some chemical in the dirt on the other side?"

"I shall explore that when I visit Mr. Chastain's establishment. Has there ever been any trouble between him and your employer?"

"No, not that I'm aware of. Once in awhile, delivery drivers have to jockey for position if they arrive at the same time, but our employees and theirs haven't had any run-ins."

This was the vein the rest of the interviews took. No real information came forth other than what Hodgkins had imparted. It was late morning now and Holmes chose to take his investigation to the neighboring warehouse.

Chastain's Furniture was laid out far differently than Vamberry's. The large loading doors were off to one side while the public entrance was in the middle. Upon walking in, one was immediately surrounded by furniture. There were sections for beds, tables, desks, chairs, and sofas. There were a few sample rooms set up to show how various furniture complimented each other, and there was a section of unfinished items where one could pick out a particular piece and order it stained to whatever shade was preferred, be it walnut, cherry, mahogany, maple, or oak.

Upon entering the showroom, Holmes was approached by a gentleman roughly his own age – that is mid-twenties – with an eager expression, flashing smile, and extended hand. "Welcome, sir! Welcome to Chastain's! The finest furniture maker and exporter in London! My name is Mr. Lyons. Is there any particular piece you're looking for, or perhaps an entire set for a specific room?"

Holmes shook the proffered hand and replied, "Not at this time, Mr. Lyons. Perhaps when I move to larger quarters. However, you may be able to assist me. My name is Sherlock Holmes. I've been inspecting the building next door, and there appears to be a problem in Vamberry's cellar, a possible leak from some underground source. I would like to inspect your cellar to see if you might be experiencing the same issue."

Assuming the use of the word *inspecting* meant Holmes was some sort of government official, Lyons was taken aback. "Oh, my! Yes, yes, I'm sure Mr. Chastain would certainly want to be made aware of any issues or possible damage. Let me take you to him so he may let you into the cellar. I don't have a key to that area."

The young salesman escorted the detective to an area off to one side where there were offices lined up against the wall. Lyons knocked on the largest of these which was labeled *Horace Chastain III, President.*

Upon the reply of "Enter!" Lyons opened the door and led Holmes inside. Horace Chastain was behind an ornate desk, obviously meant to be seen by potential clients. It was dark walnut, but its top was inlaid with various shades of lighter colours which were arranged to portray a map of the world. The gentleman was well-dressed in a modern suit of navy blue with stripes. He tended toward the stout side, so Holmes surmised the stripes were meant to be slimming. In his mid-fifties, his hair had turned salt-and-pepper and he wore it short, likely to minimize the amount of grey visible. He had a Van Dyke beard – which added to the impression Holmes had of the man's vanity, as such a cut was meant to lengthen his face, which tended toward chubbiness.

Seeing that Lyons had brought a visitor, he stood and asked, "Is there a problem, Mr. Lyons, or do you require information on a certain piece?"

The salesman nervously folded his hands in front of himself and said, "This is Mr. Holmes, sir. He's been inspecting the Vamberry building next door and has found a problem that may be affecting our cellar. I told him he would need you to let him in."

"What sort of problem, Mr. Holmes?" asked the merchant warily, his eyebrows narrowing as his head tilted to one side.

"There is a discolouration in the wall indicating some sort of foreign agent affecting the blocks. That section is also in close proximity to a floor drain and I was wondering if you also had such an arrangement and if that may be the source of the problem."

"This building has been my family's business for three generations, sir. I would know if there was a problem. The floor drain is above an old Roman aqueduct, which is certainly too large to have ever flooded, but you're welcome to take a look. I'll have my son escort you."

He rang a bell on his desk and one could hear the door of the office next door open up and footsteps quicken on the hardwood floor. In the doorway, there appeared a young man in his early twenties of moderate build and plain features. He wore a grey suit, and his deportment wasn't unlike that of a soldier reporting to a superior officer. "Yes, sir?" he asked. "What do you require?"

"Alan, take Mr. Holmes down to the cellar and let him inspect the area near the drain. There appears to be a problem next door and he wishes to ensure it hasn't spread to our side of the wall."

"Yes, Father. This way, Mr. Holmes."

As they made their way down the stairs, Holmes asked, "I take it *Alan* is your middle name?"

The fellow hesitated on a step before continuing as he answered. "Yes, Mr. Holmes. How did you guess?"

Holmes shook his head at the word "guess" but didn't comment upon it. Instead, he merely replied, "A family who carries on a name for three generations is likely to keep it going. Yet to avoid confusion in conversation, a nickname or other appellation is usually attached to the youngest generation. I noticed a paperweight on your father's desk inscribed *H.A.C. III.* I thus presumed you are in fact, Horace Alan Chastain IV."

"I see. Very astute of you, sir."

"It is my business to notice things."

They reached the bottom of the stairs and Chastain waved his hand toward one wall. "The floor drain is over there by the forge."

They made their way across the floor, stepping around crates of imported furniture and passing stockpiles of lumber and metal rods. They stopped at the drain which was located in an open area much farther away from the wall than that in Vamberry's cellar. Holmes crouched and examined the grate. It was roughly thirty inches square. He grasped it and found it easy to pull up. He peered down and, in the dim light, noted the aqueduct floor about five feet below. Looking to the young Chastain, he asked, "There appears to be little rust or crusting of the metal of this grate. How often is it lifted?"

The gentleman stood off to the side with hands clasped behind his back as he replied, "It depends on how often we empty the ashes of the furnace to be washed out to the river. I would venture at least once a week. More if production is running high, which it tends to do in spring and summer when there is a greater call for outdoor wrought-iron furniture. We've recently expanded into that area, as you will note by the enlargement of the forge. Previously we only made specialized decorative pieces – hinges or brackets for our furniture – and the old forge was quite sufficient for that. The large pieces required to build chairs, benches, and tables of wrought-iron necessitated this larger forge furnace."

This piqued Holmes's interest, of course. Higher temperatures from the new forge could easily have spoiled the wine next door if there weren't enough insulation. He stood and walked over to the new device. There was a laborer currently working at it and the detective asked, "What temperature is required to forge the iron correctly?"

The big man, sweating freely, pointed a beefy hand to a red mark on a gauge on the furnace at two-thousand-five-hundred degrees and replied in an accent similar to Hodgkins, "Right there, sir. If the rods get above that, they'll start to melt. Once they reach that point, they become pliable enough to shape the way what's called for."

Holmes thanked the smithy and stepped around where he could see the back of the forge. However, it wasn't as he expected. The forge didn't use the block wall of the cellar as its rear barrier. Instead, there was a solid layer of brick insulating the fire from the cellar wall. He reached in and felt the blocks next to the brick. They were warm and discoloured similar to the blocks on the opposite side in Vamberry's cellar, but they were certainly not hot enough to have transferred sufficient heat to spoil the wine in the crate closest to this heat source.

Chapter III

Holmes came back out from the rear of the forge and turned to Chastain. "I believe everything is satisfactory. You've had no trouble with your chimneys, I take it?"

The young man shook his head. "Nary a bit, sir. They're cleaned out every week when we're running production at full capacity. Did you suspect some problem with our heat and Vamberry's issue?"

Despite his efforts to remain nonchalant, there was an undercurrent of some sort in Chastain's question. "I just needed to check to make sure," said Holmes. "That should do it for now. You may tell your father all is well on your side of the wall."

"Very good, sir. He will be relieved, I am sure." Chastain made a half-turn and began leading Holmes back to the stairway. A thought occurred to the detective and he casually asked, "Have you met Vamberry's daughter? Hester, I believe?"

That brought Chastain up short and he turned and stared at Holmes. After a long moment, he answered, "I certainly know Hester, of course. We're in the same social circles due to our father's businesses."

Holmes nodded. "I hear she is a real beauty. I was hoping to meet her while I did this work for Mr. Vamberry, as I am a bachelor myself, and it is my understanding she is unattached to anyone."

Chastain's demeanour changed, though he fought to keep his tone civil. "Mr. Vamberry is very particular about his daughter's suitors. But I understand that she, herself, doesn't approve of her father's choices. I don't foresee a match anytime in the near future, for both of them are very . . . let us say, *headstrong*."

"What has she against her father's choices?"

"I don't know for certain, as I do not know all those to whom he has introduced her. But, in my conversations with her at social functions, I get the impression she is looking for the modern equivalent of a knight in shining armor on a white charger to take her off to some promised land where they can live happily ever after."

"Ah, I see," declared Holmes, feigning disappointment. "She's one of those dreamers with no sense of the realities of life. Too bad."

Chastain kept his back to Holmes as they ascended the stairs, but his answer was revealing. "There's nothing wrong with dreamers, sir. Where would we be without them? Aren't all inventors dreamers? The great authors of history who gave us our literature? The revolutionists and statesmen who dreamt of a better world? Without our dreams, we would be poor souls indeed."

By now they had reached the top of the stairs and Holmes was able to face his guide and prod him further. "Agreed, but even dreams must be tempered by reality."

Chastain thrust his hands deep into his pockets and rocked back and forth on his feet before replying, "Reality is determined by belief, Mr. Holmes. Do you suppose that a hundred years ago, the American colonists had any real chance of defeating the military might of Great Britain and becoming independent? But they dreamed it, they believed it, and it became so, despite all odds against it. It's those who try to quash dreams who should beware of repercussions."

Holmes put out his hand to shake that of Chastain and said, "I see you, yourself, are a furniture builder. Your callouses reveal a great deal of time spent with carpentry tools. A suitable profession for a dreamer who seeks creativity in his designs. Yet you are also a philosopher. A fine combination for a man to attract a certain type of woman. Good luck and good day."

Chapter IV

Holmes's conversation with Chastain's son had opened up a new avenue of investigation. When the detective returned to Vamberry's facility, the proprietor was off at a lunch appointment – thus, Holmes was free to perform a bit of sleuthing undeterred. He went down to the cellar and lifted the grate off the floor drain with some effort, for it hadn't been removed in many years and was held in place by the grime which had accumulated around its edges. He then lowered a small step-ladder into the hole and climbed down. What he found confirmed his suspicions. He also was presented with a conundrum as to which of two solutions he might recommend to his client.

He decided he needed to speak with Hester Vamberry. He returned to Montague Street and changed his clothing to something cleaner and less odorous than the damp aqueduct he had just quitted. Then he went to the Vamberry residence. It was a large home in a wealthy neighborhood and stood out for its beauty and architecture, much like the man's warehouse.

He was admitted by a maidservant, which surprised him as he expected a man of Vamberry's social position to have a butler. He made a mental note that perhaps he should look deeper into the wine merchant's finances. She took his card into the mistress of the house. While he waited, he noted the richness of the furniture and some fine paintings on the walls. The Vamberrys weren't afraid to show off their wealth. When Mrs. Vamberry came out to greet him, he found her to be an attractive woman, as her husband had stated. Her chestnut hair swirled atop her head in the latest fashion and accented her hazel eyes. High cheekbones ascended from full, sensuous lips, and her figure was that hourglass shape that seemed to dominate fashion magazines.

She looked from his card in her hand to Holmes, standing in her foyer. Neither his tall, gaunt figure nor his aquiline face proclaimed him to be a suitable caller for her daughter. In a firm, almost demanding tone, she addressed him. "I am Mrs. Vamberry. I understand you have arrived without an appointment to call upon my daughter. We aren't in the habit of letting strangers merely drop in for a social call on Hester. Just what is your purpose here, Mister . . . ." She looked at the card again. "*Holmes*?"

Hat in hand and in the presence of a lady old enough to be his mother, the detective nevertheless spoke with confidence in his task. "Please forgive the intrusion, Madam. I am working with your husband on an issue of possible vandalism at his warehouse, and I thought to question Hester as to any thoughts she might have regarding rejected suitors or jealous friends."

Mrs. Vamberry crossed her arms and stared at this young upstart. "I am unaware of any business problems my husband is having, and certainly Hester would have no knowledge of such things."

A voice floated down from the stairwell, causing both the detective and the lady of the house to turn. "Knowledge of what, Mother?"

Gliding gracefully down the curving stairs came Hester Vamberry. She was adorned in a dark blue dress with a white lace collar and cuffs. Her figure was trim and tall. Her auburn hair waved down her back and shoulders, framing a face even more beautiful than her mother's. Her blue eyes were bright with curiosity, and she looked at Holmes in a most disconcerting fashion.

Before the detective could even utter a greeting, Mrs. Vamberry proclaimed, "Nothing, dear. The gentleman was just leaving."

She glared at Holmes and waved her hand toward the door. Discretion being the better part of valor, Holmes tilted his head toward her to acknowledge her order, but in an attempt at maintaining some dignity, he squared his shoulders toward Hester and stared into those curious eyes. An unbidden memory stirred within. Before it came full force, he bowed graciously, stating, "Good day, Miss Vamberry." Then he turned an about-face and strode out the door.

Once again on the street, hailing a cab, Holmes reflected on this occurrence. He found it odd that Mrs. Vamberrry claimed to know nothing of her husband's troubles. He was beginning to think his client needed as much investigating as the problem with the wine, especially now that he knew how to fix the issue he was hired to solve.

His thoughts also ran to Hester Vamberry.

Chapter V

Holmes made some further enquiries into his client on his way back to Montague Street and stopped by a café to partake of a late lunch. As he thought back to the incident at Vamberry's home, he was now fairly certain he would do no more than provide the merchant a solution to stop any further wine contamination. If the man was unable to share his troubles with his wife, what other secrets might he have?

There were still nagging thoughts popping into his head regarding Hester, however. He had only been testing Alan Chastain's feelings when he made the remarks about seeking out Hester for himself. He had no intention of such a pursuit. But when he saw her, the memories of years earlier came rushing back. Memories he couldn't put aside, no matter how hard he tried, or how much of his seven-per-cent solution of cocaine that he used. The grief of the loss had been unbearable. To this day he couldn't explain how he had survived it. Even now, alone in his room . . . .

The pounding on his door snapped him from the abyss his mind was taking him down. Even as he stood to answer, angry shouts threatened to bring down the wrath of his landlord, so he stepped over quickly and threw open the door, hoping to quell the racket of his caller. Peter Vamberry pushed his way in and used his weight to pin the gaunt detective against the wall. The wine merchant's left forearm was putting pressure on Holmes's throat and his brass-handled cane was raised in his right hand, threatening to strike.

Had Holmes not been in the midst of an emotional morass, his defensive skills would have automatically asserted themselves and the shorter man would have been on the floor with one swift move. But the detective, who blamed himself for his own survival all those years ago, wasn't of a mind to care about himself. A beating, or even death, would have been preferred to living with the guilt and anguish in his heart.

In such a state he barely registered the words Vamberry shouted. "How dare you, sir? You had no right to expose my wife to the problems of my business! Being the provider and protector for my family is *my* role, and she shouldn't have to worry about how I do it. She has her own part to play in running the house and raising our daughter. There was no need for you to add to her burdens by implying that I am incapable of handling my responsibilities! You are off the case! Dismissed, I tell you!"

His tirade over, Vamberry stepped back and away from the young detective while Holmes reached a hand up to rub his throat and catch his breath. What he didn't realize, nor did the wine merchant, was that his other hand had reflexively pulled a knife from his pocket and snapped it open. Without thinking, his survival instincts saved him. He looked down and stared at the knife in his hand, suddenly shaken by the fact that he would have been ready to kill had Vamberry not relaxed his grip in time.

The elder man took another step back and toward the door, pointing his cane at Holmes. "You stand back!" he shouted.

Holmes made a show of closing the knife blade and replacing it in his pocket. Then he said, "I wish you no harm, sir. It was a defensive reflex, I assure you. I will gladly withdraw from your case. However, in the interest of collecting my fee, I can tell you how your wine was soured and how you can prevent future occurrences. If you are still willing to pay for that information."

The wine merchant hesitated. His anger wasn't yet quashed, but the practical side of his mind realized a solution to his problem was exactly what he needed to assure his wife everything was all right. Keeping his walking stick up in a defensive stance, despite the absence of Holmes's knife, he reached into his pocket with his other hand and pulled out some coins. He glanced down and counted. Looking back to Holmes, he said, "All right, you've spent two days on this problem. I'll give you one pound two for the answer."

Holmes nodded and walked over to the cabinet where he pulled out a small bottle of whisky and poured himself just enough to soothe his throat. He sat down at his table and took a deep swallow while Vamberry continued to wait by the door. Finally, he looked over at his client and said, "You need to install some bars in the aqueduct below your floor drain. They need to be wide enough to allow water and debris to get through, but narrow enough to keep any persons from traversing that way. This time of year, there is little water flowing and someone, likely a vagrant, has occasionally taken shelter down there and started up a fire to stay warm. The heat from that fire is what rose up and spoiled the wine in the crates directly above the drain."

Vamberry looked skeptical and shook his head. "No, we would have seen the smoke. It would have seeped out around the pallets."

Holmes rubbed his throat and took another swallow of the soothing liquor. "The fire would only have been lit at night when no one was working. Even if someone had been there, there are natural air currents that would carry the smoke down the aqueduct toward the river. You can check for yourself. The ashes from the last fire haven't completely washed away. I saw them myself this afternoon."

Vamberry nodded. "All right then. You've earned your fee, but you stay away from my family and don't ever come around to see me again!" He threw a quid and two shillings on a nearby shelf and stomped out the door, slamming it behind him.

Holmes downed the last of his glass and walked over to the shelf where his money lay. He used one hand to slide it into the other and stuffed it down into his pocket, mumbling to himself, "Not to worry. I've no wish to see you or your family ever again."

But wishing did not make it so.

Chapter VI

The evening meal provided by Holmes's landlord's wife was a middling affair of thinly sliced roast beef, day-old bread, overdone potatoes, and undercooked beans. Fortunately, Holmes whisky made it palatable. Afterward, he had settled into his chair by the hearth in his room and attempted to read the evening paper by the lamplight.

A knock came on his door, much more civil than his earlier visitor. When he opened it, he was a bit surprised to find his landlord's wife. The skinny old woman with the sour face and attitude to match said to him, "You have a visitor, Mr. Holmes. A *female* visitor, and you know the rules. This door stays open for as long as she's here."

She stepped aside and turned back to speak to the young lady behind her. "You heard me. House rules. All residents' doors stay open whenever a member of the opposite gender drops in, and if he tries anything funny, you just let out a yell and my old man will be here in two shakes of a lamb's tail."

The young woman nodded demurely and said, "Yes, ma'am."

Holmes couldn't believe his eyes. The last person on earth he wanted to see this night was standing in his doorway. Hester Vamberry was covered by a deep blue cloak with a hood that hid her features from anyone other than whomever she was directly looking at. And now she was looking at him . . . and he stood frozen at the sight.

She hesitated, waiting for an invitation, but the young man before her seemed dumbstruck. At last, she decided the chaperone's order allowed her to step inside, and she took a tentative step over the threshold.

Her movement toward him snapped Holmes out of his abstraction and he backed up to let her enter. He waved her toward the settee and remembered enough manners to ask if she would like some tea. She responded in the affirmative, and he was taken aback by the sound of her voice now that he heard it softly in close proximity, instead of from a distant stairwell. He shook his head and took a deep breath, resolving to treat her as a potential client and nothing more. He put the kettle on the stove and, while the water was heating, he went and sat in his customary chair opposite her.

"Miss Vamberry, please forgive the state of the room. I wasn't expecting company, least of all you. How did you find me?"

She drew back her hood and undid the top clasp of her cloak so she could shrug it off her shoulders. Smiling in a coquettish fashion, she replied, "Why, Mr. Holmes, I thought you were a detective. Can you not even deduce how I came to be here?"

Holmes's brain was starting to function again, albeit slowly. Then he answered, "I left my card with your mother."

"Yes," she said. "And she promptly threw it into the wastebasket. I retrieved it when she wasn't looking."

"But why?" enquired the young detective.

"She wouldn't explain why you came to see me, and I wanted to know. I never have strangers call upon me unless they have been sent by my father, and he always tells me when one is coming. Yet you march in, bold as brass, and request an audience. How did you know about me, and why did you come?"

Holmes attempted to take on a stern look as he faced his visitor. "Your father has already been here and admonished me for coming to your house today and causing your mother concern. If he hadn't chosen to enlighten you as to my reasons for wishing to speak to you – "

"My father," she interrupted, "is a stubborn man who believes he should do my thinking for me. I prefer to have the truth so as to make up my own mind. I insist you tell me the purpose of your visit. Were you coming to court me . . . or was there another reason?"

Could this meeting get any more painful? Even the forcefulness of her personality was so like that memory of his youth. He thought he had built up a wall against such sentiments as were rushing back at him, but his feelings must have exposed themselves in his countenance, for she suddenly leaned forward with concern. "What is it, Mr. Holmes? What's wrong?"

The whistle of the teakettle saved him from answering that question, for he had resolved never to speak of the subject that was so painful to the young student he had once been. He arose, went to the kitchen area, and poured two cups of tea. He called out to her, "Sugar or milk, Miss Vamberry?"

"A dash of both if you please," she replied.

He made hers so and came back with a cup on a saucer in each hand. He handed hers over and sat back down, taking a sip of his own before resuming this conversation. She hadn't taken her eyes off him – like a mother hen watching her chicks. She was waiting for a reply to one question or the other. He buoyed himself up and refused to become lost in those blue orbs. Then he chose to skip the latter question and answer the first.

"I wasn't coming to court you. Were that the case, I assure you I would have done so properly and arranged an introduction, rather than burst in unannounced. However, I was coming to question you regarding suitors you had declined, in order to obtain your opinion as to whether any of them might react by attempting to harm your father's business."

52

"That would be extraordinary, Mr. Holmes" she responded in bewilderment, and with a hint of disappointment which seemed to surprise her.

"Yet I have seen such actions for similar reasons in other cases I have worked." He set his cup down and chose to end this conversation as quickly as he could. "However, your father has taken me off the case. I provided him with a solution to his temporary problem and that is the end of it. You need no longer concern yourself."

He stood to emphasize the fact the interview was over. She looked up at him, surprised at this apparent dismissal. When it appeared that he would say no more, she stood and pulled her cloak back up and clasped it tightly. As she moved toward the door Holmes chose to plant a seed. "I leave you with one final thought, Miss Vamberry: Carpentry, especially the craftsmanship of furniture, is noble, creative, and artistic. It is a profession of which to be proud, as you may note in your *Gospels*. Specifically, *Mark*, Chapter Six."

She stared at him, confused by this incongruous statement. "I don't take your meaning, sir."

"Your father did share with me that your idea of a proper suitor seems to come from the romantic stories you read. I am merely suggesting you consider a different book, and perhaps you'll need to do no more than to love your neighbor."

Epilogue

Having finished his story, I couldn't help but ask Holmes, "So, were the fires below the wine crates set by Alan Chastain?"

Holmes shrugged. "I don't know, Doctor. I was removed from the case. My vagrant theory was just as viable as any other with the information I had at that point in time. If Vamberry put in the bars I suggested, his troubles from that aspect would be over."

I shook my head at this, but asked another question. "What about Miss Vamberry? Did she take your advice and give Chastain a chance?"

My flatmate shook his head. "As I said at the beginning, Watson, not all those early cases were successes. They didn't get together, and each married someone else."

Finally, I broached the subject which aroused the most curiosity in my mind. "You've never reacted to any woman in this way since I've known you, Holmes. In fact, you've never spoken of any woman at all. What happened nine years before, and what was the memory that Hester so reminded you of?"

Holmes re-stuffed his pipe and took his time at re-lighting it, as if contemplating whether or not he would answer my question. Finally, he walked over to the window, looked up toward the heavens, and replied, "That is a chapter I closed off long ago, Watson, and certainly not for publication." *

"They are not all successes, Watson," said he. "But there are some pretty little problems among them. Here's . . . the case of Vamberry, the wine merchant . . . ."

– Sherlock Holmes
"The Musgrave Ritual"

NOTE

*   The 1985 film *Young Sherlock Holmes*, transcribed by Chris Columbus, attempts to explain this missing chapter of Holmes's life in 1870, at age sixteen.

The Adventure of the
Aluminum Crutch
by Tracy Revels

"*Watson, this must cease!*"

I looked up from my breakfast to find my friend, Mr. Sherlock Holmes, holding a copy of the latest periodical in which I had recounted one of his adventures. He was scowling at me in the manner of a schoolmaster who finds himself supremely disappointed with a pupil.

"And why, Holmes? I thought it was a rather good story."

"Too good of a story," he complained. "Watson, your scribblings portray me as having unparalleled powers of deduction, not to mention unachievable levels of grooming. The business about my smooth chin and perfect linen, maintained while living upon the moor is, I will argue, a generous yet unnecessary exaggeration."

"But had it not been for you, a noble young man would have perished in the jaws of a hideous hound, and a villainous wretch afterward claimed his fortune. Surely that is worth recounting for the public."

"I will not deny its suitability for publication," Holmes said, as he picked up his morning pipe and added in the plugs and dottles from the previous evening. "But you will weary your audience with ceaseless tales of my successes."

"Would you rather I share your failures?" I chuckled, amused by the extent of Holmes's vanity. I had once found it insulting. It was a measure of the years we had known one another that I had come to view this aspect of his character with fondness.

"If they are interesting enough. Or if they have the potential for education. Consider the singular affair of the aluminum crutch."

"That case must have preceded our association," I said. "I recall you mentioning it just before you told me of the Musgrave Ritual."

"Yes, and under ordinary circumstances, I would say that it is an adventure that should never be chronicled. However . . . ."

"You have changed your mind?" I asked, even as I reached for my notebook. My friend dropped into his chair, twisting his long form into a position that would be excruciating for a less-limber man to hold. Yet I had seen him assume it before, when deep in thought, especially when recalling some distant memory.

"You may record my words verbatim, Watson, even if they are never published. This case taught me a very important lesson . . . ."

It was a hot summer's day in 1880. I was slouched in my chair, wilted from the heat, unwilling to move. All the windows were open, but no breeze stirred the curtains. The cacophony in Montague Street – where the road was being taken up – was enough to make men go mad. I found myself wishing my bank account would permit me to indulge in a weekend at Brighton, or any other spot near the ocean, far away from the choking haze of dirty old London, but at this point in my career, only a loan from Mycroft would have relieved my financial distress. My stubborn pride prevented me from making such an application.

The landlady pushed open the door to the sitting room. She was flapping a fan about her face and gave me an unfriendly look. Unlike our good Mrs. Hudson, the late Mrs. Lewis had little tolerance for my odd hours, noxious chemical experiments, and unsavory clientele.

"An Inspector Tibbett to see you, Mr. Holmes."

"Ah," I said, forcing myself to sit up and smooth my hair. "The grisly Twenshaw business. You have read of it, Mrs. Lewis?"

She grunted that she had not, confirming my deduction that she was the most uncurious of women. A few minutes later I welcomed a young, ginger-haired policeman to the room. Inspector Thomas Tibbett's attitude was one of worshipful respect, and he was grateful for a drink and a chance to settle onto the sofa. I knew at once, from a moment's observation, that he was recently married, even more recently promoted, and rather clumsy. This last deduction came from the fact that he put more of his gin on his jacket than in his mouth.

"We've heard of you even in western Sussex, sir. Reginald Musgrave lives not far from us, and he sings your praises to everyone. I know it is a great favor to ask, but can you come and help with our investigation?"

"I suspect Twenshaw would be cooler and fresher than the metropolis this time of year," I said. "But please share with me what has happened, and anything that the reporters may have left out."

The young man nodded eagerly. "I shall do my best, sir. It is perhaps obvious that we have very little in the way of crime in Twenshaw. A stolen cow or a pilfered pie is usually the extent of our mischief. The village has but a thousand residents at most, and all seem to get along. That is why we are so shocked and mortified that such a thing could happen to us.

"It was two weeks ago that a pair of little boys were wandering about the grove of trees which is known as Jenkins's Woods. Mr. Lucius Jenkins is an American who came to Twenshaw about seven or eight years ago, and built a new home, there amid the trees. He is a studious man, and rarely leaves his dwelling, but his faithful housekeeper, Miss Angel Baker, serves as his agent and lifeline to the world. He also has a ward, a little lad named Jethro. Mr. Jenkins is from the southern state of Florida and has told us that he was widowed before he arrived in our village. On my few visits to Jenkins' house, I came away with the impression that he is a man who prefers to live a retired life and devote his remaining years to study."

"He is an elderly gentleman?"

"I would place him in his late forties, perhaps."

I nodded. The young inspector seemed momentarily at a loss for words. I gently prompted him to continue.

"The boys?"

"Yes, the boys. I'm sorry. Ahem!" Tibbett coughed and collected himself. "You should know that no hunting is allowed in those woods, but the boys were being naughty and searching for bird eggs. They came across what we call a 'wych elm', a tree with a deep hollow. One boy stuck his hand inside and thought he had found a nest. What he pulled out was a human skull. The boys came screaming back into the village, and I went out along with my friend, Dr. Rook, to see what they had found. It was hard work removing the remains, sir, for the tree had grown around the corpse, but at last we were able to gather up all the evidence, which we carried back to the village and placed in the doctor's surgery.

"The bones had been picked almost-clean by insects, and of the clothing only a few faded and tattered scraps remained. Dr. Rook is a man of many interests, well-versed in anatomy and a reader of all the police journals. I doubt a more thorough man could be found, even in London. He cleaned and laid out the bones in their proper order and inspected them closely. I watched and took notes as he worked.

"'It was a woman,' the doctor told me. 'From the bones and the remaining strands of hair, I would place her between twenty and forty years of age at the time of death, though leaning toward the more youthful figure, as I see no evidence of disease. She was small, perhaps no more than five feet in height, and delicate of frame. I would call her attractive, except for this.' Here he gestured to the skull and the jawbone, which had become detached. I could tell that he was indicating her teeth. 'She was missing two, on the right side, and others were stained and decayed. No doubt she loved sweets and had little money for a dentist.'

"'Is there anything else the bones tell you?' I asked.

"'She likely died from a savage blow to the back of her head,' he added, turning the skull to show me the obvious damage. 'Death came quickly, and she didn't suffer.'

"Mr. Holmes, I hope you will not find me callous for saying how relieved I was to hear this. I had begun to imagine that the lady had climbed into the tree, perhaps while seeking shelter from bad weather, become entrapped, and starved to death.

"'I will venture one more opinion,' the doctor said. 'From the bones of her pelvis, I believe she was the mother of a child. But that is only an educated guess.'

"After that, we turned to the remains of her attire. Her dress had been made of cheap stuff, a kind of blue calico, and her petticoats and stockings were of wool. We found no belt, and just a handful of tin buttons were retrieved from the tree hollow, where they had fallen from the fabric as it decayed. There was a pair of women's boots which had been of relatively decent quality before their long entombment in the tree. A shoemaker's mark was still visible inside. We inspected it closely and decided that the stamp read *Brown's Goods, Madison, USA.*"

"'Surely this woman was an American!' I said to the doctor. 'There is a large city called Madison, in the state of Wisconsin.'

"'What on earth was an American doing here?' he asked. 'Do you think she was visiting Jenkins? She was found in his woods.'"

Here, I smiled at Tibbett's naiveté. "America is a very large nation, Inspector."

Tibbett looked abashed. "Funny, Mr. Jenkins repeated those exact same words to me. I was reluctant to even raise the matter with him at first, but after I asked around the village, the owner of The Ewe and Lamb had a strange story that I couldn't, in good conscience, fail to investigate. The Ewe is the only hotel in the village. Dr. Rook suggested that the bones had been in the tree for several years, and so I went to the inn and asked Hubert O'Conner, the proprietor, if he recalled any lady from America who might have passed through. Much to my astonishment, he did. He turned pages of his register as he talked.

"'I recall her because I almost turned her away, thinking anyone so poor wouldn't have the money to pay for her lodgings, and I don't run an institution for indigents.'

"'What did she look like?'

"'Tiny little thing, dressed in blue, cheap stuff. A large bonnet, in an old-fashioned style. She carried a baby and a carpetbag, and – perhaps this is why I remember her so well – she had a pipe in her mouth!'"

"I was astonished, though instantly I thought about the missing teeth, and how often I have seen such a gap in heavy smokers. I encouraged him to go on.

"'Well, as I said, when she asked for a room, I asked if she had funds to pay for it, especially as she was alone. She pulled out three sovereigns, slapped them on my desk, and told me I should have more respect for a lady. As if she was a lady! She had a strange accent – American, I suppose – but the coins were good, so I gave her a key. Here is her signature.'

"I looked in the record. *B. McGruder* was scrawled in a very bad hand, and the date was *March 1, 1875.*

"'How long did she stay?'

"'No time at all. She went to her room with the child and came down not an hour later. She asked for directions to Jenkins's Woods, and I pointed the way to her, warning her that it would be dark soon. She gave me a curt thanks and moved along, still carrying her child on her hip. I didn't see her again that night. She never asked for supper, nor for breakfast the next day. My girl went up to clean her room at about noon, and found it empty, with the key tossed upon the bed. The bed didn't look to have been slept in.'

"'So she vanished! Why did you not alert me or the constable?'

"The innkeeper – who, I should tell you, is a reformed felon with a prison tattoo on his hand – gave a harsh laugh.

"'She paid enough for a week! What did I care if her business took her elsewhere?'

"The fellow had a point, I supposed. I wondered what her connection with the woods had been, and the only one that suggested itself was that Mr. Jenkins, the owner, was a fellow American. And so I went to his house, where I was admitted by Miss Baker, his housekeeper."

"A word about her might be in order, Mr. Holmes. She is a singular woman who has been of great interest in the village since she arrived several years ago. She is tall and big-boned, and her strength is unmatched for a female. Once, a cart fell over on the butcher's son, and she dropped her basket and righted it before any man could step in to help. She is a woman of very few words. Her hair is wavy, and her eyes are a mysterious shade, sometimes green but often gold. She has excited many hearts among the widowers and the older bachelors of the village, but she holds her head high and her nose higher still and will give no one so much as the time of day."

"You said she has been with Jenkins a few years?"

"That is correct. I have never heard the story first-hand, but the gossip among the women is that she was a servant to another American who came to England as a sightseer and perished within a week of arrival, leaving this woman stranded with no funds or friends. Somehow, she learned of Mr. Jenkins's American origins and appealed to him. She is a wonderful cook and adept at preparing the kinds of foods Jenkins has craved since leaving his native country. The woman is also inordinately attached to the ward, who arrived to them as a baby and is now a little lad of some six or seven years. The lady adores him like a mother."

"You seem to have lost your thread again," I chided. "You were interviewing Jenkins?"

"Oh . . . Oh yes . . . I asked him if he knew of an American woman named McGruder, and he said he had never known anyone with that surname. Of course, it could be an alias, so I used the description that the innkeeper had provided, along with holding out a swatch of cloth from the dress. Jenkins turned pale but shook his head. I told him that we had found *Brown's Goods, Madison, USA* stamped in the boot.

"'Why, Madison is in Wisconsin,' he said. 'I was born and raised in Florida. Those states are a great distance from one another!'"

"I confessed it was rather a long shot, but I thanked him for his time. Miss Baker let me out, and her face was inscrutable."

I reached for my pipe. "Has any more been learned?"

"I have sent a telegram to the Chief of Police in Madison, Wisconsin, to see if perhaps the woman had a record there or was missing from her family. Other than that, what should I do?"

I gestured with the lit match. "The obvious."

"Which is?"

"The child!" I snapped. "You found the mother murdered. What became of the babe?"

The inspector turned pale. "Good Lord! I hadn't thought of it that way. If the mother was killed – !"

"There are two possibilities," I told him. "Either the child was killed as well, and its body hasn't been found, or whoever murdered the woman took the child." Tibbett was staring at me as if I had just pulled a rabbit from a hat. "When did Jenkins acquire his ward?"

"It was – let me see – before the fire at the church, and after the river flooded and – My God! It could have been about the same time the woman was murdered!"

I rose from my chair. "Inspector, I believe you should take the next train for Twenshaw. Your very interesting story has opened avenues for investigation. I shall pursue them here and follow you in a few days' time."

"Should I arrest Mr. Jenkins?"

"Not yet. But it wouldn't hurt to mention my name in the village, especially to the innkeeper."

"Why is that sir?"

"Because when I was a mere schoolboy, my evidence put him in prison! You might suggest to him that if he has anything further to add, he will want to share it with me."

Once the inspector departed, I threw on my coat and braved the putrid conditions, travelling first to Scotland Yard and later to the British Library.

My research required two days of work, but by the second afternoon I had telegraphed to Tibbett that I would be joining him for tea in Twenshaw the next day.

It is wonderful to have friends at Scotland Yard who can facilitate international communications. At the time, I had just unraveled a knotty problem for Lestrade, and saved Gregson from an embarrassing demotion. Both were more than happy to use their official credentials to open a long-distance interrogation. Through my labors, I came into an interesting collection of facts.

Americans are very fond of naming cities and counties for their fourth president, the man they consider the "Father of the Constitution". When he arrived in the village, Jenkins told his neighbors, and later the inspector, that he was from Florida. I soon learned there is a Madison County in that state, and its seat is also named Madison. Telegraphic inquiries with legal officials there painted an intriguing story.

The Jenkins family once possessed a large plantation. Jenkins's father was killed in the Great Rebellion, and his mother died after the war's conclusion. Mother and son had been destitute when their enslaved property was liberated, but after the old lady's demise, a wonderous thing occurred. Jenkins and a man named Clough McGruder, the former overseer of the plantation, suddenly became wealthy. No one in the town knew where their wealth originated, but both men were "flush", as the gamblers say. McGruder, a despicable and mean fellow, was often intoxicated, and when in his cups he bragged that he had traded an old hat and a horse for a treasure. No sensible explanation was ever offered.

In March of 1873, McGruder's good fortune ended abruptly when, in a drunken rage, he shot a black man on the courthouse square. McGruder thrown in jail. Five days later, his supposed-friend Jenkins departed from Savannah, bound for England. He never provided any legal aid or assistance to his pal. McGruder's only family was his daughter, who was nineteen years of age. Many citizens in the town pitied her, for she was in a family way without a husband.

It seemed possible – probable even – that Jenkins was the father of her child. It also appeared likely that Jenkins and McGruder had come into possession of an illicit fortune, but once McGruder was incarcerated, Jenkins made off with both shares. He stole the girl's legacy as surely as he had stolen her virtue.

No scenario could have been clearer. The offended girl had borne the child and, by great persistence, tracked her lover across the ocean to his lair to demand her share of the loot. She must have corresponded with Jenkins, and he suggested the rendezvous in the woods, where he murdered her, stuffed her body into the tree, and took the child to raise as his "ward".

I confess I boarded the train to Twenshaw that morning in high spirits, certain that I was correct in my deductions. But fate was to prove otherwise.

I stepped onto the platform at Twenshaw just as the sun was setting, for there had been numerous and infuriating delays along the tracks. Inspector Tibbett appeared happy to see me. We adjourned to a sitting room at The Ewe and Lamb, where I shared my theory with him. The inspector's face fell.

"This might explain why I never received an answer to my telegram to Wisconsin," he muttered.

"No doubt it does," I said, reminding myself that gloating would be an ungentlemanly action. Tibbett's face had turned as red as his hair.

"And I am truly sorry to hear your deductions, for Jenkins always seemed such a *good* gentleman. To think that he is capable of murder! Perhaps we should – What's this?"

The innkeeper had barged into the room. Hubert O'Conner's disreputable looks hadn't improved from the time when, as a lad, I alerted the police to the fact he was stealing specimens from our school's laboratory, a crime for which he ultimately received a brief prison sentence. He arrived towing a slender girl by one arm. He gave me a brusque nod but naturally said nothing of our previous encounter. Instead, he shook the girl roughly.

"Now, Edith: Out with it for the gentlemen. Tell them what you saw and what you took!"

The girl stepped forward. She was clearly the man's daughter, for she bore his strong features.

"Father sent me to clean the lady's room – the lady who vanished. I told Father that the bed wasn't slept in, and the key was returned. That was the truth."

"Yes," the innkeeper snapped. "But tell them the *rest* of it, which you didn't tell me until I beat the truth out of you yesterday. Tell them what you stole!"

The girl wiped her face with her apron. "The lady left her carpetbag behind. I looked through it, to see what was inside."

"And what did you find?" I asked. "Do not be afraid to tell us."

"I found five pounds," the girl finally admitted, "and some American silver coins, but only a few. There was a dirty shift, and a grey calico frock, some clothes for a baby. And a picture." She cut furtive eyes at her father.

"I took them all and hid them in an outhouse. I spent the money, and sold the clothes and carpetbag to a peddler."

"Did you keep the photograph?" I asked.

The girl nodded and pulled it from her pocket. I expected to find a picture of Jenkins, or perhaps of the woman and her baby.

Much to my surprise, it was a man, dressed in the fashion of the 1860's, with curly hair, a low beard, and a pleasant face. Neither of us recognized him. Gold lettering on the *carte de viste* informed us that the image was a product of the Bonair Studio of Richmond, Virginia. Written on the reverse was a strange message"

> *M. M. Bonfals, who traded a treasure for an old horse and a dirty hat.*

"Who might this individual be?" I asked.

"Is it even relevant?" the inspector replied.

I looked up and addressed the innkeeper. "Your apple hasn't fallen far from your tree, Hubert. It was for thievery that you were sent to prison. You have my permission to chastise your daughter, but not to harm her. If there is any report of your bad conduct, I have more information about you that might be of interest to the authorities."

The innkeeper touched his hand to his brow and took the girl away. I reconsidered the picture.

"It is late, so we shall have our discussion with Mr. Jenkins in the morning. Have you mentioned me to him, Inspector?"

"I made a point to ride by yesterday, after I got your telegram, but he was said to be ill and not receiving company. I gave the message to his housekeeper, who promised to relay it."

"Very good. I shall retain this picture. This Mr. Bonfals appears to be a jolly enough fellow – if only I could think where I have seen him before!"

I didn't sleep well that night. Clearly, there was something about the new information – as disconnected as it appeared on the surface – that disturbed me.

I took breakfast at seven, and by eight had joined Inspector Tibbett in a carriage. We passed the woods on the way, and Tibbett pointed to the general location where the body was found. He asked me if I would like to see the tree where the body was hidden. Much to his surprise, I shook his head.

"It can hardly matter now. Let us continue."

Ten minutes later, we reached the property. It was a neat villa-style home of relatively recent construction, built for convenience and comfort rather than display. The lawn needed attention, however, and I asked Tibbett if there was no staff beyond the housekeeper.

"None. Jenkins has contracts with various workmen in the village. I asked him once why he didn't employ more servants, and he gave an odd answer. He said that having people defer to him reminded him too much of slavery, and he had deep regrets of ever participating in that system."

"He is a pious man?" I asked.

"If so, only in personal devotions. He has never been seen at church, though he has been relatively generous to village charities."

We walked to the door, knocking vigorously. We waited a moment, then knocked again. Tibbett's face grew flushed.

"Surely someone is awake!"

I walked further on the drive, studying the soft earth. "Does Jenkins possess a pony and a dogcart?"

Tibbett turned. "Why, yes."

"Then your bird has flown and isn't planning to return. Look at the depths of these depressions. The cart was loaded."

The inspector's jaw dropped. He pounded harder on the door, then twisted the knob, scowling when it wouldn't yield.

"I could go back to the village and find the locksmith. Or we could break a window."

"Neither will be necessary," I said, kneeling and studying the lock. "Why do builders use these?" I muttered, removing a little velvet case from my inner coat pocket. "Even a child could pick them." I selected the appropriate tool and, with two quick twists of my wrist, the door was open.

The house was dark and silent. Tibbett called once for the housekeeper, then hushed. Our footsteps echoed as we moved from room to room. All were tastefully decorated, but there was little sign of a personality at work. I saw no photographs or portraits, no intriguing trinkets or curious rugs. The house looked like a set from a play. Only the study, which was filled with books, maps, and piles of paper, gave any impression of the man who lived there. I quickly rummaged through the books and papers.

"These seem to deal with the America war," I said. "All are works of politics and history."

Tibbett froze in his journey around a bookcase. "Mr. Holmes!" he shouted. "Look – It is the same man!"

I snatched the colored sketch from its perch, then pulled the photograph from my pocket. The images were indeed of the same man. Written beneath the drawing was another name: *Judah P. Benjamin.*

Instantly, I recalled who he was – a former member of the Confederate cabinet, now an English barrister following his escape from the southern states after the war. "Our friend Jenkins is certainly obsessed with him," I added to myself as I found other photographs and drawings of the man that were scattered about the room. "But what is the connection?"

A strangled cry sent me running into the hallway. Tibbett had been exploring the rest of the house and now he was leaning in an open doorway, his face pale, and his lips quivering.

"It is over," he said. "Jenkins is in there, in bed. He has killed himself with a pistol."

I sighed.

"It is clear. Jenkins robbed his partner, despoiled the man's daughter, and then sought refuge in England. He murdered his paramour because he didn't love her. With her rough clothes and pipe, she would hardly have made a fitting lady for his English life. When his servant informed him of our interest, he knew his time had come. He sent Miss Baker and his child off on some journey, to spare them finding him. A sad but predictable conclusion. Well, let us view the final scene."

I stepped past the inspector, walking into the bedroom. It was a modest chamber, with a single bed in which the body rested. There was a neat bullet hole from a derringer pistol in the man's right temple. The gun rested some distance away.

I hesitated, for a moment questioning my eyesight. Then I stepped forward and gently pulled down the sheet that had been drawn to the man's chest, in the process exposing his body, which wore only a short nightshirt.

You have seen me angry, friend Watson, but you have never seen me in a *rage*. I suspect it is a terrible thing to witness, and I was a younger man at the time, with less control over my reactions to idiocy. I spun on the inspector with a savage fury.

"You *fool*!" I shouted. "You utter *ass*! Why didn't you tell me the man was crippled?"

I pointed to the gentleman's legs. Both were withered. By their appearance, they had been almost useless to Jenkins in his lifetime. I noted an aluminum crutch leaned against the wall.

"His left leg is much shorter than his right," I continued. "He has surely been lame since childhood. Why did you not tell me?"

The young inspector cowered like a whipped dog. "I just . . . didn't think of it. I am so used to seeing him this way, and you never asked about his legs and . . . ."

"What about his missing *arm*?" I thundered. "Did that not strike you as a significant detail?"

The right sleeve of the dead man's nightshirt was empty.

"I . . . I suppose not. It was a tragedy for him, I know he said it was amputated just before he came to the village but . . . Why does it matter?"

"For two very important reasons," I snapped. "The first is that he couldn't have murdered Miss McGruder. How would he have navigated his way into twisted, tangled woods? How would he have possessed the strength to strike her with a heavy object? And most importantly, how would he have lifted a dead body, folded it up, and stashed it in a tree?"

The inspector's face was so red it looked primed to explode. "I suppose he could not."

"And as for the second – you say he committed suicide."

"Well – there's the gun on the bed, and there is the wound to his right temple and . . . oh. I see your point. I don't suppose he could shoot himself with his left arm, and then toss the gun so far to his right."

"I have no more business here. The killer is Miss Angel Baker, who for reasons unknown to us wanted vengeance on both these individuals and is now in possession of their child, and possibly their fortune."

I was incensed I walked back to the village. A brief interview with the station master confirmed that Miss Baker and Master Jethro had departed on the afternoon train, the previous day. No doubt I had crossed paths with them on that platform!

They had a day's lead on me, and who knew what type of alias she would adopt or where she would travel. I could have given it my attention, but I wasn't blessed with my talents solely to rectify the mistakes of others.

All during the journey home, I gnashed my teeth in frustration. The servant had killed the man and his lover. There was no other logical deduction. She clearly possessed the physical strength to do so – I recalled Tibbett's story about the cart. If Tibbett had been as descriptive of Jenkins, I wouldn't have wasted time and our felon would be behind bars.

The only consolation was that it seemed the woman meant the child no harm. The offense was committed against the mother and father. But what offense was it? And how did it connect with the photographs of Judah P. Benjamin? What role did he play in this? Why did Miss McGruder carry an old photograph of the man, with a different name inscribed upon it?"

Then it came to me, just as the train approached London. What a fool I'd been! The name written on the first picture was *Bonfals*. That word in French means "*good disguise*". McGruder bragged of gaining his wealth by trading a horse and an old hat for a treasure. Perhaps the men aided the fugitive Benjamin in his escape through their state and received largesse for their assistance. But I would never know. To dwell on such frustration would be to grind the wheels of the mental machine. Therefore, I trudged back to Montague Street, swore that I would never speak of the matter again, and turned my mind to other things.

A month passed. Then, to my great surprise, a letter was forwarded to me from that idiot in Twenshaw. Here – you may read it for yourself:

My Dear Mr. Holmes,

Reginald Musgrave, who lives not far from our village, has made you famous in the neighborhood. When Inspector Tibbett told me you were coming to our house, I knew I had to act immediately. Ever since the body was discovered in the tree, Jenkins had been ill. Guilt, remorse, and fear were acting upon him, and he kept whispering that he should be arrested for the crime, when he had never known Becca was in England. I convinced him to stay in bed and rest, and I gave him a heavy draught of laudanum. Then, just before Jethro and I departed, I shot him dead. I could have placed the wound correctly, but it was my final gift to him, to show he was not a suicide. He could be buried in hallowed ground even though, God knows, he did not deserve such a privilege.

I offer my story not because I seek forgiveness or even understanding, but because I respect you, sir, and I have read in the papers that Inspector Tibbett made a mess of things. You are no doubt furious with him and wish to know the truth, so I will provide it.

My real name is Laura Stokes, and my father was Reverend John Stokes, a Negro minister. Before he was a freedman, my father was a slave on the Jenkins's plantation, where he was cruelly treated, frequently beaten, and often starved. He was even forced to take two women as wives, for old Colonel Jenkins viewed his enslaved people as livestock, and wished them to breed. When freedom came, my mother chose to move to Jacksonville, and I went with her. We were forgotten by white folks in Madison, but Father cared deeply for us, and visited when he could. He loved me no less for having been the child of his "assigned" second wife. He was a good man, one who urged us to forgive those who had harmed us, and to live in peace with all people.

And yet in March 1873, Father was gunned down by a drunken white man, in broad daylight, on the courthouse steps! My father was beloved for his work and his goodness to both races, while McGruder was despised as a bully and a

67

town drunk. You should know that our state had just elected a Republican governor who did not hesitate to sign the death warrant when McGruder was convicted. Yet McGruder's execution was not enough for me to feel that Father had received justice. I blamed Jenkins as well, for he was the one who kept McGruder drunk and disorderly.

Jenkins fled to England when his friend McGruder was arrested, but I did not sleep until I tracked down McGruder's daughter, who gossips in Madison said was carrying Jenkins's child. I went to her and, in the guise of a humble freedwoman, offered to work for very little pay. I called myself Angel Baker. I won her confidence – soon she trusted me with many secrets, including the one which explained Jenkins's sudden wealth: Judah P. Benjamin, the Confederate Secretary of State, had fled into Florida at the end of the war. He arrived at the Jenkins's plantation one dark and rainy night in 1865, begging for aid. The Yankee soldiers were in pursuit, and he was desperate to escape them. Old Mrs. Jenkins made him a suit of common farmer's clothes, while her son and McGruder, the overseer, scouted a safe route for him to follow. McGruder gave Benjamin his hat and nag of a horse. Benjamin left behind a locked satchel, asking Mrs. Jenkins to guard it until his return.

Jenkins and McGruder wondered what was in the satchel, but the old lady refused to allow them to open it. As soon as the breath left her body in 1870, they cut into the bag, finding gold coins and jewels. Clearly, Benjamin had been afraid such a fortune would betray him, should he be detained and questioned. Jenkins invited McGruder to live on the plantation again, and McGruder's daughter Becca – who was a pretty girl, except for her bad teeth – fell in love with Jenkins. That foul man promised McGruder a fair division of the spoils but instead plied him with alcohol and lied about how much money they possessed. The day McGruder shot my father, he was drunk on Jenkins's whisky. As soon as he learned McGruder was arrested, Jenkins packed all the treasure and fled to England, leaving a broken-hearted Becca – who had become his mistress – behind to mourn.

Though I had sworn myself to revenge, I had a weakness. I longed for children but been told by a doctor I could never bear them. When Becca gave birth to Jethro that summer, my hard and angry heart began to soften. I turned from wanting

68

vengeance to dreaming of the treasure, and scheming as to how I could achieve it so that Becca and the baby and I could live in comfort.

I suggested the plan of action for Becca to follow. I told her that I should go to England, find Jenkins, and attach myself to him as a servant. Once I had taken the measure of the situation, I would bring her over to confront him with his child. I had a little money of my own, and Becca sold off the trinkets Jenkins had given her to buy passage for me to travel to England alone. As you now know, Jenkins was a man of a rather distinctive description, and my quest did not take as long as I had anticipated. I did not reveal my origins to him, but my southern voice was clearly a salve for he led a lonely life. He paid me exceptionally good wages, and the local butcher rewarded me handsomely for saving the life of his son when a cart fell upon the child. Every penny I received was hoarded to bring Becca and Jethro across.

Soon, all was ready. I sent Becca the ticket to come to England. I instructed her not to tell anyone what her mission might be, and to take a room at the inn and meet me in the woods that night. She came as I instructed, and there, in the darkness, as little Jethro slept on a blanket, I told her the truth – who I was, what I had planned, and how my heart had changed from hate to love. I told her that we could confront Jenkins and threaten him with the exposure that he had stolen Judah P. Benjamin's treasure. Benjamin was alive and working in England – he could take his own legal revenge. The shame of the revelation alone – for Jenkins had become obsessed with the famous man – would no doubt bend Jenkins to our will. He would give us what we asked to make us go away.

The one thing I had not accounted for was Becca's feelings for Jenkins. A thousand times she had proclaimed her hatred of him, how she would murder him with her own hands if she could for abandoning her. But now, so close to seeing him again, she changed her mind. I told her he was even sicker and weaker than he had been at home, that an arm had been amputated, but this news only inflamed her.

And then, Mr. Holmes, she began to abuse me. She called me every vile and filthy name that has ever been applied to my race. She screamed she was glad my father had been killed, and that she would shoot me with her own gun. She pulled a

69

derringer from her bosom. A shot rang out but went wide. I
seized a heavy, fallen branch. She had turned and was trying
to reload the gun. I crashed the branch down upon her head.
Her brains glistened in the moonlight.

May God forgive me.

I knew I would hang, that no one would defend me. I
picked up her body, folded her like a quilt, and shoved her into
the hollow of the tree. Little Jethro had just awakened and
begun to cry. I bundled him up and carried him back to the
villa and gave him just enough mother's cordial to make him
sleep. Then I slipped back to the inn and returned the key. I
thought of taking Becca's carpetbag with me, but a noise in
the inn startled me, and I ran off without it.

Jenkins was away on business, and when he returned, I
concocted a story of how I had found the child abandoned on
our steps, wrapped only in a blanket. Jenkins knew of my
fondness for children, and agreed to let the little boy stay,
taking him as his ward. He never knew the child was his own.

Now you have the truth. Two wicked people have
perished from this earth, but their son shall not suffer for their
perfidy. I have decided I want nothing of their Confederate
treasure, for it was earned on the bloody backs of my people.
I took only enough money to transport us back to America,
where we shall live in peace under new names. I am strong
and able and can work hard to support my boy. I will make
sure Jethro grows to be a good man, one that all people will
be proud of.

Very Sincerely Yours,
Miss Laura Stokes
a.k.a Angel Baker

At this point I shook my head, wondering how she proposed to claim
the child as her own, if she was black and the child was white. Surely
people would question the arrangement. And then a postscript fell from
the folds of the paper. It seemed that the lady had anticipated the question.

Please do not waste your time in seeking us, thinking that
our novelty might set us apart. My father and my mother were
both people of mixed race, the offspring of enslaved women
and lecherous masters. As a result, my own skin is of a lighter
hue, my nose is straight and my hair only wavey, rather than

70

curled. It is quite easy for me to "pass" as white in my own nation, as I did in yours.

"Remarkable!" I cried at the end of the narration. Holmes shook his head.

"Deplorable."

"Holmes!"

My friend smiled ruefully. "It taught me an important lesson: A true detective must *see* and *observe*. He must also learn to ask piercing questions of witnesses who only see, to learn what there is to observe. A few pointed inquiries would have immediately exposed the flaws in my assumptions and prevented the murderess's escape."

I looked back at the letter. "Will you be incensed with me if I say that I am glad you failed in this case?"

"In truth, Watson," my friend's lean cheeks took on the slightest of hues, "I am grateful that I did as well. But I have never forgiven that fool, Tibbett."

"What is he doing now?" I asked. "Surely he is no longer a policeman."

"Tibbett was widowed in 1890 but has since remarried. His new lady is a local heiress, and Tibbett currently lives the life of a country squire, spending his days hunting fowl. If his eyesight is as weak as his wit, our feathered friends are in no significant danger."

"Here's the record of the Tarleton murders and the case of Vamberry, the wine merchant, and the adventure of the old Russian woman, and the singular affair of the aluminium crutch . . . ."

— Sherlock Holmes
"The Musgrave Ritual"

The Most Winning Woman
By Liese Sherwood-Fabre

In the spring of 1895, Holmes and I had just sat down for breakfast when Mrs. Hudson, our faithful landlady, arrived with a small paper-wrapped box for my friend. After he took it from her and studied the writing upon it, the color drained from his lips and his hand shook as he used his kipper knife to slice the string around the box. I rushed to the tantalus and returned with the brandy bottle, adding a drop or two to his morning tea.

From my place behind him, I observed his slow, deliberate moves to unwrap the parcel – as if it might contain some gruesome offering. His cautious efforts called to mind the grisly "present" of two severed ears as recounted in the matter of the cardboard box. Fearing what he might uncover, I decided a sip from the brandy bottle might not be out of line for myself as well.

When the contents were finally revealed, however, a wave of disappointment passed through me. The box contained a folded, yellowed document, and two other sheets of paper underneath.

Holmes took a sip of his fortified tea and studied first the older document before removing the other two. One, I could discern, was an official death certificate. The second, a letter written in the rather crude and awkward hand of an uneducated person.

After reading the letter, he passed all three to me without a word. I took them to my seat and let my breakfast grow cold while I read them. Holmes also appeared to have lost his appetite. He merely steepled his hands, his elbows resting on the table, and watched me as I perused the lot.

The original document was a life insurance policy for a Mr. Jameson Windom. It listed the beneficiary as a Margaret Windom. The death certificate was also for a Jameson Windom, with the cause of death listed as consumption. Finally, I turned my attention to the letter:

Dear Mr. Holmes,

You are so famus now, you might have foregotin me, but I am keping my promis to you. I am sending you a kopi of my Jameson's deth certifikat to show you I did not kil him and he dyed in his bed of konsumshun. Our dauter Margaret will reseve the insurans moniy.

72

Pleez now reles me from my obligashun.

Yours truly,
Mrs. Grace Windom

When I finished, I raised my gaze to meet his, but could tell his thoughts were elsewhere.

"Holmes?" I asked. He started and shook himself as if to settle his thoughts back into the present. "Was she one of your clients?"

His mouth turned down into a grimace. "Hardly. She was . . . I'm not sure how to categorize her. An almost-murderess, I suppose, would be the best. Had I not intervened, Mr. Jameson Windom wouldn't have made it to his next birthday. And their daughter, Margaret . . . I suppose she would have been the next victim."

"Good Lord." I drew in my breath. "Why was this packet not sent from a prison? This woman is free?"

"I said she was an almost*-murderess. As you can see, her husband died of consumption, and her daughter lives to inherit his insurance – although I will confirm that Margaret thrives. The last time I saw her, she wasn't yet two. Imagine that. The girl is now a young woman of seventeen or so." He glanced at the ceiling. "Where has the time gone?" Refocusing on me, he asked, "Do you recall I once told you that the most winning woman I ever met poisoned her children for the insurance money?"*

"You mean, Mrs. Windom – ?"

He waved his hand, brushing away the words I'd pronounced. "No. No. I'm referring to Mrs. Josephine Reynolds – a particularly charming woman with as black a heart as ever lived. She was hanged for her crimes, but I regret not being able to bring her to true justice."

He finished his tea and pushed his plate back. I had to say, my appetite had disappeared, but my desire to hear the full explanation overwhelmed me.

Following a long moment of contemplation on the scene outside our window, he turned to me. "Given that Jameson Windom is now in his final resting place, I feel I can now share the full details of the package's contents." He glanced around the room as his attention returned to the present. "Let's retire to our places by the fire. You may need the warmth, for it is a very cold tale indeed."

Once in our customary places, Holmes stuffed his pipe from the tobacco in his Persian slipper resting on the mantel beside him. The pipe's smoke drifted toward the ceiling where it curled about on the early-morning breeze coming from the opened window. The room's cheery atmosphere contrasted so with the dark, grim tale he then recounted . . . .

As you know, prior to our arrangements here at 221b, I let rooms in Montague Street, and had already done work for Scotland Yard as well as some private clients. My reputation also was growing, thanks to my assistance to Reginald Musgrave, and it was actually through him this case arrived at my doorstep.

Jonathan Barnes arrived with a letter of introduction from Reginald in the fall of 1880. Reginald didn't explain in his missive the exact nature of Barnes' problem. He only noted that Barnes was a tenant on his land, was an honest, hard-working soul, and needed my help.

The man was terribly distraught and couldn't stand still. Pacing back and forth in front of me, he shared how his brother had passed unexpectedly two weeks earlier. "It weren't right, Mr. Holmes, how Malcolm died. The man had barely passed thirty. He was a bricklayer and strong as an ox. A week-and-a-half ago, I gets a telegram from Lila, his wife, saying he died of dysent'ry. Me poor mum and da were beside themselves. Lord Musgrave – God love 'im – gives us the money to get to London for the burial. But when we arrive, we find Lila's already put 'im in the ground. She sent the telegram two days after poor Malcolm had gone from this earth."

"Dysentery? Had she called a doctor? Did you speak to him?"

"She said she did call a doctor, only's it was too late. Showed me the death certificate he signed. Cause of death: Dysent'ry."

"Do you have the name of this doctor?"

"I copied it from the certificate, but here's the queer part, sir. My brother made enough to keep 'em in house and victuals, but not much more. She was wearin' *new* widow's weeds – not secondhand. I don't know much about those things, but my mum, she's a seamstress, and she said it was the latest style."

"And did you share any of this with the authorities?"

"I tried, sir, but they weren't interested. Said people die of the dystent'ry all the time. That the water or food can go bad here in the city, and nothin' can save the poor wretch what comes across it."

"You have shared some very disturbing turn of events. I will research your brother's death further. Now share with me your particulars, including those of your brother's widow. Once I have more information, I will contact you through Lord Musgrave."

After noting the name and address of the widow Barnes and the doctor's name, he took his leave, and I went to work.

The doctor's surgery in Whitechapel was located next to a chemist's shop and near a pub. His practice barely met the definition of "doctor" or "surgery". The anterior room was filled with the inhabitants of that slum, experiencing all kinds of afflictions. His attendant, a woman in a filthy, blood-spattered apron, fairly curtsied when I entered.

"Dr. Kinston is with a patient at the moment," she said, over the screams coming from behind a door, "but I'm sure he'll attend you straightaways, sir."

The doctor had a similar, obsequious manner. "'Ow can I help you, sir? You look fit enough. Got a young lady in trouble? I can fix it."

His offer to perform an illegal act immediately marked the man's unscrupulous nature, and I considered the possibility he was involved in Malcolm Barnes' untimely demise.

"I understand you signed the death certificate for Malcolm Barnes. What do you recall of his condition?"

"Barnes?" The short, scruffy man squeezed his eyes together as if trying to recall. "I sees so many, sir. Do you have an address?" When I provided that bit of information, his face brightened slightly. "Yes. I do recall. A bad case of the dysent'ry. His wife called me in. Such a pretty, young thing she is. Won't have no trouble finding another husband, that one. I gave him some laudanum for the pain. Next day, his wife come in to tell me he passed in the night and asked for a certificate. Said she needed it for the insurance."

"Do you recall anything odd or different about the man's illness?"

Another puckering of his face and a shake of his head. "No. See a lot of dysent'ry here. People die of it every day. Course, they have other reasons. Only last week, a woman died givin' birth. Baby boy died too. They brung in a man run over by a wagon in front of my surgery." He shook his head. "Couldn't do nuthin' for him. Expired right there on my table. Happens all the time. You'd be hard-pressed to find a family in this area that ain't lost a loved one or two this past year. Consumption, dysent'ry, cholera. Sees it all the time. People die here."

While Barnes might have indeed contracted dysentery and passed from natural causes, the doctor's apathetic response to a patient's death suggested two items: The first being that he hadn't actually viewed the man after he succumbed, and that most likely his wife would be the only one with another first-hand knowledge of his last breaths.

Given the doctor's attitude in response to my attire, I changed my dress for that of a laborer's pants, shirt, and cap.

Mrs. Lila Barnes lived not far from the surgery. The woman wasn't at home, and after some inquiring, I learned she was most likely to be found at a knitting club located a few streets away. I found it strange that a woman who had so recently lost her husband would attend such a social meeting, and after gaining directions to the club, sought her out there.

The club met in an upper room in a public house called The Wolf and Badger. The pub itself was next to a stable with wagons for hire. I was very pleased when I learned this, because there is no better source of information regarding the local population than a publican, and here, the group was right in its midst.

The pub appeared the same as any other in that part of the city with sawdust on the floor that hadn't been changed in years, scarred tables and benches scattered about the room, and the scent of stale beer and gin that burned one's nose. Given the still-early hour, the place wasn't full, but those occupying the bar and tables were a rough lot served by an even-rougher-looking man. Upon entering, I shouldered my way between two men at the bar. No sooner had I ordered a gin than a woman passed through toward a set of stairs at the back. She was dressed in mourning clothes, and when the man returned with my drink, I asked, "Is that Malcolm Barnes' widow? I thought I recognized her."

"No," the man said and wiped the bar in front of me. "That be Amos Hardy's widow. She should be gettin' out of her deep weeds soon. Been gone almost a year now. About half of 'em are in black. I think that's what they do – knit shawls, scarves, and the like for the newly bereaved."

"Surely not all of them are widows?"

"Some have lost a son or daughter, like poor Mrs. Sanders. Both her babies. Or mother or father."

This bit of news immediately struck me. Here was a "club", if you will, for mourners.

"How many women are in the group?"

"I don't count 'em."

"Well, then, how many are up there right now?"

"Twenty, maybe."

"Don't you consider it odd there are so many widows in one place?"

The man had been wiping a glass with a rag, but at my question, he stopped and stared me straight in the eye and responded to me with the same observation as the doctor earlier. "Are you daft? People die here every day."

Despite the assertion by these two men concerning the death rate in this part of London, I couldn't help but feel intrigued by this knitting club for mourners. I turned to follow the woman up the stairs.

The barman, however, put a restraining hand on my arm. "Where do you think you're going?"

"I was hoping to speak to one of the women."

At that point, he squinted at me, scrutinizing me from my head to my toes. I had the feeling that my working man's clothes didn't pass muster

76

with him. "They don't like strangers botherin' them, and I don't like it either. I think it best you leave. Now."

The last two words were spoken in a louder voice and appeared to be a signal to others. Several patrons soon surrounded me, and while I was certain my skills would have served me well against any one of them, at that moment they outnumbered me. Knowing discretion is the better part of valor, I took his advice and exited the premises.

Once outside, I considered my next move. I was certain this knitting club required further investigation, but it didn't seem I would easily gain admittance. Not a single man had ascended the stairs.

I was thus pondering alternatives when a woman in plain clothes passed by me and into the tavern, providing me with a plan. While I couldn't gain entrée into this group, I *could* make the acquaintance with a woman who was already a member.

After another hour, the knitting circle appeared to break up, with its members exiting as a group. With most in their weeds, they appeared like a murder of crows flying out of the pub and into the streets in various directions.

The last to leave was the street-dressed woman I'd seen entering earlier. She was a handsome woman with a fine figure and her hair done up in curls. Her clothes were of a finer quality than those usually found in this district, with a well-turned ankle and a sharp eye. Those widened when I approached her.

"Excuse me, Madam, for being so forward," I said and bowed to her. "My name is Neville Adams, and I'm hoping you could help me."

"Mrs. Josephine Reynolds. How can I be of assistance?"

I took a coin from my pocket and showed it to her. "I'm looking for a Mrs. Barnes. Her neighbors said she might be here. I owed Mr. Barnes this coin and hoped to pass it to her."

"Yes, poor Lila," she said, making a tsk-tsk sound. "She had quite a shock, losing her husband so suddenly."

"I assume now that he's gone, she'll be needing such help. Perhaps you can share her address with me so that I can repay my debt."

She glanced up and down the street, but all the club members had disappeared from the immediate vicinity. "If you like, you can give it to me, and I will pass it on to her."

When she reached for the coin, I pulled my hand back and put it in my pocket. "Excuse me, dear lady, but I prefer to give it to her directly."

"Of course," she said and curled her fingers into her palm before lowering her arm. "You may be glad to know, Mr. Barnes left his wife well provided for. He had a life insurance policy which left her more than one-hundred pounds."

Having already worked several cases with Scotland Yard, I knew that much money represented at least a year's wages for someone in Barnes' former line of work, and I expressed my surprise and delight in learning of the man's foresight. "But how do you know of her good fortune? Did she share it with you?"

"Someone else in our little circle told me."

She had a warm way about her. Her large brown eyes widened as she glanced into mine, as if encouraging me to linger longer with hers. After a moment's reflection, I said, "I have neither kith nor kin left here nor elsewhere. If I were younger, you might call me an orphan. As it is, I am simply alone in this world, and I would be honored if you would join me in a meal."

At this pronouncement, I saw a spark for the merest of seconds – very fleeting – before her eyes softened even more, and she said, "I, too, am alone in this world. I had a husband and three beautiful babies – a happy family. First one, then the other, then the other of our children fell ill. The doctor said it was a stomach fever. They died within days of each other. My poor husband was so distraught, he took to drink and one night, after leaving a pub, fell into the path of a speeding carriage and died as well." After expressing my sympathies, she added, "I think I would very much enjoy accepting your invitation."

When she turned back toward the pub, I hesitated, explaining the publican had taken a disliking to me earlier. She gave a little laugh and said, "You needn't worry. They are suspicious of newcomers, but if you're with me, there'll be no problem. I'm on good terms with him."

With that, I let her pull me in. As predicted, the publican's scowl at my appearance switched to grim acceptance when Josephine smiled and nodded at him. Without a word, he sent two glasses of beer to our table, followed by two bowls of stew, which I had to say was flavorful, although slightly watery and with more onions than I enjoy.

Throughout the meal, she quizzed me about myself, getting my full name and where I was living and working. Her approach was subtle. A less-astute man would haven't even been aware that he was sharing this information, for she was truly a beguiling woman. After we had finished our meal, we lingered over a second beer, and I chose this moment to return to my true interest.

"When I was here earlier, I learned of a group of women who meet upstairs. To knit."

She bobbed her chin. "After I lost my family, I sought some form of solace. A chance to meet with others who had experienced similar heartbreak. When I learned of another recently widowed woman, I invited her to my home, and we found knitting a great comfort. It kept our hands

78

busy, but we could also share with each other. Soon, we were inviting more and more women and chose to move into the room upstairs."

"Your group has been successful, from what I can see. I saw several head up the stairs."

"Yes. Together we get through and learn to live again by helping each other."

Following the second beer, we left the pub, and I offered to accompany her home, given the hour. She accepted, and soon we were leaving the worst of Whitechapel into a still-impoverished, but modest, area. The air didn't carry the stench of decay so prevalent in the other area, and I found her company rather pleasant. Her rooms were above a sundries shop. At the steps, she turned to me and thanked me for the meal.

"My landlady allows me access to the kitchen to prepare my own meals. Let me repay your favor with a home-cooked dinner."

Knowing I still had much to learn about her group, I agreed to come in four days' time. In the meantime, I planned to make my way upstairs at the pub to discover any secrets it might hold. Given Josephine Reynolds' obvious arrangement with the publican, my access would have to be by some sort of subterfuge.

And there was still an examination of any connection Dr. Kinston might have had with Malcolm Barnes' death.

My first move was to rent a room near the pub where I could observe all those entering and leaving. It also served as a place to store my disguises – the first of several such rooms I've since arranged throughout my career. That was where I transformed into Victor, a down-on-his-luck blacking salesman. Each day, Victor would spend his time in a corner of the pub with his sample case, nursing a pint and observing the women's comings and goings to the second floor.

By the middle of the third day, I had determined a pattern, suggesting the knitting club's room would be empty around suppertime when these women would return home to prepare dinner. Because I was to meet Josephine the next day, I decided it was time to discover what lay above.

Such an effort, however, required a diversion to occupy the barman long enough for me to make it up the stairs and inspect the club's rooms. I left the pub early on the third day and watched all the women leave. Then, returning in my blacking salesman dress, I burst in with a shout.

"I did, it! I made my quota! Drinks for all!"

I slapped several shillings onto the bar, and the other patrons rushed to be the first to get their free beer or gin. Having completed this step, I waited for the group to finish their first and then their second or third. One group of patrons, who probably had their share and more, became very boisterous, shouting and pushing each other. At that point, I created the distraction needed to slip upstairs. When one from this group rose to make his way to the bar again, I casually extended a foot, causing him to trip and fall into another. The second turned to the first and landed a blow to the man's jaw. The first returned the favor.

Soon, the entire room was filled with men giving and receiving punches. The barman attempted to stop the brawl, but was soon the recipient of a few uppercuts of his own. When one particularly fierce jab sent blood spurting from his nose, I took the opportunity to push my way to the stairs and onto the upper floor.

The cries and crashes echoed up the stairs and made the boards underneath my feet vibrate. From the intensity of both, I calculated I had some time to explore this second floor.

And it appeared I would need it, for several doors lined both sides of the hallway. The first two were empty, but the third one I tried was locked. I checked over my shoulder. The commotion downstairs was still going strong, and I had time to pick the latch.

Despite the evening hour, the moon and a corner gaslight provided enough illumination for me to make out a plain room with chairs lining three sides. The fourth side included two cupboards. A table with three bowls stood in its center. What the chamber didn't contain was any evidence of knitting. No bits of yarn covered the floor, no forgotten needles or other knitting items, nothing. As I've noted, the absence of an object can be a clue as much as one present. In this case, clearly these women weren't as they professed, and the answer most likely lay in the room's center – the bowls and their contents.

Approaching the table, I noted no scent from the bowls, only the sour smell of beer seeping through the floor from the bar below. While the room was too dim to make out the liquid's color, I could tell it was dark but transparent. I dipped my finger into the solution intending to taste it but thought better. Instead, I considered what I might use to carry a bit back with me. How I cursed myself for not having a stoppered bottle with me. From that day forward, I always carried one in my breast pocket for such occasions.

I did, however, have a kerchief in my pocket and soaked some of the liquid in that. A rubbish bin containing some damp papers stood at the far end of the table, and I wrapped the kerchief in them. Thankfully, I had brought my blacking sample case with me and used that to transport the rather sloppy mess.

I now had only to make my way back downstairs without being noticed. Unfortunately, the noise from the brawl had diminished, suggesting the melee's more rowdy instigators had been ejected. I checked

80

the window. I would survive the drop, but would most likely be detected when I landed.

As a further complication, I could hear footsteps on the stairs. I surveyed the room in a desperate search for somewhere – anywhere – to hide. Its sparse furnishings offered little concealment. The footsteps grew louder and closer, and I knew that my time was running out. Racing across the room, I opened one cupboard and found it full of boxes. I pulled them out and squeezed into the empty space with only seconds before the door opened.

The voices of two men echoed through the knitting club's room.

An unfamiliar voice said, "See, I told you. There's no one up here."

"There's something wrong, I tells you," said the publican. "Josephine always locks it."

"She just forgot today. You lock it, and let's get back downstairs afores there's another blow-up."

"I don't have it."

The other asked, "What do you mean you don't have it?"

"Josephine didn't give me one. You're the one watching the place. Didn't she give you one?"

"I'm just a watchman. You're the owner. You don't have a key to your own place?"

"She paid me to let her change the lock."

"Well, come on. There's no one up here. That's all I need to know. I want you to tell her we came up here. Checked everything out."

Their voices were already drifting down the hallway when I finally worked my way out of the cupboard. As I did so, I hit one box, and its content scattered about the floor with a *thud*. I froze, uncertain whether the two men heard the noise, and afraid to move in case they did.

My greatest fears were confirmed when the watchman asked, "What was that?"

"Probably one of the rowdies has come back and lookin' for another row. I best get down there."

"I think it came from Josephine's room. I'm going to check."

"Come with me. I'm going down before my pub's in ruins. I may need your help."

After a moment's hesitation, the watchman said, "All right, but I'm not goin' to take care of Big Tuck this time. The more he drinks, the meaner he gets."

"What are you complaining about? I helped you earlier."

"But . . . ."

Their voices drifted down the stairs, and I quickly righted the box and gathered the papers that had spilled from it. Other than the bowls on the table, these were the only other items in the room. I tucked a few into my breast pocket for later review, returned the box, and made certain the room was as I had found it.

I still had to find a way downstairs, but the publican had given me an idea. Stepping to the window, I pulled it open and shouted until those lingering about responded, "Free gin at The Wolf and Badger! Hurry before it runs out!"

Soon, the noise from those now crowding the pub and demanding their gin rose through the floorboards and echoed down the hallway. As the shouts increased, I let myself out of the room, making certain to lock it behind me.

I crept to the stairwell and peeked down into the pub. A gang of men crowded around the bar, shouting and gesturing at the barman, demanding their gin. He swung a shillala back and forth, keeping them from passing over the bar while shouting back that he didn't know what they were talking about. I considered simply slipping out during the melee but felt I owed the barman for having created two disturbances in one hour. When his back was turned away from me, I slapped some coins on the bar and said, "Take care of these men. Gin for all!"

As those already in the pub pushed forward to join those who had come in from the street, I shouldered my way through the crowd and out the door.

After changing in my rooms near the pub, I returned to my quarters in Montague Street to study what I had found in the clubroom.

I analyzed the bowl's liquid first. This turned out to be a rather simple task because now that I could examine the papers from the bin, I found a watermark: "*Lady Abigail's Fly Paper*". With the studies I had already completed on poisons, I knew this type of fly paper carried not only arsenic, but also a bit of sugar, quassia to give it a bitter taste, and brown coloring to make its presence obvious. The papers would be soaked in a saucer of water, to attract and kill flies and other flying pests. Added to someone's tea or coffee, it would be deadly.

The bowls I examined contained no such creatures, and the women would have no need for three bowls of it in one room. To state the obvious: This club was preparing poison.

And the papers in my breast pocket provided the reason: Insurance money. I'd escaped with three insurance policies: One for Harris Thomas, with his wife Amanda listed as the beneficiary, and another for Jameson Windom, naming his wife Grace as heir. The third sent a frigid chill down my back, for it listed my persona, *Neville Adams*, as the insured, and Josephine Reynolds as the recipient. I recalled our conversation at the pub and all the information she had extracted from me that day. My name, address, and other bits were now part of a policy underwritten by the Essential Insurance Company.

But how did she do it without my signature?

Checking the last page, I found a thumbprint in place of a signature. The two other policies carried similar prints.

With a magnifying glass, I studied each and determined they all belonged to the same person. Only recently, Sir William Herschel had published his treatise on fingerprints and their use in contracts in India. I had conducted my own research on the subject and came to the same conclusion as Sir Herschel: Each person's prints were unique and immutable.

The chill down my spine grew as cold as ice as I contemplated the savagery of this group of women. They were purchasing burial policies for their husbands (and perhaps strangers with no kin, like my persona *Neville Adams*). These weren't substantial amounts – about a laborer's annual wage – but more than they would ever see at one time. With the poison they had extracted from the flypaper, they ended the insured's life and collected the benefits. I then recalled a comment Josephine made that took my breath. "*My babies died of a stomach fever.*" This group wasn't content to eliminate their husbands or strangers. Their own children were at risk.

Staring at the policies lying on my table, I contemplated the fate of the other two men. Were the policies in the box that I spilled in the room the next in line to be collected? Tomorrow, I, as Neville Adams, was to dine with Josephine. Was that to be my last meal?

I sprang from my chair, ready to grab my coat and hat, and race to the addresses listed on the documents. I was halfway to the door when I checked my watch. It was half-past one in the morning. If they had been dosed at dinner, it would be too late. I could only hope Amanda Thomas and Grace Windom preferred to administer it in their husband's morning coffee or tea.

And if they *had* ingested the poison?

I needed more of a plan, and a counter-poison would be the first step. My extensive research into poisons included their antidotes as well, and I knew hydrated sesquioxide of iron was recognized as appropriate for arsenic. Just as now, I turned to the chemistry equipment in my rooms and spent the night preparing the compound.

I finished just before dawn and had only enough time to make it to both the Thomas and Windom residences before the men left for work. Because the Thomas residence was slightly closer to my rooms, I stopped there first. My heart dropped to my stomach when I spied a black wreath hanging from the door. I was too late. Death had already visited the house. Hoping the garland was for someone else, I rapped on the door.

Amanda Thomas, already in widow's weeds, answered the door. The woman was a slight woman with a week-old bruise on her left cheek.

"Is Harris here?" I asked in a workingman's accent. "We's gots plans for today."

"Ha – Harris pa-passed away last night," she said, and dabbed a black handkerchief against her eyes.

"Lord, no! What happened?"

She raised her hands to suggest she had no idea. "He had these terrible pains. I called the doctor. He said it was dysent'ry."

"Oh, that *is* a turrible misery. Me uncle died of it. I'm so sorry. Since I'm here, can I pay me respects?"

I peeked over her shoulder with the goal of possibly getting a glance at Thomas' remains. Her response filled me with even greater dread.

"They already came for – for him," she said with another swipe of her eyes. "The doctor said it weren't safe for him to be in the house with our children. They already were feeling poorly. He said I shouldn't have anyone in."

Her words hit me in the face like a pan of cold water. Not only were these women eliminating family members, but selling their bodies to body-snatchers. "Resurrectionists", as they preferred to be called, weren't above purchasing corpses (no questions asked) for resale to medical schools. I had to stop this fiendish enterprise before the Thomas children suffered the same fate as their father.

I put my hand over my mouth and nose as if I were afraid of the miasma that filled the few rooms. "Harris was a decent chap," I mumbled through my fingers and took my leave. "I'm sorry for your loss."

The Windom residence was in an even poorer part of Whitechapel, if that was possible, up two flights of rickety stairs. To my great relief, no wreath adorned this door. A woman with a small girl on her hip answered my knock.

Mrs. Windom was as thin as a broomstick, as if life had already drained her of all vitality. Her blonde hair had been pulled back into a knot at the base of her neck, but most of it had escaped the bun and hung limply down her back. From the doorway, I caught the scents of old food, mold, and despair.

When I asked for her husband, she said, "He's sick. I think it's the dysent'ry. Has dreadful pains. Can't keep nuthin' down."

My heart squeezed in both terror and elation. I was too late for Harris Thomas, but perhaps I would be in time for Jameson Windom. I shoved past her and rushed through the cramped, filthy front room to a dilapidated iron bed covered in a threadbare quilt. The face of the man in the bed was as gray as the pillow on which he lay. I pulled the stoppered antidote bottle from my coat pocket, forced the man's lips open, and poured about half its contents down his throat. He coughed and sputtered, but the compound stayed down. As my panic over the man's fate faded, I found my energy dropping. While Windom wasn't out of the woods, I knew I'd only saved him for the moment unless . . . .

Replacing the stopper with a slightly shaky hand, I spun on my heel and faced Mrs. Windom. She'd followed me into the little bedroom, spouting a barrage of insults and threats. At my sudden movement, she quieted long enough for me to address her.

"Madam – and I use that address loosely – if you don't wish me to call the police immediately for the attempted murder of your husband, you will cease your jabbering."

The glare she gave me in response provided the most animation I'd seen in the woman, but she remained silent.

"Thank you," I said and pointed to the other room. "Now, if you will accompany me to the other room, I wish to have a chat with you. Your answers will determine both your fate, and that of your husband'."

We sat down in two flimsy chairs at an even more unsteady table. A dirt-smeared glass window let in a thin sliver of light, making the interior even grimmer than when I first entered.

The babe in her arms whimpered slightly, and she bent her head to coo at the child. "This is Margaret," she said. "She's been poorly too." My eyes widened at that remark, but she quickly added, "It isn't dysent'ry. She just needs more to eat. I can't – can't . . . feed her right. If I can't get her more milk . . . ."

Despite her low status, I realized the poor woman still had some compassion – if not for her husband, at least for her child. Perhaps in her mind, one death was justified to save the life of another. I withdrew the policy on her husband from my coat pocket, placed it on the table, and glanced toward the bedroom. "But this is not the answer."

Her eyes rounded at the sight of the policy. Then her lips trembled. "I wished I'd never heard of that knitting club or Josephine Reynolds! I knew a woman who lost her husband. She came into a fortune after he died. Said it was from his insurance. She was the one who introduced me to the group."

She went on to describe the scheme I already deduced, but with a few wrinkles I'd never suspected. The "club" was highly organized and efficiently run through Mrs. Reynolds' oversight. The members pooled their funds to ensure that all were paid on time and would hold a lottery to see whose insured was next. When one woman collected on a death, they split the proceeds according to contributions. As I had already learned, they also sold any remains to the body-snatchers – unless there were relatives or other family members insisting on a funeral. Their meetings involved a review of the current policies, maintaining all policies up to date, holding lotteries, and extracting the arsenic from the flypaper.

"No one at Essence Insurance ever checks the mark," she said with a shrug when I asked how they could purchase such policies without the person's knowledge. "They are happy to collect our money."

A low groan from the other room drew me there to check on the latest surviving victim. His eyes were open, but he seemed disoriented. I was able to get him to drink a bit more of the antidote. His wife watched from the doorway.

"What's that you givin' him?" she asked.

"An antidote. Something that counteracts the poison."

"You still goin' to turn me into the coppers?"

I glanced around the room, my gaze resting on the child in her arms and the meager furnishing in the front room. "That all depends. If you'll help me, I'll see about another means of ensuring your future."

"What's I gots to do?" she said with a squint toward me.

"At the moment, I need more information. What's the name of the person who collects and sells the bodies?"

She brightened slightly, as if proud of her knowledge. "That's an easy one. Name's George Tolliver. Has a cousin that has a wagon for hire near The Wolf and Badger. That's how we gets word to him of a death. Hire the cousin's wagon for a delivery at some address."

"Do you know a Lila Barnes?"

She nodded. "Her husband passed less than a month ago. Tolliver picked him up the same day he died. They like 'em fresh as they can."

I took a piece of paper and a fountain pen from my coat pocket and wrote down what she had told me in the form of a confession. It stated she had tried to murder her husband for insurance money by serving him arsenic in his coffee. After reading it to her, I said, "Make your mark and put your thumbprint there."

She pushed back from the table, her eyes growing wide. "You said you'd help me. I ain't signing that. They'll hang me for sure."

"Only if I give it to the authorities. Consider this my own insurance policy to protect your husband – and child. I said I would help you, and I will. But I need assurance that you will not try to harm either in the future. I will keep watch on all of you. If there is ever a suspicious death, I will take this confession to the authorities, and you will have to answer to them – and to God." Leveling my gaze to her, I said, "Now make your mark."

She crept back to the table and did as I commanded.

After leaving her with more of the antidote, I put her confession and insurance policy in my coat pocket and stood to take my leave. "Breathe a word of this to anyone, and the confession goes straight to Scotland Yard."

As I stepped out onto the dirty street, I took a deep breath of the fetid air and exhaled slowly. Compared to that in the Windoms' rooms, I felt as if I were breathing in the spring countryside. What I had learned of Josephine Reynolds' scheme and the organization she had created almost rivaled that of another individual of whom I am aware. She had recruited the women in the knitting club, developed a means of selling policies and ensuring their collection, and a process for disposing of the bodies that had operated for some time without raising suspicions.

With Jameson Windom's fate assured for the moment, I turned to my own. After changing into my laborer's clothes and tucking more of the antidote into my coat pocket, I headed to her rooming house. When I reached her street, I kept a vigilant search of all around me. A sense of dread had settled between my shoulder blades as if I carried a target there. Along the way, I contemplated the how her pleasant face and outwardly compassionate personality masked one of the most devious minds I'd ever met. Perhaps it was best that I met such a woman so early in my career, for I took this lesson to heart: One cannot make assumptions by outward appearances, and Josephine Reynolds proved the rule.

As before, she was all smiles and flowers when she answered the door and led me to the small dining table in the kitchen. She'd prepared a curry dish and served us both, along with a beer. I observed her while she labeled the meat and gravy onto two plates. The same with the beer – she served two glasses from the same container. While I couldn't imagine her poisoning herself, I still didn't trust the items weren't contaminated in some form. Pretending to drink the beer and moving my fork in the curry, I gave the appearance of eating without ever ingesting any. I often went without food in the middle of a case, and so felt no loss – especially when my very life depended on it.

During the meal, Josephine charmingly shared about her day, and even mentioned the death of the husband of one of her knitting club members – to which I expressed my sympathies. All the while, I observed her studying me whenever she thought my attention lay elsewhere. Was she waiting for me to show signs of arsenic poisoning?

When I remained with no symptoms by the end of the meal, she suggested we take a stroll. Once on the street, she linked her arm in mine, and I let her lead us up one street and down another toward The Wolf and Badger.

"Let's have another beer," she said, tugging at my arm to lure me in.

Once seated, two beers arrived at our table. At that moment, I realized the depths of the publican's involvement. The barman's personal attention clearly indicated this beer would, for certain, do me in. I pretended to sip the drink while we chatted. After what I considered an appropriate amount of time, I rose, doubled over, and complained loudly about stomach pains.

"My gut's on fire!" I said in a loud voice. I turned to her. "The curry must have been bad!"

I lurched forward, knocked over the table with the beers, and shouted, "I'm going to be sick!"

The publican and another patron were at my side in an instant. "Let's get you to the street. I'll not be having you soiling my place."

The two grabbed me under the arms and dragged me from the establishment, Josephine following behind me, crying in a distressed voice about my sudden illness.

Once in the street, I had expected them to throw me to the ground and leave me in my misery. Instead, they pulled me up the street toward the corner. Josephine continued close behind, murmuring consolations about my condition and directing them to take me to a doctor.

"I can't stand to see him in such pain!" she wailed.

As we reached the corner, a wagon turned from a side street and rattled toward us, and I could feel the men shift their course to lead me directly into its path. I had to react quickly, or I would meet the same destiny as Josephine's husband.

I fell to my knees to slow my progress, but it had little effect. The two men continued to drag me to my fate. From my prone position, I could see a crack in one of the horse's hoofs, and the reek of the street's muck filled my nostrils. With only seconds to spare, I pulled my knees under me and pushed upward. The sudden shift of my prone-to-standing position destabilized the other two men. Because he was closer to the street than his companion, the publican fell forward and under the horse's hoofs.

The wagon's driver pulled back on his leads, causing the animal to rear slightly and dislodging its cargo: The remains of Harris Thomas.

The screams from those in the street, the wagon's horse, and other transports passing by called a local officer to the scene. His whistle summoned still more nearby policemen to the street, and they arrested all those involved – me, the wagon driver, the barman, Josephine Reynolds, and the good Dr. Kinston. I learned later Josephine had signaled the barman to send for the doctor as soon as we'd arrived, so that he would be johnny-on-the-spot for signing my death certificate.

While I was still making inroads into Scotland Yard at this stage in my career, I had created a few – among them Inspector Lestrade. When I laid out the full extent of this woman's organization – the knitting club with the various insurance policies, the production of arsenic, the connection to the Resurrectionists, and the help of Dr. Kinston in providing the death certificate – the arrests that followed led to convictions and the execution of Josephine Reynolds and her various accomplices.

Josephine and seven other women from the club hanged for their offenses. Their leader's meticulous records proved to be their undoing. The payments they had made to the various policies and the amount each collected provided the basis for conspiracy charges. Allegations of murder were simply a matter of tracing the bodies – again, thanks to Josephine's records – to the various medical facilities. Additional corpses were exhumed if the deceased was buried. Together, they afforded the evidence needed to substantiate arsenic poisoning. The family of Malcolm Barnes recovered his remains from one of the London hospitals and gave him the proper burial they desired. Interestingly, the amount of arsenic he'd ingested actually preserved the remains, making the return less-upsetting – once they clothed the man to hide the students' dissections.

By the end of Holmes's recounting of the events, the tobacco in his pipe had long since extinguished. Mrs. Hudson had carried away the remains of our breakfast and laid out our lunch, but after this tale, I found I had little appetite.

I shook my head, "To think of the tragic loss of life caused by this woman, and the number of orphans created. Surely the courts showed some mercy to those women with young children?"

"Mercy?" my friend's voice hit a note of incredulity. "What mercy did these women show to any of them? What alternative did the courts have but to take them away from their families? At least the children, orphans though they became, had an opportunity to reach maturity and make something of their lives. Many would have most likely served as additional insurance income to these depraved women. My only regret was that Josephine Reynolds could only be hanged once for all the murders she engineered."

Pausing for a moment to consider this observation, I glanced back at the morning mail which had started the retelling of this case, and a thought occurred to me. "And what of Grace Windom? Did you keep your word to her?"

"I wrote to Reginald and explained her role in helping me destroy this murderesses club and solving the disappearance of Malcolm Barnes. For her part, I requested he provide Mr. Windom with some form of employment and to monitor the health of both Barnes and his daughter Margaret. Thankfully, he was very diligent in providing periodic reports on their welfare. You'll be glad to know Margaret will soon be married to

the local blacksmith, and the remittance from her father's insurance (which I will ask Reginald to confirm was of natural causes) should serve nicely for her dowry."

He studied the scene out the window and sighed. "Out of that horrifying tragedy, at least one good did come."

"I assure you that the most winning woman I ever knew was hanged for poisoning three little children for their insurance-money . . . ."
– Sherlock Holmes
The Sign of the Four

Mrs. Farintosh's Opal Tiara
by Brenda Seabrooke

I've long been fascinated by Sherlock Holmes's cases which occurred before I met him. In April 1883, when Miss Helen Stoner consulted Holmes, she stated that Mrs. Farintosh had recommended him. I longed to hear about the earlier case, but I had to wait, as we were immediately occupied on the journey to Surrey to aid Miss Stoner. Later, when we were on the train back to London after revealing the truth behind the deadly speckled band and its resultant rough justice, I waited a suitable amount of time, and as soon as we were settled and the wheels began to roll, I asked, "Regarding Mrs. Farintosh, who recommended you to Miss Stoner . . . ?"

"You never forget anything, do you, Watson? Oh very well. I see I'll get no peace until I tell you about that case."

"It will while away the journey back to London," I said . . . .

Early in December of 1880, just before you and I met on New Year's Day, I lived in Montague Street, around the corner from the British Museum. I wasn't as busy as I am now. I'd already retired for the night when I received a telegram asking me to come as early in the morning as possible to call on a Mr. Farintosh, who had a most urgent problem. I replied I would be there at nine, and then returned to bed without a thought as to what his problem might be.

The address wasn't far, but in the interest of time, I took a hansom to John Street, just off the Strand near the Waterloo Bridge, and stood before a narrow three-story house, built of dark brick, with carved stone pilasters and an attic. The door was opened by a proper butler, whose name I later learned was Paxton, a solid fellow who looked as though he might wrestle horses, but was excellent with overcoats and umbrellas as well. "You are here about the missing tiara?"

I nodded, though I didn't yet know what the urgency was for my summons. A missing tiara sounded less urgent than a missing person or a murder.

The butler ushered me into the morning room where the entire household awaited me – fourteen people, one or more of whom may or may not have taken the tiara. I hadn't faced an audience of that size since I was onstage as Marzando the Magnificent's assistant, and never as a consulting detective. I felt like an understudy opera singer performing *Aida* for the first time.

The room was well-appointed, with floor-to-ceiling windows for the meager December morning light. They were hung with yellow silk draperies patterned with latticework. Yellow, green, black, and white were used for the rug and upholstery, and the walls were painted a cheerful yellow. A large six-sided terrarium, lush with greenery, stood on a table near the windows.

A man stepped forward and identified himself as Gilbert Farintosh, pronounced *Fairn-tosh*, a Scotsman who spoke the Queen's English. He asked me to follow him to his library, where he closed the door and turned to me in order to explain the reason for the telegram.

"My wife's tiara is missing."

I almost told him that was regrettable but beneath my services when he wrung his hands most anxiously and said, "Please let me explain. I know the problem must seem trivial to you, although the tiara is quite valuable."

"It hardly seems to be as urgent as you seem to think it," I replied.

"Please. I'm neither wealthy nor titled. I must earn my way. I'm a junior in the Foreign Office. My superiors have honored me by issuing an invitation to their annual Christmas Ball. All of the women will be resplendent in their gowns and tiaras, a way of evaluating them and by extension their husbands. This tiara has been in my family for more than a century, since an ancestor brought it back from India. It may hold the key to my advancement."

I hoped that Foreign Office promotions weren't based on tiaras, but I didn't doubt it. "I assume you have searched for it already. When was its loss first discovered?"

"Late yesterday. The tiara is made of silver set with truly resplendent opals. My wife went to the locked cabinet where she keeps it to see if the silver needed polishing again. The box in which it's kept was there, but was empty."

"I see. Opals. *Upala* from Sanskrit, meaning 'precious stone'. Was the box itself kept locked?"

"It was, as was the cabinet."

"Where are the keys kept?"

"Lenora has an intricate little box with a trick opening. I gave it to her for a courtship present. Only the two of us know the secret to open it. That key and the cabinet key were both undisturbed in the trick box."

A locked box in a locked cabinet with keys hidden in a secret compartment in a puzzle box. My interest was piqued by now. "What measures have you taken to find the tiara?"

"I gathered everyone in the dining room where I thought the tiara was least likely to be hidden, because people are in and out of it all day. My wife and I then searched the servants' quarters in the attic. We found nothing. We then made our way down from floor to floor, but the answer was the same: The tiara had vanished."

"No one left the room while you were searching?"

"No. Paxton kept stern watch over the room. Only the children were asleep."

"They are how old?"

"Gil, Jr. is five, Susan is three, and little Petey is just over a year. We checked the nursery as well as their beds in case some diabolical person had hidden the tiara there. We were thorough, I assure you. We even looked under the beds to be sure the tiara hadn't been attached to the bottoms. I knew of no one I could turn to. I didn't want the police involved, or the news to reach the newspapers. I remembered hearing your name once mentioned in passing in the hallways at work, and that you are a consulting detective." He spread his hands. "And here we are."

"The difficulty of this case seems to be the time of the theft. We only know it was missing late yesterday. When was the last time your wife looked at it?"

"Sometime after we received the invitation to the ball. My wife thinks it was on the fourth. She remembers that was a Saturday, and the joint for Sunday dinner was delivered that day."

"Today is the tenth. You found the tiara missing on the ninth. That narrows the time of the theft to five days. Now I need to meet the rest of your household."

We adjourned back to the morning room where I met Mr. Farintosh's brother, Harold, two years younger than Gilbert, who appeared to be about our age, Watson. Also present was Harold's wife, Bess, and sitting quietly beside her was Mrs. Lenora Farintosh, who was younger than I expected after having three children – all of them seated beside her. Her sister, Sylvia Somers, was probably around twenty-three. Gilbert Jr.'s governess, Miss Ida Ayers, was a pleasant but plain young woman of perhaps thirty-one, and Nanny Frakes was a cheerful cushiony woman of middle age.

The staff consisted of Paxton, the butler, Mrs. Bowles the cook, whose quarters both were off the kitchen 'tween floors, Mary the parlour maid, and Edith the cook's helper. From time to time, part-time workers came – window-washers, chimney sweeps, knife sharpeners, pot-menders – but none since October when the house was cleaned for the winter.

I stood near the terrarium while Farintosh introduced me to the household and explained what I would do. I watched them while I pretended to look at the scene in the glass box: Mountains covered in

93

velvety smooth green moss, where ferns and other moisture-loving plants formed a dell with a ceramic dragon hidden in it. A circular mirror stood in for a lake with a pair of tiny glass swans swimming on it. Someone had spent considerable time on this creation.

Mrs. Farintosh noticed my attention. "My sister made that with the children."

"Clever," I said. Her sister blushed prettily.

"We did it last week," Miss Somers said. "The day it rained. Sunday I think it was."

"I put the swans in," Susan whispered from her seat beside Nanny Frakes. "On the other side."

Nearly the floor, seemingly stuck to the back of one of the table legs, was a bit of ferny green.

Farintosh finished relating to the household that they must tell me everything they could remember about the five days between the last appearance of the tiara and the previous night.

"No matter how trivial," I added. "I will start with Mrs. Bowles, followed by Nanny Frakes and Miss Ayers. Please remain in this room until your turn, and pray do not discuss the case."

Nobody seemed unduly alarmed at being questioned. I chose the cook first because her duties would need to be attended to soon. Mrs. Bowles was a substantial personage in a blue-print dress, covered by a capacious spotless white apron. I suspected she was a dab hand at pastries and the like. Her plain features were framed by a ruffled white cap.

"I never go upstairs 'cept on special occasions," she stated without preamble, "and there's been none since the house was turned over."

"That was in October."

"Yessir." She nodded emphatically.

"Have you heard anything about the tiara?"

"Only what's been said 'bout it missin'."

"You haven't seen anything suspicious in the five days since Saturday last?"

"Nossir." She nodded again.

"If you think of something, let Mr. Paxton know."

"I will, sir."

"Thank you. You may go."

Nanny Frakes raised her eyebrows at the door as she passed Mrs. Bowles, who gave her a nod.

"I'll be quick," I said as the door closed. Nanny Frakes was about forty. She wore a brown-print dress with another snowy apron.

94

"I don't know anything about the tiara. I didn't know it was missing until Mr. Farintosh came in the nursery last night, after they discovered it were gone."

"I thought as much. If you think of anything let Mr. Farintosh know. You may take your charges to the nursery now, and send in Miss Ayers."

She nodded and returned to the morning room. In a second or two, Miss Ida Ayers knocked on the door Nanny Frakes closed behind her. I'd made a list of their names and made a brief note as we talked.

The governess was dressed more modishly than the previous two – no apron, her dress of a striped merino wool with a lacy collar, a gold watch pinned to her bodice. As governess, she had more access in the house than the previous two, but she knew no more than they did.

"I've never seen the tiara and wouldn't know it if I did," she declared, her brown eyes opened wide. "This is my first year here."

"How do you find the household?"

"Gil, Jr. is a precocious little boy eager to learn. Susan will start her lessons next year."

"And the adults of the household?"

"Mr. and Mrs. Farintosh are lovely people." She refused to say more.

I asked her to tell Mr. Harold he was next, and he entered within seconds. He was a lesser version of his older brother, as if one print had been made, but the ink had faded on the second copy. His dark hair was receding, his eyes a pale gray, his nose slightly pinched. His face was marred by a thin black moustache. His shoulders had mimicked his moustache's droop, sloping under his fashionable gray-on-gray coat. His voice was somewhat nasal, indicating a possible obstruction of his airways.

He, too, had noticed nothing amiss. He accompanied his wife on carriage drives in Hyde Park several times in those crucial five days. "She's in the family way," he said with obvious pride. "I'm scarcely two years younger than my brother, but he already has three children."

And also a promising career and a house on a fashionable street were the words left unspoken.

He was between positions, he said, doing a little speculating. I managed not to prick up my ears at that, because obviously living in his brother's house, without a job and a baby coming, he had need for money, but he shot that theory down in his next sentence.

"I'm not in a rush. Our great-uncle's estate is almost settled. We both have expectations, as he died without other heirs beside the two of us." He leaned back as if enjoying the inheritance in advance.

I thanked him and bade him to ask his wife to come in next. He turned at the door and looked as if he wanted to tell me his wife didn't need to answer my questions, but thought better of it and slouched out.

Bess Farintosh was a petite woman with dark brown curls, held in place by carnelian combs. She wore a voluminous gown of soft wool in a shade of russet that set off her dark eyes and pale coloring. Several years younger than her husband, she still had a fresh dewy look, even after living with him. Perhaps she, too, had expectations, or possibly she hoped her brother-in-law would be knocked down by an omnibus and the tiara and all that accompanied it would become hers.

"I haven't seen anything of that old tiara," she said in a breathy voice. "Lenora should take better care of it if it's so valuable."

I refrained from saying that she'd locked it up twice and hidden the keys well while she explained to me how she went to bed early, arose late, and nibbled dry toast until noon. "After that, if the weather is fine, my husband takes me for a drive in the park, and then I may read a magazine or a novel, or nap until dinner."

I nodded to be polite. I've no knowledge of the ways of women in the family way and didn't know if this was the usual for ladies who need not work.

"Please ask Miss Somers to come in next," I said as she slowly progressed to the door.

While awaiting Miss Somers, I looked around the library at the comfortable appointments, the leather chairs, the walls of books, the mahogany desk with ornate dagger letter opener, utilitarian inkwell, and a small globe that no doubt omitted Krakatoa, Zanzibar, Okinawa, and other islands of no importance to the Queen. The room was dark, lit only by oil lamps on sconces set into the wall. The sole outside light came from the hall through the glass transom over the door.

Miss Somers strolled in. She wore her blond hair in plaits wrapped around her head, perhaps in Viking style. Her eyes were green, and she wore a dress of the same color.

"Confound it, Watson, how do you describe all these details when you write our case studies?"

"Well, it isn't easy. I take notes. Sometimes I go back and fill in from memory."

"I took notes, but only to remember where they all were roughly during those five days."

96

Miss Somers sat demurely in the green leather chair and waited for me to finish appreciating her beauty she had packaged so well. "I am Sylvia Somers," she purred when I didn't speak.

"Indeed. Tell me of your activities during those five days from last Saturday until yesterday."

"Twice, I think, I went driving in the park with Harold and Bess. One day, I went with my sister to look at silk embroidery thread, but we didn't buy any."

"Why is that if you needed the thread?"

"I don't like embroidery, and my sister couldn't make up her mind between the greens or the mauves." She pursed her lips.

"Did you know where the tiara was kept?"

"Vaguely – somewhere in their rooms?"

"Had you seen it before?"

"She wore it at her wedding."

Interesting that she spoke of her sister as *her*, *she*, or *my sister* – never by name.

She had no more to add. I asked about the terrarium she had made with the children.

"I thought their little eyes would enjoy the greenery during the winter when there's no color, and the sun sets almost before it rises."

"Did you put it together, or did the two older children?"

"It was a combined effort. We even let little Petey put in some of the moss. I had to rework a lot of it later after they were in bed, but they had fun doing it."

"What day did you make it?"

She pursed her lips again, thinking. She must have been told that was a pretty pose. "It was Sunday, as I've already stated. Gilbert bought the terrarium the week before when I suggested it."

She had nothing to add. Like the others, she'd seen nothing, heard nothing. "Ask Mrs. Farintosh to come next, please."

Her sister hurried in a few minutes later and sat down with a swirl of her skirts. She appeared to be in motion even when she was not. "Do you have any clues yet?" she asked anxiously.

"Some things have come to mind, but I need more information."

"Watson, are you taking notes?"

"A few. I can't possibly remember all these details, and I marvel that you can."

"This is not a case that you helped to solve."

He was being generous. "I can't remember so many little things, like the fallen fern, when I haven't experienced it myself."

97

"You would remember that whether you experienced it or not."
"Somehow I doubt that."
"I do not."

"What kind of information?"

"Since your oldest son is five, I assume you've been married for at least six years."

"Nine. I was nineteen, Jason was twenty-two."

"How long has your sister lived with you?"

"Three years. Our parents both died within weeks of one another. My father was a lawyer in Evesham. We used the inheritance for a debut for her, but she 'didn't take', as they say. She's twenty-two now, and I don't know what to do about a husband for her. Gilbert has invited young bachelors to visit from time to time, but again nothing happened. I do wish she would make more of an effort to please."

"Are you close?"

"Not in years past, because I was older, but now that she's grown up, and we can share more activities."

"Such as?"

"She's interested in embroidery. We often go to match silks."

"Do you enjoy embroidery?"

"I hate it. I much more enjoy gardening. Gil bought the terrarium for me, but she insisted on doing it with the children. How could I say no? They gathered the moss from the scrap of a garden out back. I do think I shall add violets, both purple and white."

"Any other activities together?"

"We walk in the park."

"Did you walk much during these five days?"

"The weather wasn't clement enough this week. We were going to look at embroidery materials one day, but then rain blew up. Why these questions about my family?"

"I need to understand the background of the household. Did you engage your servants when you acquired this house?"

"Yes. My husband inherited it from his father. His mother died young. We were living here with his father when he died. There's some ancient property in Scotland, but I've never seen it. We engaged all the servants ourselves, except for Mrs. Bowles. She was here already. When my husband's father died, his butler retired, as did the maids. Edith was engaged after we moved here. Paxton came then, and later Mary."

"And you have no reason not to trust them?"

"None at all. Paxton is the only one who even knew about the tiara. He has polished it several times. He seems pleased to be with a family who

98

has a tiara." Her mouth curved in a fleeting smile until she remembered she might never see the tiara again. "Interesting how people value their meager holdings. I'm sure the wives of dukes and earls never even bother to count their tiaras."

"Their staffs may do that for them." I returned to the questioning. "You are quite sure no one entered your house during those five days?"

"No one."

"Perhaps some kitchen deliveries?"

"The meat delivery had been made before I looked at the tiara that day. The vegetables had been delivered earlier. They are due again tomorrow."

"What do you think happened to the tiara?"

She turned her blue eyes, clear as water, to mine. "I really don't know. I've lost sleep trying to figure out if I removed it in my sleep."

"Are you prone to sleep-walking?"

"No, not at all, but I can think of no other way it could have gone missing. Oh, Mr. Holmes, please find it!" Her eyes glistened with tears. "It means so much to him! He thinks he needs it to advance at the Foreign Office. We have enough if he never gains another step up. We could make do with fewer staff! I've told him this, but he feels it's a blot on his ability."

"Do not worry. I shall find the tiara for you, and in time for the ball tonight. Now, if you could ask Paxton to come in."

Paxton, perhaps more than any other member of the staff, knew what the loss of the tiara meant to the family, and it had happened on his watch. He was understandably worried, but in the tradition of butlers, kept his feelings to himself.

"Meat deliveries were made on that day for both the weekend and the rest of the week. In addition, vegetables were delivered. I supervised both. No tiara went out that door, I can assure you."

"I'm sure you can, but I must leave no carrot unturned."

Not only was I surprised at Holmes's levity, but also at its use during an investigation. Later, he told me he was attempting to relieve the butler because by then he already knew what had happened to the tiara.

"Yes, sir."

"Tell me about yourself."

"I was born the youngest in Alfriston on the coast. I didn't want to go to sea as my brothers did. Our father had been lost in a storm on the Channel. I was seven and frightened of the sea from that day on. At age nine, I began running errands and doing odd jobs at the pub, and later at the Mirleton, the large country house owned by the Gaylon family." He stopped abruptly.

I didn't question him further. No doubt some unpleasantness had happened, as it often does with these houses and their casts of characters. "What do you think happened to the tiara?"

"I cannot say, sir, but I am reasonably sure it didn't leave the house – certainly not through the kitchen during deliveries. Mary and Edith are two honest girls, and Mrs. Bowles is the soul of goodness."

I nodded and asked him to tell Mr. Farintosh I would like to speak to him.

"Very good, sir." He left silently as butlers do, and Gilbert Farintosh entered.

"Well, Holmes, I hope you have some indication of what happened to the tiara."

"I do, but first, I need to look over the house myself."

He nodded. "It is near the noon hour. Shall we wait in the dining room? I've ordered a light collation if you care to join us, or I could have it brought here."

"Perhaps later. A cup of coffee would be excellent."

"I'll see to it."

I waited until they were all in the dining room and Paxton brought me coffee. I took the cup and saucer with me and drank as I descended to the kitchen.

"Lord, Mr. Holmes, I wasn't expecting you," Mrs. Bowles said as she removed a pan from the mountainous stove. The kitchen was warm with pots bubbling and delectable dishes laid on the long wooden table.

I put the cup down. "Excellent coffee. I'm just getting the lay of the land, so to speak."

I walked around the kitchen, opened the door, and looked out into the courtyard. "The dustman comes once a week?"

"Twice, sir. He came on Monday, and again on Thursday, but no tiara went out of this kitchen. I check the barrels myself. There's no telling what people will drop by accident late at night. Once I found a silver comb."

"I'm sure the tiara didn't escape your eagle eye."

She stirred a pot and bobbed a curtsy. "Thank you, sir."

I took a few moments to question Mary and Edith. Neither contributed anything of value, except that the former described how she cleaned the house, specifically confirming how she had cleaned the legs of the table where the terrarium sat.

In a ragbag off the scullery, I found an interesting piece of silk. I folded it and slid it into a pocket. Mrs. Bowles' and Paxton's rooms were locked. I didn't need to know more than where they were located on the half-floor between the basement and the next.

I climbed the servants' stairs, noting they were of better quality than many I'd seen. I started at the top floor, glancing into the rooms of the two maids with their neat possessions and pictures of family. I noted one had a photograph of a young man in a uniform in a plain frame on the cabinet beside her bed.

The next floor down held the nursery, the schoolroom, and the rooms of the governess and nanny. I didn't disturb them. Still on the back stairs, I perused the next floor, where the rooms of Gilbert and Lenora were somewhat larger and more tastefully decorated in blues and mauves. All was as I expected. I looked in the cabinet, now left open and empty of its charge, the tiara. The box was there, but locked. I looked for the trick box and found it under folded handkerchiefs. The design was Chinese, and I had no difficulty in finding the secret compartment where the two keys lay in a small velvet bag. I replaced them and moved to the sitting room. Nothing to see there. I crossed the hall to the sitting room, now by necessity a bedroom for Sylvia while Harold and Bess occupied the next larger bedroom. She must have hated giving up the bigger room. Beyond, I found a series of even smaller rooms into which the children would move when they outgrew the nursery.

I took the main stairs this time, passing through the morning room, where I prepared my revelation. I didn't bother with the drawing room, but opened the dining room door. The low murmur of voices stopped, some in mid-sentence. The longcase clock in the hall struck half-two.

"Did you find it?" Harold demanded as if it were his tiara.

"Yes," Sylvia echoed, "did you find it?"

"Would you all please assemble in the morning room? Just the family." A frown flitted across Paxton's face, quickly replaced by a bland look. Farintosh could tell him whatever he wished later. I withdrew, leaving them to follow me.

They took the same seating as before, in a rough semicircle with Gilbert and Lenora in the center, Sylvia on the left curve facing Harold, and Bess somewhat recessed between the two brothers. They looked at me with expectant eyes.

"I have been all over the house," I said, "looking for places where a tiara could be hidden if it weren't smuggled out."

Sylvia let out a little scream. "Do you mean some – some *housebreaker* has been inside these walls, endangering our persons?"

"I have found no evidence of that."

"Have you found evidence of the tiara?" Harold asked with a smirk. He obviously thought I hadn't.

101

"According to all of you, no one has entered the house, except for those who live and work here during the time the tiara was last seen on Saturday. Supplies brought to the kitchen were overseen by Paxton, who assures me that nothing left the kitchen that day and yesterday, when Mrs. Farintosh opened the box in which the tiara is kept to see if the silver needed polishing. Is this correct?"

Harold shrugged. Bess nodded. Sylvia said, "Mmm". Lenora nodded, and Gilbert said, "That is what we believe."

I took out my handkerchief and unfolded it to show a tiny frond of a small green fern. "I found this behind the leg of the able with the terrarium."

"Mary must not have seen it when she cleaned," Lenora said.

"Careless of her," Sylvia said. "You must speak to her, Gilbert."

"It was actually stuck onto the leg, and completely unnoticeable in the shadows thrown by the lamps and the windows."

"I'm sure all of the debris from the making of the terrarium were cleared away," Sylvia said. "I put down newspaper before we started for that purpose, but it's possible that I missed a tiny piece."

"You didn't come here to complain about the housekeeping, I hope," Harold complained.

Sylvia smiled at him.

"No, that isn't my purpose. I'm here to find the Farintosh Tiara, and that I have done."

Gilbert sat straighter in his chair. "You have?"

Lenora looked relieved, no doubt because she felt responsible, and also the family's standing had been salvaged.

Sylvia let out a trill of laughter. "What a relief!"

I removed from my pocket the silk wrapping I'd found in the scrap bag. As I unfolded it, the family gradually realized what it was, but I needed them to confirm. "Is this the silk in which the tiara was wrapped?"

Sylvia arose and walked over to feel the silk to identify it. "I believe so," she said as she sat back down.

I gave her a brief look to see if subterfuge were present. It was not.

"Where did you find it?" Harold demanded.

"It was stuffed into a ragbag in the pantry. Any idea how it got there?"

"Obviously the thief put it there," Harold said.

"It must have been one of the maids," Sylvia said. "I can't imagine Cook climbing those stairs unless summoned."

"Or that's what we are meant to think," I said.

"Tell us where it is, if you know," Harold challenged.

"And who took it," his wife said in a small voice. Harold gave her a sharp look.

102

I leaned over and opened the top of the terrarium, reached in, and started piling moss into one corner.

"Oh, you're ruining it!" Sylvia cried. "The children will be so disappointed."

"What has been unmade can easily be remade." Soon I uncovered the stones that propped up the moss. Amidst them was the tiara, the mirror of the small lake in its curve. I drew it out of the terrarium and turned it so they could see the opals like glowing moons in the silver frame. Bits of moss and fern tendrils, along with some of the dirt from the underside of the moss, clung to it.

I held it out to Gilbert. "Is this the Farintosh Tiara?"

He took it and showed it to his wife who turned it over to look inside at the engraving. "Yes," she whispered. "Oh yes! See – There is the engraved Farintosh Coat of Arms." Then she said to her husband, "Please ring for Paxton."

The butler immediately opened the door, his stoic face smiling with relief.

"Please see that it is cleaned," she instructed him, "and don't let it out of your sight."

"Very good, Madam. I will watch it as a mongoose watches a cobra."

"Well, that's a little sinister," Sylvia remarked when he'd left.

"Now for the best part," Harold said. "Who *is* the thief?"

"That I cannot say. I was asked to find the tiara, which I have done. It has been restored to the family, and Mrs. and Mrs. Farintosh may now go to the ball in splendour. It is barely half-three, which gives you plenty of time to make your preparations."

"Wait!" Bess interrupted. "How did you know it was there?" She'd been quiet throughout the revelation, and appeared somewhat worried.

"Madame, I eliminate the impossible and what remains, no matter how odd, has to be the solution. With no outsiders in the house, the theft therefore must have been done by an insider who had no opportunity to remove the tiara from the premises. The plan from the beginning, no doubt, was to do so later when the household was no longer under intense scrutiny. The terrarium was a brilliant place of concealment. Now, if you have no more questions, I'll be on my way."

No one could think of anything to ask at that point. I bowed to Mrs. Farintosh. "Enjoy your ball tonight."

I nodded for Farintosh to accompany me, since Paxton was occupied with restoring the tiara.

I entered the hall ahead of him. He closed the morning room door behind him. "If you could step into my library a moment . . . ."

I led the way, and he closed the door quietly behind him. "Well – Who did it?"

When I didn't reply he said, "Was it the servants?"

"No."

"Then who?"

"Do you really want to know?"

"Was it my brother?"

"No, but possibly only because he hadn't thought of it yet."

"Surely not Bess."

"No."

"Then – "

"If you have properties in Scotland, I think it would be wise for your brother and his wife to go there so their child will be born a true Scot. If you have another place, your sister-in-law should go there."

"I take your meaning, sir. Thank you. I'll see to it."

His eyes looked sad, and I wondered if earlier discordant incidents, perhaps not of this magnitude, hovered around the edges of this family, and suddenly appeared more sinister in the light of the tiara's theft.

"Enjoy the ball tonight."

"Thank you. We shall." He bade me good afternoon, and I thought to myself that Sylvia accomplished something in the theft of the tiara: Gilbert Farintosh could no longer feel comfortable in his extended family, if he ever had.

"I wonder if they really enjoyed the ball?"

"Mrs. Farintosh no doubt did. I'm sure her husband went through all the motions of it, but the jealousy within the walls of his house had to be on his mind."

"How did you know it was the sister?"

"Harold spent all of his time with either his wife or at his club. That isn't to say he couldn't have done it, but I didn't think he was devious enough. He wore his stupidity on the outside of his coat.

"Sylvia's sweetness on the other hand, came with little pinches of pepper."

"Yes, but how did you know she did it?"

"It was her idea to make the terrarium with the children so they could see greenery in winter's bleakness, and she usurped her sister's involvement. The maids had assured me that they regularly cleaned the legs of the table it sat upon. One of the children had spilled some of the water for the plants on the table top, and it ran down the leg before anybody could wipe it up. Mary said she wiped all of the legs all the way around. She would've seen a bit of fern.

104

When the household slept, Sylvia crept through the house carrying out her plan. I suspect she took the tiara Saturday last when her sister and brother-in-law were at a party to which she wasn't invited.

She hid the tiara in her room, and then had the brilliant idea to hide it in the terrarium. Lenora couldn't say no to the children. After they planted it, Sylvia slipped down late one night during those five days before tiara was found missing and disguised it as part of the mountains. A clever plan. She didn't see the tiny bit of fern, nor did she realize on the day that I visited that it hadn't been there long enough to turn brown, so it couldn't have been there the previous Sunday."

"She may have planned to retrieve it that night while her sister was at the ball, perhaps to wrap it as a Christmas gift for someone and take it and other parcels out of the house that way. With a mind that devious, one need always to anticipate such behavior before more ruin is caused."

"Holmes, you should write an agony aunt column for the newspaper! You solved the problem of the Farintosh tiara and gave advice on the domestic front. Well done!"

"Ha!" He looked out the window at the beginnings of spring, a far distance from December in London. "I found the tiara and the thief, but I can't always solve human problems."

"At least you gave Farintosh some suggestions for dealing with his relatives."

"I did, to the best of my ability. I hoped it would be the solution for him. One must consider the safety of children around such aberrant personalities."

The train began slowing as we came into Waterloo Station, and I wondered if this was the case that made Holmes wary of women, or if it had happened earlier.

"I have heard of you, Mr. Holmes; I have heard of you from Mrs. Farintosh, whom you helped in the hour of her sore need. It was from her that I had your address . . . ."

Holmes turned to his desk and, unlocking it, drew out a small case-book, which he consulted.

"Farintosh," said he. "Ah yes, I recall the case; it was concerned with an opal tiara. I think it was before your time, Watson.

— Miss Helen Stoner and Sherlock Holmes
"The Speckled Band"

A Case of Duplicity
by Gordon Linzner

I had shared a flat with my new friend Sherlock Holmes for close to a year and still, every day, discovered some new aspect of his personality. Whether these involved his chemical experiments, the occasional indoor target practice, or the late night tunes he played on his Stradivarius, such activities could prove equally charming, fascinating, frustrating, and irritating.

I would not have traded those early years for anything.

Late one morning in October 1881, with the noon hour rapidly approaching, Holmes and I sat relaxing in our rooms in Baker Street. This had become our usual habit when he wasn't actively working on a case. I nibbled absent-mindedly at the remains of our morning's hard-boiled eggs and rashers from a plate on the side table, then leaned back in my chair. My free hand clutched a copy of *The Daily Mail*, as well as something more, in front of me.

Holmes's lean form, draped in a purple dressing gown, sat hunched over his cluttered desk. His back was toward me as he occasionally puffed on his favorite pipe, made of oily black clay. He spent the morning sorting out a final bit of paperwork for his personal files concerning the Brook Street Mystery, which he had resolved but a few days earlier.

Abruptly, without so much as turning around or raising his head, Holmes announced, "You needn't to hide your copy of *Sporting Life* from me, Watson. We all have our little hobbies, as you well know."

I lowered my reading material to blink at the nape of my friend's neck. "I have no idea what you're talking about."

On the contrary, I knew exactly what he meant.

With a shrug, Holmes set aside his paperwork and spun around in his chair to face me. "Trying to hide a copy of *The Sporting Life* within the folds of yesterday's *Daily Mail* accomplishes nothing. The pages don't quite match. In any case, it isn't as though I'm not already aware of your excessive gambling habits."

"That's a bit harsh," I protested, even as I separated the two publications and placed the *Mail* next to the plate of rashers. "I consider this a mere distraction. An occasional bet helps me to break up the monotony of a day-to-day post-war life."

"Only occasional? Was it not just over a month ago that you were forced to cancel certain travel plans due to a lack of funds? On the positive side, it was overspending your pension income on such activities that forced you to give up your hotel room in the Strand to share this flat with me. That is a fact for which I, at least, feel increasingly indebted."

I shrugged at his flattering statement which I knew, though I had been friends with the consulting detective for only a few months, was sincere.

"I will confess," I admitted, "I am perhaps not always as cautious as I should be in my betting habits. I blame that partly on my reliance on a wound pension, rather than having to earn a living from a real occupation. Then again, the risk of overplaying one's hand is, in itself, part of the thrill."

Holmes leaned forward. "If you desire some help controlling such urges, I would, for example, be willing to keep your checkbook under lock and key. That would give you one more step in the process to consider."

"I hardly think we need go that far," I began.

Abruptly Holmes turned his head, waving a hand for silence. After a moment, he hastily began tidying his desk. This action consisted primarily of shoving the papers upon which he had been working into the uppermost drawer.

"Holmes!" I exclaimed. "Are you all right?"

He nodded. "Couldn't be better, my friend."

"Then what – ?"

"We have a visitor on the way." He nodded toward the window of our flat overlooking Baker Street.

I straightened in my chair, folding my copy of *The Sporting Life* and laying it atop *The Daily Mail*. "What gives you that idea? You can't even see the street from this angle."

Holmes gazed at me with a sardonic smile. "Would you care to make a wager on our possible client?"

I snorted. "A wager with you? You must believe my gambling skills to be dicey indeed! Even I know better than to counter your abilities. Although how you can know about a visitor at our doorstep is beyond me."

Holmes raised a finger in mock admonition. "Surely you are aware of all those street noises below, even with our windows shut and a strong October breeze rustling what few leaves remain on the trees."

"Of course I am. Those horse hooves clattering along the street have been echoing back and forth all morning. One can hardly miss the sharp cries and laughter of urchins as they race by. I hear nothing unusual in any of that."

"And what of those hoof-beats that a minute ago paused directly in front of our residence?"

"Eh?" I began rising from my chair to take a glimpse out the window.

"No, stay where you are, Watson. Close your eyes. Listen closely."

Sure enough, as I concentrated, I could clearly make out the heavy clomping of hooves almost directly below us, unmistakably the sound of a carriage as it started to move down Baker Street once again.

Meanwhile, Holmes had removed his purple dressing gown, replacing it with a slightly more formal jacket. I hastily followed suit, and had just finished adjusting my collar when I heard two sets of footsteps making their way up the flight of stairs.

There came a sharp rap on the door, followed by our landlady politely calling out, "You've a visitor, Mr. Holmes. She seems rather anxious to talk with you. Are you prepared to receive company?"

"I am indeed, Mrs. Hudson," Holmes answered, standing alongside his desk. "Pray show the lady in. The door is unlocked."

The woman standing behind Mrs. Hudson didn't appeared to be much older than our landlady herself, though she moved more hesitantly, as if reluctant for the attention. Mrs. Hudson stepped aside, ushering the visitor in, and then asked, "Will you be wanting a fresh pot of tea for your guest, Mr. Holmes?"

Holmes cocked an eye at the newcomer. The latter shook her head slightly.

Holmes then addressed the stranger directly. "You do look a bit weary, Miss – ?"

"The name is Dowling," she replied. "Miriam Dowling. And yes, Mr. Holmes, you are right, perhaps a cup of tea would be in order."

Holmes nodded toward Mrs. Hudson, who then made her way back down the stairs. Returning his attention to our visitor, he pointed to the chair opposite the fireplace.

"And what is it that brings you to our humble abode, Miss Dowling? It is Miss, is it not, since you didn't correct me on my use of the title, and I see no wedding ring. Ah, but wait! I do detect a faint indentation on your ring finger. You may be recently divorced, for you aren't wearing mourning clothes, and from your reaction to that observation perhaps have chosen to consult me regarding said gentlemen's well-being."

"It is a bit late for that, Mr. Holmes," she answered with a slight, weary smile. She lowered herself to the visitor's chair. "Miss or Mrs, either title suits me. I have been a widow these past three years."

Holmes raised an eyebrow as he took his own seat. "Of course. My apologies for making that assumption. Still, it would appear that you only stopped wearing the ring more recently. Might I assume, therefore, that you now have another man in your life? Are you perhaps preparing to move on?"

Before Miss Dowling could answer, I had already risen from my own chair. I intended to slip out of the room, if need be, to allow Holmes and his client more privacy.

Holmes glanced in my direction, then raised his hand. "Incidentally, the gentleman sharing this space is my good friend, Doctor John Watson. He has proven of some valuable assistance over the past year. I trust you will not mind including him in our conversation."

I looked from my friend to his potential client. "I don't wish to intrude . . ." I began.

After a brief hesitation, the woman offered another faint smile. "Not at all, Doctor," she replied. "Given the circumstances, I could use all the assistance I can get. The fact is, I'm not sure exactly what kind of aid I need." She turned back to Holmes. "I have a mutual friend with a certain Mrs. Farintosh. I have been informed that you were able to assist that unfortunate woman last year, clarifying a similar confusing situation regarding an opal tiara."

"Ah!" Holmes replied with a nod. "Indeed. That case did possess one or two minor points of interest." His tone, however, indicated to me that he had, in truth, not found the Farintosh incident to be much of a challenge.

Mrs. Hudson arrived back upstairs in person by that time, bearing a fresh pot of tea and an extra porcelain cup. Her housemaid had been sent off on an errand earlier in the day, and wasn't expected back for at least another hour. Holmes chatted with our visitor over some idle details in his recently published monographs on the human ear.

Once Mrs. Hudson departed, however, Holmes ended the side chat on mid-sentence to lean forward, hands clasped on knees, anticipating Miss Dowling's tale . . . .

I first met Jason Carter *(Miss Dowling began)* at a friend's wedding reception. We had reached for the same slice of cake, resulting in a brief, though polite, exchange of words. "You take it," he offered, and I protested, insisting that he had been there first. This discussion continued, despite there being several more servings available. In the conversation that followed, he confessed to being a lifelong bachelor, but insisted it wasn't by choice. A woman of whom he had been exceptionally fond had died of consumption a few months earlier. He was still recovering from the loss.

Jason was a few years younger than myself, and my motherly instincts were aroused. I therefore invited him to freely share his problems with me at any time. He seemed particularly grateful for the opportunity, which he later took advantage of. My sympathies were soon replaced by deeper feelings, and our friendship developed over the ensuing weeks into real love.

Jason, like any man, wasn't without his flaws. From time to time he complained of financial difficulties, though as far as I could tell they were somewhat frivolous. I myself had been left a decent amount by my late husband, enough to survive on quite comfortably. Jason said he worried about not pulling his fair weight. He feared that when we eventually married he would appear to be taking advantage of me, despite my reassurances to the contrary. You know how some men can be, Mr. Holmes.

(Holmes nodded, his face void of expression. I watched his long, thin fingers slowly start drumming on the armrest of his chair.)

Jason grew prone to mild sulks. To spare me, he sometimes spent more time than necessary in one of the local pubs. I tolerated this habit for his sake, as the one serious flaw in our otherwise charming relationship.

About a month ago, he arrived at my flat bearing a huge bouquet of roses and insisting that we should dine that evening at Pagini's to celebrate. What, exactly, we were celebrating he never made clear, beyond claiming that he had at last been offered, and readily accepted, a new and handsomely paying employment.

His working hours proved to be quite erratic. On some days he did nothing at all, idling in a nearby park or the local pub when not spending time with myself. On others, he might disappear the entire day, or even two or three days in a row. His income varied just as wildly. Moreover, Jason's attitude began taking wider swings, switching back and forth from a deeper depression than his previous moods had been prone to, to expressions of almost maniacal pleasure . . . .

Miss Dowling's narrative, while obviously moving, tended to sound a bit mundane, even to myself. I couldn't help wondering when, if ever, the woman would get to the point of her story. I glanced at Holmes and saw his own eyes beginning to glaze over. Despite of having achieved several recent successes over the past months, and before we met, this was still an early stage in his career. He could hardly afford to turn down work, even if the problem appeared sadly unchallenging. I straightened up in my chair. At last, I felt my presence might indeed be of use, by encouraging my friend to take on the case.

Then Miriam Dowling dropped a detail that made any interference on my part unnecessary.

"I took the risk of making a handful of small, discreet inquiries on my own," she continued softly, as though embarrassed by her actions. "That is how I learned Jason had been involved in some possibly questionable duties at the behest of an elderly Russian."

Holmes had been slowly leaning further back in his overstuffed chair during the woman's recitation, legs crossed, sometimes staring at his fingers. Upon hearing this last statement, however, he sat bolt upright.

"Did you say it was an elderly Russian woman?"

Miss Dowling shook her head. "A woman? No. I had assumed it was a man. Of course, I hadn't encountered the stranger in person. Since you mention the possibility, however, I suppose it could have been a woman."

"Do you have her name?"

"Only a last one. Belinsky."

Holmes drummed a forefinger against the arm of his chair. "That sounds close enough. I shall now require considerably more detail about her – or him – from you."

"I'm afraid I don't know much more," Miss Dowling admitted. "It was only this morning that I learned by chance that Jason and the Russian planned to meet near one of the disused docks in the East End tonight, around midnight. That's why I hurried over here this morning, in hopes that a man of your skills might discover what is going on."

"And so I shall, Madam! Can you at least give me a more detailed description of your friend, Jason, so I know for whom I'm looking?"

"I can do better." She reached into her purse. "I've brought you a photograph, since my descriptive skills are somewhat lacking."

Holmes accepted the picture, poring over it quickly. "Very well. If you have nothing further to add, I shall be in touch."

Once his new client had provided her address and made her way back into Baker Street, Holmes leaned back in his chair, shutting his eyes. He remained thus for several minutes, unmoving save for the tapping together of his fingers.

Reluctant as I was to disturb my friend's concentration, I also knew him well enough by then to tell when something deeply bothered him.

"Holmes?" I asked softly. "What is wrong?"

My companion glanced up, rolling his eyes. "The case of the old Russian woman," he muttered. "I thought I'd completely cleared that up. It would seem to be quite the coincidence for aspects of it turn up again, now."

"Eh?"

Holmes sat erect. "I'm talking about a case that happened a year before we met, Watson. Several Londoners had been taken advantage of by an elderly Russian woman going by the name of Lada Babinski. She claimed her family had been murdered by the Ukrainians some decades earlier, which left her the last of her line."

111

"This woman not only escaped the threat to her life," I asked, "but eventually escaped to England?"

"Just so." Holmes reached out to grasp his pipe, lighting it before he continued.

"One of the affected families called on me to look into the situation. It didn't take much investigating on my part to uncover Mrs. Babinski's true age as being closer to twenty, several years younger than myself. The Russian accent wasn't entirely accurate, and our impersonator had never even set foot in the Ukraine. Furthermore, it turned out the Babinski persona had been adopted by a young Englishman named Ronald Wainwright, impersonating an elderly foreign woman in order to gain maximum sympathy from his victims. Doing an excellent job of it, as well. I personally picked up several tips on disguise by observing him, which has later proved useful in my own line of work."

"So," I replied, "our client is justified in thinking the elderly Russian was a male."

"Her response indicated it was more of an assumption on her part, but came off as nonetheless accurate. To continue, once I confronted him, Wainwright agreed to help me resolve a much more serious matter, involving a particularly depraved character by the name of Oswald Brigham. It was Brigham who had drafted the young man into his unfortunate lifestyle, and that proved to be but the tip of the iceberg. This foul criminal ran a variety of unsavory activities, and not only in London. Many of them were far more serious and life-threatening than simple scams.

"In gratitude for Mr. Wainwright's help in resolving the situation, I agreed not to expose the young man to prosecution if it could possibly be avoided. In turn, he would be obligated to adopt an honest lifestyle. I offered my assistance in so setting him up, including arranging for him to have a legitimate employer. Naturally, the young man readily agreed. I continued keeping an eye on his activities for several weeks afterwards, until I was satisfied that he'd truly settled in."

"And has this Wainwright fellow has kept his promise since?" I asked.

"As far as I have been aware, yes, he has. Until now, at least, with this doubtful affair coming to light." He rose and began rummaging through his desk. "We may save some time by first calling on Scotland Yard to confirm this Brigham character is still in prison, and then visiting Ronald Wainwright himself this afternoon. I believe I still have his current work address on file in one of these drawers."

I studied Holmes in anticipation.

He knew the answer for which I was waiting. "Watson! Of course you are more than welcome to accompany me on this little excursion. Unless you've more pressing engagements?"

"I believe I can clear the rest of my day," I replied, offering a thin smile.

Holmes had, as stated, indeed been responsible for getting young Ronald Wainwright his employment at the woodworking shop. The detective had, after all, salvaged both the owner's reputation and his business two years earlier in an unrelated case. That businessman, still grateful, was now only too happy to grant his benefactor a few minutes' intrusion into the privacy of his office, as well as taking up the time of one of his staff.

"It's been some time since we've spoken in person, Mr. Holmes," Wainwright noted, once the owner left us to speak in confidence. "I trust you've been enjoying your career – solving crimes and all?"

"Moderately so," Holmes admitted. "And yourself?"

"I'm doing quite well, indeed. I have a wife who loves me, an employer who watches out for me, and a new circle of friends made up of honest men, one and all."

"I'm very glad to hear it," my friend replied. His tone grew more serious. "I regret bothering you at work, but I have a question or two that badly need your response."

"I shall always be willing to assist you, Mr. Holmes. Whatever I can do." Despite such openness, however, the young man looked a shade uneasy at the gravity of Holmes's tone.

He grew more so as Holmes recounted, in detailed summary, that morning's visit with Miss Dowling.

"I swear to you, Mr. Holmes," he whispered, once my friend finished, "whatever it is your client may have told you, it is none of my doing. If nothing else, I would not risk my wife's happiness by such foolish actions."

"Are you saying," I blurted out in surprise, "that Mrs. Wainwright knows nothing of your past?"

"Oh, she knows right enough, Doctor Watson. I told her everything. Which is all the more reason I trust that you and Mr. Holmes will keep this little chat between the three of us. Or even the fact of our meeting this afternoon. I am, of course, extremely grateful that you decided to call on me here rather than at home. If Emily thought for even a moment that the famous detective Sherlock Holmes suspected me of falling back into my old habits – Well, who knows how she might react?"

113

Holmes folded his arms across his chest. "Such a revelation will, hopefully, be entirely unnecessary by its falseness," he said. "Although, if I understand you correctly, you think the best way to protect that young woman from the lies by which you once made your living is to lie to her now?"

Wainwright turned away, startled. "I'd never lie to Emily, Mr. Holmes. Well, not exactly. I just don't see the point in telling her things she doesn't need to know."

"Let us say I believe you," Holmes offered. "And to be fair, I do not presently lean toward one side or the other of this question. Would you have you any idea who this new Russian imposter might be who used a name similar to the false one you did? That villain who recruited you, Oswald Brigham, the monster who drew you and many others into a life of petty deception, currently remains in prison, with little likelihood of an early parole. Watson and I made certain of that earlier this afternoon. Who else, then, might we be looking for?"

The young man spread his hands, palms upward. "If I knew the answer, I would certainly tell you. I'm not saying Mr. Brigham didn't have other young men as gullible as me under his mentorship. You were equally aware of that fact. But I personally knew none of them, neither by name nor face. He deliberately kept us apart, likely to prevent us from rebelling against him. None of us were mentioned at his trial, especially not myself, for which, as I've told you more than once, I shall eternally remain indebted to you." Wainwright lowered his voice to a whisper, glancing at the door of the office lest some other employee grew curious. "I would be more than happy to assist you again, Mr. Holmes, as long as you continue to keep my wife and new friends out of the matter."

"We shall see if your offer is necessary, Wainwright. One more thing . . . ." Holmes held out the photograph of Jason Carter, provided by Miss Dormer, for Wainwright to examine. "Do you recognize this man?"

Wainwright peered at the picture closely, then shook his head. "He doesn't look familiar, I'm afraid. I will certainly keep an eye out for him now, though, if you like."

Holmes slid the photograph back into his coat pocket. "That appears to be unnecessary for now, but I appreciate your offer. Watson and I are finished here, for the present. I only needed to confirm you were indeed not involved in this matter. My apologies if you felt threatened. I had to be certain."

Wainwright let out a shaky breath. "I understand, Mr. Holmes. I pray you resolve things swiftly." He flashed a quick, nervous grin. "Is there any chance you might satisfy my newly aroused curiosity once the case is settled?"

114

"If it is possible, and reasonable, I will certainly do so," Holmes confirmed. He gave a brief bow and turned to leave.

I offered Wainwright a last bemused glance myself and shrugged, before hurrying after my friend.

"So," I said, once we were out of Wainwright's hearing, "do you believe that young man?"

"I don't disbelieve him," Holmes replied. "You may have noticed how I rearranged a few minor details of our client's story."

"I did indeed." Although I'd only accompanied Holmes on a handful of investigations in the brief time we'd been together, I had already learned never to correct him in front of a potential suspect, or even a witness.

"Which means," Holmes continued, "that he does, indeed, know nothing of the events I described as relayed to us by our client. Either that, or the young man has become far better at concealing his reactions since the last time we met."

"What is our next step, then?" I asked.

"Later tonight, near midnight, I shall personally visit to the deserted dock that Miss Dowling mentioned. I should at least be keeping an eye on this Jason Carter. For his sake, if no other reason."

I nodded. "Should I accompany you armed on this adventure?"

Holmes paused, then shook his head. "Much I would welcome your company, Watson, the answer is no. I think it best in this instance to go alone, using one of my less-reputable disguises. The sight of two of us hanging about in such a desolate area may rouse suspicions."

"Are you certain that's wise?"

"I'll have my own revolver on me, never fear. I'll be taking some other precautions, as well."

"What if, after this, the matter still isn't resolved to your satisfaction?" I inquired, concealing my disappointment.

"In that case, tomorrow, during prison visiting hours, the two of us shall call on Mister Oswald Brigham himself to search out more direct answers. Now, however, since we missed lunch, I suggest a hearty meal is called for. Let us return to Baker Street, and I may even indulge myself with a short tune or three on my Stradivarius to set the mood before I head back out."

It was nearly two o'clock in the morning when at last I heard Holmes's familiar tread on the stairs leading to our first-floor flat. I had spent most of the evening in my usual reading chair, unable to sleep – eager, even anxious, to learn what if anything my friend might have discovered. Much of that time I'd alternately skimmed through the previous day's newspapers for any stories I might have missed and gone

115

over what notes I had jotted down regarding the current day's adventure. This latter habit I had recently picked up as an inexpensive way to amuse myself.

"Watson!" Holmes exclaimed cheerfully as he entered our sitting room. "You're awake! Excellent!" The shabby rags of his disguise that clung to his tall, lean form looked a bit worse for wear since than when he'd left a few hours earlier.

I glanced at the clock on the mantel, pretending I hadn't already done so every few minutes. "Is it that late?" I exclaimed. "I was about to retire for the evening."

Holmes gave a slight chuckle but didn't openly challenge my obviously false statement.

As he stepped into the light, I had a clear view of the clotted blood covering his forehead, chin, and lower jaw, as well as the stains on his shirt.

"You're injured!" I tossed my paper aside and leapt up to assist him.

He waved me off. "It's only a few scrapes and bruises, my good fellow. These are nothing compared to what my three attackers suffered."

My eyes widened in surprise. "Three, you say?"

Holmes couldn't conceal a wince as he pulled his left arm free of his shabby disguise. "I confess to having had a little help."

"Sit down, Holmes." I pointed to his usual chair. "Let me examine you properly."

"If you insist." He winced again, lowering himself to a sitting position.

I retrieved my limited medical supplies from my room, mostly splints and bandages, and took up my position alongside my friend. "Tell me what happened tonight, while I examine these injuries. I wish to hear it all."

Holmes nodded. "I fully intend to share these details with you – though, on the whole, I usually prefer keeping my failures to myself." He then let loose a deep sigh, demonstrating regret, or pain, or likely both, before diving into his narrative . . . .

Picture the scene again, Watson. In this very room, this morning, the two of us listening as Miriam Dowling told her desperate story. Ah, I see that look in your eye. I therefore admit, technically, I refer to *yesterday* morning. I beg of you, try not to interrupt me. The mere fact that you are tending to these modest injuries will prove distracting enough.

What you likely didn't notice at that time was that more than a few aspects of her presentation didn't quite come together. As emotional as she appeared to be when Mrs. Hudson first led her into our chambers, I couldn't help but notice that, the deeper she dove into her tale, the more rehearsed her phrasing, and the details, felt. I have had some small experience in the theater world myself before settling on my present career, and easily recognized certain nuances in the cadence of her words. The final touch was her emphasis on that callback to a previous case of mine, the one I described to you after she'd left. That action of hers was obviously intended to draw me into the case more fully, should the rest of her tale not prove enticing enough to hold my interest. She did indeed revive my attention, though likely not quite as she expected.

It was because of her less-than-subtle reference, among other hints, that I made that small detour when we stopped by Scotland Yard to check on the status of Oswald Brigham. Prior to our proceeding to Ronald Wainwright's place of employment, I felt I needed to leave a personal note for Lestrade. That dark-eyed, ferret-like man may not be the brightest of London's detectives, but he is competent enough. For this type of assignment, he is well-suited. I provided him with brief but hopefully tantalizing description of my plans for the evening, along with the strong suggestion that it would be well within his interests to also look around those abandoned docks at that hour.

You needn't scowl, Watson. That expression doesn't suit you at all. I have already made clear my reasoning for turning down your company this evening, if not in every detail. Regarding my personal safety, if my assumptions about the situation were even remotely accurate, having an additional police presence in the area would also prove useful.

As it happened, even though I was keenly aware that a deserted pier at midnight might prove to be – and almost certainly *was* – a trap, and even as I had kept my Webley revolver easily accessible in the right-hand pocket of my coat and my senses at their keenest, I still found myself suddenly put upon by a trio of thugs.

One of the three men pinned my arms tightly against my sides from behind, while a second came rushing toward me, swinging a long metal rod. By turning my head quickly, I managed to avoid the worst of the impact, at the same time landing a sharp kick of my own in the man's more sensitive area. The rod's wielder staggered backwards into the third approaching attacker, throwing both to the ground. This startled my initial captor. His grip loosened enough for me to turn, and we exchanged several blows. Finally, I freed myself completely, spun around, and reached deep into my pocket to wrap my right hand around the Webley.

At that moment, fortunately, Inspector Lestrade, along with half-a-dozen of his men, showed up to surround us. I didn't need to draw my revolver, let alone fire it.

Relax, Watson. I told you that I was never in any real danger. Not physically. Well, not much. During the brief discussion Lestrade and I

117

subsequently had with my attackers, before he had the three men taken away, I confirmed what I had already surmised.

Those men had no intention of ending my life. A single gunshot at that close range could have accomplished as much. I was instead being set up as a murderer. They were playing a part in a long game. The plan, I gathered, was to use my eventual indictment to overturn Oswald Brigham's internment by demonstrating that I, not he, was the real criminal. The conceit was ingenious, although I doubt strongly it would have worked. The result would have been a minor inconvenience at most.

Who was my so-called victim supposed to be, you ask? Why, none other than Miriam Dowling's alleged beau, Jason Carter! Well, to be clear, there never was a Jason Carter. That name had been assigned to a member of Brigham's organization who apparently had been considered expendable.

Fortunately for him, Lestrade's men found the would-be Jason Carter tucked in the back of a carriage behind the pier, unconscious, heavily drugged, barely breathing, but still alive. My attackers had been instructed to ensure the evidence against me would be as fresh as possible.

Jason will no doubt share more than a few interesting tales with Scotland Yard, once he regains consciousness.

Lestrade arranged to have me dropped off here a few minutes ago, while he sent a squad to Miriam Dowling's residence. I would have insisted on accompanying them, but was fairly certain the woman had already fled those quarters, as a precaution – assuming, of course, that the address she gave us was legitimate. I admit, I feel a bit foolish for not checking all of her information before I started my investigation. Another lesson learned the hard way. I hope that Lestrade's men can track her down, but I suspect she may have already fled the country.

Must you wrap that bandage so tightly? Ah. You're right, Watson, of course. I'll happily endure this small inconvenience over the possibility of a scar, however faint. The latter could affect my future efforts at disguise.

Off to bed? If you insist, Doctor. It has indeed been a long, trying day, and there's no telling what tomorrow may bring.

Lestrade called at our Baker Street roomss a few hours later, shortly after dawn. Holmes was deep asleep, and I refused to wake him. Instead, I wrote down as many details as the inspector was willing to share, and passed them on to my colleague mid-afternoon, when he finally stepped out of his bed-chamber. They seemed to me to contain little information that Holmes didn't already know, or at least deduced.

Holmes apparently agreed, since he put my notes aside after a brief scan.

"I still don't understand why you couldn't at least tell me something of your plan," I grumbled as I removed the bandage from his forehead. Holmes had been right, as usual. His wounds were minor, and would leave no scars.

"My dear Watson," he replied, "in the few months that we've shared these rooms, I quickly learned how poor you are at keeping secrets. A certain tic to your cheek, an extended pause before replying to a question – these things and more tell me all I need to know. If I can read those signs, so might others."

"Why even invite me to tag along on your cases then?" I asked, peeved. "If you think I'm giving away vital clues."

"For your companionship, first and foremost," he said warmly. "Your ability to act as a perfect sounding board. Your fascination with my work. And your excitement at the hunt – almost as great as my own."

"You might be taking things a bit far, Holmes."

"Am I? I've often observed you spending time writing up synopses on even the most tedious of my cases."

"There is always something of interest to be found in the solution of a crime," I countered.

My friend leaned back quietly in his chair, his unlit clay pipe in hand. Then, adopting a warmer tone, he advised, "Rather than wasting your time and money on such nonsensical activities as gambling, Watson, you might consider organizing your notes of our adventures and offering them to some of the criminal journals on newsstands. That could supplement your army pension, and gain you a bit of fame as well. Such distractions might also help relieve your mind of your wartime nightmares. Spare me that look! Don't imagine I haven't occasionally heard you moaning in the night from your upstairs quarters."

I had in fact considered taking up such activities. And yet . . . .

"I wouldn't wish to intrude upon your privacy."

"You have my full permission," Holmes replied. "I ask only that you exercise caution regarding the confidentiality of certain clients. And perhaps omit the less impressive cases, such as this one." He paused. "Speaking of which, is that a carriage I hear a carriage pausing outside our residence?"

"Holmes!"

He winked as he lit his pipe.

"But there are some pretty little problems among them. Here's the . . . adventure of the old Russian Woman . . . ."

– Sherlock Holmes
"The Musgrave Ritual"

The Adventure of the
Fraudulent Benefactor
by Mike Adamson

In the long years of my acquaintance with my friend, Mr. Sherlock Holmes, my skills as a doctor have featured to one degree or another in a fair number of cases, whether in terms of my rendering a medical opinion or indeed services, for I have patched up Holmes times beyond reckoning. However, long before I began my career as a General Practitioner, a situation arose that called for some manoeuvring at a medical level, and while my role was perhaps the minor part compared to Holmes's understated theatrics, it qualifies as an affair worth relating at some length.

The summer of 1881, generally cool as the British Isles had been for most of a year, had faded to an autumn markedly warmer than average, in which we could take pleasure in mild evenings perfect for pleasant walks in the parks of London. In these kind days, Holmes and I could look back on our recent adventures with some satisfaction, and for my part, I was frequently assured that my choice to room with the eccentric genius of Baker Street had been the right one. But matters often came upon us unheralded. and one evening, as we returned in the early dusk of the season, I sensed Holmes's attitude shift as he reviewed a letter slipped under our door from the last post.

"What do we have?" I remarked as I shrugged out of my coat.

"An invitation to a minor intrigue," Holmes mused as he scanned down the handwritten message. "This will bear some consideration. Indeed, it will be necessary to bring you up to date, for it relates to a case upon which I worked prior to our meeting. Light the fire and get some tea on, there's a good fellow, and I shall do my best to explain."

Soon the kettle was boiling, and the hearth blazed up cheerily. Mrs. Hudson had left an evening snack of cold beef, bread and butter, and cake, and when Holmes and I sat by the fire, he began his tale.

"It was in the July of '80 – about the time you were braving the Hell of Maiwand – that a case came before me, which called for some rather specific playacting. Do you recall, in the matter of Dr. Trevelyan's resident patient, a few weeks ago, I remarked that catalepsy is not a difficult condition to mimic?"

120

"I recall something to that effect," I replied. "I confess to being curious as to the circumstances that would compel you to enact such a malady."

"The client of the moment was a medical man, a young fellow by the name of Morton Mainwaring. Leaving Guys with a first-class qualification, he had not been long in general practice when he was lucky enough to be taken on as a junior partner – his stake bought by his family – in a sanatorium by the name of Greenacres, out at Barton Mills. A convalescent home for general surgery cases, they also catered to the more perplexing conditions resulting in long-term incapacity. Dr. Mainwaring felt he had observed a certain malpractice on the part of his senior partner." He paused to set aside his empty cup and plate and select a pipe from his rack. "The senior, Dr. Eugene Durand, wasn't the sort to trifle with, especially where matters of diagnosis and propriety were concerned. Dr. Mainwaring felt that many, especially long-term, patients were being over-medicated and, worse, hindered in their recovery for the purpose of extending their residency at, of course, the expense of their families."

I frowned with a shake of my head. "Such medical misconduct in order to extort fees from patients' families is not unknown. The General Medical Council takes complaints most seriously. May I ask why Mainwaring didn't pursue it through the normal channels?"

Holmes struck a match and drew his pipe to life. "He was very early in his career and felt it unlikely to do his future prospects any good, should he take to task a man as senior and respected as Durand. Even should his case be proven, he might as well tear up his diploma or practice medicine in the Outer Hebrides, as the closed shop of the respectable establishment would never again look kindly on a whipper-snapper who had embarrassed his superiors, no matter the cause. And he would be letting down his family, who had sacrificed for those very prospects." Holmes puffed with pleasure for a few moments. "But he was and is a man of conscience. His medical ethics are the bedrock of his conduct, so he couldn't ignore his suspicions. He had heard of my investigations via gossip at his club, brought the case to me, and I infiltrated the clinic to obtain a surreptitious viewing of their records."

I smiled at once. "Disguised, I take it, as a catalepsy patient?"

"Just so. Concentration is required to imitate the catatonic state, while the rigidity of the body can be enhanced with skilfully placed supports under one's clothing. Such deception will not hold for long, of course. It was necessary to be in and out quickly, so I enlisted the services of a physician friend from Barts to act as my case supervisor. He placed me temporarily, a single night, as an interim before going on to more permanent care elsewhere."

"Which gave you time to make a nocturnal reconnaissance of their offices in search of damming evidence, then be back in bed with your cataleptic episode passed when next checked by the night nurses."

"Precisely. I regret to say I was unable to locate the evidence I was after. Dr. Durand is very careful with his paperwork."

"Could it not be that perhaps Dr. Mainwaring was simply mistaken in his perceptions?"

"I doubt it. He impressed me as a keen, knowledgeable man, highly motivated in his vocation, and he believed strongly enough to sell his partnership once more and return to general practise, as he couldn't in conscience participate in what he believed to be a corrupt institution."

I nodded as I absorbed the facts. I finished my tea and set aside the cup to find my own pipe and take a pinch of black shag. "And if I have come to know you at all, Holmes, I know you cannot abide a case that lies unresolved."

Holmes's eyes sparkled as he gestured with the letter. "Dr. Mainwaring may have laid before me the opportunity to reverse my previous disappointment. And with your help, Watson, we shall endeavour to do precisely that."

I gave a small, tight smile as I pressed the tobacco into the bowl. "May I ask what has changed that prompts Dr. Mainwaring to renew your acquaintance?"

Holmes turned the letter to the gaslights and scanned it once more. "Apparently, he has a patient on his current list who tells of a relative who spent time at Greenacres, recovering from a postoperative infection, and the same story emerged. A lengthy stay, complicated by clumsily removed stitches, which aggravated the wound, thus extending the recuperation. Too many drugs were prescribed – the patient suffered severely, when he was denied those opiates at last."

I clicked my tongue with a scowl. "Not what you expect from a professional establishment. Any competent senior student should be able to snip out old sutures with only the most trifling discomfort, never mind worsening the injury. As for overprescription, it can be a fine line, as each case must be handled on its own merits. But a repeating pattern suggests something deeper. What else?"

Holmes raised a brow. "Of course, there's more. He happened to cross paths with a nurse who served for some months at Greenacres and was also perturbed by the professional conduct there. It's far from the purview of a nurse to criticise the administration of a hospital and, desiring to keep her occupation, she kept her tongue firmly between her teeth – but her eyes open. During an evening of candour, she told Dr. Mainwaring of a strongbox kept by Dr. Durand in his office's closet, which she had

122

accidentally observed, late one night, to be taken out and opened. She was working in an adjoining wing, and the senior man had failed to close his office curtains as the evening drew in. She caught a clear view of Dr. Durand as he took down the box from the closet shelf, unlocked it, and removed various volumes in which he made notations, then returned books to box, and box to shelf. Dr. Mainwaring feels this may be Dr. Durand's 'other set' of books – the *real* accountancy ledgers, which record the truth of his organisation."

I smiled through my pipe smoke. "Worth another crack?"

"Indeed. On the last occasion, I changed my appearance considerably, so there is no question of being recognised. A further brief stay in the guise of a cataleptic may pay dividends."

"An ideal condition, as it precludes communication with the individual during an episode. So long as the staff are satisfied, they will allow you some unsupervised periods in which to drop the act."

"A diversion would also be desirable, which you are admirably positioned to provide, Watson. Also, if we are to pull off the plan I have in mind, we shall need an extra pair of hands – and I know just the man."

Under an assumed name, I sent a telegram to Dr. Durand, seeking to briefly board a special patient prior to moving him on to long-term care elsewhere, and was made welcome by return, both for the patient, myself, and an orderly who would be travelling with us to manage said patient. With this assurance in hand, I contacted a coach company in Mildenhall to have a carriage meet us at the appropriate station upon the appointed day to convey us to Greenacres. I had to marvel at how simple duplicity really was, as I took on this alias – one Dr. Stewart McAllister, late of the Royal Army Medical Corps, and enjoyed the opportunity to affect the accents of my native land. Holmes coached me on the details of the case, and we were soon ready to place his plan in operation.

A couple of days hence, we departed London for Cambridge with valises packed with the makings of the disguises the matter called for. Holmes had hired a collapsible wheelchair, and we were accompanied by the redoubtable Inspector Tobias Gregson of Scotland Yard. Holmes had invited him along during his leave for a spot of "sport", promising him a professional laugh or two, on the understanding that the local constabulary would of course have jurisdiction.

In Cambridge, Holmes effected his transition in a cheap hotel room, becoming a round-shouldered character with sunken cheeks and an unhealthy pallor, a wispy, retreating hairline and hands that trembled. He remained strictly silent, and we had little difficulty in vacating the hotel unseen to return to the station, Gregson pushing the chair in the guise of orderly and myself having taken on the role of supervising physician. I bought us tickets on the eastbound line, and we reached the country station of Kennett some forty-three minutes later.

The coach was waiting as instructed and we helped Holmes aboard with great care. Gregson folded the chair and placed it upon the luggage rack, then we set off northward through mild and hazy weather. We went through the village of Herringswell, passed by Tuddenham Mill, and soon turned east by a private track. Greenacres lay upon the south bank of the River Lark's picturesque sweep, in the wooded country toward Cavenham Heath, and the rambling old manor house in its gardens and orchards soon appeared to us.

I had to admit, it was a superb locale for a sanatorium, with both the peace of privacy and the beauty of nature to soothe the afflicted. Yet that very isolation also offered the opportunity to abuse the trust of those it served, and I had to wonder quite what offences occurred that were never reported. Allow corruption to fester, and anything is possible.

A nurse greeted us as we disembarked, and Gregson got Holmes into the chair at once, a broad hat concealing the latter's features. Holmes had rather the simple part at this point. All he must do was behave in a withdrawn manner, as if deeply emotionally disturbed by his episodes of catalepsy, and leave the rest to me.

Dr. Eugene Durand met us in the reception hall as the coach growled away on the gravel drive. He was an impressive man, very tall and very broad in his girth, with the full beard of a patriarch, though still with the dark gloss of youth. He spoke very softly, however, and gave a firm, dry handshake. "Dr. McAllister, so good to meet you. We have accommodations ready: A private ground-floor room for your patient, an upstairs room for yourself – one of the servants' quarters, I'm afraid, so there's a fair few stairs to climb – and your man here has a spare billet with the groundsmen and stable lads. Let's get your patient installed, and you can tell me more of his case."

Gregson pushed the chair as we ambled through the great old house. I expanded with the lyrical ease of the writer I would become and enjoyed the brogue of Scotland upon my tongue. "Mr. Davies was a green-grocer from King's Lynn. He moved to London to work with his brother's family around Covent Garden. He has suffered from epilepsy since childhood, though seizures are fairly mild and infrequent. But a couple of years ago, he began to exhibit catalepsy also. He presents the typical 'waxy' flexibility of the limbs during an episode, slowing of respiration, and lack of alertness or response. Episodes can last from an hour or two to most of a day or night. It has taken a grievous toll, both physically and emotionally. I'd say he's one of those rarer cases that progresses from the early

124

depressive state to the physical condition quite rapidly, to use Kahlbaum's terminology. I've prescribed both mild electrical application and sessions with a hypnotist, and have noted an improvement over the last several months. As his physician, I've undertaken to see him safely home to his family in King's Lynn – thus the need for temporary accommodation on the way. Our travel was already arranged when some difficulties arose, which delayed their readiness to receive him."

"More than happy to help, Dr. McAllister."

"And your rates are very fair indeed. We appreciate your assistance."

"We've had a few catalepsy cases in the past – one last year for a brief stay, the same sort of thing. I'm only sorry we can't be of greater help." Durand smiled and leaned closer to speak in an almost conspiratorial way. "If the family should find they have taken on more than they can manage, Greenacres is always available to take the strain."

"That's most kind, Dr. Durand. I'll be sure to make this clear to them. As you can see, Mr. Davies isn't a small man by any means, and the physical strength needed to assist him when in the *rigour* of the malady is not to be underestimated."

Holmes was installed in a small private room overlooking the back gardens. It was clean and tidy, with that distinct "hospital" feel – all cream walls and white blankets, the usual metal-framed bed, and a vacant vase awaiting flowers upon a side table. Holmes was taken over by a pair of nurses, who had him into pyjamas and thence to bed in a twinkling.

Durand invited me to his office for tea at four to further discuss the case. Then he departed on his afternoon rounds, and a junior nurse showed Gregson and me our accommodations. The top floor was deserted at this hour, the nurses and orderlies all hard at work below, and when we had privacy, I tipped a wink to Gregson. "Well, as Holmes would put it, the game's afoot now!"

Gregson was ensconced in accommodations in the grounds, a converted stable from centuries gone by, and I wouldn't see him until later. With Holmes settled, I made myself scarce, reading in the staff common room during the afternoon until my rendezvous with the top man. His sumptuous office was on the first floor, overlooking the front gardens and carriageway. It occupied a corner position in the central wing, and I saw at once that its side windows lay opposite those of a ward in the southwest wing, from which Dr. Mainwaring's nurse friend would have made her inadvertent observations. Opposite, the closed door of Durand's cloakroom and ablutions reminded me the crucial evidence was almost within touching distance. However, I covered my prior knowledge with a

125

professional smile, and we sank into matching leather wing chairs in a bay window as an orderly brought in a silver tea service.

"You have a most impressive nursing home here, sir," I began genially. "I wonder at the costs involved. This estate must be worth a pretty penny."

"The gift of the late Lord Jarvis Barton. His line ended when his only son developed a wasting sickness. I don't think it was ever properly diagnosed. He made a gift of the estate to the Coleman Trust on condition it be used to support medicine, and I'm proud to have been its director since '76. But you're right, of course: Such a kingly gift is one thing – the day-to-day finances of its operation quite another. We have a charitable function and are supported by charities in return, but a large part of our income is covered by patient fees. I'm glad to say we have been able to maintain over ninety-percent occupancy at all times."

I could abruptly see why Durand was so keen to take patients: This establishment was apparently being run as a business, and keeping his rooms full was the only route to success. My first thought was whether the dubious practices reported were due to personal skimming, or simply a dire need to maintain residency. At that point, I was willing to keep an open mind, yet the very luxury of Durand's office made me wonder. He was fitted out the equal of any Harley Street specialist, down to the solid gold pens upon his desk.

"Do ye no find it difficult to care for so many?" I asked, letting my brogue thicken. "Qualified staff must be hard to find, given competition from the major hospitals."

"This is true." We sipped our tea in silence for a moment. "We offer a competitive wage and a less-trying environment than a city hospital." He waved a hand almost dismissively. "But tell me about yourself, Doctor. You must have some interesting stories to relate."

This was my cue. Holmes had known this moment would come, and we had discussed at length what I should say. I built upon my military experience, could speak in detail of India and Afghanistan, of life in the Army Medical Corps, with absolute credibility, giving merely a different regimental affiliation. I kept my summary brief but alluded to dissatisfaction with both the military wage and my success to date in civilian practice.

Durand nodded politely and at last gave a genial smile. "Bravo, Dr. McAllister! You seem a man after my own heart. You really must dine with me and my senior staff this evening. I'm sure they would be as enthralled as myself by your stories of doctoring on those wild frontiers."

"I'd be delighted," I returned, raising my cup in salute.

Holmes's distraction was in hand. While I spoke at length of my experiences out east, Durand and his key players would be together in one place, and I was more than certain that Sherlock Holmes could melt unseen through the corridors upon his covert mission. Indeed, when I left Durand's office I paid him a visit – "Checking on my patient." – and told him exactly where to find the room and its closet.

"Excellent progress, Watson," he said softly, propped up on pillows in his room as the afternoon light spoke of coming dusk. The door was ajar for nurses to look in from time to time, and we kept our comments brief. "I saw the staff roster on our way in, and have already overheard sufficient to know that at midevening, after patient meals have been served and removed, there is a lengthy, quiet spell before last medications. I trust you will be on hand to supervise those."

"Sugar pills only," I assured him.

"Then, while the general staff have their own dinners and you're keeping the senior people entertained, I shall sally forth. I shall need only a few minutes to assess the contents of that trunk, but picking the locks will take longer."

"I'll keep them in the dining room as long as I can."

"Good man. And if I'm found wandering, I'll feign confusion, even a full-fledged episode, and they should simply return me to my room, albeit under closer scrutiny from that moment on. Be of good heart. With a little luck, we'll have the facts soon."

I kept Holmes's surety in mind that evening as I presented in the private dining room to greet the senior staff – the doctors who worked with Durand, the matron, and ward sisters. We met at eight, rather late for a main meal, I felt, though perhaps I had simply become used to living by my own schedule. After cordial introductions, we enjoyed an excellent dinner: Bouillabaisse complementing a fish main course, and lemon meringue desert, accompanied by a crisp white wine. Dr. Durand certainly set a fine table, and once again I was forced to consider Dr. Mainwaring's assertion that he did so at the expense of his patients. Conversation ebbed and flowed. Hospital business was strictly avoided, and there was much discussion of the impending rugby football season – apparently the hospital boasted several excellent players amongst its orderlies, porters, and stable hands who participated in local matches.

But as dessert went down and coffee, brandy, and port were offered, Dr. Durand steered the conversation to my own exploits, and I was invited to speak regarding my time on the subcontinent. I took a glass of port and a seat by the fire to expand on the points I had mentioned earlier. Well pleased with my narrative, I held my audience's attention until almost half-past-nine, speaking of the military medical system, the deplorable state of health among the tribesmen we encountered, and the difficulty of caring for wounded among the heat, dust, and flies of those tropic uplands. Much of my own feelings – of coming to terms with my wound and my slow recovery – coloured my words. My listeners, I felt, sympathised deeply, such that when I at last ran out of anecdotes, I received a polite round of applause and a handshake from Durand.

That's it, Holmes, I thought to myself. *That's as long as I can give you.*

I moved to tap my pipe out into the hearth, but before I could say goodnight, a duty nurse hurried in and whispered to the matron, who in turn whispered to the top man. He turned to me with an apologetic shrug of his huge shoulders. "It seems your patient has had an episode. Perhaps we should look in on him."

"Mr. Davies managed his dinner well enough and was napping comfortably when checked about ten-minutes-past-eight," a young nurse in starched uniform and wimple said softly as we approached Holmes's room. "All was quiet. I made another round at a quarter-to-nine, and at that point Mr. Davies was sleeping soundly. I looked in once more after staff supper, and he had gone into an episode, so I sent word at once."

In his room, the oil lamp was low, and Durand turned it up as we entered. Holmes lay in a rictus, the seizure mimicked with fine attention to detail – a facial grimace with teeth clenched, arms above the covers locked in an unnatural, unrestful position, and he breathed very slowly. I adjusted the position of his right arm with some difficulty, knowing he had a hard rubber support under the sleeve of his pyjamas to emphasise the so-called 'waxy' nature of the paralysis. "Thankfully, he seems spared the dementia that often accompanies the malady," I said softly, taking his pulse. "There are grounds for hope that he'll live a substantially normal life if we can ease him over the bad patches."

Durand nodded his patriarchal head. "I can't help feeling he would be better cared for here. Are you sure the family can cope?"

"I'll be honest when it comes to advising them," I said frankly. "I appreciate that they want their loved one at home, but to see him in such a state may well break their hearts, as well as overtax their abilities. If they reach that decision, I'll be happy to bring him back."

"Thank you, Dr. McAllister. Well, there's little we can do but cater to his needs in the present and have faith that the electrical and hypnotic treatments will prevail."

"I'll sit with him a while and administer his medications when he comes out of this," I whispered, and Durand said goodnight, ushering the nurse out. I heard their steps recede, turned down the lamp once more, took a seat by the bed, and at last cleared my throat softly. "All clear, Holmes."

An eye opened, and the body relaxed as if by magic. "I seem to have struck gold, Watson," he whispered.

"Tell me!"

"After the ten-past-eight check, I arranged pillows and blankets to provide the impression of a sleeping body in a mostly darkened room, then took to the halls with my picklocks and a notebook and pencil. Using alcoves and store-rooms as convenient cover, I evaded the duty nurse and orderlies, ascended by the main stair, and made my way to Dr. Durand's office. The room wasn't locked, and I secreted myself within to take an oil lamp from a wall bracket and retire within the small cloakroom. There, I turned up the flame and located the strongbox in question. The lock was very professionally made and took me ten minutes to open. The contents, however, were well worth the wait."

"Whatever has Dr. Durand committed to record?"

"They appeared to be ledgers, balancing income and expenditure quite extra to those the government might ever see. Sums of hundreds, indeed thousands, of pounds are in play, and the books are updated on a monthly cycle. This leads me to believe that Dr. Durand is mobilising excess funds from his overzealous provisioning of services to patients and disposing of them in discreet, careful payments to undisclosed parties. The obvious assumption is that these amounts are accruing in bank accounts, whether locally or abroad. One other point: A small velvet bag contained some fifty pounds in sovereigns – a considerable sum."

"So, no indication as yet of where the funds are going?"

"I'm afraid not. The doctor is more careful than to file receipts for his shady transactions."

I let the Holmesian sarcasm go unchallenged. "Then what do we have to work with?"

"Not enough to satisfy a judge or jury. The ledgers can be confiscated by the police – perhaps turning up fortuitously during a warranted search – and stand in evidence of undisclosed financial activity, but when the character of a pillar of the community like Eugene Durand is called into question, it will take a lot to convince twelve good men and true of any misdeed. Dr. Mainwaring's allegations will no doubt be borne out at least in part by the records of patient admissions and releases and of drugs prescribed, and no few families would likely come forward to corroborate on the grounds of simple overcharging. Yet it all smacks of scandal, of dragging through the mud a man who, ostensibly, has devoted his life to his fellow human being. It's *bad form,* Watson, and society will see it that way. The burden of proof lies with the accuser. Therefore, if we are to

129

expose and put an end to wrongdoing in this establishment, we need more."

"What would suffice?"

"A confession would be excellent."

"Twice in one day, Dr. Durand has suggested you should remain under his roof. That might just cross the boundaries of concern for a patient's wellbeing and enter the realm of applying pressure to financially benefit the institution."

Holmes thought with a faraway stare for long moments. "Could you manoeuvre a conversation without revealing that we are even aware of the ledgers, to induce him to admit to his double-dealing?"

"It won't be easy, but I'm willing to try."

"Good man! In that case, we shall need friend Gregson's assistance to-morrow. Take me for a wheelchair stroll in the gardens in the morning, and I shall formulate a line of argument you might pursue."

Good as his word, Holmes had a strategy mapped out for me to consider the next day. "Mr. Davies" slept well enough after his episode, managed breakfast, and was quite fit to be taken for fresh air in the sprawling gardens of the estate. First, I called upon Gregson and found him reading a yellowback in a sunny patch by the converted stables. I whispered him an update, and we returned to the main house to collect Holmes. With a broad hat and a rug over his knees, the detective was propelled into the back gardens for a stroll past topiary hedges in the first drift of leaves from oaks and birches beginning their turn to red and gold.

We took a seat at a bench a hundred yards from the house, and with the privacy of distance, Holmes coached me on lines of conversation that might draw out Durand. I nodded over the points, recited them back to Holmes, and framed them in my own words until I was comfortable with the thrust of argument to be followed. "Right," I said at last. "Dr. Durand will be done with his morning rounds shortly. I would imagine I could intrude upon his tea break for a word."

"First, we must return to Gregson's lodgings," Holmes replied. "I've been in this makeup as long as is practical and must have access to my kit."

"Easily done." Gregson pushed the chair along a gravel walkway, and we were soon at the old stables, now devoid of residents as the staff went about their chores. I watched Holmes cleanse his face, drawing away the wig and false scalp, and soon chuckled as I saw his intent – for Dr. Durand would never know quite the predicament in which he found himself until it was too late.

130

Half-an-hour later, I strolled into the manor to leave a message at the office that I needed a word with the top man, that he could find me in the rose garden – and that our business would not wait.

The considerable bulk of Dr. Durand appeared along a garden path at half-past-ten. He wore a flustered expression and clearly didn't appreciate his routine being disrupted. "Really, Dr. McAllister," he began without preamble, "you're more than welcome to visit my office if there's business to discuss."

I rose from an ornamental bench and glanced around the trellised rose garden. The wheelchair was parked at my side, where "Mr. Davies" slept, head bowed under his broad-brimmed hat, his breathing slow and regular. Our orderly stood some way off, hands in his pockets, staring out across the lawns.

"Well, now, Dr. Durand. I felt a touch of privacy was in order, for the matters are more than a little delicate."

"Delicate? In what way?"

"Well . . . Consider how things look to an outsider."

"What things?" Durand's patience was wearing thin.

"Do you have any idea the talk there's been among your ex-patients, and indeed your ex-staff? Certain irregularities haven't gone unnoticed, I assure you."

"Irregularities?" His eyes fairly blazed, though he kept his voice down, throwing a glance at our orderly's back. "Whatever are you talking about?"

"Let me explain. You have a most impressive organisation here, Doctor. I'm looking for a decent situation, one with the opportunity to amass some personal remuneration. As I told you yesterday, neither military nor civil practice have been particularly rewarding for me to date. I have some capital, a bequest, which I'm looking to invest. I'm asking if you would care to take a further partner in this establishment."

Durand spread his large hands in a gesture of incomprehension. "I'm always open to investors, especially those who bring valuable medical skills to the group. But what has this to do with irregularities and talk?"

"Greenacres has developed something of a reputation, Dr. Durand. A reputation for charging rather more than a fair price – or, to be more specific, for delaying patients' release well beyond the point at which they could be sent home . . . or, indeed, manufacturing reasons for extending their stay. Keeping up your occupancy, I believe you implied. Then there are the ex-patients, those who go through the discontinuation of opiate drugs. Really? They were fit to leave hospital but required narcotics at such a level?"

131

"On occasion!" Durand grunted, fists on his hips. "I'd be glad to show you the case files if you would care to review them!"

"All in good time," I went on smoothly. "But let us be frank with each other, Doctor. So impressive a nursing home, so well appointed in every sense. I've never known a hospital yet that wasn't scraping for pennies, yet here you are, doing surprisingly well. If I'm to invest in your concern, I want to know precisely what I'm getting into."

Now, Durand stared at me from narrowed eyes, clearly torn between caution and a desire for the money I was offering. "This is a respectable establishment, Dr. McAllister. Oh, a few ex-patients and ex-staff might have something to carp about, I don't deny it. But there has never been a moment since I set foot on these grounds that my every attention has not been focused solely on the well-being of my patients."

"Are you . . . sure? I've heard tales of medical incompetence and clearly unnecessary overprescription. It's difficult to escape the conclusion that patients have been kept in a drugged state days longer than their recovery might demand, solely to continue accumulating residency fees."

"That is a slanderous accusation!" Durand hissed, fists balled.

"Not if it's true." I gave a soft laugh. "Come now, Dr. Durand. I'm offering to bring three-thousand pounds to the coffers of this enterprise. I merely wish to know at what rate I will be recompensed, and in what manner."

Durand's bluster was arrested at mention of the sum, and he shrugged his great shoulders. "No such policy exists, I assure you. And should patients be accommodated a little longer than the letter of their case demands, so much better will be the care they receive."

I snorted softly. "I've heard tell of a patient whose release was delayed weeks, involving the infection of an operation site – a stitch-line abscess – due to incompetently removed sutures. The patient's indisposition was extended long enough for his occupation to be in jeopardy. I'm told a complaint to the General Medical Council was seriously considered."

"I recall the case. We parted on good terms. I was unaware of any dissatisfaction on his part."

"Nevertheless," I pressed, "were I to announce that Greenacres was under investigation for extortion and malpractice, I have no doubt a great many would come forward to provide a very damming testimony indeed." I prodded his great chest with a blunt finger. "I'm not seeking to do so, Dr. Durand, but if I'm to be party to these excesses – to suspend the spirit and letter of my very Hippocratic Oath in the name of largess – I want to know the return on my investment will be worth my time and trouble, not to mention mortgaging my conscience!"

"All right," he snarled, eyes flashing, beard bristling. "All right, damn you! Yes, we have kept patients longer than medical needs demanded so as to continue to amass fees! Yes, we have kept patients in the bliss of opium longer than necessary for the same reason, plus the cost of the drugs *and* a profit on them! We've collected thousands of pounds in fees over and above legitimate costs, so you can expect your investment to be comfortably repaid over time, on the sole condition that you occasionally participate in this scheme and keep your mouth strictly *shut* about it!" He put big fists on hips and stared down at me. "There – is that what you wanted to hear?"

I let his words fade into the rustle of the breeze in the turning leaves, then gave a short sigh. "I'm entirely happy with that," I said calmly, and stepped back.

In the wheelchair, the figure stirred, the hat lifted off, and a hand rose to the hairline to detach scalp and wig and draw them away, revealing a shock of fair hair and a young face. A warrant card appeared from a pocket. "Inspector Tobias Gregson, Scotland Yard. And you, sir, have just confessed to a crime."

Durand gaped, glanced around, and backed away, clearly panicking, and our orderly turned back from the trellises at the edge of the rose garden, drawing away a blond wig to reveal dark hair around an early widow's peak. "My name is Sherlock Holmes, Dr. Durand. I doubt you've heard of me. I'm a detective, and this is my second foray within Greenacres on the trail of suspicions of malpractice going back years. Thank you for accommodating us with a confession to this undercover police officer."

Durand's gaze swept me. "And I suppose you are not Dr. McAllister, either."

"Doctor John Watson," I announced, doffing both hat and accent. "Former Captain, Fifth Northumberland Fusiliers, retired."

Gregson rose from the wheelchair, produced handcuffs, and snapped them onto Durand's wrists. "I'm outside my jurisdiction. In this moment, I'm making a citizen's arrest, but it'll become official the moment I pass the case to the Mildenhall boys."

Surrounded by three pairs of accusing eyes, Dr. Durand sank to the bench and gave a shuddering sigh. "Who put you up to this?" His words were flat and sad.

"You will have the opportunity to face your accuser in court," Holmes replied mildly.

"This is entrapment!"

133

"'Entrapment is an imperfect legal construct,'" Holmes pontificated. "While it might be argued that in approaching you with a fallacious claim to seeking investment in your criminal enterprise, Dr. Watson trapped you into confirming our suspicions, it is equally true that his actions don't bear upon your previous offences, and many a judge would be inclined to overlook the technique and focus on the confession. After all, an actual crime would have to have resulted from the ploy for it to qualify as police entrapment, and it manifestly did not."

"But don't you understand?" Durand looked up at us with eyes abruptly guileless. "It isn't just me. Several of the senior staff are active participants. To take all of us into custody would strip the hospital. Patients would be without expert care."

"Obviously, this will be taken into account," Gregson murmured, though, by his tone, he hadn't in fact realised this.

"And for what?" Durand threw up his cuffed hands. "I admit, we have played fast and loose with our oaths as doctors, but ask yourselves: *Why?*"

"Financial gain seems the entire motive," Holmes returned without hesitation.

"It's a business of pounds and shillings, yes. But money is a liquid commodity and can be made to flow where it's needed."

"What do you mean?" I asked softly.

"Doctor . . . Watson? You strike me as an especially earnest fellow and a good doctor. Have you been in general practice?"

I shook my head. "Direct from Barts to the Army. Out to India and back within a twelve-month, shot up." I palmed my shoulder almost unconsciously.

"Then you haven't had a chance to see at firsthand the realities of health among our own community. I assure you, it is *dire.*"

"I'm aware of the difficulties faced by ordinary people, especially the poor."

"Then ask yourselves how so many lower-class people pass through Greenacres. How could they possibly afford a week's convalescence in the country? It's simple: Because three-quarters of the cost of their stay is tagged onto the bills of well-to-do patients, who typically never even realise they're being overcharged." He nodded sagely. *"They* are only interested in positive outcomes, not whether their bill is a few pounds more than it need have been. I promise you, no one has ever suffered, gone hungry or cold as a result of any bill I have ever served."

"You claim to bend the law in the name of altruism?" Holmes asked.

"I do, sir. Unreservedly. And you'll find the same conviction among my staff." He looked me in the eye. "Three-thousand pounds is a lot of money, Dr. Watson. A lot of good could have been done with it in the here and now. It would have taken some careful bookkeeping, but I could have paid you a dividend of a couple-of-hundred pounds-per-year for the rest of your days in return."

"But what about the luxury of your circumstances?" Gregson asked, spreading his arms to encompass the estate. "A country residence, whose upkeep alone must cost hundreds of pounds per year. And you set a very fine table."

"Charitable donations from a number of pillars of the county more than pay for maintenance, and there is a stipend from the government that goes toward the wage bill. The books are up to date and balance properly, I assure you. Anything *else* goes through a separate accountancy."

"Yes, we're aware of your second set of ledgers," Holmes mused. "And the cash kept in gold?"

Durand's eyes widened in surprise. "Confound your intrusion, sir! It is a violation of trust!" He sobered a moment later. "Petty cash. Gratuities to staff. Quick payments as may be needed."

"But what of medical ethics?" I asked, a hand extended in a heartfelt gesture. "We have a duty to do our very best for every patient, no matter who they are. Patients have suffered in a medical sense – injury, addiction, prolongation of illness. This cannot be acceptable."

"Therein lies the balancing act, Dr. Watson. A question of weighing the evils. A patient or two goes through somewhat more than they should have in exchange for others receiving care that would otherwise have been beyond them. I am in no doubt that we have saved many a life by virtue of proper and timely care, lives that would have otherwise foundered amid cold, neglect, and hardship. To me, this is acceptable. I regret the necessity, but have come to terms with it."

I looked at Holmes and Gregson, and my expression must have told all, for Holmes beckoned us out of earshot of Dr. Durand. When we huddled by the rose trellises, he raised a brow wryly. "Gentlemen, we are in a profoundly cleft stick here. I would remind you at once that with Inspector Gregson officially off both duty and his 'patch', and Watson and myself civilians not bound by regulation, we aren't in fact legally obliged to follow through on our findings. So we may ask ourselves the pertinent question – " He glanced back at Durand, and Gregson and I followed his nod to take in the dejected figure. "Has Dr. Durand done more good than harm with his enterprise?"

Gregson cleared his throat self-consciously. "You're suggesting that we . . . walk away from this case?"

"I'm saying that, as we have the choice to do so, we are obliged to weigh the pros-and-cons very carefully indeed. We came up here on the trail of a fraudulent practitioner. We have confirmed the crime and

135

identified both the methodology and the chief perpetrator. If we present this case to the authorities, Dr. Durand's career is over, along with several of his staff. The hospital will be taken over by others appointed by the Coleman Trust, no doubt with increased external oversight to prevent irregularities in future. From the autocratic perspective, correctitude will have been asserted. But what of the human and ethical perspectives?"

After a moment's difficult silence, I shook my head gravely. "This is a confounding ethical position for a doctor to be in. I remember a lecture at Barts in which our professor told us there is barely a doctor alive who has never put the cost of a poor man's treatment on a rich man's bill. It may not be spoken of openly, but it's far from unknown. My concern is with those patients who are physically harmed in the process. In all conscience, I cannot ignore that. Yet at the same time, to close down Dr. Durand's enterprise will almost certainly cost lives among those in direst need." I shrugged my shoulders helplessly. "I frankly don't know what to do."

Holmes nodded simply, fists on his hips. "Gregson?"

The inspector blew out his cheeks in a noisy sigh. "A good copper knows when a warning is enough. Ten minutes ago, I'd have said this business was far beyond that point, but now . . . ." He glanced back at Durand.

"Very well." Holmes seemed to meditate for a long moment. "Watson, would a promise to simply *do better* when it comes to patients' suffering from all this salve your conscience?" I gave a tight-lipped nod, a little reluctantly. "And Gregson, would you be willing to deliver a stern warning from the police perspective?" At his agreement, Holmes too nodded. "Very well, gentlemen. We're decided. We hold the power in this moment, and it is our mutual choice to *not* bring this matter to the attention of the Mildenhall Police. However, we may do so at any time – and that possibility more or less ensures the improvements of which we spoke. Let us inform Dr. Durand."

He rose as we approached, and Gregson unlocked the cuffs without a word.

"Listen very carefully, Dr. Durand," Holmes said softly.

A carriage was ordered for us, and we departed for Kennett after lunch, all three walking this time, our luggage in the wheelchair as we waited on our transport.

"It's an unusual feeling," I commented as we watched the coach approaching through the trees along the driveway. "Making the judgement call as to the merits of a situation and deciding who goes free or suffers. I don't think I'd be a magistrate for all the tea in China."

136

"Knowledge is power, Watson, and with power comes responsibility." Holmes had his unlit pipe between his teeth and his deerstalker comfortably in place. "I have very rarely allowed a miscreant the luxury of a second chance, but, just occasionally, it is warranted."

"An interesting experience," Gregson agreed. "Usually, we trim up a case like a Christmas turkey and present it to the courts in the hopes they have a taste for it. They don't always. But this time . . . ." He shook his fair head. "For what it's worth, I think Dr. Durand will be tightening up his dealings to avoid the kind of unfortunate events that put us on this trail. And that's as much as we have a right to hope for."

I had filled my pipe as we waited and took up my case as the carriage crunched into the gravel forecourt. "Well, he knows we'll be quietly reviewing his patient releases in future. What do you say, Holmes?"

"For all your misgivings, Watson, I profess a sense of having done the right thing here. I believe Dr. Durand is a good man who has gone to unfortunate lengths to extend the beneficence of which he is capable. But, with some adjustments, his stretching of both ethics and law may indeed be tolerable." And with that, he hefted his cases to board, and we heard not another word about Dr. Durand and the Greenacres convalescent hospital from that day forth.

"And the catalepsy?"

"A fraudulent imitation, Watson, though I should hardly dare to hint as much to our specialist. It is a very easy complaint to imitate. I have done it myself."

– Dr. John H. Watson and Sherlock Holmes
"The Resident Patient"

The Adventure of the
Dead Rats
by Hugh Ashton

My friend Sherlock Holmes could never be described as one of the tidiest of men. Mrs. Hudson, our long-suffering landlady, was forced to endure a state of continued disorder that would have driven many other women into a terminal decline.

Quite apart from the presence of piles of paper covering almost every available surface, and the frequent presence of strange objects, often exhibiting clear evidence that they had been used in the commission of acts of violence, there was usually an almost impenetrable fog of tobacco smoke which mimicked the London fogs outside the room. I confess that I was not entirely innocent as regards the last, but the emissions from Holmes's pipe far outweighed my more modest offerings.

Mrs. Hudson, however, no doubt mollified by the handsome sums that Holmes and I paid in rent, appeared to be largely unruffled, confining herself to mild remonstrations and clucking sounds.

For my part, I learned to tolerate most of the eccentricities that surrounded me, but towards the start of my acquaintance with Holmes, his occupation one morning as I entered the room after my constitutional tested the limits of my patience.

"What on earth are you doing?" I asked him, as I saw him stooped over the dining table, on which the remnants of our breakfast had been pushed to one side. "Is that a dead rat?"

"Indeed it is," my friend assured me. "*Rattus norvegicus*, to be precise. A fine specimen, is he not?" He indicated the lifeless rodent, in the belly of which, judging by the bloodied scalpel lying beside the corpse, he had made an incision.

"This is intolerable!" I exclaimed. "The dining table – Indeed, our sitting room! – is no place for anatomical examinations. I demand that you remove this rat to a more suitable location before Mrs. Hudson sees what you are doing and throws us onto the street – an action that would be fully justified, in my opinion."

It wasn't often that I became angry with Holmes, but this latest exploit had, as I say, overstepped the boundaries of my tolerance.

Almost sheepishly, Holmes gathered up the rodent and surgical instruments.

"Would you have the goodness to move the bottles of prussic acid and strychnine from the chemical bench and return them to their places on the shelves?" he asked me.

I did so, and he deposited his burdens on the space thus vacated.

"Now tell me," I demanded, "where did that rat come from, and why are you so interested in it?"

"To answer your first question, it was sent by messenger, in the box you see there, a little after you went out. The answer to your second question may be found in the note that accompanied it." He removed a paper from the top of the pile before him. "Here, you may read it for yourself."

I took the paper, and read:

The Fir Trees, Artington, Guildford

"Dated yesterday."

Dear Mr. Holmes,

Please excuse the contents of this package, which I assure you I wouldn't have sent had I not considered it necessary to do so. As you will see, it is a Brown Rat, which I discovered deceaced outside the kitchen door of our house. This is far from being the first specemin of its kind that I have discovered in recent days.'

I broke off. "This is more than a little ridiculous, Holmes. Does this man, for so I take the writer to be, expect you to behave like the character in Robert Browning's poem and charm the vermin? Surely there are rat-catchers in Guildford?"

"Read on," Holmes commanded.

As you may imagine, I am angered by the fact that some twenty of these rodents have been deposited outside my door (for I cannot concieve how they all crept there to make it their final destination in life) over the past week or so. I have hidden the existence of these objects from my wife, and instructed the servants not to mention them, as I am sure that she would be upset by these events. Would you have the goodness to examine the enclosed in order to determine the cause of death. If I make so bold, the assistance of your friend,

139

Doctor John Watson, may be of value in this. Unless I hear
from you otherwise, I intend calling on you this afternoon.

Yours sincerely, Mortimer Maberley (Capt., retd.)

"Well, Watson, a pretty little puzzle, is it not? Twenty rats, all deceased in mysterious circumstances, all located at the same spot."

"And no obvious cause of death, I take it? No wound or injury?"

"Not that I can discern. Come, perhaps you would care to examine the *corpus delicti*? Captain Maberley seems to be under the impression that your professional expertise may be of value here, and I cannot say that I entirely disagree with him."

"Very well," I answered, "though my last experience of dissecting a rat was some years ago, in the early stages of my medical education."

It was the work of only a few minutes to confirm Holmes's observation that there were no visible wounds or injuries on the body of the unfortunate rodent. A few more minutes, during which I found myself praising Holmes's skill in dissection, revealed no obvious damage to the internal organs.

"Almost certainly poison, I would say," I declared. "Impossible to say when or where it was administered or what type of poison was used. Are you really intending to take on this case?"

"I will at least listen to what this Captain Maberley has to say to us. What do you make of the letter itself?"

I picked up the letter again and addressed myself to it, attempting to obtain information from it in the fashion which I had often observed with Holmes. "The handwriting definitely has a masculine flavour to it," I started. "And although the language is fluent and accurate for the most part, I do notice that there are one or two errors in spelling, such as how he spelled '*conceive*', '*deceased*' and '*specimen*'. I would say that this is the writing of a man who is unused to expressing his thoughts in writing."

"Indeed so. The paper, the ink?"

"I see nothing remarkable there."

"Both are of exceedingly poor quality. As you can see, this has been written with a steel nib, not a fountain pen, and, moreover, one likewise of poor quality. The address on the package containing our visitor was written in a different hand, possibly feminine, but also using the same pen and ink, and also, by the appearance, unused to writing. The number of our house is missing, the package being simply addressed to *Sherlock Holmes, Esq., Baker Street, London*."

"It seems that you are well enough known for the carrier to be able to deliver it," I smiled.

Holmes ignored my last and continued. "The rat here was in a cardboard box, originally used for some other purpose. The remnants of a label saying *nderby and Sons, Ltd., London SW* still adhere. I would venture that this is *Enderby and Sons*, the well-known suppliers of female apparel. The wrapping paper has been previously used for wrapping." He put his nose to the paper and sniffed. "I would say onions. The odour was quite noticeable when I first opened the box. Is our Captain Maberley one of the tribe of whom it is said that they have long pockets and short arms? Enderby's isn't the cheapest of emporia, and the address would seem to indicate a certain level of prosperity. Perhaps we may deduce that Maberley has risen from humble beginnings to his present state, and still retains a certain caution in the way that he spends his money. And why, you may ask, would he ask the cook to write the address?"

"The cook?" I confess to being baffled by this last statement of Holmes.

"If the paper used to wrap the box was originally used to wrap food, then it would certainly have been left in the kitchen. Who better, then, to address the package?"

"And why did he not address it himself?"

"Perhaps he didn't wish his wife to know of the existence of this plague of rats." Holmes's face took on that characteristic smile betokening the welcome of a problem to be solved. "There is something about this business that intrigues me. Let us welcome the Captain when he arrives this afternoon."

"In the meantime, I suggest that we remove all traces of this – " I indicated the rat. "Mrs. Hudson would, in my opinion, be perfectly entitled to turn us out onto the street if she were to discover that we were dissecting vermin on her furniture." I sniffed the air. "At least it isn't producing an odour at present, but I fear that it will do so very soon, and we should take steps to dispose of it at the first opportunity."

"Very well," said Holmes. "In any case, I fear there is little more we can achieve with regard to a solution without more information from Captain Maberley."

Suiting our action to the words, we were soon able to make the room presentable to Mrs. Hudson. The rat was concealed in the coal-scuttle, to be disposed of in an alley by either Holmes or me, dependent on who left the house first.

Captain Maberley made his appearance at half-past-two precisely. He was somewhat short in stature, with close-cropped greying hair and a small moustache. I noticed a certain stiffness in one leg as he took his seat in the chair that Holmes reserved for clients. Remembering what Holmes had marked earlier about the Captain's spending habits, I remarked that the boots, though originally of good quality, had aged, and appeared to have been repaired, more or less skilfully, on more than one occasion.

"It's very good of you to see me, Mr. Holmes," were his first words, delivered in an accent which had more than a touch of the Midlands counties about it. "I told myself several times that such a great man as yourself would hardly be interested in such a trivial matter as this, but I assure you that this business has been somewhat of a trial to me."

From my acquaintance with Sherlock Holmes, I could tell that this speech caused him some amusement, but this wouldn't have been obvious to any person who didn't know him as well as myself.

"Pray continue, Captain Maberley," he invited our visitor.

"Perhaps I should tell you a little about myself. I was born in the city of Derby, and joined the Army as a boy. I fought as a sergeant with the Sherwood Foresters in Egypt, and would you believe, they gave me the Queen's Commission and a medal for something I did. The same business that gave me this," tapping his leg. "It still pains me in wet weather – not that I'm one to boast about what I did, but it took me up in the world, it did. I married Mary, the widowed sister of one of my fellow officers, soon after my promotion, and I have to confess to you that there were words in the Mess about the match."

Holmes raised a quizzical eyebrow at this, which Maberley took as a request for further explanation.

"You see, Mr. Holmes, I wasn't of the same class as them. They'd been brought up all proper, and knowing which fork to use at dinner and all that. And the idea of a former ranker sitting at the same table as them wasn't altogether to their taste, as you might say."

"It didn't seem to prevent you being promoted," I remarked.

"I was good at my job," he replied. It wasn't a boast, but a statement of simple fact. "But I knew that I'd never get past Captain, and that was good enough for me. I took my pension and retired to the house in Guildford which had been left to my Mary by her parents." He paused. "I have to tell you that once again, those neighbours where I now found myself barely tolerated our existence. Indeed, if Mary's parents hadn't lived in the house before, I don't think we would have been tolerated at all. For myself, I don't mind too much, but it has broken my wife's heart to be shunned by those families with whom she grew up."

He spoke with a certain resignation, rather than with bitterness, and it was hard not to feel some pity for this man who had given so much for his country.

142

"You wouldn't consider removing from there?" I asked, and for the first time in his narrative, there was a flash of anger from Captain Maberley.

"I would not give them the satisfaction!" he exclaimed. "In any case, Mary would never agree to leave her childhood home."

There was a silence, wherein we digested what we had just been told, broken by Holmes, who addressed himself to our client.

"May we talk about the rats?" he asked.

"If we must," was the reply, accompanied by a shudder. "I have always hated the beasts, since I was a child. They disgust me more than I can say, and I have never made any secret of it to anyone. " He paused. "About three weeks ago, as I was leaving the house for my morning cigar – I should perhaps explain that a cigar of a morning is a habit I developed as a young man, and I still continue to practice it, although Mary is somewhat worried about the effect of the smoke on the health of Douglas, her little boy from her first marriage, and for that reason I only smoke my cigars outside the house."

"Most considerate of you," Holmes remarked.

"Thank you. In any event, I noticed a dead rat just outside the front door," replied Maberley, shuddering once more at the memory. "It repelled me, but I forced myself to turn it over with the aid of a stick. Even so, I could discern no injury."

"How did you explain its presence to yourself?" asked Holmes.

"It may be un-Christian of me, but my first thought was to assume that the rat had been killed by poison, and placed at my door by my neighbour, Sir Lionel Malpas."

"You have a reason for ascribing this action to him?" Holmes asked.

"Sadly, yes. He is a man who is known throughout the district for his bad temper and general dislike of almost everything. I fear that I am a special object of his dislike."

"Lionel Malpas," Holmes mused. "The name is familiar. Watson, would you be kind enough to hand me the Index from the shelf behind you? Thank you. Ah yes, my collection of Mr. Malpas. Ha! Yes, indeed, Captain Maberley, you are correct in your report. He was bound over regarding a quarrel over a card game at the Albermere Club some years ago, and only escaped prosecution for assault on another occasion involving his carriage and that of another by buying off the case with a large sum of money. A man of clearly strong passions, and of a temperament to put his thoughts into action. Pray continue," he invited Maberley.

"Well, Mr. Holmes, after breakfast I requested our gardener to dispose of the rat, after first informing Cook of our unwelcome visitor, and cautioning her to say nothing about the rat to my wife."

"Your wife shares your antipathy to the creatures?" Holmes asked.

"She does, though I confess my dislike is stronger than hers. No, my reasoning was that she would be upset by the action of our neighbour, whose family were friends with her parents. Indeed, she and Sir Lionel used to play together as children."

"Indeed?" murmured Holmes. "And I am to take it that these visitations continued?"

"Indeed they did," was the answer. "One, two, or on one occasion, three corpses of rats have been left beside the door."

"Always in the same place?"

"Indeed so. I had my suspicions, and one night I kept watch, intending to catch the villain in the act. I saw nothing, and yet, at my feet the next morning, I saw two of the loathsome creatures. It seemed a ridiculous affair to take to the police, and I feared they would simply disbelieve me and take the word of Sir Lionel. I then remembered your name, which had appeared in one of the weekly papers, and fearing that my story would appear ridiculous to you without further proof, I requested the gardener to package the rat for dispatch to you, and – "

I interrupted his narrative. "Pardon me, but do you smell smoke?"

"I smell nothing," our visitor replied, but Holmes indicated with a nod that he did.

"It appears to be coming from outside the room," I said, and rose to cross to the window overlooking the street. "It is indeed a fire," I reported. "It would appear that smoke is issuing from the house across from here which has remained empty for so long. I can now see the fire-engine approaching. It would appear that there is no danger to life from what I can see."

"Perhaps some tramp or idler has been lodging in the empty house," suggested Maberley, "and an ember has fallen from his fire, and set alight the débris that accumulates in such places

"Very likely," concurred Holmes. "Watson, perhaps you would be good enough to close the window. The smell is becoming quite strong."

"I confess that my sense of smell is rather weak," said Maberley. "Ever since I got that knock on the head in Jaipur. In fact, I really can't smell anything at all unless you hold it right under my nose."

"Is that so?" I enquired. "Yours sounds like a most interesting case."

"If I had a sovereign for every doctor who has said that to me," he laughed, "I would be a tolerably rich man by now."

"You were saying?" Holmes invited as I closed the window and returned to my seat. "You were saying that you ordered your gardener to package the rat and address it to me?"

"Strictly speaking, it wasn't he who addressed the package. Lomax is almost unable to read or write, and so it was Cook who addressed the package before passing it to the carrier."

"Not you?"

"If Mary had seen the package addressed to you, she would immediately wish to know why I was communicating with you, Mr. Holmes. Your name is hardly unknown. I fear I am very poor at dissimulation, and the truth, as I have said earlier, would cause her some considerable distress. If the writing on the outside of the package wasn't mine, she would express little interest in its contents. I wrote a letter which I requested be enclosed with the package, and – well – here I am."

"I see," said Holmes. "And what is it that you require of me?"

"Would it be possible for you to visit my house on Saturday? Mary will be visiting her sister at that time, so she will not know of your visit. I would like you to confirm my suspicions that Sir Lionel is at the bottom of this."

"And then?"

"I intend to bring him before the courts. It is intolerable that Mary and I should be subjected to this harassment."

"Perhaps I will take this case," agreed Holmes. "There is, however, the small matter of my expenses incurred in the matter, and my professional fee."

The other's face fell. "I am not a rich man," he said, "though if you were to see the house and style in which I live, you might fancy otherwise. The money is all my wife's, largely held in trust for young Douglas when he comes of age."

"No matter," smiled Holmes. "I have yet to demand a fee of a client that he or she cannot comfortably afford. In some cases, as Watson will confirm, I have been known to remit fees altogether. Art for art's sake."

"That is a weight off my mind," said Maberley. "Then you will come?"

"Indeed I will," said Holmes. "There are aspects of this case that present themselves as being of great interest."

Our visitor thanked Holmes profusely and saw himself out, explaining that he was expected back before the evening.

"Well, what do you make of him?" Holmes asked me.

"As the Bard so rightly observed, '*Some have greatness thrust upon them*'," I answered. "Poor Captain Maberley, I am sure, would have made an excellent sergeant-major. But giving him a commission, and making

145

him mingle with those who are his social superiors – I am all for giving others their due and recognising their achievements, but I fear that the mores of our society don't always permit such advancement to be a success for those involved."

Holmes chuckled. "Your views never fail to surprise me, my friend. So here we have a man from humble beginnings, living on the money supplied by his marriage, and disliked by those around him. Though," he mused, "being disliked by Sir Lionel Malpas would seem to me to be more of a recommendation than otherwise."

"And what do you expect to achieve by visiting The Firs?"

"I don't know at present. No doubt all will become clear when we visit the scene of the incidents."

On Saturday, we took the train to Guildford, and then a cab from the station to the end of the road on which The Firs was situated.

"We aren't going to see Captain Maberley immediately," Holmes replied in answer to my question. "First, let us pay a call on Sir Lionel Malpas."

Sir Lionel's house proved to be an imposing red-brick building in the late Gothic style. As we neared the house along a winding drive flanked by yew hedges, Holmes appeared to be somewhat abstracted, his head bowed, and absent-mindedly using his stick to poke at and disturb the dead leaves and other vegetation by the side of the path.

Upon our approaching the steps leading to the front door, the door itself was abruptly flung open to reveal a tall bearded red-faced man clad in a crimson dressing-gown, brandishing a heavy blackthorn stick.

Seemingly unperturbed by this vision, Holmes mildly enquired if he was speaking to Captain Mortimer Maberley.

"Damn your insolence, man!" came the furious reply. "My name is Lionel Malpas, and I have no connection with the man whose name you have just had the impertinence to utter!"

"Why, what has he done?" Holmes enquired.

"What has he done? I will tell you what he has done. First, when offered the Queen's Commission, he didn't have the common decency to know his place and refuse it. '*Captain*' he styles himself! I refuse to recognise that title. Next, he had the temerity to seek the hand in marriage of my childhood playmate and sweetheart, Mary Upton. And lastly, with the Devil knows what lack of respect and propriety, he moves into the house next to mine," pointing with an angrily shaking finger. "I tell you that the man should be horsewhipped, and his very existence is an affront to the whole neighbourhood!"

146

"Thank you," Holmes replied in a mild tone. "Can you tell me," smiling, "if there is a path that leads between this house and that of Maberley?"

"Your impudence knows no bounds, sir! Would I allow such a path to continue to exist, given what I have just told you? Now be off my property forthwith, before I set the dogs on the pair of you!" As if in answer to this threat, the sound of baying dogs arose from within the house.

"Thank you," Holmes replied, tipping his hat in salute, a gesture that seemed to infuriate Sir Lionel still further.

We turned and walked down the yew-tree avenue.

"I believe he was on the point of apoplexy," I remarked when we were out of earshot of the house. "From a very superficial observation just now, I fear that I don't give him long to live."

"A most illuminating discussion, nonetheless," was Holmes's answer.

We reached The Firs, which, as its name suggested, was flanked by two magnificent specimens of the Douglas Fir. The house itself, though undoubtedly handsome and of good quality, was on a smaller scale than that of its neighbour, but presenting a less gloomy and more cheerful aspect.

Maberley himself opened the door to us.

"Two this morning," were his first words to us. "I have left them where I discovered them. I will take you there."

"Excellent!" said Holmes. "Lead on."

As we walked through the house, which was furnished in simple, but good, taste, Holmes mentioned that we had just called on Sir Lionel Malpas.

"We found him to be as you described him," Holmes remarked.

"A singularly unpleasant individual," I added. "A few words from him were enough to confirm the opinion you gave of him earlier."

"He implied, however," said Holmes, "that a path used to exist between the two houses. What do you know about this?"

"I know that at one time there was a path, and that Mary and her family used to visit the next house using it. However, since we moved here, Sir Lionel has erected a stout fence between his property and ours. There is no path any more. Ah, here we are." We stopped in front of a door. "Please excuse me if I don't come any further. I explained my antipathy to these creatures, did I not?"

"You did," Holmes assented.

"Very well, then. Gentlemen, if you could prove that it is indeed Sir Lionel who is responsible for this, I will be most grateful." So saying, he

147

opened the door. "I'll be in the drawing room when you have completed your examination," he informed us.

We stepped outside, where, as we had been told, two dead rats lay before us on the bare earth. They were large examples of the type, and had they been living, one would have assumed they were in perfect health. A superficial examination was enough to inform us that they were deceased, and furthermore there were no wounds visible which might have been the cause of death.

I bent over to examine the corpses more closely. "Holmes, do you smell anything?" I asked him. "I believe there is an odour of which the source is something other than these unfortunate rodents."

With a look of distaste, Holmes stooped. "You're right. A smell of coal-gas. I noticed that gas was laid on as we came through the house." He cast around and discovered a stout twig which, to my astonishment, he placed in the mouth of one of the dead rats, and used it to open the jaw, peering inside with the lens he held in his other hand. "As I thought," he exclaimed, as he repeated the process with the other corpse. "But here, why here?"

He straightened himself and looked around. "Halloa, what do we have here?" he asked, pointing to a small crockery dish beside the steps.

"I do not know," I said.

"It is the solution to the mystery, I feel. There are only two more links needed in the chain to complete the story." He then strode off, back in the direction of Sir Lionel Malpas' house.

"Come here, Watson," he called. "See here." He was standing by a stout board fence, some six feet or more in height, through which it was impossible to discern anything. "Now," he said, "do you go this way," indicating the left, "and I will go the other. Call when you discover anything of interest."

"What do you consider as being of interest?" I asked.

"You will know what is of interest when you see it," was his enigmatic reply.

More than a little irritated by the vague nature of this mission as it had been presented to me, I set off in the direction indicated. I had hardly taken a dozen steps, I suppose, before I heard Holmes's voice calling me.

"I have it," he said when I joined him. "See here – there is the remains of a track that was here in the past. Undoubtedly this is the path which the children used to visit each other. But more interesting still is this." He pointed to the ground at the foot of the fence. "A fence may be difficult to climb over, but for certain creatures, it is easy to go underneath it by digging a tunnel. And that is exactly what we have here."

"So, the rats aren't dead when they come into this garden?"

148

"Indeed not."

"But why do they come here from the other garden?"

"The cook will no doubt tell us," was his answer, as he led the way back to the kitchen door.

Maberley's cook, a Mrs. Danby, proved to be in the midst of creating an apple pie, a task she was happy to abandon when Holmes produced a half-crown from his pocket and displayed it to her.

"Tell me," Holmes asked, "do you ever put out bread and milk or any other food for hedgehogs, or other animals?"

"Not me, sir," she answered. "That would be the girl."

"The girl?" I asked.

"Yes, sir. Little Jilly, the scullery maid. She comes in to give me a hand two or three days a week, though I have to say that she's that small, and quite frankly, sir," pointing to her head, "she's not all what she should be up there, so she's not as much use as you might think. Anyway, she came from the country somewhere, and she said that they always used to put out a little something for the hedgehogs – 'urchins' she called them – at night, and asked me if I minded. Well I didn't really, seeing as how it was only a few scraps of bread that had gone stale, and a bit of milk which like-as-not was already on the turn. So she used to use an old dish and put it out before she went off of an evening."

"Thank you, Mrs. Danby. That has proved most illuminating."

"Thank you, sir," she answered, pocketing the half-crown.

"And now for the drawing room," Holmes said to me.

"Well?" asked Maberley, rising to greet us.

"I am sorry to say, sir," Holmes told our client, "that Sir Lionel Malpas, much as you, or indeed Watson and I, might wish him to be guilty of placing the rats outside your door, is innocent of that offence."

"Can you tell me more? Specifically, how you reached that conclusion?" Maberley asked. "Some brandy to refresh you and Doctor Watson?" he offered.

"Thank you, no," he replied, and I declined as well. "I will be brief, as we must return to London shortly. First, let me remind you that there was no mark of violence or injury pertaining to these rats."

"They were poisoned, then?"

"They died from poisons, yes, but that poison wasn't deliberately administered. The drive to Sir Lionel's house is flanked by yew trees, as you have no doubt remarked."

"Ah yes," said Maberley. "I was told as a child that the berries of the yew were poisonous."

"Interestingly enough, that is incorrect. The leaves are poisonous, to be sure, and so is the seed. The berries themselves are apparently edible, though I have never put this to the test. It is perfectly possible – indeed, it is likely – that rats, foraging in the undergrowth below the trees, ingested some fallen needles, and perhaps also some berries and seeds. While a small amount might not necessarily kill them outright, it would certainly spell their eventual doom. Victims of the yew do not give up the ghost immediately, but will die within a few hours of ingesting seeds or leaves, even dead leaves, of the tree or bush. I discovered traces of yew foliage in the mouths of this morning's victims."

"I see. But how and why did they get into my garden over the fence? And why did they die outside my kitchen door?"

"As to the how, the cunning beasts had dug a tunnel under the fence at the point where the path had once been, and therefore the vegetation was thinnest and it was easiest for them to dig. For the why, you must ask your scullery maid Jilly, who has been in the habit of leaving out food for hedgehogs. This almost certainly was a reason for the rats, having ingested a fatal dose of yew, to visit your garden on a regular basis."

"I see. But then, why would they die there?"

"You remarked that you lacked a sense of smell," Holmes said. "You would therefore have been unaware of the fact that the gas pipe under the soil was leaking. The combination of yew poisoning and town gas proved fatal, The animals were rendered insensible and immobile by the gas, unable to steal away to die, and probably died without regaining full consciousness, but after a brief period of convulsions of the body and limbs, as was obvious by the marks on the ground around the bodies. In conclusion, other than the charge of maintaining poisonous material in the form of yew bushes, it is impossible to accuse Sir Lionel of anything. I am sorry if this isn't the outcome you wished."

"Can I merely say that it is a most unexpected outcome? I thank you for your swift resolution of the matter, and I expect your account soon, which I will be happy to pay. It hasn't been pleasant to think of another man, even one such as Sir Lionel, as being guilty of what I had fancied him as doing."

"In this instance," smiled Holmes, "there will be no charge. This has proved a happy break from my usual routine, and I am sure that the change of air today will have improved my health. However, sir, I cannot speak for an improvement in your health if you do not arrange to have that leaking gas pipe repaired at the earliest possible opportunity. Come, Watson, let us away."

It was two weeks after the events recorded above that I observed in *The Morning Post* the notice of the death of Sir Lionel Malpas from apoplexy.

"Your diagnosis when we met him was correct, then," Holmes said when I informed him of the news. "It isn't often I say this of anyone, but the world will be a happier place without Sir Lionel in it. Let us hope that Captain Maberley and his wife are now able to lead a more peaceful life – one without Sir Lionel and without rats."

"I believe that my late husband, Mortimer Maberley, was one of your early clients"

– Mary Maberley
"The Three Gables"

The Laodicean Letters
by David Marcum

Chapter I

"I'll wager that you haven't seen one of these before!" crooned the hunchbacked man.

He had a beatific smile upon his wide face as he leaned upon the counter. From the other side, Sherlock Holmes stepped closer with enthusiasm, while I took a moment to study our surroundings.

The space was small – no more than a dozen square feet – and to call it a shop was charitable. Flaked paint on the front door spelled the words *Winslow – Antiquities*, but the room in which we stood had nothing more than an empty scarred counter, a shelf with a few collapsing old books that looked to be from the early sixties, and some forgettable trinkets in the window consisting of various nicked and dinged maritime devices – a brass telescope and astrolabe, for instance – and a grimy-looking gasogene of ancient manufacture.

The window was dirty and would need the better part of a day to clean, should one choose to do so, but judging from the equally dusty interior, such was not one of Mr. Winslow's higher priorities.

Holmes was leaning closer, shifting slightly to one side in order to catch what light he could from the front window. He was examining an ancient-looking document, curled and ragged at the edges. To assist, Winslow reached and shifted a lamp closer.

"The Laodicians?" asked Holmes, looking up.

"An early Christian church – from the Apostolic era. They were located in Laodicia, on the river Lycus, in Phrygia – now a part of Turkey. It was then one of the Asian areas under Roman control. The river itself is something of a curiosity. It flowed west from Mount Cadmus before vanishing into a chasm in the earth. However, after half-a-mile or so it reappeared. After flowing by Laodicia – "

Holmes tapped his finger on the counter beside the document, pulling Winslow back to the shop. "Thank you," he said. "My ancient Greek is quite rusty, and this isn't quite the modern incorrect version now taught in our universities." He straightened up. "Fifteen-hundred years?"

"If the text is to be believed, it should be two-thousand."

"Also years?" I interrupted. "That document is truly two-millennia old?"

Instead of receiving an answer, Holmes said, "I gather there's more to this than simply letting me read an ancient letter to a long-gone people."

"I thought you'd enjoy seeing it, Mr. Holmes," said Winslow. "And a few others like it as well."

Having been awakened early that February morning and urged into a cab before I'd had breakfast and coffee, I needed to know more.

The sun had not yet risen when Holmes knocked on my door. It had been a bitterly cold night, and I was still wrapped tightly in my blankets. I decided that continued sleep was my first priority and ignored Holmes's second knock. Then, as I should have expected, I heard the door open, and I sensed through my closed eyelids that a candle was being carried into the room. In seconds, I was awakened by a tugging at my shoulder.

"Arise, Watson!" Holmes cried. "The game is afoot – something a bit unusual. Not a word! Into your clothes and come!"

Five minutes later we were both in a cab and trundling through the silent streets on our way to the City – specifically, some unnamed lane that ran from north to south between Houndsditch and Leadenhall Street.

"Winslow's is a most peculiar place," Holmes was explaining while I struggled to follow. "I discovered it when I first came up to London. The shop itself isn't much to look at, but for those who know, it's a gateway to academic and historical treasures. He specializes in documents – the more ancient the better. Many is the time that the British Museum has decided they want this or that added to their collection, and they've recruited Winslow to their cause. He is a most effective agent.

"It was through the Museum that I first heard of him. In those early days when cases were few, I devoted a great deal of my time to study, attempting to gather all knowledge that I might need for my chosen profession. On one occasion, for instance, I was hired by a Manchester businessman with notions of social advancement to locate a rumored first draft of *Vortigern*. Have you heard of it? In 1796, it was touted as a lost Shakespeare play, before it was revealed to be a hoax, perpetrated by William Henry Ireland, the prominent forger. Jacob Sherwood, my client, had the notion that the forgery must have been copied from an original legitimate work, and based on a recommendation from a friend of his for whom I'd done a small service, he hired me to find it.

"The Museum scholars scoffed at the notion of a legitimate earlier version of *Vortigern*, but they pointed me toward Winslow, and it was fortunate that they did, for it was my introduction to a whole new area of study. After I had located the lost legitimate *Vortigern*, I did some further work for Winslow, helping him to authenticate that Shakespeare also actually wrote *The Birth of Merlin* and *Locrine*. From there – "

153

At this point, I had to interrupt. "Wait – Are you saying that there are other Shakespeare plays – *legitimate* plays – that are out there, unknown to the general public?"

Holmes nodded. "But like the suppressed books of the Bible, there are reasons for them to be hidden away."

This comment soon turned out to be of tangential relevance, although we didn't know why then. Before I could ask further questions about these earlier cases – for I knew that chances were high Holmes might never discuss them again – he raised a hand. "We're here."

Inside, we found the shop empty, but Holmes called out, and in seconds a door behind the counter opened to reveal Winslow. "Thank you for coming," he said in a high-pitched voice. "I knew that you wouldn't mind such an early summons."

With his twisted spine, he was no more than five-feet high. He had a long rectangular head, a full beard spilling over his chest, a little knuckle of a nose, and small round glasses over merry dancing eyes. He presented a warm dry handshake and seemed delighted to meet me.

"I'll wager, Doctor, that you were asleep not half-an-hour-ago." His eyes twinkled in the dim light.

Before I could affirm it, he continued, nodding. "Ha! Young Mr. Holmes isn't the only one who can observe and make a deduction! Never fear, Doctor! In a few moments, I'll have some breakfast for us and a bit of tea. Or perhaps coffee will be more to your liking? I see from your expression that is your preference. Coffee it shall be! But first – " He turned back toward the doorway. " – let me retrieve the reason that I've asked you here."

"An invitation to breakfast," Holmes said softly. "He already likes you."

Winslow was back in just a moment, placing the ancient-looking parchment on the counter.

After Holmes's examination and our discussion of the Laodiceans, I was still puzzled. "It's an ancient letter, then?" When they both nodded patiently, I added, "What is the significance?"

Winslow smiled, as if I were a bright pupil who had potential after all. "Let us adjourn to my parlor and we'll discuss it further."

"An honor, Watson," murmured Holmes as we rounded the counter. "You've passed a test. Distinct! Not everyone is invited into the inner sanctum."

Crossing through the doorway was as if we had entered another realm of existence. Whereas the front shop had been plain, bare, and dirty, Winslow's private quarters could only be described luxurious, although in a curious way. The furniture was old, but solid and beautiful. There were

154

fine rugs on the floor, and a number of lamps lit to make the room bright and cheerful. There didn't seem to be a speck of dust – which was surprising, as the vast majority of the space was given over to a truly impressive amount of old books and documents. Their familiar and peculiar and comforting smell was quite apparent.

The room had no windows, and every wall had built-in floor-to-ceiling shelves of some dark-stained wood. Tabletops and several desks all had books stacked on top, but neatly – very much unlike my friend's methods of filing, where leaning piles of papers were mounded against one another to form flying buttresses constructed of paper, with additional support from other sinister criminal souvenirs best left unnamed. Amassed dust was a constant source of disagreement in Baker Street, as Holmes wouldn't allow Mrs. Hudson to clean around his carefully hoarded documents, and therefore I was often set to sneezing or racing to open a window (when the weather allowed) when he went hunting for some hidden or misplaced sheet. No such dust was evident here.

Winslow rang a bell, and an elderly woman shuffled in from a door at the rear of the room. After inquiring our preference, our host told her, "Coffee please, Mrs. Harris. And perhaps a bit of breakfast as well?" She smiled, nodded, and withdrew.

We were directed toward a grouping of chairs surrounding a low wide table, upon which were three other documents, all somewhat similar to the one we'd just seen in the shop. Winslow had carried that one back with him, and laid it to one side of the others.

"Mrs. Harris and her husband run the house," Winslow explained to me as we were seating ourselves. He waved a hand toward the surrounding room. "The rest of the building is laid out along these same lines – each room filled with books and papers. I have more volumes arranged in the other rooms of this floor, and the same in all the rooms upstairs as well. A lifetime of scholarship and accumulation, you see. The Museum is drooling to have it all, you know, just waiting for me to slip from my mortal coil." He glanced at Holmes. "This is all willed to them, but there are others who covet what's here." He lowered his voice. "Should I one day end up deceased before my time and under suspicious circumstances, Mr. Holmes, you must be certain to check on Colonel Carruthers' alibi!" And then he laughed gleefully. Holmes smiled and nodded in return, but I could see that he was filing the thought away, should it ever be necessary for further consideration.

At that moment, Mrs. Harris returned from some other part of the house, skillfully carrying a large tray containing a coffee pot and cups, as well as dishes of eggs, bacon, and toast. She began to set them on a round dining table to one side of the room, the only such flat plane free of Winslow's accumulated detritus.

Winslow apologized for making us relocate so soon after we'd found our seats. We settled at the table in front of our plates and enjoyed the excellent breakfast. After we'd had a few moments to satisfy our initial hunger, our host resumed the conversation.

"What do you know of the Lost Books of the Bible?"

Holmes frowned, and I suppose I had the same expression on my face. While he ticked over the facts he'd stored in his brain attic, I spoke. "I've heard of a few – *The Gospel of Judas*, for instance, or *The Gospel of Thomas* – Doubting Thomas, I've always supposed."

Winslow shook his head. "No, those aren't 'Lost' Books. Rather, they were simply suppressed, or left out of the Canonical Bible for various reasons. *The Gospel of Judas* relates Jesus' story from Judas' perspective, while *The Gospel of Thomas* – and some do attribute it to the famed doubting disciple – is a collection of Jesus' sayings. There are dozens of such suppressed books – *The Book of Enoch*, *The Wisdom of Solomon*, *The Gospel of Nicodemus*. No, I refer to the *Lost Books* of the Bible."

"Such as the Laodicean document you just showed us."

Winslow nodded, pleased. "Exactly! Now drink up – No coffee around the texts, if you please! – and rejoin me across the room."

We did so, and in moments we were again seated at the small table which held four documents – the Laodicean letter we had seen before, and three others, all of similar appearance. Winslow leaned forward and picked up two of them, handing them carefully to Holmes. "This is the one you previously saw, and the second is something called *The Prophecies of Iddo.*"

"Shouldn't we be wearing gloves to touch them?" I asked, before realizing that I was second-guessing an expert who had spent his whole life around such items. If he wasn't being more cautious, who was I to question him?

Winslow smiled and shook his head. Holmes, meanwhile, had retrieved his glass from an inner pocket and was studying the documents with great interest. Then he looked up, asking Winslow, "May I see another?"

The crooked man leaned forward awkwardly and retrieved a third sheet, extending it to Holmes. "*The Annals of Jehu*," he said. The he explained to me, "Detailing the story of Jehoshaphat."

Holmes was looking intently at one document and then another. Then he said, "And the fourth?"

Winslow raised his hand. "A moment – First, what are your thoughts about what you've seen so far?"

156

"Clearly these purport to be some of the 'Lost Books' to which you referred – although as Watson pointed out, if they were truly the ancient texts, you would have been more careful, and you might not have let me handle them at all. That factor alone seems to call their authenticity into question. However, my quick study indicates that they would appear to be authentic. The parchment seems ancient, and without chemical tests, the ink also appears to be very old. But again, I say that your rather indifferent handling of the documents implies that they are forgeries."

"And here is another reason," said Winslow, leaning forward and handing Holmes the fourth and final document.

Holmes barely had it in his hand before he barked, "Ha!" and shuffled the sheets so that he could compare the new one with another already in his hands. After just a moment, he laid those two back on the table, facing my way, and handed me his magnifying glass. One look told showed even me enough to understand their thinking.

"They're identical!" I cried. "There are *two* of the Laodicean documents!" I looked closer. "I cannot believe just how similar they are – down to the irregular shapes and folds small tears at the edges, to the age spotting of the parchment in the exact same places, and to light and dark variations in the ink." I looked up at Winslow. "This is how you knew they were forgeries? Because of this duplication?"

He nodded. "But," I continued, "how do you know that one of these isn't the real thing? Or that the other two documents aren't real?"

"Because of the way I received them." He leaned back and re-settled himself in his chair, as if getting comfortable for a story, now that he didn't have to reach for any more sheets on the table.

"There are essentially nine 'Lost Books'," he explained. "These, as I mentioned, represent three of them: Paul's *Epistle to the Laodiceans*, *The Annals of Jehu*, and *The Prophecies of Iddo*. These 'Lost Books' are mentioned at different places in the Old and New Testaments, and Biblical scholars have worried about them for years. These aren't like the various books that were removed from the Bible entirely, or acknowledged by some and placed into the *Apocrypha – The Book of Tobit, The Book of Judith, Ecclesiasticus*, and so on. These untold tales, if you will, are referenced specifically within the Biblical texts, but they have never been found.

"Paul references his letter to the Laodiceans in *Colossians* 4:16. Jehu's narrative of Jehoshaphat is mentioned in *Second Chronicles* 20:34, and Iddo's prophecies are also discussed several places in *Second Chronicles* – 9:29, 12:15, and 13:22, I believe. These other untold narratives are – " Here Winslow raised a hand and counted on his fingers, repeating one when he reached the sixth and final entry. "*The Book of*

Jasher, The Acts of Solomon, The History of the Prophet Nathan, The Records of Gad the Seer, and two other letters from Paul to the Corinthians and the Ephesians.

"In addition to these books, there is another lost 'treasure', so to speak: *The Book of The Chronicles of the Kings of Israel.* The Hebrew Bible refers to some twenty of these works that no longer exist. These were apparently a very detailed history of that Iron Age period from which numerous other Biblical narratives may have been drawn. We're talking about a thousand years before Christ – kings you've heard of like Saul and David and Solomon, and others far more obscure: Zimri and Omri and Pekah and Ahaz."

Winslow smiled – I found that he smiled a great deal. He raised his hand again. "I can hear your thoughts, young Mr. Holmes: Enough with the history lesson. Why have I summoned you this morning – beyond giving you the opportunity to examine some interesting documents?" He glanced my way. "You are a very patient listener, Doctor." He then pulled a folded letter from his pocket – modern and rectangular shaped, I noted, and on paper and not parchment – and handed it to Holmes.

"Two days ago, I received this." Holmes took the letter, and then, after carefully studying it front and back, he handed it to me. It was handwritten in block letters on plain cheap paper.

"As you can see," continued Winslow, "the anonymous author says that he'll be in touch in one week. He is offering to sell me the entire recently discovered *Book of The Chronicles* – all twenty volumes – for the fee of fifty-thousand pounds. A paltry sum, considering their historical value – should they be legitimate. As evidence of the seller's good faith, and his '*respect*' for my '*professional integrity*', as he puts it, he included Paul's letter to the Laodiceans, Jehu's narrative, and Iddo's prophecies, with the idea that I would return them or buy them at additional cost when the negotiations for *The Chronicles* commences."

"Wait," I asked. "There are *two* copies of the Laodicean letter. Did the sender accidentally include both?"

"I like you, Doctor," said Winslow. "You ask the right questions. No, he did not. When I received the initial package, there were only the three separate different sheets. It was only yesterday, when I discussed the situation with another collector, that I learned that he too had been sent some of the 'Lost Books', along with the same offer to buy *The Chronicles*."

Holmes looked up, surprised. "Another collector? I was under the impression that your collection was unique."

Winslow shook his head. "Oh, no, Mr. Holmes! Mine is only a patch on what my brother has accumulated."

158

It's a rare treat to see Sherlock Holmes surprised, and this was one of those instances. His eyebrows raised dramatically, and a boyish grin settled on his face. "You have a *brother*?" he exclaimed, almost happily.

Winslow grinned as well, nodding emphatically. "I *do*!" he cried. "Lord Carringer! I'd wager that you never suspected I could have so notable a sibling, did you, Mr. Holmes?"

And indeed, apparently Holmes had not suspected it, for his surprise from a moment before continued unchecked.

"And you say he also received an offer similar to the one sent to you?" I asked, rather needlessly.

Winslow nodded. "He did. It's not well known at all that we are related, so I suspect that the forger had no idea we'd compare notes. When I received my copies of the documents, I was skeptical, but they are really excellent and convincing. I was immediately curious about *The Chronicles* – but I don't have the funds to purchase them. I then set out for my brother's home in Mayfair, where I found that he'd also received three documents as offerings of the legitimacy of the entire offer: A copy of the Laodicean letter, as well as Paul's two lost letters to the Corinthians and Ephesians, also with perfectly ancient parchment and ink, and written in old-style Greek.

"My brother had been intrigued as well, and half-convinced of the legitimacy of the offer – for lost ancient documents *are* found every once in a while, you know, so it was possible. As you can see from the letter, the author was vague as to where he claimed to have obtained them, but that would have been established during negotiations."

Winslow lowered his voice. "My brother seemed somewhat surprised to see me, and I wonder if he would have shared his good news if I hadn't arrived on his doorstep when I did. However, it turned out to be of great value to both of us to compare what we'd received, as the duplicate Laodicean letters were enough to throw doubt on the whole offer."

"Why do you think the sender was so careless?" Holmes asked. "Surely if he's forged this many of the 'Lost Books', he could have forged one more, instead of repeating one of them."

"My brother, Edwin, and I discussed that. We feel that one of these copies of the Laodicean letter – either his or mine – was a first draft, and that it contains some flaw that we haven't yet seen. It's obvious to the forger, but not so much to anyone else. And given the circumstances – that both of us initially thought we were the only ones to receive an offer – we decided that he must have decided to use the flawed copy. He also likely made similar secret offers to other collectors as well, to generate a number of private sales, rather than start some sort of bidding war. There may very well be any number of these forgeries floating around. However he did it, he certainly created something that would satisfy extensive examination. We wouldn't have known, had we not placed the duplicates side by side."

"Is that the nature of collectors at this level?" I asked. "Would you normally keep something like this to yourselves?"

"Secrecy is our way, Doctor," said Winslow, "and as I said, it isn't common knowledge that Edwin and I are brothers. We had something of a falling out when we were quite young – mostly repaired now, but I went my own way then and have lived my own life."

"What about the other collectors?" asked Holmes. "Those who might also have received an offer?"

"Really, there's only one other at our level: Colin Wright. His collection isn't as extensive as that of my brother and me, but its specialization, particularly in ancient Biblical texts, is second to none."

"And have you asked him about this?"

Winslow shook his head. "No. When Edwin and I discussed this late last night, we felt it was likely that Colin has also been approached, but then I suggested that we involve you, Mr. Holmes, and we decided that your investigations, and the impressions you receive directly from Colin, would be of more value than anything I could tell you second-hand."

Holmes nodded, and then held up the letter. "The Biblical letters aren't folded – they must have arrived in a flat box. May I examine it?"

"Certainly." And he pointed to a shelf near the door to the dingy front shop area, where a flat heavy-looking cardboard box, about sixteen-inches square, was resting on a shelf, atop a pile of much newer-looking documents, all with squared edges. "The string is inside it. I cut it instead of untying it."

"Excellent," murmured Holmes as he retrieved it. Then he returned to his seat and put it under intense scrutiny. After a moment, he set it aside, disappointed. "No return address. The label is written in block letters, using a moderately worn modern-day pen and typical blue ink. The wrapping paper and twine are available anywhere in London, and there's nothing special about the knot. There's nothing of interest in the box as well – no curious soil or seeds or scraps of anything that might give a clue to the sender's location." He looked toward Winslow. "The letter – was it originally folded, or flat like the sheets?"

"Folded as you see it – lying on top. And there was no packing material. The documents fit close to the walls of the box without being folded, and the box is so shallow that they would have essentially stayed in placed without the possibility of damage, unless the box itself was crushed."

"And the cardboard is heavy enough for that to be unlikely," added Holmes. "Besides, the British mail system is extraordinarily careful of its deliveries." He looked again at the outside of the box. "Typical postage, and mailed in Charing Cross. That, too, tells us nothing. It's nearly certain that questioning the clerks there would reveal that they have no memory of this anonymous-looking package." He shook his head. "This will need to be approached from a different angle – assuming," he added, "that is why you asked us here this morning? To determine who sent these documents to you and your brother."

Winslow nodded. "That's correct. If these are forgeries – and they appear to be – then they're the best that either Edwin or I have ever seen. Someone – Colin Wright, or another amateur collector that I don't know or recall – may buy a set, and they may then achieve some sort of legitimacy which they do not deserve, terribly confusing future scholarship." Winslow sat up straighter. "Can you see your way to looking into this?"

"Of course. First thing, Watson and I will need to visit your brother. Can you provide his address?"

Winslow shared a house number in Half Moon Street, and then Holmes abruptly stood, our business here apparently finished. He gestured toward the documents. "May I take these with me?"

Winslow frowned – the first time I'd seen him do so – but nodded, in spite of his seeming reluctance to let them get away, and Holmes put the four sheets into the cardboard box in which they'd arrived and wadded the string into his pocket. I stood, and then our host pulled himself upright and shook both of our hands. I thanked him for the breakfast, and he led us back through the shop and to the front door. "I look forward to your report, gentlemen," he said just before letting us out.

Chapter II

The sun had risen further as we walked south, although the light didn't penetrate very deeply into the narrow lane. Holmes was silent as we turned into Leadenhall Street, and still when it became Cornhill. He only spoke when we reached the Bank, and then just to say, "I thought that we would be able to find a cab easier here than if we'd turned toward Whitechapel or Spitalfields."

I agreed. The street there was full of them, hansoms and growlers discharging men in fine suits as they prepared to enter the massive buildings around us and carry out the Empire's tedious but demanding financial business. It always amazed me that this area, arguably the richest part of the richest country in the world, the center of so much of the world's monetary activity and accumulation and conservation of capital, was just a few hundred feet from possibly the poorest part of the metropolis, where people lived in filth and poverty and squalor, jammed dozens to a room (when they could find one at all and didn't live on the street) in conditions that should be unacceptable if anyone in these rich surroundings bothered to give any thought to it.

From just a few years of being associated with Holmes's cases, I'd already been educated enough as to what went on in much of the East End, and I was aware that it was only a matter of time until the accumulating pressure between these two vastly disparate but adjacent worlds, rubbing against each other with increasing friction, would ignite. But I kept such thoughts to myself, aware that it was all too easy to be accused of being a radical or a socialist or a revolutionary for taking too much of an interest in one's fellow man. Society would adjust, as it always did, and such suffering would be alleviated, but it would not be painless.

Only in the cab did Holmes share his thoughts with me as we traveled up Cheapside to the Holborn, and so on to the west. "I cannot profess to have the level of expertise attained by Winslow, but I'll confess that I would have been fooled, as he nearly was as well."

"I ask again," I said, "is it not possible that one of the Laodicean letters is the real thing? Why should they both be forgeries?"

He shook his head. "The odds are greatly against it. One of the two letters is certainly a forgery. If that forgery – either the one sent to Winslow or the other to his brother – is a fake, then it's very likely that the other two documents that were included with it are fakes as well. And if that set is fake, then why shouldn't the other Laodicean letter also be a hoax, contrived for the same purpose? It is unknown right now why a duplicate of the same letter was sent, but I favor the prosaic explanation – the sender didn't know that the two men were brothers, and thought that as rival collectors they wouldn't communicate or compare notes, so it wouldn't matter. Perhaps, as Winslow said, one has a flaw that we haven't spotted. Maybe the forger didn't have enough false documents prepared to make up a full package, so he used the flawed sheet, thinking that it wouldn't be noticed."

"It sounds as if this fellow is a master forger – it was only his careless use of a duplicated sheet that gave rise to any doubts. There doesn't seem to be any way to track him – certainly not by the package he sent. I suppose you don't want to wait until the next letter arrives, to arrange for the sale, with the hope that it will provide some way to locate him." I nodded to the box, sitting in Holmes's lap. "What will you do?"

He shook his head. "I know someone who can possibly help us. Perhaps we should have spoken to him first, but Winslow's brother seemed to be the next likely port of call. Hmm . . . ." Then he knocked on the roof of the cab with his cane, asking that the driver stop for a moment at the next post office. By now we were well along Oxford Street, and it only took a moment for us to pull over. Holmes handed the box to me and jumped down. He was only inside for a moment before he returned, taking back the box as we lurched into motion, resuming our course to Mayfair. Seeing my unspoken question reflected on my face, he said, "I've sent a message to someone who owes me a few favors, arranging an appointment with an expert when we finish speaking with Lord Carringer."

I nodded as he fell silent once more, knowing that all would eventually be explained. Or so I assumed. It usually was, although there were occasions when I was still left a bit in the dark, and no amount of asking would reveal additional details if it was felt that they were not my business.

In those days, Half Moon Street, at the bottom edge of Mayfair, was not a place where I'd had much chance to visit, although that changed in later years. Number 13, on the east side of the street, was nearly identical on the outside to our rooms at 221 Baker Street, but it was a world away. It had the same number of floors as our lodgings, the same width, and the front door at ground level was also on the left side of the building. The bricks were the same dun color, and there was also wrought-iron metal-work outside the first-floor windows, though such was true for many homes in London. But the faint ring of the bell sounded with unmistakable *gravitas* when compared with the functional tone at our own door, and the austere butler who answered was nothing like our dear landlady, instead being cold and intimidating. When we presented our cards, he looked, sniffed, and announced that we were expected, and that he would inform the master to see if he was available. Then he invited us in, leaving us standing in an entryway of the same dimensions and layout as our own in Baker Street, but under a vastly different froth of expensive decoration.

In a moment, the butler returned and then led us through to a room that was the located where Mrs. Hudson's parlor would be, but it was a very different place indeed. There, a tall handsome man in his fifties was standing to greet us, a peeved expression on his face. "Thank you, Cain," he said, and then nodded in our direction.

He was about the same age as his brother, but otherwise they couldn't have been more different. Winslow had been bent, clearly that way since birth, while his brother, Lord Carringer, had grown strong and tall. Both had the same thick gray hair, and they wore similar glasses, perched on similar noses, but whereas Winslow's eyes were friendly and amused by life, Lord Carringer's were pinched and squinted, surrounded by lines that did not come from laughter. He saw my examination, no doubt matched by Holmes's, and he spoke in response.

"Robert and I are twins," he said, as if he'd had to explain it before, "but our lives have taken far different paths, initially at Robert's insistence, but I soon understood his reasons – for taking a different last name, for instance – and eventually I came around to agreeing with his way of thinking. But that isn't why you're here," he added, gesturing to the box in Holmes's hand, and then to a similar one on a small side table. "I presume that you'd like to examine what I received."

Holmes agreed and stepped forward, pulling out his glass as he did so. It gave me a chance to look around the room. It wasn't very crowded, with just a few chairs that were more for decoration than comfort. I realized that Carringer hadn't invited us to sit, and perceived that he also didn't intend to offer us a great deal of time.

"Your brother has a vast collection," I said, feeling rather awkward. "He indicated that it fills most of his house – and he also implied that yours is greater. I take it that you don't keep it here in your home, as he does."

Carringer's mouth tightened, as he apparently didn't feel like discussing it with a stranger, but he replied, "I have some items here – upstairs – but the majority are in the building next door – Number 12, between this building and the hotel. I have opened doorways on each floor between this building and that one, allowing for access between them. It's there that my staff maintains the collection. Both buildings have been improved – together they are now like a fortress."

Then he glanced at Holmes, who had been looking at each document – both Carringer's and Winslow's – before laying them aside and studying the second box.

"These were likely mailed at the same time – they're virtually identical. Besides the duplicate Laodicean letter, there are two others, both different, and both seemingly authentic, although I suspect otherwise. Your brother said that these are supposed to be two of the letters written by Paul – one to the Corinthians, and the other the Ephesians."

"That is correct."

"And if they were authentic, is there anything about them that's surprising – and earth-shaking doctrinal assertions that would rock the Church?"

"Not at all. They are simply reiterations of various policies and beliefs that Paul shared in his other epistles. They have some of the same sniping and disagreements about procedural disagreements with Peter that the Biblical letters contain, but nothing that would need to be suppressed, or that might cause some kind of Holy War."

Holmes nodded. "So it's likely that the forger simply wants to collect some money for the supposed value of these documents, and isn't trying to spook anyone into buying and suppressing them so that a conflict can be avoided – for religious folk are so easy to inflame about the least little things."

"That's correct. For instance, there was the incident at Antioch, as described in *Galatians* 2:11–13, wherein Peter described a confrontation he had with Peter over the fact that Peter, who used to eat with the Gentiles, stopped doing so after meeting with some men sent by James, Jesus's brother, because they weren't considered acceptable. Paul argued that *all* men were acceptable. To Paul's disgust, the people of Antioch, along with the disciple Barnabas, sided with Peter – which subsequently led to a falling-out between Paul and Barnabas as well."

"Even today," I noted, "such small things can cause wars. Are you sure there's nothing of this nature in any of these letters – even if they are forgeries?"

"No, nothing at all. Just references to Paul's past visits, and adjurations to stay strong and keep to the faith."

"Your brother mentioned Colin Wright," said Holmes. "That he would also be someone who would also likely receive an offer to purchase the lost *Chronicles* of the Israeli kings. Do you agree?"

Carringer nodded. "I expect so – but we decided not to approach him, once we agreed to seek your assistance in the matter. I would be curious," he added, "to know what documents *he* received – whether he has yet another copy of the Laodicean letter, or any of the others that Robert or I received, or if he was sent copies of the rest of the 'Lost Books'."

"Your brother told us of the others. Not counting these, I believe that the others so far unaccounted-for relate to Jasher, Solomon, Nathan, and Gad."

"That's correct."

"Are these all Old Testament documents, or further New Testament letters?"

"Old Testament. Jasher is mentioned in both *Joshua* and *Samuel*, Solomon in *First Kings*, and both Nathan and Gad in *First Chronicles.*"

Holmes indicated Carringer's set of documents. "Do you mind if I take these with me? It may aid in tracking down their source."

Carringer appeared, like his brother, as if he would initially object, but then with a sigh he waved a hand. "Take them. I don't believe that they're legitimate, so do what you must."

"And Mr. Wright? Where can we find him?"

"That is both easy and difficult. Colin's home is nearby – No. 2 Tilney Street, just near the Park – but he's also out of the country right now. He has been for three months, at least. He's on a buying trip, I believe, seeking the journals of a brutal Wallachian ruler from the mid-1400's – some chap who massacred tens of thousands of Turks and Muslim Bulgarians four-hundred years ago. The last I heard, Colin is in Hungary, southeast of Sibiu, in the Carpathian Mountains. Some place called Poenari Castle – *Cetatea Poenari* as they say locally – near the Arges River. Much further than I would go . . . ." He pursed his lips. "But I can provide a letter of introduction. Perhaps his secretary, Roger Melrose, would be willing to confirm whether he's also received a box. He knows more about Wright's collection than Wright does – he's the real expert – and he'd also be interested and appreciative to know if the documents are fakes."

He moved to a small desk at one side of the room and composed a short note, which was then folded and provided to Holmes. Then, with our business at an end, he rang a small bell, and when the butler arrived, he instructed him to show us out. With no further words spoken, we found ourselves back on the quiet street. Holmes, shifting both cardboard boxes under his harm, led the way up to Curzon Street, and then west and north the short distance to Tilney. Pausing at the corner, he unfolded Carringer's note before passing it to me. It was addressed to Colin Wright or Roger Melrose, simply stating that Carringer had recommended that we speak with either one of them regarding a matter of some interest.

No. 2 was much nicer than the property we'd just left, with white stone at street level and red brick stretching three stories above. It was slightly wider as well, and its clean lines had a very solid elegance about it. Knowing something of Lord Edwin Carringer's rumored wealth, Colin Wright's finer house seemed rather indicative of his more-extensive resources.

His door was not, however, answered by a butler. Instead, it was opened by one of the two men we were seeking: Roger Melrose, a rather stout fellow in his early thirties. He was a smiling man, with his face having a natural turn to pleasant and open interest. We introduced ourselves, and he seemed to have heard of Holmes, for he ushered us in immediately without any request to first state our business. He glanced curiously at the two cardboard boxes in Holmes's arms, both of which were turned to hide the address labels, and asked that we step through to a well-appointed sitting room on our left as we passed through the immaculate entry hall.

Again looking toward the two boxes, Melrose motioned toward a small rectangular table, offering us seats which we accepted, and brandy which we declined. He sat down across from us, perched upon the front of his own chair and leaning forward. With his hands on the table, the fingertips pressed lightly upon the surface like two matching five-legged spiders, he asked, "What can I do for you, gentlemen?"

When Holmes didn't immediately answer, allowing the silence to build for an awkward moment, Melrose leaned back and clasped his hands.

He began to make unknowing washing gestures, squeezing and turning one hand within another, and then reversing himself. Was it a habit, or an expression of nervousness related to our unexpected visit? I looked at him again, more closely.

He was well-dressed, with brown hair parted in the middle. He wore no wedding ring. His wrists were pale, as if he spent a great deal of time inside – something to be expected if his days passed working with rare documents – and his face was rather florid, possibly from enjoying the bounty of Colin Wright's table a bit too well. Other than a small cluster of three small *acrochordons* at the outer corner of his right eye, there was nothing unusual about him that I could see, although I had no doubt that Holmes had observed a great deal more – perhaps where Melrose had grown up from certain subtle aspects of his speech, or his daily activities as revealed by the callosities on his fingers.

Holmes, still without speaking, handed Melrose Lord Carringer's note and, while the secretary read through it once, and then again, Holmes opened one of the boxes, still obscuring the label, and pulled out the four documents that we had taken from Winslow's shop, saying without explanation, "We understand that you are Mr. Wright's 'expert'. What do you think of these?" I thought that his tone seemed a bit abrupt, but he surely had his reasons. He pushed the sheets across the table, but Melrose made no effort to reach for them. Holmes then took out the two sheets from Lord Carringer's box, laying them beside the others. It was then that Melrose spoke.

"May I ask who said so?" he countered, laying down the note and folding his hands back together.

"Certainly." Holmes reached a hand forward to tap the note, now lying on the table. "As you see, we have just come from Lord Edwin Carringer's residence in Half Moon Street. It was he who said so, and suggested that we speak with you. He's aware that Mr. Wright is out of the country, and he indicated that as you are knowledgeable in this area, we should seek your opinion." He glanced down toward the sheets, adding, "He received these various parchments as part of a negotiating tactic toward purchasing a larger item. These were sent as proof of the legitimacy of that item."

"And the larger item?"

"I would prefer to reserve that information at this time."

Melrose nodded, unclasped his hands, and pulled the sheets closer. The light was good in the room, and he had no apparent difficulty in making his examination. He looked at the first sheet, turning his head with interest and making a small humming noise to himself. Then he pulled over another sheet, and another. One of the letters to the Laodiceans was the second document he examined, and when he reached the second duplicate letter, which was the fourth in the stack, his eyebrows went up in surprise. He raised his head to look toward Holmes. My friend, however, made no explanation or comment, and Melrose returned to his intense studies.

Finally, after nine or ten silent minutes, Melrose pushed the papers back, gently gripped his hands once more, and said, "An initial examination would lead one to think that these are genuine – if there weren't two identical copies of the letter from Paul. After that, one would be inclined to think that forgery is involved. Of course, one of the two letters might still be the real thing, and there's nothing to say that the other documents aren't *bona fide*. Still, tests would need to be made, an evaluation to the most exact scientific standards . . . ."

Holmes raised a hand, his tone still surprisingly abrupt. "Did Mr. Wright also receive such a package?"

Melrose glanced at the two cardboard boxes, lying on the table. "It isn't my place to comment on Mr. Wright's affairs," he said, although there was some very slight hint of disingenuousness in his tone. Or perhaps it was my imagination. Holmes's manner throughout the interview had carried an equal hint of antagonism, and possibly Melrose was simply responding in kind.

"That's unfortunate," said Holmes. "I had hoped that you might be able to provide some information to that would make our task a bit easier."

"Is that so?" Melrose responded, now with something of a sneer in his tone. "Surely you understand my position, gentlemen. You both arrive with a note from Lord Carringer, seeking confidential information, although he has never been a great friend to my employer. At the same time, you don't seem willing to share very much information with me in return. There are *two* boxes there, but surely only one of them was mailed to Half Moon Street. Whose address is on the other? Why are you so careful to keep that information hidden? You indicate that these letters were sent in relation to an offer to purchase some larger item, but you refuse to say what that is. If my employer also received such letters and a similar offer – and I'm not confirming that he did – then it's my duty to protect his interests and not take a chance on spoiling his efforts to obtain the same item – should he choose to do so. I will say, however, that it is of interest that there was a duplicate of Paul's lost letter. That seems to be a rather careless mistake on someone's part, doesn't it?"

"I think that we can agree on that," said Holmes. He stood and retrieved the various documents from Melrose's side of the table. "I believe that our business is finished." As he spoke, he sorted the sheets, this time putting three in one box and three in another, as they would have been originally received before one of the duplicate letters was left with Winslow by his brother. This did not go unnoticed by Melrose. Then, with a nod, he turned and left the room. I followed, with Melrose trailing behind. Holmes opened the front door, and we went outside. Without comment, Melrose closed the door behind us, while Holmes led the way to our right, where we soon reached Park Lane, just across from Stanhope Gate. There, Holmes pulled me to one side, a sudden urgency in his voice.

"Watson, make your way back and find someplace – a door or areaway – where you can keep an eye on Wright's house. If Melrose leaves, do your best to follow him, and when you get a chance, send word to Baker Street where you end up. Hopefully he won't depart through the back entrance until I have a chance to find help."

"What is going on?" I asked, surprised at the abrupt shift of tone. "What did you see?"

"I recognized him," said Holmes, "but I cannot recall exactly where. As soon as I find some assistance, we'll follow that thread. Now – take your post!" And with that, he turned and vanished to the north alongside the eastern edge of the park.

Chapter III

Without waiting to watch him out of sight, I slipped back into Tilney Street, being as cautious as I could. By then it was late morning, and the sun was bright that day and nearing its apogee. The street wasn't very long, just enough to hold half-a-dozen buildings on each side, and No. 2 was near the center, so there weren't a lot of choices in terms of places to hide. I was fortunate that nearly across the street was a building whose areaway gate was unlocked, allowing me to slip down and out of sight. I tried to prepare some sort of story in case my presence was questioned, but fortunately no one from inside the house ever seemed to notice me.

I was there for slightly over half-an-hour, and in that time, no one came out of No. 2, and there were no indications of activity. No one looked surreptitiously from a curtained window. There were no deliveries, and no servants departed on errands – suspicious or otherwise. I realized that we didn't even know if there were servants in the house, and I had no instructions about what to do if one of them left. At least, I hoped, I would recognize Melrose if he departed, even in disguise, as he would have trouble hiding his stocky shape.

I didn't know what Holmes expected: Would Melrose withdraw surreptitiously to pay a visit to some confederate in connection with the document scheme, or would he instead boldly surge forth with luggage, making a mad dash for the Continent? And what had Holmes seen that suddenly caused him to be so urgently and immediately suspicious?

I was still worrying about what to do if Melrose actually came outside, and how I would follow him down this quiet street without being seen, when a lad sidled into sight from the west. As he approached, I could see that he was rather disreputable, with an appearance that didn't fit with this neighborhood. However, as was usually the case, instead of being chased away, he would be ignored and left to carry out his business – which I was sure involved instructions from Sherlock Holmes.

In fact, when he approached, I recognized him as Tad Willocks, one of Holmes's regular Irregulars. I had first learned of these deputized agents a couple of years before, soon after finding out that Holmes was a "consulting detective", as he called his profession. Typically we dealt with an older boy named Wiggins, who served as the group's leader, but I often encountered many other members of the group as well.

Tad didn't appear to be doing anything but ambling down the street, without purpose, but I knew that he was looking sharply from side to side. That was how he spotted me, and soon he had joined me in the areaway.

"Mr. Holmes found me near Portman Square," he said. From that, I knew that Holmes had quickly walked north toward Baker Street until he located one of the Irregulars. "It only took a few minutes to round up more of us and send us back this way. Clive is behind the house, watching the mews. Has the man come out?"

"Not by way of the front. I haven't seen anything at all. I can't vouch for the back."

"Not to worry. Before walking up and finding us in the Square, Mr. Holmes paid a beggar, Blind Steve, to keep an eye on the entrance to the mews. He didn't see anyone come out."

"Blind Steve didn't see anyone?"

"He ain't blind." He didn't add any irony to his comment. In fact, he seemed almost irritated that I didn't already know about Blind Steve. "Mr. Holmes is waiting for you in a cab at the corner of Mount Street, across from the fountain."

I nodded and left Tad there, aware that he and the other Irregulars would do a better job than I could following Melrose if he decided to leave. Returning to Park Lane, I turned north, and in moments I'd spotted Holmes, standing impatiently beside the hansom. After we'd climbed in, the driver gigged the horse into motion, and Holmes began speaking immediately.

"After I left you, I engaged this cab and turned toward Baker Street. Along the way, I found the boys and sent them this way. Then I continued to our rooms, where I consulted my scrapbooks."

The cabbie had set a fast pace, and he barely slowed when we turned right into Oxford Street at the Marble Arch. "I knew that I'd made an entry about Melrose, but it was so long ago that the information initially eluded me. Thank Heaven for those books, Watson! Even a brain attic that is trained to hold many facts will only stretch so far."

"And who is this fellow?" I asked. "Apparently he must be fairly notable to generate such immediate urgency."

"He is – and he's kept a low profile for quite a while. I last heard of him in '77, when he peddled a supposed *fifth* copy of the Magna Carta, apparently found in a West Country manor that had been a monastery before their dissolution under Henry the Eighth. The British Museum was in a bidding war with Cornelius Vanderbilt. I was able to inform the Museum of the truth, but Vanderbilt went ahead and paid a fortune – three-quarters-of-a-million. This was just before his death, and in the confusion that followed, the lawyers decided it was easier to let the man go than try and recover the money. Can you imagine, Watson – being so rich that being bilked of that amount could simply be ignored?"

"And this forger? Did you hear nothing more from him until now? And if he made that much money from Vanderbilt six years ago, why does he need to carry out another scheme so soon?"

"An excellent question. I suspect that he enjoys the excitement more than the monetary reward. No, I've heard nothing more about him, although I've made periodic attempts to see if he's surfaced anywhere. Coming across him this morning was a complete shock."

"What was it? His appearance? The way he held and moved his hands, or perhaps the skin tags beside his right eye?"

"Very good. Yes, it was both of those things – plus his general description. Brown hair parted in the center, stocky build, traces of a Manchester accent. That, and the man's association with possible forged documents, made it highly likely that we'd unexpectedly run across Archie Stamford – for that is his true name."

"I wonder that he was able to obtain Colin Wright's confidence."

"Well, from what I've heard, Wright has more money than sense. He's spent the last twenty years buying whatever he could, outbidding private scholars and collectors and notable institutions. I'm sure that we'll find that Wright's past secretary left for some reason, and Stamford saw an opportunity to take his place."

By then, we had progressed some distance across central London, staying on Oxford and New Oxford Streets when practical, and taking side streets when the mid-day traffic became snarled. In Holborn, we turned north along Southampton Row toward Russell Square, and I thought to ask about our destination.

171

"You recall the telegram that I sent earlier? I was checking on the location of someone – another noted forger who I helped to corner back in my Montague Street days: Elliott Baines. I wired to someone that I know in Whitehall, asking permission to interview him."

"Interview him?" I asked. "Permission? Is he in prison? What prison will we find in this neighborhood?"

"Not prison. Rather, he's under semi-permanent house arrest, at the pleasure of Her Majesty's Government. There are times when having a forger comes in handy, you know, and at the end of the day, Baines was quite willing to trade some of his freedom for Government service instead of a lengthy stay in Newgate."

As I pondered this, we completed our journey, stopping in front of No. 48 Doughty Street. As we climbed down, Holmes must have noticed my expression. He smiled. "Yes, you're correct – this address does have some historical notability. Do you not recall who lived here?"

I shook my head, frowning – and then I remembered. "Dickens!" I cried. "In the early days – He wrote *The Pickwick Papers* and *Oliver Twist* and *Nicholas Nickleby* while living in this house!"

"That's correct," agreed Holmes, belying the idea he's once suggested that he only kept facts in his brain attic that might have relevance to his investigations. "Apparently the building was in some danger of being torn down, and the Government stepped in, secretly, to save it, while also making use of it as a facility to house the occasional favored miscreant. There's some talk of converting it into a museum, but not yet. For now, Baines is the grateful resident, and he's kept rather busy. But let us go inside – by now he should be expecting us."

As we approached, the door was opened by a slim man in his late thirties, in a dark suit and with a tidy military mustache. It was easy to understand that he was a government agent, set in place as a caretaker for both the house and the resident. He stepped aside to let us enter.

It was a lovely little building, three stories with dark brick, and I felt a small thrill as I crossed the threshold. Charles Dickens had long been a hero of mine, and I particularly enjoyed his first three works, composed in this building. But before I had a chance to consider looking around and taking a moment to appreciate the ambience of the author who had lived here and then moved away years before I was born, we heard quick footsteps from the back of the house. In seconds, we were confronted by curious scarecrow of a man – tall and disheveled, his gray hair and beard both long and wild, his clothing unkempt and shabby, and his manner frenetic and vaguely hostile.

"So, you've come to gloat!" he said upon facing Holmes, planting his feet abruptly.

172

My friend shook his head, looking faintly amused. "You know better than that, Elliott. When offered this opportunity, you leapt for it. It's better than prison, and you have your own chef. These are much better rooms than where I found you, and you have important work that makes use of your skills in a positive way, rather than simply moving from one shady venture to another."

"Perhaps, perhaps. But it isn't just about the work. There's the thrill of the *game*, Mr. Sherlock Holmes. I think you, more than most, can understand that. Here I'm no more than a dull craftsman. I might as well be a cobbler making shoes. I should join a guild!"

Holmes laughed. "I should like to see such a guild, and who would be in it!" His expression sobered. "Elliott, we've run across someone who could be a member of that group alongside you."

"We?" asked Baines, looking my way. "This one?"

"Not him. This is Dr. John Watson, my associate."

"And are you a genius like Holmes here? A single-minded bloodhound?"

I shook my head. "No sir, not a genius. Instead, I have determination."

Holmes nodded. "That's it, indeed. Now, Elliott, we won't keep you long. Can you show us into your workshop? I want to ask your opinion about a few documents." And he lifted the cardboard boxes.

Baines nodded, his curiosity ending the cranky bantering. He took us deeper into the ground floor to a room in the back of the house, with a window looking out upon a small garden. I wondered if this was where Dickens had worked.

Holmes, again keeping the addresses on the box hidden, removed the sheets of parchment from each and handed the stack to Baines, who took them, adjusted the lamp on his desk, picked up a large magnifying glass, and began his examination. Meanwhile, I used the opportunity to look around the room. There were several high tables along the walls, each stacked with a number of sheets, some ancient looking, rather like what we had brought with us, and others along the lines of official government documents, both British and representing a number of other counties. The dates on these ranged from recent to several hundred years earlier. Many were in languages that I couldn't read, but I saw some that purported to be treaties, or grants of land transfers, or official-looking bonds and currency. Interspersed among all of them were a number of pens and brushes, bottles of ink, paints and dyes, rubberized erasers, balls of discolored putty, and knives that almost appeared surgical in nature. There were, however, no signs of the past presence of Mr. Dickens.

Baines immediately became deeply involved in the documents, studying both the front sides with the writing and the blank backs as well. Murmuring softly to himself, he often turned the sheets so that the writing upon them was upside down. He reached and grabbed a pad and pencil, making a series of neatly written notes. In fifteen minutes, he was ready to report.

"Forgeries, all of them," he said, "but all of them excellent. Although they purport to be from different Biblical eras, there are a few similarities – very few and very subtle – in the lettering that that show they were written by the same hand. I'm probably the only person on earth who could have seen it."

"And do you know who this person is?"

"What? Oh, of course. And I assumed that you did too. It's Stamford. He's made a specialty of this sort of thing. Haven't heard about him in several years – though in my current digs, I don't get out to gather news like I once did."

"He's surfaced," explained Holmes. "These were sent to two different collectors to give legitimacy to a bigger offer – he's offered to sell a larger work: *The Chronicles of the Kings of Israel.*"

Baines whistled. "Well, that's ambitious, isn't it? I wonder . . . ." He drifted off for a minute, and then looked at Holmes. "One thing you should know: These are all forgeries, but the text seems legitimate. What I mean is that they are *copies* of some original work. It seems as if Stamford has somehow acquired some of the *real* Lost Books of the Bible – and if he has these, he probably has others, maybe even the actual *Chronicles*. And that could be dangerous."

"How do you mean?" I asked, thinking that neither Winslow nor his brother, Lord Carringer, had intimated any indications of danger.

"What I mean is that many of the existing and accepted Biblical books aren't original – they're supposedly drawn from *The Chronicles*, in the same way that Shakespeare took some of his plots from previously published works. For example, *Romeo and Juliet* originally came from Arthur Brookes' 1562 poem *The Tragical History of Romeus and Juliet*, and *Hamlet* was first told as the story of *Amleth* in Saxo Grammaticus' *Gesta Danorum*, or *Deeds of the Danes*. You'll notice that *Amleth* is an anagram of *Hamlet*.

"*The Chronicles* may very well tell a different kind of story than what one finds in today's Holy Texts that were based upon it – to the point that they say something that might start a war! Oh, you think I exaggerate, Doctor, but surely you know enough about people to realize how passionately they feel about this kind of thing."

174

I nodded, knowing that he was correct. The masses did tend to cling to their religions, and they could become quite irate, and often violent, when this was challenged. And sadly, they chose to cling to their weapons as well.

"Fortunately," said Holmes, "we have a line on tracking down these items and keeping them from causing any problems." He began to collect the sheets back into the boxes. "Many thanks for your help, Elliott. I'll be sure and notify Whitehall of your cooperation."

"Yes, do that. For what it's worth." Then the prisoner, for I supposed that's what he was, waved a hand toward the stacked tables. "For every piece of work I finish, they send two more. I'm not sure that my debt will ever be paid, nor my sentence completed – but perhaps a miracle will occur. Good hunting, Mr. Holmes! Come back some time and tell me what happened – and if you can, bring the original documents with you when they're recovered. I'd enjoy seeing them."

Without committing himself, Holmes nodded and led me outside to our waiting cab. He instructed that we should next travel to Baker Street where, he told me, he'd see if there was any word on Stamford's latest activities. He was silent throughout the journey as he arranged his thoughts. I, too, considered what we had heard and learned.

When we arrived, Holmes told the driver to wait, as we might be leaving once again. He was correct. Upstairs was a small boy, Ike Denton, perched in Holmes's chair like a prince upon a throne, swinging his feet back and forth a foot above the floor. He had a message from Tad Willocks as to Archie Stamford's location. "The man you had us watching left not five minutes after Dr. Watson. We trailed him to Waterloo, where he caught the local to Farnham. And Mr. Holmes – he had several large trunks with him!"

I perceived that this was important, for a known forger fleeing the home of a notable collector with substantial baggage was highly suspicious, implying that Stamford had moved from creating documents to stealing them.

What follows next is quickly told, although there were still a few surprises before the tale was fully revealed. Our waiting cab briskly conveyed us to Waterloo, where we were in time to catch an express that bypassed all of the local stops to which Stamford would have been subjected. As such, we reached the Farnham station just ten minutes after Stamford disembarked. Before we'd left Baker Street, Holmes had written a pair of concise telegrams, sent by way of Mrs. Hudson, seeking official assistance, and we were met on the platform by Inspector Silas Beckett, who we had last seen the year before when Holmes solved the brutal murder of the divided linguist. Beckett had received word from Scotland

175

Yard to provide assistance as needed, and I quickly sketched the situation while Holmes ascertained from the nearby cabbies that Stamford had just hired one of their fellows to carry him and his trunks to a farm not far past Waverley Abbey. Beckett beckoned to one side, and three constables who had been standing there joined us. Hiring two cabs, we were soon on Stamford's trail.

We caught him as he was climbing down from his cab at a rundown farmhouse, talking with a little careworn woman who turned out to be his much put-upon old mother. As he had in the past, the man we had first met as "Melrose" had retreated here when things became too hot for him. He was quickly placed under arrest, causing a surprising torrent of vile cursing and spewing epithets to pour forth from the lady's wicked and filthy mouth. On principle, Beckett took her into custody as well, although it was later determined that she was likely innocent of any charges.

The trunks contained unexpected treasures: The cream of Wright's collection, as well as a vast amount of cash. It seemed that during the weeks when Wright was away from London, traveling in the dark places of the Continent, Stamford had been quite busy, dismissing the servants and quietly selling what he could of Wright's collection before moving most of the rest to rooms he had rented in another part of the city, leaving the house on Half Moon Street nothing but an empty shell. Using his exceptional skills, he had also forged documents to transfer the entirety of Wright's funds to himself. Most daring of all, he had created a new will, in which Wright apparently left everything to his secretary, Melrose. This took on additional significance when a telegram was found among Stamford's papers, notifying the perfidious secretary that Wright had been killed two months earlier while in the Carpathian Mountains, his body savagely assaulted near the *Cetatea Poenari*, apparently attacked by some kind of large animal which had torn out his throat and drained him of blood. Seeing a unique opportunity, Stamford had gone to work, day and night, to thoroughly loot his late employer's assets.

Ready to flee at any moment, but not yet finding it necessary, Stamford had come up with another plan: To forge a number of lost Biblical books and sell them to Wright's collector competitors. He was a master at quickly creating these documents, and when he had enough of them ready, he sent the boxes to Lord Carringer and Winslow. As suspected, he'd made two copies of the Laodicean letters, one with a small flaw, and rather than take time to create another, he'd simply included the flawed copy in the box to Winslow, not realizing that he and Lord Carringer were brothers and would compare the packages.

Of greatest interest were the originals from which Stamford had made his copies. Wright, whose money made him a very effective collector, had in fact been able to purchase all nine of the Lost Books, along with the fabled *Chronicles of the Israeli Kings*, from a source in Egypt. Where they had been located before that was never determined, as Stamford claimed not to know. The true and original stories upon which many of the Old Testament books were based were quickly found to be so shocking and divisive, and contrary to the established Biblical versions known so well by so many, that they were hidden away as soon as possible within the bowels of the British Museum, where a number of other similarly dangerous items were kept. Holmes was briefed on the contents of the ancient writings, but he felt that I would be better off not knowing.

"It's for the best, Watson," he'd said. "They should never be read. The world is not yet prepared. In truth, I'm sorry that I saw them."

I resented this attitude, treating me like a child, but I also suspected that he was correct, and that once I had seen what the original versions related, I might never forget them, to my own dismay. In the end, I ceased my entreaties to learn the truth.

"Yes, sir; near Farnham, on the borders of Surrey."
"A beautiful neighbourhood and full of the most interesting associations. You remember, Watson, that it was near there that we took Archie Stamford, the forger.

– Violet Smith and Sherlock Holmes
"The Solitary Cyclist"

A Case of
Exceptional Brilliants
by Jane Rubino

"The ideal reasoner," Holmes remarked one evening, "does not only seek out the facts in a case, but must make certain that what is essential isn't obscured by the irrelevant. Only then can a precise chain of events, linking cause to effect, be established."

"An unforeseen coincidence may prove to be as essential as a relevant fact."

"There is always the possibility of coincidence, of course, but coincidence cannot be relied upon. It cannot be ranked with analysis and deduction."

"And yet," I argued, "coincidence, when it does occur, may be the most vital link. In the case of Miss Westphail's necklace, for example."

"Ah, yes," Holmes conceded, with a smile. "The exception that disproves the rule."

Not for some time after Holmes and I had settled into our rooms at Baker Street did I fully understand the nature of my new companion's profession. That it was something out of the ordinary, however, I concluded from the disparate set of callers whose visits required me to surrender the sitting room so that they might consult with Holmes in private.

One visitor, who came rather often, was first introduced to me as Mr. Lestrade, a well-known detective, and as the weeks passed, and when I learned of Holmes's profession and he placed a greater confidence in my discretion, I was no longer excluded from their *tête-à-têtes*. At these sessions, Mr. Lestrade, who I'd learned was a Scotland Yard Inspector, would mention some police matter, and while not asking directly for Holmes's advice, he would bait his tale with features were most likely to pique my friend's interest. Holmes would then draw upon his own knowledge of the history of crime and suggest a course most likely to resolve the matter. At times, when Holmes was laying out his theory of a case, I would see an expression of bemusement or distrust pass over Lestrade's sallow features, and yet Holmes set the detective right too often for the Scotland Yarder to entirely dismiss my companion's *modus operandi*. And on those rare occasions that a case ended in failure,

Lestrade was too decent to crow – perhaps because he knew that where Holmes failed, no one else could possibly have succeeded.

From the earliest days of our acquaintance, I observed that Holmes had his own set of habits and idiosyncrasies, and one of them was to indulge in long rambles that took in every part of London, high and low. These weren't always aimless. Rather, they were Holmes's manner of acquiring that thorough working knowledge of the city which might serve him in his profession. Occasionally, when the weather was fair, he would invite me to join him, and so it was that on a Friday evening, in the middle of June of '83, Holmes laid aside his violin and I laid aside my book, and we set out on a leisurely stroll.

It was nearly ten before we returned to Baker Street to find Lestrade sitting in an armchair, puffing at a cigar, his expression one of weariness mingled with agitation.

"Lestrade!" Holmes threw off his coat. "You have been absent from these rooms for more than a week, and yet tonight you have been warming that chair for more than an hour. Your cigar," he added, nodding at the accumulation of ash in the ashtray. "Your grim look portends a matter of some importance. I hope it may be resolved in a week's time. Sainton is to give his farewell concert at the Royal Albert Hall on the twenty-fifth."

"I would be happy to think that it may be resolved at all."

"It is something particular, I take it."

"'Particular' doesn't begin to express it," declared the detective.

Holmes reached for the cigar box, settled in his chair, and lit one of his own. "Then express it in any way you wish."

"It is burglary, Mr. Holmes. Burglaries, I should say – three in five days' time."

"And what has been stolen?"

"Gems. Of considerable value."

"In that case, I'm surprised you aren't here to report a murder."

"Murder!"

Holmes waved at the stack of newspapers on the hearth. "Only a declaration of war or a sensational murder will eclipse the theft of valuable jewels! Yet, as I have seen no reports of assassination or war, there ought to have pulp enough and ink enough for burglary, unless a reporter has been abominably negligent. Any respectable editor would have done away with a fellow who overlooked a single noteworthy burglary – and you say there have been three?"

Lestrade nodded, grimly. "It is always difficult to know how much to feed the press. Too much may drive our burglar to ground and then we will never get the darbies on him. And it hasn't been twenty-four hours since the second and third, though the press must hear of them soon enough, since the second burglary – "

Holmes held up his hand. "It would be best to have them in order. The first was five days ago? What was stolen?"

"A dozen or more rings, and pair of antique diamond-and-sapphire brooches."

Holmes gestured for Lestrade to continue.

"The brooches belonged to Lady Metcalf, the wife of Sir George Metcalf. You know how it is, Mr. Holmes – at this time of year, all of the finery kept in a country estate safe is brought to town to be paraded about, since there is ball or crush or grand dinner six nights out of seven. Lady Metcalf had been going over her finery, and found that the catch had broken on one of the brooches, and a stone had come loose from its setting on the other. She asked around among her set who was the best fellow to put them to rights, and was given the name of Mr. Joseph Verlander, an elderly jeweler who has a shop at Greville Street, in the neighborhood of Hatton Garden. Verlander gained his reputation as the best gem-cutter in all of London, but his trade is, for the most part, buying, selling, and restoring of fine pieces, and is one of the few who will undertake the repair of antique jewelry. Lady Metcalf sent a note around to the fellow, describing the problem, and an appointment was made for her to bring the items to his shop on Monday last, at noon."

"Was Lady Metcalf accompanied on her errand?"

Lestrade nodded. "By her maid and a footman, but they waited in the carriage while she went into the shop."

"Was anyone in the shop when Lady Metcalf arrived?"

"Verlander was tending to a young couple who were looking over a tray of rings, and his young assistant was in the work-room at the back."

"The assistant's name?"

"Mr. Cree. And he is an apprentice, really. Verlander is getting on and not as nimble as he once was, and Cree seemed a clever lad and eager to learn the trade."

"Has he been with Mr. Verlander very long?"

"Little more than two months."

"And has he been an apt pupil?"

"Verlander says that he is sharp enough, though not without his lapses. There was one mishap when Cree attempted to treat pearls with a weakened solution of acid, which splashed up and left him with a scar upon his forehead. In all other respects, however, Verlander says he has come along nicely."

"Is he the jeweler's only employee?"

"There is a girl of all work – Susan Gryce is her name – who does a bit of cleaning and gets his tea, but she is often sent out on errands during the day, and wasn't in the shop at the time of the incident."

"Do the employees live on the premises?"

"Gryce has the attic, and Cree has a pair of rooms on the first floor, above the shop. They had been Verlander's, but he is arthritic and can no longer manage the stairs, so he made up a small apartment for himself at the back of the shop, beside the work-room and kitchen, and offered Cree the use of the first floor."

"If the work-room and kitchen and the jeweler's quarters are at the back, the shop itself cannot be a very large one."

"No, it isn't large, just a long, narrow room with the counter above display cases along one side, and a curtain to screen the rooms at the back."

"The entrance to the shop will be on Greville Street. Is there another?"

"Yes, a rear door opens onto yards with a market just beyond. Just inside is the passage and stair to the upper floors where Cree and Gryce lodge, and they both have a key to this door so they may come and go, since the front door is locked when the shop is closed."

"Pray, continue."

"Verlander called upon his apprentice to wait upon the couple so that he might see to Lady Metcalf. She produced the brooches and asked him if they might be put to rights by Thursday – last night – as she meant to wear them to a ball. Verlander had just laid them on the counter when a dirty vagrant shambled into the shop, begging for a sixpence. Verlander hobbled around the counter to shoo him off, but the fellow stood his ground and became disruptive and foul in his language. Cree hastened to aid his employer, but not before the young patron hurried his sweetheart out of the shop. Lady Metcalf attempted to pacify the beggar by offering him a shilling. He snatched at it and bolted, and when they all turned around, they saw that the lady's brooches and half of the rings were gone."

"So, the young lovers flee, the beggar decamps, and several valuable items of jewelry are gone. What *was* their value, by the way?"

"The brooches were appraised at twenty-thousand a few years ago, and Verlander states that the value of the rings wouldn't be less than seven- or eight-thousand."

Holmes knocked the ash from his cigar. "What next?"

"Lady Metcalf was near to hysterics and Cree ran to her carriage to summon her maid, and then went to see to the back door and hurried off to fetch a constable, who kept all in order until I arrived. You can imagine what a blow it was to Verlander. I have rarely seen a fellow brought so low."

"Could the jeweler or Mr. Cree or Lady Metcalf give an accurate description of the beggar?"

"Only to say that he was a dirty, shabby object."

"And the name of the affectionate pair who fled just after he arrived?"

Lestrade scowled. "They had given no name."

"If they had, it would have been a false one. You understand that it was all a play-act, Lestrade. Lady Metcalf's visit to this jeweler wasn't impromptu – she had certainly written to Verlander and made an appointment. When she arrives, a young couple is looking over a tray of rings. A beggar enters and causes a disturbance that draws everyone's attention away from the rings and the two valuable brooches laid out on the counter. Verlander and his assistant attempt to eject the fellow, whose unruly conduct appears to drive away the young couple. After they are gone, the vagrant is persuaded to depart, a shilling richer for his performance."

"Do you say that the young couple and the beggar were in league with one another?" I ejaculated.

"One provides a distraction while the others make off with the gems. It is a fairly common dodge."

"But they – the young couple and the beggar – would have had to know of Lady Metcalf's appointment."

"Quite so. And since she had written to the jeweler, that information could only have come from someone inside the lady's household who saw the note before it was posted, or one of Verlander's two employees, who saw it after it was received. So you have four collaborators, at very least."

"Which makes my task all the harder," Lestrade grumbled.

"Perhaps not, Lestrade. Prudent thieves prefer to work alone, or with one single tried-and-tested accomplice. But here we have a snug little gang: The beggar, the young couple, and whomever informed them of Lady Metcalf's visit. Which of the four will take custody of the gems until they are converted to pounds? Will all agree that they should be moved quickly, or will some want to hold back until a police investigation has cooled? And how will a mere twenty-eight thousand be divided? A single thief has only himself to satisfy, but it may be source of disagreement to a gang."

"'Mere'!" scoffed Lestrade.

"It is a considerable sum for one or two, perhaps," Holmes conceded. "But it must be divided among at least four, and perhaps not evenly – the brains may expect more than the limbs. If there is a fence, he will want a share as well. And there is another matter, Lestrade: Lady Metcalf made the appointment only days ago, and as you note, it is a particularly busy time of year, and so it is entirely possible that something may have occurred that would cause her to change the appointment, or to cancel it, which would alter this gang's scheme as well."

"I don't understand you," said Lestrade.

Holmes stubbed out his cigar and sat back in his chair, his fingertips pressed together. "I must wonder whether this gang was brought together solely to make off with Lady Metcalf's brooches, or whether they had merely taken advantage an irresistible opportunity, while waiting upon a more ambitious scheme."

"You may not be far off the mark, Mr. Holmes," declared Lestrade, "for one of last night's burglaries was a shocker, and it was no pair of brooches this time, but the single largest stone of its type."

Holmes sat upright. "You don't mean the Cavendish Emerald?"

"A right good guess, Mr. Holmes!"

"I don't guess, Lestrade. The largest of its type? Such stones are in museums, or privately owned, and at present, no great gems are on display in museums. Therefore, it must be privately owned, and the Cavendish Emerald is the only great gem that fits the description. It had been kept at a bank vault, but it was reported quite recently that His Grace had a display case made so that he might exhibit it at an engagement party he was to give, and there was talk that afterward he would turn it over to a lapidarist to have it cut down and a set of baubles made for his bride."

Lestrade nodded. "The engagement party was last night – "

"The affair that Sir George and Lady Metcalf were to attend."

"Yes. And it was a grand one – more than two-hundred of the best names invited to a ball, a supper, and then a display of fireworks in the great park on the grounds of Cavendish House. The emerald was set in a glass case, a six-sided chamber bolted to an iron stand, and secured with three stout locks. It was placed at the top of the grand staircase, just beyond the reception hall and two guards were posted beside it. It was never to be unattended."

"Then it should still be there. But, of course, your next statement will begin with, 'While everyone was at the park watching the fireworks display . . . .' Am I correct?"

Lestrade gave a wry laugh. "While the guests went out to watch the fireworks display, the guards stood at their post, and the servants went down to their supper. Not an hour later, one of the maids went up to ask the guards if she might bring them something to eat, and found the two lying senseless upon the floor, a neat opening cut into the glass, and the stone gone. She immediately ran down to the servants' hall, and they all rushed onto the scene. A few attempted to revive the guards, while the Duke's man went to alert his master, and one of the waiters ran out to notify the police. We were at Cavendish House in half-an-hour, and you

183

can only imagine the uproar! Two-hundred guests, and the Duke's own staff of eighteen, and several more hired for the evening from an agency – waiters and tweenies, for the most part – and there were the pyrotechnical men. And I had but five officers and a woman searcher."

"I don't imagine the prospect of being interrogated and searched endeared His Grace to his guests. Two-hundred, you say, and at least two-dozen servants. Your people cannot have got to them all."

"A dozen, perhaps, were overlooked. Upon learning of the theft, some of the women fell into a faint and had to be attended to, and even before I arrived, the Duke had dispatched several of the men-servants to comb the grounds."

"And the residence itself – was that searched?"

"You must know Cavendish House, Mr. Holmes – that grand place along Piccadilly. It would take two-dozen men a fortnight to go through every chamber and closet and cupboard."

"And what did the two guards tell you?"

"When they were revived, they said that one of the young men brought them champagne – compliments of the Duke to toast his engagement."

"Drugged." Holmes was silent for a moment. "That was only last night, Lestrade, and yet you say it was the second theft of three? Lady Metcalf's brooches were the first – "

"And the third came in the early hours of the morning, while I was still on the scene at Cavendish House. I was summoned to Hamilton Place, to the town home of the Earl and Countess of Selby, which is only a half-mile or so from the Duke's residence. They had attended the ball and had waited their turn to be questioned, and it was near dawn before they were permitted to leave. When they returned home, the Countess went straight to her dressing room and saw immediately that her jewel case was gone."

"What was taken?"

"All but what she wore to the Cavendish Ball, and a diamond tiara kept in a bank vault. Some pieces have been in the Earl's family for generations, and she hasn't been shy about showing them off. Her likeness, wearing the gems, can be found on cabinet cards, and in the dress and fashion magazines."

"But she didn't show them off at the ball."

"No. She was well-decked out, but the heirlooms were in her jewel case, and the case was on her night table." Lestrade shook his head. "I will never understand these rich folk. When the family are all at home, they lock the finery away, but when they go off for an evening, it is left lying about."

"Sometimes a fashionable address in town gives a false sense of security, but few homes, Lestrade, and few safes, are proof against a determined thief. I daresay that, given an hour free and clear, and a few choice instruments, I could have made off with the lady's jewels. Where were the servants?"

"The lady's maid and the Earl's gentleman had been waiting in the kitchen for the master and mistress to return. The others were still in bed."

"And none of them heard anything?"

"Nothing at all."

"And you saw no evidence that the door or windows were forced?"

Lestrade shook his head. "But the lady's dressing room is entered through her bedchamber, and the bedchamber has a long window that opened onto a terrace – "

"Secured with those English fasteners that a child could open, and on a floor just low enough so that a nimble fellow could climb from beneath, yet high enough for him to drop himself from above."

Lestrade groaned and nodded.

"Now you may call it guesswork, Lestrade, but would it be out of the question to suppose that the person who burgled Lord Selby's residence was one of the servants hired for the Cavendish Ball? And also one of the actors at Mr. Verlander's shop?"

"You say that all three crimes were the work of the same gang?" I cried.

"I say that it isn't impossible. The emerald is an exceptional prize, but when Lady Metcalf's gems are within reach, what resourceful thief would hesitate? Or hesitate, having made off with the emerald, to hurry on to Hamilton Place – no more than a brisk ten-minute walk, if my geography serves – and burgle the Selby residence?"

"The thief may have been among those who avoided a police interrogation by joining in the search of the park," I said. "Or, perhaps, he was brazen enough to offer to summon the police."

Holmes nodded. "Excellent, Watson! Either role would have allowed our burglar to conceal the emerald, invade the Selby residence, and vanish long before you, Lestrade, had even begun to interrogate His Grace's household. You have but one advantage, and that is the fact that what has been taken – antiques, heirlooms, a lump of emerald larger than my fist – are unique, and that makes them more difficult to be moved quickly. Every jeweler, gem cutter, pawnbroker, auction house has been notified, I trust?"

"They have."

"It is now after eleven. Nothing more can be done tonight. If it will not interfere with your investigation, tomorrow, I will call – "

"Upon the Duke, yes. I have mentioned your name to him, and he said that you may call at eleven."

"It's very kind of His Grace to be so liberal with my time, but it is my intention to call at Mr. Verlander's shop."

"Well, you cannot see Verlander until tomorrow sunset, Mr. Holmes. He observes the Sabbath – he allows young Cree to conduct business, but spends his day at his temple or in prayer, and I am afraid it may take a good deal of praying to have those gems turn up."

"It will be Mr. Cree then. Good night, Lestrade, and don't hesitate to inform me of any fresh developments."

"What do you think?" I asked, when the little detective departed.

"I think Lestrade has come up against a cunning and resourceful opponent."

"Opponent? You said it was the work of a gang."

"Yes, but a gang is a body – eyes, ears, limbs, but only one brain, and this one has iron nerves and sharp wits. It is clear that the emerald was the object, and yet he was quick to take advantage of opportunity."

"Do you think the gems can be recovered?"

Holmes shrugged his shoulders. "The jewelry are antiques that offer the best return if they are kept intact, so I doubt that they can be moved quickly. A fence hesitates to take what he cannot break up or melt down."

"But the emerald can be cut down. And Lestrade says that this Verlander is the finest gem-cutter in all of London. There may be some attempt to bribe or bully him into breaking them down to what a fence *can* move quickly. It's a pity that you must wait a day to see the jeweler."

"It's a pity I have no antique gems lying about to snare our burglar."

With that, Holmes reached for his pipe and waved me off to bed.

It wasn't yet nine o'clock the next morning and I had just finished my shave when I heard a knock upon the door. "Come, Watson! We have visitors – two ladies – one of which has already made our acquaintance. Be quick, for I have asked them to pause in their singular narrative until you may come down to hear it."

I quickly threw on my clothes and hurried down to the sitting room to see two black-garbed ladies perched on the settee. The elder appeared to be sixty or thereabouts, wearing untrimmed walking dress and an old-fashioned coal-scuttle bonnet. Her companion was much younger and more smartly dressed, and this lady, I did, indeed, recognize.

"Miss Stoner!" I greeted, for it was our client of only months before, the step-daughter of the wicked Doctor Grimesby Roylott. "Or do I say 'Mrs. Armitage'?"

"No, it is 'Stoner' yet," she replied. "Percy and I had first planned to marry at the end of April, but I didn't think it was fitting to marry the month of my step-father's death, and my aunt," she added, with a nod and a smile toward her companion, "is superstitious and didn't like for us to marry in May, and so we delayed our wedding until this month."

"You will remember Miss Westphail, Doctor," said Holmes, as he settled into a chair. "These ladies have had a very unusual experience, and one which I am certain you'll find interesting – particularly as it may relate to the account of last night's visitor. If you wouldn't object to beginning your tale again, Miss Stoner."

"Since my step-father's death in April," said that lady, "I have remained with my aunt at Harrow, but we came to town last week and took a suite at the St. Pancras Hotel, so that I might be fitted for a wedding dress and attend to a few matters of business regarding the disposition of Stoke Moran."

"And when is the wedding?" asked Holmes with a smile.

"Next Tuesday. It will be a very small affair, just my aunt and Percy's father and one of Percy's university friends and his wife. My aunt is somewhat sentimental in the matter of weddings and insisted that I keep to a few of the old traditions, so I will have something old and new and blue, and for something that is borrowed, my aunt asked me to wear a string of amber beads that were given to her many years ago."

Miss Westphail drew from an embroidered handbag, a small oblong box, opened it, and lifted from a layer of cotton wadding a strand of faceted amber beads strung on gold wire, and fastened with a tarnished filegree catch. "It has no value beyond sentiment, of course, but I thought it would do for a borrowed token on Helen's wedding day."

Holmes took the strand and held it up, turning it this way and that while the lady spoke.

"It was given to me many years ago by – Well, by a young man who had asked for my hand. Thornton – John Thornton was his name. He was appointed ship's surgeon on the *Guiding Star*, a post that would pay well-enough for us to marry on when he returned, and before he left, he gave me this necklace. He had spied it in a pawnshop window, and I don't believe he paid more than a pound for it, but he said that it would look well with my hair – my hair was quite golden when I was Helen's age – and that I should have a diamond ring when he returned. I waved him goodbye in Liverpool, and that was the last I was ever to see of him."

Miss Stoner patted her aunt's hand, gently.

Holmes rose, took the item to the window, and held it up to the light. "It is quite an old piece, I see. And the beads all have peculiar scratch marks on one side – was that the case when the necklace was given to you, Miss Westphail?"

"Yes. After John was lost, I put it away in a drawer, and there it has been ever since, but if Helen is to wear it on her wedding day, I thought that I ought to have it polished and perhaps re-strung, and so on Thursday afternoon, Helen and I took it to a shop on Greville Street – "

"A Joseph Verlander, correct?" said Holmes, with a glance in my direction.

"Yes. He was recommended to us at our hotel, though we didn't see the gentleman, only his assistant – an odd-looking man – because we understood that his employer was unwell. I showed him the strand and he seemed – " Miss Westphail's lips trembled and she fell silent.

"I am sure," Miss Stoner said, mildly, "that Mr. Verlander and his associate are accustomed to the very best clients, and such a small commission – "

"The young man's conduct suggested that your request was beneath them."

Miss Stoner nodded.

"I apologized for the trifling nature of the request," Miss Westphail continued, "and asked if he might just look over the strand and see if the scratches could be polished. He took it and examined it in a cursory fashion, and then – more to appease us than anything else, I believe – took up the jeweler's loupe he wore hanging around his neck, and studied the beads again, casually, at first, and then with a greater scrutiny, studying each bead in turn."

Holmes drew out his convex lens. "Pray, continue."

"He said that something might be done with it if I would leave the necklace, but Helen was to have her likeness done, wearing it, that afternoon – the scratches wouldn't show up in a photograph – and so we offered to bring it back yesterday morning."

The lady's remark met with silence, and we all looked toward Holmes, who now studying the piece with great intensity. "I daresay," Holmes said in a low voice, as he ran his lens over the string of beads, "that the young man told you it wouldn't be convenient for you to come yesterday morning, and suggested that you bring it today instead."

"Why, how could you know that?" cried the elderly lady.

Holmes pocketed his lens and resumed his chair. "But you came to me first because you wanted to know why a commission that was beneath the usual trade was suddenly of such interest?"

"Not only that, Mr. Holmes," said Miss Stoner. "Because he didn't only seem to have a sudden interest in the piece, but he actually made my aunt an offer for it. Mr. Cree – that was his name – said that the business had many wealthy and eccentric clients, and there is one who has an affection for old pieces of amber. Mr. Cree assured us that this gentleman would give a thousand pounds for my aunt's necklace."

"Good Heavens!" I cried. "A thousand pounds!"

"For a strand that didn't cost one," said Holmes. "And what did you tell Mr. Cree?"

"I didn't decline the offer. I agreed to consider it. My own circumstances – Well, I have been no stranger to economy," said the lady with a smile of resignation. "And yet – "

"And yet, your niece encouraged you to submit the matter to me before you came to any decision."

"Yes."

"What time is your appointment this morning?"

The lady consulted the gold watch pinned to her bodice. "An hour from now."

"Very well. I would like you to keep the appointment, but there is something you must do, and I will ask that you carry out my instructions to the letter."

"Certainly," said Miss Stoner. "We will do whatever you advise."

"When you arrive for your appointment, the young man will again ask whether you might consider selling the piece, and you will say that you have decided against it, you are interested only in having it restored. He will bow to your decision, and tell you that the necklace must be left in order to be polished. Do not give over the necklace right away, but ask him a number of questions – what he will use to take out the scratches, whether it ought to be fitted with a new clasp, and so forth. Prolong the process as far as you can. Have no fear that you will interrupt other matters of business. They do very little trade on Saturdays. You will then hand over the necklace to the young man and return to your hotel."

Miss Westphail leaned forward and laid her hand over Holmes's. "I think you've seen something that we have not."

Holmes patted her hand, and then turned up her palm and laid the beads upon it. "If you do as I say, it will all be clear very soon."

I rose to see the ladies out when Holmes said, suddenly, "One moment! One question more: I have heard something of Mr. Verlander's apprentice, that an accident at work that left him with a scar on his forehead. Was that why you referred to him as an odd-looking fellow?"

"Yes, and that he has pierced ears."

The remark seemed to make a strong impression upon my friend, but he only repeated his instructions to our visitors and bade them good morning.

I helped the ladies into a cab, and returned to our sitting room to see a shabby young workman in a faded waistcoat, rough shirt, and cloth cap emerge from Holmes's bedchamber.

"Go take up your hat and coat," Holmes said as he sat down at his desk. He scribbled off several notes, rang for the page, and then donned an old pea-jacket and stuffed a few tools into its pockets.

"I think you have seen something I have not," I said.

"I have inferred something, at least. Come!" he said, when he had dismissed the page. "Think of the narratives we have been told in the last day. Did any particular small detail strike you?"

"Well – the was the offer of a thousand for a strand of old, scratched beads . . . ."

"That is hardly a small detail. Think of Lestrade's account. Nothing singular or odd?"

"It is all very odd."

"Well, I hope to make sense of it soon."

In the street, Holmes whistled for a hansom and directed the cabbie to Leather Lane. "Now, Watson, we have little time to rehearse your role, but I depend upon you for the time I will need." He then explained what I was to do, and had me to repeat back his instructions until he was confident that I thoroughly understood my role.

We alighted where Leather Lane met Greville Street. "There!" Holmes pointed the sign – *Joseph Verlander, Purveyor of Fine Jewelry* – which distinguished the jeweler's establishment from the other tenement shops along the street. "Ah – I see that our fair clients have arrived."

A hansom drew up in front of the shop. Miss Stoner alighted and helped her aunt down, and the two entered.

"You will wait at the opposite pavement and watch the transaction. Place yourself where you have a clear view through the window. The ladies will surrender their necklace to Mr. Cree and depart, and he will retreat to the back of the shop. Wait a few minutes and then enter. He will hear the ring of the shop bell and must come to wait upon you. Then do as I instructed you. When you have finished, return immediately to Baker Street. I may want you to entertain our guests until I arrive."

With that engimatic remark, he turned on his heel, retreated into the dense pedestrian swarm, and vanished.

I watched from the opposite pavement as Miss Stoner and her aunt engaged the young assistant for nearly twenty minutes. At last, Miss Westphail surrendered the necklace and the pair were ushered out of the shop. Upon their departure, Cree immediately darted to the back of the shop. I waited five minutes and then crossed the street and thrust open the door so that the bell would give a sharp ring.

In a moment, a sturdy, dark-haired young man – for he couldn't have been more than twenty-four or -five – came from the back room. "Sir, how may I help you?"

"Mr. Verlander?"

"No, sir, I am his associate, Mr. Cree. Mr. Verlander will not be here at all today."

As Holmes had predicted, the young man seemed impatient to dismiss me. "I am sorry to hear it," I said. "I had hoped to see Mr. Verlander."

"You might try one of the tradesmen along Hatton Garden."

"Yes, I suppose," I drawled, "but it is a very particular commission, and I was recommended expressly to Mr. Verlander as the best person to repair the settings in some of the pieces before I decide whether to surrender them to Sotheby's or to Christie's."

That seemed to pique the fellow's interest. "What sort of pieces, sir?"

"It is a *parure* – diamonds and rubies set in gold. A pair of combs, a pair of earrings, a necklace."

"Five pieces? If I may ask – how did they come to you?"

"The set has been in my family for eighty years or more, and passed most of that time in a bank vault. Upon my mother's death, they fell to me, and while they are beautiful and no doubt quite valuable, I have no use for them. And to be frank, I do have use for what they might bring."

"And they are yours absolutely? There is no possibility that their provenance might be challenged."

"None whatsoever."

"Perhaps you might bring them this afternoon? Mr. Verlander has been schooling me in the trade, and I believe that I can at least give a fair assessment of what needs to be done to put them to rights."

"I am a very busy man. I must leave town this evening and don't know when I will be back again."

"If the pieces are what you represent them to be, they should take precedence. Is there no possibility of bringing them this afternoon?"

I glanced at my pocket watch and made a show of considering the proposition. "I might get them from the bank," I said, slowly. "But the Capital and Counties Bank closes at one o'clock on Saturday, and I must be able to return them before then. Perhaps you might accompany me to Oxford Street and examine them there?"

"I cannot leave the shop unattended. It isn't yet eleven. You may be at the bank in half-an-hour, and it will not take me fifteen minutes to examine them for you. That is more than enough time for you to have them back at the bank before one o'clock."

"Perhaps," I replied, "if I go immediately – Very well! Shall we say noon?"

The young fellow shook my hand and bowed me out of the shop and, following Holmes instructions, I sprang into the nearest cab and returned immediately to Baker Street.

No less than three handsome carriages idled along the pavement in front of our address, and I entered to find our landlady in a state of considerable agitation. "Dr. Watson!" she cried. "Wherever is Mr. Holmes? His callers have been waiting this half-hour at least, and I don't know what to do about them! They don't mean," she added, in a horrified tone, "to be asked to luncheon?"

I was saved from a response by the appearance of Holmes himself, still in the workman's garb, a rough canvas sack slung over one shoulder. "I see from the procession that our visitors have arrived. I wired Lestrade in the hope that he might join us after his small matter of business is concluded, but perhaps we ought not wait."

I followed Holmes up to the sitting room and found a party of six, three gentlemen and three ladies, whose elegant attire and air of dignified affluence pronounced them to be people of some standing. "Ah, Your Grace!" Holmes greeted, cheerfully, and turning to me, he said, "His Grace, the Duke of Cavendish and his fiancée, Miss Fiske, Sir George and Lady Metcalf, and Lord and Lady Selby. My friend and colleague, Doctor Watson."

"Mr. Sherlock Holmes?" His Grace said, coldly. "You were asked to call at Cavendish House."

"Forgive me, Your Grace, I was otherwise engaged."

"Evidently Inspector Lestrade didn't convey the importance of the matter."

"I assure Your Grace that he did. Shall we sit?"

The party looked around at our homespun furnishings and remained standing.

"As you like. Perhaps it is best to stand, since the matter will not take long and I am a very busy man." Holmes then drew from his pocket a ring of skeleton keys. "Ah, forgive me – It's the wrong pocket," he said, and reaching into the other, he produced a pair of large, glittering brooches. "I believe that these are yours, Lady Metcalf," he said.

"Why – Why – ! " sputtered Sir George, and Lady Metcalf cried, "My brooches! I had given them up for lost!" And then she clasped them to her breast and burst into tears.

Holmes then slipped the canvas sack from his shoulder, laid it upon a table, and drew out a small jewelry box. "And for you, Lady Selby," he said as he handed it to her. "Allow me to offer a bit of advice: When you have an evening's engagement, don't leave this lying on your dressing table. And I believe there is something more . . . ."

He made a show of probing inside the sack. "Ah! Here it is!" He then drew out a large, rough dark-green stone and presented it to the Duke.

"It is the emerald! By all that is holy! Mr. Holmes, however did you – ? Here it is, Alice!" he said, pressing it into the hands of his young fiancée.

There followed a moment of profound silence, and then all six of our visitors, possessed by the same impulse, broke into a burst of applause. My friend had often expressed an aversion to displays of adulation, and gave credit for the success to the efforts of the official force, but I could see that he was pleased.

To our landlady's great relief, our noble callers departed soon after, and she was spared the ordeal of producing a luncheon that would satisfy the palates of such distinguished visitors.

They weren't gone very long when Lestrade appeared, his features white and grim. "It was as you said, Mr. Holmes. That clever fish leapt at the bait and called upon the gang to be ready."

"Then why so glum, Inspector?"

"Because we have the couple and that sham beggar, but Cree slipped through the net!"

Holmes uttered a bitter curse, and then shrugged. "Well, Cree isn't the type to allow this setback to deter him from his natural turn for crime, and so I must believe that we will meet again, and as Mrs. Howitt once wrote, '*pleasure deferred is not pleasure lost*'. As for the emerald and the baubles, that has been put right, and I think that I must surrender these to you." Holmes drew from a pocket a dozen exquisite rings. "Mr. Verlander will think of a Scotland Yard detective as an answer to his prayers. And I have no doubt the press will have you covered in ink."

"That ink will be misapplied," I said when Lestrade has left us.

Holmes only smiled and shrugged.

"But how were you able to recover the gems?"

"With the assistance of you and the ladies, who all played your parts quite well. Miss Westphail surrendered her necklace to Mr. Cree, and you gave him only time enough to put it away in his safe before you entered the shop."

"How do you know he had a safe?"

"Because I saw it. While Miss Stoner and her aunt were prolonging their business with Mr. Cree, I made my way into the shop by way of the back entrance, and hid myself in stairs leading up to the young man's rooms. When he placed the necklace inside, I was hidden not six feet away. Your ring at the bell obliged him to return to the shop, and while you

193

detained him, I got into the safe – I have made that trick a particular hobby of mine, since it's necessary in my profession – took possession of its contents, and was out of the shop before you had concluded your performance. When you left, he did as I expected, and as I told Lestrade to await – he called upon his confederates who would, upon your return, enact the same little drama that got them Lady Metcalf's brooches." Holmes sighed. "Lestrade arrested the young couple and the beggar, but I am afraid there may not be evidence enough to hold them, unless his powers of bluff are sufficient to bully them into a confession."

"And yet, Cree has escaped."

Holmes lit a cigarette and nodded. "An interesting fellow, our young Mr. Cree. His name isn't 'Cree', but 'Clay'. His grandfather was a Royal Duke, though the dukedom has been extinct for more than half-a-century. He has education and brains enough to make his name in some legitimate profession, but there may be a dark strain in even the most noble lines. If Lestrade hadn't been so slow to fix his nets, he might have had him, but I daresay when an hour passed and you didn't return, his suspicions were aroused. He quite likely meant to make off with the jewels and abandon his confederates to their fate, found the safe empty, and fled, empty-handed – though I would advise Mr. Verlander to examine his inventory – deeply regretting a significant loss."

Holmes reached into his pocket and drew out the amber beads, dangling them from a fingertip.

"Miss Westphail's necklace? That certainly can't be compared to the Cavendish Emerald."

"No, indeed. There is a powerful lens on my desk, Watson. Take it up and examine the scratches upon these beads."

I did as Holmes asked and, carrying the strand to the window, I held it up to the light and studied the peculiar scratches that marred one side of each bead. "It appears to be writing. '*Napoleon*' – "

"'*Napoléon à sa chére Joséphine*,'" said Holmes. "Extraordinary workmanship. It vanished so long ago that its very existence had begun to take on the mantle of myth. I believe the French Government will pay handsomely for its return, and considerably more than a thousand pounds."

"But would Miss Westphail part with it?"

"My opinion is that the lady will do what is right."

Holmes's opinion proved correct. Miss Westphail's shock at the discovery, and her understanding of the value of the piece, didn't sway her conviction of what was right. She was even willing to forego any reward, and asked only that a plaque be laid by the piece: *Returned to the French Government by Mr. John Thornton and Miss Honoria Westphail*. Holmes, however, had some acquaintance with an influential member of government, who negotiated on Miss Westphail's behalf and secured for her a sum that ensured she would no longer be a stranger to economy.

It was some time after the entire matter was settled that I recalled Holmes's question to me. "You asked whether anything Lestrade had said had particularly struck me – some small detail.

"Lestrade stated that when it was discovered that the brooches and the rings were lost, Cree went to summon Lady Metcalf's maid, and then went to the shop to see to the back door. Why should he do so? The young couple and the beggar had run out the front door, presumably with the jewels. What motive would Cree have to search and secure the back rooms?"

"The confederates didn't have the gems – *He did!* And he ran up to his rooms to lock them away. As you saw when I produced them, what was taken could fit in a pocket."

"So, the gems are restored to their rightful owners, the French Government receives a curio of great value, Miss Westphail is rewarded, Lestrade is lauded in the press – there is nothing left for you."

"Ah, well. *L'homme c'est rien, l'oeuvre s'est tout.*"

"I have had one or two little scores of my own to settle with Mr. John Clay," said Holmes.

– Sherlock Holmes
"The Red-Headed League"

NOTES

- *Sainton is to give his farewell concert at the Royal Albert Hall on the twenty-fifth.* Violinist Prosper Sainton gave a farewell concert at the Royal Albert Hall on June 25th, 1883.
- *My aunt is superstitious and didn't like for us to marry in May.* The old saying was "*Marry in May, rue the day.*" Ancient superstition dictates that a May marriage is unlucky.
- *John Thornton was his name. He was appointed ship's surgeon on the Guiding Star.* Transporting emigrants to Australia, the *Guiding Star* was lost in early 1855. John Thornton was the ship's surgeon.
- *As Mrs. Howitt once wrote, 'pleasure deferred is not pleasure lost'.* Mary Howitt was a prolific nineteenth-century author whose work was primarily directed at young readers. She is most well known for her poem *The Spider and the Fly*.
- *The amber necklace.* There are a few variations of the Napoleon's "*love necklace*" tale. One was featured as an episode of Paul Harvey's *The Rest of the Story.* The story itself is said to be absolutely true and absolute myth.

The True Account of the Dorrington Ruby Affair
by Brett Fawcett

Inspector MacDonald of Scotland Yard was ushered into the room . . . Holmes was not prone to friendship, but he was tolerant of the big Scotchman . . . .

– Dr. John H. Watson
The Valley of Fear

"[A]rguably [MacDonald] is the most human of all the policemen in The Canon and seems to arouse more genuine affection in Holmes even than Stanley Hopkins of The Return, *or, save at supreme moments, the old sparring-partner Lestrade . . . [He seems to be the same person as] the leading adversary faced by [Doyle's] brother-in-law E.W. Hornung's Raffles –* 'Mackenzie, o' Scoteland Yarrd an' Scoteland itsel'!'"

– Owen Dudley Edwards,
The Valley of Fear
(*Oxford Edition* Explanatory Notes, pages 180-181)

"Chemistry: *An instinctual, apparently unanalysable, attraction or affinity between people or groups of people.*"
– *Oxford English Dictionary*, c.1600

Chapter I

I awoke one morning in the summer of 1883 coughing violently. The heat alone was oppressive, but the air also tasted acrid, and I could feel my eyes burning. As I clumsily got out of bed and attempted to shake off my sleepy stupor and realized that what was aggravating me was a thin, almost invisible smoke streaming through the sides of my closed bedroom door. I stumbled out of my room and downstairs to identify its source.

Holmes was seated in his mouse-coloured dressing gown at his laboratory, and was pouring a blue liquid from one glass vial into a clear liquid in another one. He was enveloped from the fumes that streamed from the latter vial. I snapped at him in rather strong language and demanded to know the meaning of this as I marched towards the closed window and threw it open.

"I have been sent a letter inviting me to a case," sighed Holmes, setting the two vials down and capping them both. He picked up the second vial again and examined its contents. A thinning piece of paper was floating in the fluid inside. "The crime is utterly unworthy of my attention, so I'm trying to redeem this morning by conducting an experiment on the letter to see whether it can be completely destroyed, leaving no trace. Hydrochloric acid is normally reliable for such annihilation. It can dissolve almost anything, from most metals to several parts of the human body. Nevertheless, the paper has so far failed to fully disappear. Hydrofluoric acid is also quite powerful – though you must handle it very carefully, since it can dissolve glass – so I'm attempting to see if they can eradicate the paper when mixed together – "

"Without so much as opening the window, or at least waiting for me to depart?" I fired back, wiping tears from my eyes with the backs of my hands as I angrily returned upstairs to my bedroom. But as I dressed, and as the odour dispersed, I found myself growing curious about the details of this apparently worthless case. When I finished, I descended from my room once again to find Holmes already dressed and seated for breakfast, where I joined him, being sure to look as cross as possible.

"I am truly sorry, my dear fellow," he greeted me. "I'm too accustomed to conducting my chemistry experiments alone. During my university days, I met someone who would have been a worthy companion for these scientific pursuits, but that partnership never materialized, and I have subsequently developed the habits of a solitary alchemist with no one's health to worry for but his own. Your ire is utterly justified, Watson, and I implore your forgiveness."

Placated, I began buttering some toast. "How could you be so confident that the case wasn't worth your attention?" I asked.

"You have seen the reports of the theft of the Cliveden Plate?"

"Of course!"

"The Duke of Westminster is dissatisfied with Scotland Yard's progress and wishes for my help."

"Why not accept his invitation? I imagine the reward he would offer would be lucrative."

Holmes grimaced as he sipped his coffee. "It has all the hallmarks of a smash-and-grab theft. When no genius has gone into planning a crime, no genius is required to solve it. All that is necessary is thoroughness, and the man the Yard has put on the case, Inspector Sam Brown, is nothing if not thorough. It is necessary work, and we can rejoice that Scotland Yard has the resources for it – What they lack in creativity, they make up for in dedicated manpower. – but it is also tedious and requires no particular cleverness. Give me a comparatively trifling case that nevertheless

198

stimulates my imagination before bothering me with a high-profile task that promises nothing but dullness."

Holmes's wish would be granted about an hour later, when the landlady informed us that an inspector from Scotland Yard was here to see us. I half-expected this to be Sam Brown, here to restate the invitation to Holmes to take up the Cliveden case. Instead, the sandy-haired, craggy-faced man before me was one I had never met before. He was around twenty-four years old, and, while it was difficult to believe someone that young could have already risen to the role of inspector, something of the gravity and even dourness with which he carried himself made him seem older than he was. He was tall, thin, and gaunt, though something about his bearing suggested considerable physical and moral strength. He wore rather unfashionable tweeds and carried a Gladstone bag.

"Mr. Holmes?" he asked, looking at us both. He had a flinty Scottish accent, and there was the faintest hint of a nasally sniffle in his voice. (I am a doctor. I notice these things.)

"The very man," said my friend, "and this is my associate, Dr. Watson. To what do we owe this visit?"

The Scotsman shook our hands. "I'm Inspector Alec MacDonald. I've heard your name mentioned among my colleagues in tones which suggest you are more important to them than they choose to let on. I have a problem that's bothering me, but it isn't significant enough – yet – to bring to the other Yarders. Based on what I've gathered about you, I had a feeling you might be interested in it."

I could sense that Holmes was instantly impressed, and it was a reaction I shared. The fact that MacDonald could correctly infer so much about Holmes and his (at the time) carefully concealed importance to the Yard said a great deal for his abilities as a detective. Holmes invited him to take a seat and explain his conundrum.

"It's a very fresh case, Mr. Holmes, so I may not have all the information you need as yet."

"That very freshness is precisely why it was wise for you to come to me now. The early hours of a case are the precious ones."

"Do you know anything of Lord Ashworth Dorrington?" MacDonald asked.

"Only that his cousin, Arthur, works for the British government as a civil servant." [1]

"Lord and Lady Dorrington own many properties, but recently, including last night, they were staying at Dorrington Hall near Windsor. That is where he stores his prized possession: A ruby given to his grandfather, Sir Arthur Deering, by King George IV in 1826, upon Sir Arthur's elevation to the peerage. Lord Dorrington is intensely protective of this ruby. Two winters ago, when he was living at Dorrington Lodge on the Isle of Wight, he heard that a neighbour had recently had a jewel stolen, and became so anxious that he relocated himself and his ruby to Dorrington Castle in Devonshire for several months. Currently, the ruby is kept in a safe hidden behind a portrait of Sir Arthur which hangs in the Dorrington Hall library."

MacDonald opened his bag, in which I could see a small portable camera, and produced a photograph of the library, a long, narrow room with an open window in one wall and the painting of Arthur Deering hanging between two shelves on the opposite wall. "I went to a rather advanced school in Aberdeen that trained its students in photography," he explained, "and I still dabble in it. I thought some pictures might help you appreciate the situation.

"Last night, the estate was burgled. The butler, Niven, was asleep in the servants' quarters, but was roused by a noise and came to the library to find the intruder sneaking through the room. Niven described the prowler as medium-sized, wearing a flat cap and a scarf over his face, and as having a jemmy in one hand, a bag in the other, and a rectangular metal box sticking out of his pocket."

"His burglars' tools, no doubt," remarked Holmes.

MacDonald nodded agreement. "When the thief saw Niven, he leapt out the window and he fled the property before the household could be roused. It appears all he had been able to stuff into his sack was a small clock and a pair of dusty tomes he snatched off the library shelves. In other words, it's such a petty crime that my being called in to investigate was little more than a formality."

"Yet something about it has obviously struck you."

"Indeed, Mr. Holmes. Of course, the first thing Lord Dorrington did was rush to his safe to check on his ruby, which he was relieved to find was still there. The thief had discovered the safe, but it seemed he was unable to open it and eventually gave up, contenting himself with whatever else was at hand." MacDonald showed us a photograph of the safe. It was covered with scratches and scrapes, but was fundamentally undamaged. "It seems like an inexperienced crook snuck in, found himself in over his head, and was interrupted before he could do any serious damage to the estate."

I could see Holmes's mind already at work, but he nevertheless asked, "And what bothers you about this, Inspector MacDonald?"

MacDonald scratched his chin thoughtfully. "First off, Mr. Holmes, Lord Dorrington has a dachshund, Nicholas, who patrols the area. This morning, he was found deep in sleep. I explored the property and discovered some dog biscuits distributed around the area. It smells as if they'd been soaked in *somnol*. The thief must have left them earlier in the day to ensure that the poor creature had devoured enough of them by nightfall that he'd be too deep in sleep to be a bother during the break-in. To me, Mr. Holmes, that suggests a burglar of some experience and skill. Yet – look at these scratches, Mr. Holmes. It seems as if he tried to jemmy the safe open. But any reasonably experienced cracksman would know instantly that there was no chance that a safe like this could be jemmied open. There are too many deadbolts. In fact, to me, it looks as if all he did was drag his jemmy across the door several times."

I could tell from Holmes's face that he had already reached the same conclusion. "In fact," he remarked, "these scratches try to make it *appear* he had tried to force it open and gotten frustrated."

"Exactly, Mr. Holmes!" MacDonald nearly shouted. "It feels somehow stage-managed to me."

MacDonald may have lacked Holmes's gift of insight (and, I would later discover, his breadth of knowledge), but he possessed something of the instincts and observational talents that set great detectives apart from the rest. Seeing their investigative minds at work together was like watching the operations of an industrial machine.

"Further, look at this." MacDonald produced a photograph of the library window from the outside. "See that spider web under the windowsill? If the thief had climbed in through that window, he would surely have torn that web apart. But if he didn't enter through this window, he must have climbed through one in another part of the building. That means he would have gone through Dorrington Hall, passing by bedrooms, the kitchen, the dining room – rooms filled with jewelry, silverware, and all manner of other valuables – but didn't stop until he reached the library. Why would a thief go *there* looking for booty? The only explanation is that he somehow knew the ruby was stored there – but, if so, why was he supposedly so ill-prepared to steal it? There's something very off about all this, Mr. Holmes, and it's haunted me enough that I felt compelled to ask your opinion."

MacDonald was right. This once-innocuous situation was growing more nefarious. Like a dark alley filled with unsettling noises, it may not have been clear yet exactly what evil lurked in this strange event, but it was an evil that had grown increasingly palpable.

"And where is Lord Dorrington now?" asked Holmes.

"As a matter of fact, I accompanied him to London. There's a meeting of some of the Lords for the next two weeks to discuss England's relationship with Scandinavia, so Lord Dorrington is staying at his private flat in Campden Court Grove. The attempt on the ruby left him nervous enough that he didn't want to leave it behind, so he put it in a lockbox and brought it with him. He even sealed the lockbox so he could always be certain it hadn't been opened when he wasn't looking."

Another photograph: Lord Dorrington, a bow tie beneath his round, bald head, smiling as he held a lock box filled with cotton, upon which sat a ruby whose brilliance shone through even in grainy black-and-grey. The next picture was of that same lockbox, now closed and with a large wax seal with "*Deering Ton*" imprinted on it over the keyhole. Holmes looked at the photographs, but his mind seemed elsewhere.

"A supposedly botched burglary the night before he happens to go to London?" he wondered. "Had the ruby been stolen from Dorrington Hall, the countryside would be swarming with police, and there would be few places for the thief to hide. But Dorrington is spooked into bringing it with him into the city, where a bandit can effortlessly disappear among the masses. I begin to see the calculations behind this crime, Inspector MacDonald. We must get to Campden Court Grove at once."

In the cab ride to Lord Dorrington's flat, I noticed a curious change in Holmes's disposition. His manner towards MacDonald had gone from being appreciative and admiring to chilly and distant, and he barely acknowledged him during the short trip. Had something the Yarder said or done caused him to disappoint Holmes? I could tell that MacDonald was also perplexed by this, though he said nothing.

The carriage dropped us in front of a white, neoclassical structure on the corner of a street crossing, with one street running along the front of the building and one running along its east side. It was surrounded by a high gate, the spokes of which resembled long Zulu spears that had been forged in iron. We were admitted by a punctilious porter with a thin mustache and ascended to the third floor, where Lord Dorrington kept his rooms.

Dorrington, still dapperly dressed and wearing his bow tie, was seated by an open window. On the table next to him sat the wax-sealed lockbox and also a gold-plated box, from which he took and lit a cigar. He blew smoke rings out the window as he eagerly listened to MacDonald explain Holmes's inferences, utterly unworried by the fact that dangerous forces could have followed him here. The paradoxical fact soon emerged that, while Dorrington was terrified of losing his jewel, he was attracted by the prospect of being in proximity to crime.

"Jolly exciting!" Dorrington declared when MacDonald finished. He had a distinctive, high pitched voice which made everything he said seem slightly shriller than he must have intended. "I can't imagine how anyone expects to purloin anything from a flat as well-protected as this, but I'm thrilled to imagine that they might try! I'm something of a student of, eh, literature about lawbreaking, you see. I've even dabbled in writing some grisly stories featuring an investigator who's a bit like that Dupin fellow. Oh, I'll admit, an aristocrat's life can be rather dreary. The lower classes don't appreciate how lucky they are to have the excitement of crime lurking about them, enlivening their existence."

As if responding to this, a muffled but resounding *Bang!* rang out from outside the flat door. If the reader has ever heard someone shot at close range, then the noise I have described will be recognized.

We all leapt to our feet, Dorrington throwing his still-lit cigar out the window with a look of delight. Rushing out the door, we headed down the hallway and around the corner from where the noise seemed to have come. At the end of that hallway was a closed door, which MacDonald practically ripped off its hinges.

Inside was a narrow charwoman's room containing a sink, mop, bucket, and soap. It was filthy, covered in black dirt, shattered glass, waxy chunks, and splattered blood. A smoky odour hung in the air. It was as if someone had shot someone else in that tiny space, only for them both to instantly disappear. The sickening darkness of this situation had grown thicker.

Behind us, a crowd gathered. The porter was there, looking horrified, as was the robustly-built charwoman, presumably drawn here away from a cleaning job somewhere in the building. A slight, white-haired man and a thin fellow with a Van Dyke beard, whom I took to be other residents of the flat, were also present. The older man had scarlet blotches on his hands that looked like eczema. The bearded man had slightly bulging eyes and I quickly diagnosed him as having Graves' Disease. Amidst the shocked murmuring, I heard MacDonald sniffle and nearly sneeze in reaction to the atmosphere of the room. (I am a doctor. I notice these things.)

"No bullet hole," growled MacDonald, looking around the small closet. He turned to the porter. "Did anyone leave the building?" The porter shook his head emphatically. His superior attitude had utterly vanished.

Holmes turned sharply towards Dorrington. "Do you have the ruby with you?"

Dorrington's eyes widened. The thought that occurred to him was clearly more horrifying than the prospect of a gruesome murder.

"Out of the way!" ordered MacDonald, and we cut through the crowd (which followed, hot on our heels) to rush back to Dorrington's flat, the door of which was still open.

The gold cigar box now sat alone on the desk.

Dorrington screamed and nearly collapsed. The bearded man grabbed him and attempted to steady him to his feet.

MacDonald turned back the crowd. "You'll all have to be searched!" he ordered.

But Holmes ran into the room, threw the window open, and stuck his head out it. "The robber is out here!" he shouted back at us.

MacDonald and I looked at each other. "How do you know?" I asked Holmes.

His head still stuck outside, he called back, "Because this window was open when we left! There – I see him!"

We rushed up behind Holmes and looked where he was pointing. Sure enough, several streets away, a street urchin with the strongbox under his arm could be seen bolting at full speed through the crowd.

"No way we can catch up to him now," MacDonald grumbled.

"No?" Holmes asked, pulling back from the window. There was a curious twinkle in his eye. "That thief didn't leap out this window, MacDonald. Can you really conceive that a human being, however lithe, could have climbed that gate, pilfered the ruby, jumped back down three floors to the street below, and then run as far as he did in the time we were out of this room? Someone inside the flat – undoubtedly the same person who created that distraction – threw the box out the window to his or her confederate below, and impulsively slammed the window shut after it to try to conceal how the theft occurred."

MacDonald nodded slowly, turning a suspicious eye upon the crowd by the doorway. "But who?" he asked.

Holmes chuckled. A bit of his warmth towards MacDonald had returned. "You are an amateur photographer, yes?"

MacDonald frowned. "I fail to see the relevance, Mr. Holmes."

"Surely you know that, for more high-quality images, a technique has been developed to produce a sudden, blinding flash of light."

"Aye, yes! Magnesium powder is ignited. It creates a bright blast, one that's horribly noisy and malodorous – " MacDonald stopped, Holmes's point clearly having gotten through to him.

"Supposing," Holmes continued, "one were to stick a lit candle in a heap of magnesium powder, particularly in a small room, the effect when the flame of the candle was low enough to ignite the pile beneath it would be rather like an explosive gunshot, no? There would be smoke, ash, and pieces of the candle blasted everywhere, I predict. And if a vial of blood happened also to be placed on that pile, would it not be thrown against the wall, shatter, and leave sanguinary splatter and shards of glass all around – precisely as we observed?"

It was a perfect explanation. The lingering powder in the air must have been the cause of MacDonald's sniffle. Everyone stared attentively at Holmes as he casually proceeded.

"Watson, why are scientists advised to wear gloves when handling substances like magnesium powder?"

"Because direct exposure to the skin," I answered, "can cause irritations or . . . rashes."

All eyes turned towards the white-haired man nervously scratching the red skin on his hands. He was already a smaller man, but he seemed to physically shrink under our collective scrutiny. Dorrington, who had somewhat regained his composure, looked especially venomous.

"Tell us your name, sir," ordered MacDonald, calmly but firmly.

"Noah Barks, sir," he answered with a shaky voice.

"You'll need to explain yourself, Mr. Barks."

Barks gulped and took a deep breath. "All right, Detective," he mumbled, wringing his hands, "you've caught me. I have foolishly fallen into debt and, in my retirement, lack any source of income that would enable me to pay what I owe. I decided to burgle Lord Dorrington's flat," he continued, hanging his head, "in hopes that whatever I found would be worth enough to cover what I owe. I hired a pauper named Willie Perowne to be my confederate, arranged the distraction in exactly the way this gentleman suggested, then ran into Lord Dorrington's room, grabbed the most valuable-looking box I could, and threw it out the window to Perowne. We are to meet in three hours to split the loot together."

"For shame!" snapped Dorrington, but MacDonald silenced him with an upraised hand.

"You'll have to come with us, Mr. Barks. We'll arrange to have Mr. Perowne taken into custody as well – "

"Inspector," Holmes interjected. "I would advise against that."

Some Yarders would have resented this interruption. MacDonald raised his sandy eyebrows, but was clearly open to hearing Holmes's insights.

"If Mr. Barks had actually planned this heist, he would need to possess a reasonably high degree of familiarity with chemistry and the handling of dangerous materials. Yet anyone with even a passing knowledge of the properties of magnesium powder would know to wear gloves when exposed to it. As Dr. Watson has observed, Mr. Barks neglected to do so.

"Further, would the mastermind of this elaborate caper really be expected to make such an amateur mistake as to close the window after throwing the strongbox through it when he had found it open, thus drawing attention to how the theft was committed? That speaks to impulsiveness and nerves, not the meticulous mind that must have been behind this crime.

"Finally, Mr. Barks claims he tossed the most expensive-looking box he saw out the window. Yet a gold-plated box was right next to the rather plain-looking strongbox. Mr. Barks would have no way of knowing it was filled with cigars – and, even if he had, those are, if I'm not mistaken, not inexpensive cigars, and could also raise some considerable funds for Mr. Barks if he were to resell them."

Holmes turned to Barks.

"I gather that the real villain here is using you as a pawn. If you are willing to go to prison rather than reveal his or her identity, I further gather that you have been threatened with harm if you tell us the truth. Please accept my assurances, Mr. Barks: We can help you and protect you if you are honest and straightforward with us."

It was clear that Barks was wrestling internally over what to do next, but something about Holmes's decisive and confident demeanour finally won him over.

"I am ashamed to admit," he ruefully began, "that I was telling the truth about my finances. I haven't been prudent with them in my retirement, and have been in great distress for months, wondering how I'm going to pay off my creditors. Two evenings ago, I went for a walk, hoping I could think my way into a solution to my problems as I strolled. After a few minutes, I came upon a beefy man in a long brown coat and a wide-brimmed hat waiting in my path. As I made my way past him, I felt him jab the barrel of a gun in my back. 'Go where I tell you,' he ordered in a low, menacing voice. I was frightened, but saw no alternative to obeying him.

"His directions steered me towards a mansion on Little Ryder Street. There was something eerie about the place: The exterior was of Gothic design, and well-maintained, but every window had pitch-black shutters, giving it an atmosphere of living death. My unwelcome companion knocked in a particular staccato rhythm at the door, and another thug, this one wearing a long white jacket, admitted us.

"I found myself, not in a home, but in a small office. There was no furniture in the room except for a stool and a desk with a lamp and an ashtray upon it. The ashtray was full of cigarette remnants, each of which had been smoked down to the butt, and every butt had a logo of a yellow diamond on it. Behind the desk was another door, in front of which stood a third hulking figure clad in a long black jacket holding a box.

"Seated at the desk was a heavily built man with a neck like a bull, thick, black eyebrows, and wild, untamed gray hair. I have traveled much in my time and have had occasion to see tornadoes and typhoons, and something about this mammoth man, both his physical strength, his intelligence, and the emotions I felt radiating off him, reminded me of the violent forcefulness of those phenomena. I felt he could tear through any barrier in his path. His face, which reminded me of an angry bulldog about to attack, glowed with sweat, and he was chewing on a smoldering cigarette butt. Oddly, he was wearing two dress shirts underneath his jacket, one buttoned up over the other. Beside the desk was a skinny man with thick glasses holding a stack of papers. He reminded me of a scarecrow. The thin man placed one of his papers on the desk before the large man, who glanced down at it before focusing his fiery eyes on me.

"'Noah Barks, is it?' He had a coarse accent, and his voice was deep and raspy. I nodded meekly.

"The man pulled an envelope from his desk drawer and laid it on the table. He then announced it contained a particular sum – exactly half of what I needed to pay off my debt, down to the farthing. 'Take it,' he said, with an unpleasant smile. 'I know you need it.'

"I hesitated but shakily picked it up and pocketed it. The man's cruel smirk grew wider and more wicked.

"'You will receive another envelope, containing an identical sum, when you finish your job,' he informed me, the tone a master takes with his servant. He then instructed me on how, and when, to arrange the distraction you witnessed this morning, assuring me that everything I needed – the powder, the vial of blood, the candle, even a box of Lucifer matches – were contained in the box his henchman was carrying. Once everyone else on the floor had gone to the source of the blast, I was then to rush into Lord Dorrington's flat, look for a locked strongbox, and toss it out the window and over the gate before he returned.

"It was clear I was being ordered to take part in criminal activity, but I saw no other solution to my financial woes, and, further, feared that the gunman behind me wouldn't let me leave that room alive if I declined.

"'What if I am found out?' was all I could bring myself to say.

"My unwelcome employer puffed at his cigarette butt with obvious impatience, as though my course of action in that situation should have been obvious to me. He then provided me with the story I just unsuccessfully attempted to fool you with. 'Say nothing about myself,' he added, 'and I can promise you a degree of protection for your brief stint in prison – and you can still expect the rest of your debt to be paid. But should you say anything . . . I cannot promise this protection. I'm told some prisoners manage to smuggle knives into prison somehow.' The way he glared at me made his meaning as clear as his words."

As Barks recounted this, it was clear that the force of the threat was re-asserting itself in his mind, and he trembled visibly as he concluded, "They then practically threw me out the front door and, as I hurried home, I passed the Tyburn Tree, thought of all the criminals that have hung from it, and shivered as I imagined what my own fate would be if I ran afoul either of this sinister creature or . . . or of the law."

207

"You've taken a great personal risk to share this, Mr. Barks," said MacDonald assuringly, "and it's taken courage on your part to do so. If you can help us nab this scoundrel, I'll put in a good word for you with the magistrate, and you may be spared any time in gaol."

"He doesn't deserve your kindness!" whined Dorrington, who clearly had no sympathy with or appreciation for the situation of being short on funds.

MacDonald leveled a steely stare at Dorrington. "Would you rather punish this gentlemen, my Lord," he asked, "or recover your ruby?"

Chafed but chastened, Dorrington fell silent, shoving his hands into his pockets and clearing his throat.

"Now, Mr. Barks," continued MacDonald, "kindly escort us to this house on Little Ryder Street."

"But his rash needs to be treated before it becomes worse!" I protested.

"We haven't the time for that now, Doctor!" MacDonald rebutted.

"In fact, we do," countered Holmes, who had been deep in thought throughout Barks' narrative. "Before we descend upon this fateful building, I strongly urge you to fetch a couple of your best constables. We are dealing with a man who is used to having an alternative plan, and we can be certain he has some means of escape provided for in case Scotland Yard should ever knock on his door. You'd be well-advised to have the manor surrounded. Watson, Barks, and myself will meet you there in half-an-hour."

MacDonald thought for a moment, then nodded and took his leave.

"And Lord Dorrington," added Holmes, "I will need to borrow your cigar case."

The bemused Lord reluctantly acquiesced to this request. I washed Barks' hands in the sink of the charwoman's closet as thoroughly as I could and treated it with an ointment that the porter was able to procure from a nearby chemist. Afterwards, as Holmes said, the three of us headed to Little Ryder Street. Barks was right: The mansion had an oddly sepulchral ambience about it, its undeniable neo-medieval beauty notwithstanding. MacDonald was waiting for us on the street with two constables, who were introduced to us as Sergeants Druce and Clyde, and who were assigned to guard the sides and back of the mansion.

Once the constables had taken their positions, the rest of us went to the front door. Taking a deep breath, Barks knocked at the door several times and in an odd pattern, presumably the one he had heard when he had first been brought to this menacing place.

A minute later, a bulky man in a brown jacket opened the door. The moment the two men saw each other, the huge thug swore and tried to slam the door. Before he could, MacDonald had thrown himself against it and pushed the man backwards, throwing the door open upon him. Holmes and I rushed in, finding ourselves in the office Barks had described. Holmes charged through the next door into the main building while MacDonald and the thug scuffled against the desk, knocking over the full ashtray which had sat upon it. I hurried after Holmes.

Almost as soon as he was through the door and we found ourselves in a grotesque archive filled with cupboards and bookshelves, he ducked to avoid the swinging fist of a black-suited brute who had been waiting for him just inside, out of our sight. Holmes lunged backwards to avoid the blow, but quickly snapped forwards and fired a left hook into the nose of the crook, who doubled backwards and crashed to the floor.

The thug in the white jacket, who had been lurking on the other side of the door, dashed forward, almost taking Holmes from behind. I threw myself upon the ruffian in a rugby tackle. We tumbled to the floor, but I found myself on top of him. He thrashed violently and I could sense his superior strength would be hard to suppress for long, so, gathering all my strength, I drew back my fist as far as I could and drove it into his snarling face. The hulking body went limp beneath me.

Holmes came up alongside me and offered his hand to help me up. "Good show!" he commended me. My war wound felt as though it were screaming at me in pain, but I thanked God I had kept in fairly good shape, and that my rugby skills hadn't entirely left me.

Behind us, MacDonald was dragging the ringleader in, his arms having been wrestled and handcuffed behind him. Our victory assured, we took a moment to consider our grotesque surroundings.

As I have said, this wasn't only a mansion. It was also a bizarre museum. The furniture consisted of one couch, two writing desks covered with papers (and both of which also had fully ashtrays and one of which had a chessboard), and several wooden chairs which were distributed erratically around the room. Every inch of the walls was covered by stacks of boxes or by shelves stuffed with documents. Some were books: Encyclopedias, editions of *Bradshaw* and *Who's Who*, university textbooks (particularly on the topic of physical science), biographies (concentrating on prominent wealthy figures), and so on. As far as the loose papers were concerned, they included receipts, maps, blueprints of buildings, personal letters, medical reports, train tickets, newspapers going back decades, and nearly any other kind of documentation that might be useful to one interested in blackmail or in organizing crimes of any description. It was clear that most of these documents had either been stolen or retrieved from rubbish heaps. There were also some locked cases, in which I assumed that various purloined goods were stored.

We heard scuffling noises from the back of the building. and a moment later Clyde and Druce had dragged in the two men Barks had described. The skinny man's eyes darted everywhere rapidly, while the larger snarled and stared like a caged animal. He was every bit the force of nature that Barks had described.

"You were right, Mr. Holmes," explained Druce. "There was a secret passageway installed that would have let them escape out the side of the building, had we not been there to snag 'em."

"Would you be so kind," asked Holmes politely, "as to have our hosts – aside from the gentleman accompanying Inspector MacDonald – sit down on this lovely settee?" He gestured at the couch.

The three policemen, and even the criminals we apprehended, looked puzzled, but the constables obliged, and the two captives were rather ungently escorted to the couch.

Holmes produced Dorrington's golden case and offered both men cigars. They looked skeptical, and the scarecrow-like man declined, though the bull-like man accepted one. Holmes lit them both, took and lit another one for himself, and sat down on a nearby chair. I am confident in saying that, other than himself, everyone in the house was thoroughly confused.

"I appreciate you taking the time to speak with me," Holmes began. "I am something of a connoisseur of crime, and I so seldom get to speak with experts on the subject. Besides, I can admire what the Americans call a 'self-made man'.

"What do you know about me?" It was clear that the bull-like fellow had done a great deal of work to conceal his identity, and was both incensed and intrigued that someone had already learned so much about him.

"It is a simple matter of retroduction – reasoning backwards from effects to causes," Holmes explained, puffing at his cigar. "Your plan involved spooking Dorrington into bringing his ruby to London, and distracting him with the possibility of an exciting crime investigation so you could steal it. This shows that have done extensive research on Lord Dorrington. You knew that he was coming to London today, that he takes his ruby with him when in fear of thieves, and that he is fascinated by the idea of murder (as portrayed in the penny dreadfuls, at least). This, in turn, shows what a diligent researcher you are. I even gather, " he added, pointing at the bespectacled man on the couch, "that you have a secretary or research assistant to help you with all your information.

"This is something of a leap, but I also infer that you have not always been as wealthy as you are now. Lord Dorrington has, with respect, never had to work for his money, so he doesn't always appreciate what he has –

you may have noted how expensive these cigars must be, and yet he thoughtlessly threw one out that he had barely smoked – whereas you, I am told, smoke your Golden Gem cigarettes (for, based on the yellow diamond symbol on each of the artifacts in your ashtrays, that is the brand, no?) right down to the butt. You appreciate a high-quality cigarette, but you will not spend more than you need to. You aren't smoking *very* expensive brands like Sullivan, I observe, though you can surely afford to do so – and you don't let them go to waste. This suggests someone who understands the value of money and of frugality, which is a trait more associated with those who have come from poverty and earned their fortune.

"Finally, you wear two shirts, despite the, if you'll pardon me, questionable sartorial taste this involves. Why? I posit that you always have an alternative plan. If one shirt gets dirty, you have another one ready – another skill you may have learned in your less prosperous days. In the same vein, if one of your operatives is caught, you offer them a substitute story that, as much as possible, protects them and, more importantly, yourself. If the police come to your base of operations, you have a secret passage installed so you can make a speedy and surreptitious exit." Holmes pointed at the chessboard on the writing desk with his cigar. "Even your recreation involves scheming and preparing for contingencies.

"This even extends to your *modus operandi*. Based on the testimony I have heard from one your, *ahem*, unwilling servants, and from what I observe about this household, I predict that you don't maintain a large army of employees. Not only would this be too expensive, but it also involves much greater risk of betrayal in case one of them is apprehended or simply becomes greedy. Instead, you hire people to play small roles in your larger scheme. They don't understand the larger plan, or even necessarily the meaning of what they are doing, but you pay them handsomely, threaten them severely in case of failure or disobedience, and, in some cases, when you need an insider who isn't already a criminal, you dig up what you can use to blackmail them to do your bidding. Theirs is not to reason why. Theirs is but to do and die.

"You hired a burglar to break into his home, simulate an attempt to break into his safe – this way Dorrington knows for sure that its location has been discovered – and to steal some other miscellanea so the burglary didn't appear to be a targeted attack on the ruby itself. This would cause Dorrington to demand a parish-wide search for the thief, which would be too risky in case your agent was caught and betrayed you. This was timed such that it would occur just before Dorrington came to London, so he would bring the ruby with him. Then, knowing the ruby would undoubtedly be in some kind of strongbox, you paid and threatened Mr.

Barks to distract Dorrington. I presume your research revealed the extent of his gambling debts – and to throw any strongbox he found out the window. Finally, you hired someone to catch the strongbox and to bring it to you. None of them understood the overall scheme. Each was merely a chess piece mindlessly making the moves you required. But that strategy enabled you to pull off an impossible theft with minimal risk to yourself."

Both men on the couch looked deeply ambivalent. The skinny one looked both irritated and worried. The larger one seemed to be wavering between being angered, being impressed, and being pleased that his work and intelligence were finally being rightly appraised and valued. Holmes took a deep puff at his cigar.

"The ruby will be found on these premises. You're going to be imprisoned for stealing it anyway. You may as well receive the acclaim you deserve among scholars of crime like myself by describing your process for us."

Holmes had made an impressive demonstration. The description we had heard of this villain's visible impatience, and the intense chewing upon his cigarette as he answered Barks' uncomprehending question, must have revealed to Holmes that the man before us wasn't used to having someone understand the brilliance of his plans, and also that he was almost literally champing at the bit to brag about them.

The man knitted his black eyebrows. I could tell that Holmes's gambit was working. His lanky associate gave the fat man an imploring look, but he ignored it, inhaled on his cigar, and grinned.

"You're right, sir," he answered, his gravelly voice between a growl and a purr. "It's good to be appreciated. I'm Chester Murdock, and this here," he added, indicating the scarecrow "is Thomas Clark – " The thin man visibly flinched as his name was mentioned. " – who not only helps with my research, but is also in charge of storing and fencing our, eh, *winnings*. Sometimes I'll twist the arm of an insider to get what I need, like I did with that wretch Barks, but, normally, Clark or I will go to some disreputable pub like the Castledown Tavern and hire street crooks to do odd jobs for me. For the ruby mission, I got a redheaded pickpocket named John Creighton, whom I'd been told had a talent for housebreaking, to do the job in to break into Dorrington Hall, and I found a former district messenger named Russell Galler – who got busted once for robbing from a client – to run the strongbox to me here. Paid 'em both handsomely for it, and warned them what would happen if they deviated from their task."

I could see that Murdock was falling back on yet another plan: Give the police the names of everyone he used in his enterprise, not only so that they could also be arrested and share the blame for his crimes, but also in hopes that a judge would take his cooperation into account and lighten his sentence. And it didn't stop there: Murdock spent the next half-hour elucidating other large scale heists he had orchestrated, including the robbery of the Cliveden Plate. As he discoursed, Clark hung his head and put his hand over his face.

Holmes glanced at us. MacDonald had lost his usual serious expression. He bore the look of a child who had just seen a magic trick for the first time.

Everything from that point on was a formality. Clyde went and fetched Inspector Brown, the officer originally assigned to the case, and more constables. (Brown remarked when he arrived that he wasn't surprised that an amateur had solved this case, as his own brother had better detective instincts than he did and yet had chosen to become a priest rather than a policeman.) [2] Murdock, Clark, and their three bodyguards were arrested, the mansion was searched, and numerous hidden treasures were revealed. Among this booty was the Cliveden Plate and the still-sealed strongbox containing the Dorrington Ruby. After Holmes checked with his magnifying lens to confirm that the seal had not been broken or disturbed in any way, the strongbox was returned, along with the cigar case, to the relieved Lord. MacDonald received all the credit for the arrest, despite his insistence that Holmes also receive official recognition. Barks was never formally charged with complicity in a crime, since MacDonald was good to his word and spoke up on Barks' behalf to the relevant authorities. The police were unable to locate Creighton, but apprehended Galler.

But what surprised me was that, the moment the case ended, Holmes once again became indifferent and even cold towards MacDonald, even growing irritated when I mentioned his name. Even in those early days, I knew that Holmes wasn't much given to friendship, but MacDonald seemed like someone whose mind and energy had synthesized with his own, and I couldn't tell why he had no interest in investing further in that relationship.

Chapter II

On a warm afternoon two weeks later, however, he would have occasion to see MacDonald again when the inspector was once more in our Baker Street flat, wearing tweeds that were somehow even uglier than the ones he'd worn before. I can only describe his manner as being utterly bewildered.

"I didn't expect to call on you about the Dorrington Ruby again," he said in a tone that was almost apologetic, "but there's been a development that – Well, the whole country will hear of it within a few hours, I'm sure, but I expected you'd like to hear it first.

"For the last two weeks, as the Scandinavian discussions have carried on, Lord Dorrington has not let the strongbox out of his sight, even bringing it with him to the House of Lords. The meetings formally ended yesterday, and this morning I accompanied Lord Dorrington back to Dorrington Hall in Windsor, keeping an eye on his strongbox and the seal all the way. But once Dorrington had opened his safe to return the jewel, just as I was getting ready to return to London, he opened the strongbox and let out an even greater cry than when he first saw it missing from his flat – a terrible, choking sob. The strongbox fell from his hands and landed open on the floor."

MacDonald shook his head vigorously, as if trying to wake himself from sleep.

"Mr. Holmes, it was *empty*! Dorrington stumbled over to me, coughing and wheezing from the shock, his eyes already red and streaming with tears. He yelled at me over and over that I had let this happen. I said nothing. I couldn't believe what I had seen."

"Is Murdock being interrogated?" Holmes asked.

"Yes, as are Clark, Barks, and Galler. But what can they tell us? I saw that ruby go into the box, saw it locked and sealed with wax. Then I saw that same wax seal broken and the box opened, and saw that there was no ruby there. What could any of them have done, Mr. Holmes? How could they have taken it, even if they were to confess to it? *How?*"

MacDonald was, I could tell, a man who lived by his wits and senses. He didn't know how to deal with doubting both of them at once. Holmes seemed to perceive this as well. "Do you have a photograph of the strongbox?" he asked in a tone that was almost soothing.

The question seemed to snap MacDonald out of his stupefied state. "I've something even better," he answered, once again professional and focused. He reached into his Gladstone bag and fished out the strongbox itself, the wax seal broken and the cotton inside still bearing an imprint where the ruby had rested.

"My father was a mechanic, so I know something of machinery, and I cannot find any hidden compartments or trap doors in this contraption – but I'll be greatly relieved if you can," he added, handing it to my friend.

"Know that you will hear from me immediately if I do," smiled Holmes, analyzing the wax seal under his magnifying lens and murmuring that it was undoubtedly the same seal as before. And, since that appeared to be the end of the matter for now, MacDonald took his leave, still clearly agonizing over this puzzle.

214

"To think that this case seemed so satisfyingly closed not half-a-month ago," I remarked.

"'*Sorrow never comes too late, and happiness too swiftly flies,*' Watson," Holmes quoted, still contemplating the strongbox. "By the way, I advise you to spend a few hours outside these rooms." It wasn't an order, but I knew he wouldn't make such a recommendation lightly, so I took the opportunity to play some billiards at my club.

I returned just after nightfall. A faint but somehow familiar smell permeated the sitting room. Holmes was seated cross-legged in his dressing gown, smoking his pipe silently, and he somehow appeared more melancholy than usual. Knowing he wouldn't respond, I wished him a quiet and perfunctory goodnight before going to bed.

The next morning, he still seemed pensive at breakfast, which he ate fully dressed.

"I have telegraphed MacDonald," he informed me, "asking him to meet us here this evening."

"Have you identified the robber?"

"Effectively, yes. There is one piece of information I must acquire before he arrives, but I am . . . confident about my conclusion." With that, he abruptly rose and left without another word.

I spent much of the day musing over what Holmes could have concluded. As I was having lunch, the thought crossed my mind that, while MacDonald claimed to have seen the ruby being locked in the strongbox, that was the only assurance we had that this had actually taken place. Could it have been that the disappearance of the ruby was some sort of insurance fraud on Dorrington's part – a fraud that MacDonald was somehow party to? Was *that* why Holmes had withdrawn from MacDonald – because he had inferred that there was something corrupt about him?

Holmes returned in the late afternoon and sat down opposite me. I opened my mouth to ask him about my theory, but he spoke before I could.

"Do you recall me saying that I once knew someone in university with whom I could have potentially conducted my chemical experiments – who could have done chemistry with me?"

"Yes, and it surprised me, because you said you didn't mix much with the men of your year."

"Not with the *men*, no."

My attention was immediately piqued. Holmes continued:

"One morning, after a rather low-church liturgy at the university chapel which had been presided over by a guest preacher, I noticed a young woman looking at a stained glass window depicting the crucifixion. It was unusual enough to see a young woman at the university in those days, but there was also an intensity about her examination that reminded me of the mood that came upon me during my own investigations. I decided to approach her and ask what had caught her attention.

"She introduced herself as Marjorie Tattersby. Pointing to the stained glass image of the Blood of Christ running down the cross, she told me there was something remarkable about how the artist had generated the vibrant red colour of the blood and went on to explain how she suspected this had been achieved. You once remarked that my knowledge of chemistry is 'profound', but you ought to revise that to 'eccentric'. I know a great deal about the chemistry of the human body, but my knowledge in other areas is riddled with lacunae. Her explanation of how a skilled chemist could create colours in glass revealed a great command of chemistry in aspects where my own knowledge was deficient, and I felt that merely having this conversation was an education in itself.

"I remarked that it was unusual for a woman to be allowed to study there. She additionally revealed that her father wasn't just a major donor to and guest lecturer at the institution, but he had also been the chaplain who preached that day: Reverend James Tattersby of the Anglo-American Missionary Society. As a concession to the reverend, his daughter had been allowed to informally take some classes on chemistry, art, and medieval history.

"Since we knew we would be in each other's vicinity that year, we discussed the possibility of embarking on certain chemical investigations together. The next time I went to chapel, however, she wasn't present, and I never saw her again. I gathered that, assurances to Reverend Tattersby notwithstanding, the prevailing attitudes about women in higher education had driven her out."

He winced at least twice while recounting this.

I listened attentively during this story for any notes of romantic affection for Miss Tattersby on Holmes's part, but none were forthcoming. Instead, it was clear that the emotions he had felt towards Marjorie Tattersby were similar to those he experienced with Alec MacDonald: An admiration and spontaneous connection that could have become friendship. Yet that had been unexpectedly, and no doubt painfully, ripped from him in the case of the lady. Perhaps his memory of that disappointment was why he had held himself aloft from MacDonald, and, indeed, why he avoided friendship in general. However, it wasn't clear to me why he had chosen to share all of this.

"I discovered where she works today," he continued, but just then it was announced that MacDonald had arrived and was waiting for us outside. Holmes strode briskly into his room and returned moments later wearing a false beard. He pulled a book off his shelf, tore a page out, folded

216

it up, and stuffed it in his breast pocket before accompanying me downstairs. MacDonald had kept a cab waiting for us, and Holmes gave the driver an address on Ivy Lane before we climbed inside.

"So, Mr. Holmes," asked MacDonald, his voice more eager than I had heard it before, "do you know what happened to the ruby?"

"I'm fairly sure I do, yes."

"How was it stolen, then?"

"When you have eliminated the – "

I groaned. Holmes smiled.

"It never left that box. Not, at least, until Lord Dorrington opened it."

MacDonald stared.

"I apologize. That is misleading. It is impossible that the ruby could have been stolen from the box because the box was never opened. What in fact happened was that the ruby never entered the box."

MacDonald's face darkened. "I saw it go in, sir! Are you suggesting I am lying?"

I wondered briefly: Had Holmes arrived at the same theory I had?

"Goodness, no! But accompany me down this path, MacDonald. What did the butler, Niven, describe the burglar in Dorrington Hall as carrying with him?"

"A jemmy, a sack, and a metal box, likely for burglary tools," MacDonald recited methodically.

"Think, Inspector: He needed the jemmy to open the window and to scratch the safe door, and the sack for whatever quarry he stole, but why would he need his burglar tools? What would be the purpose of adding the additional baggage of lock-picking and safe-cracking equipment if he had no intention of opening a safe? Unless, of course, he decided to go above and beyond what Murdock required of him and to *also* open the safe for his own purposes."

MacDonald's sandy eyebrows knit together. "But supposing he did open the safe – He still left the ruby there."

"Did he?" Holmes asked airily. "How did Lord Dorrington react to the discovery that the ruby was missing?

"Well, as I said, he was so upset that he choked and coughed and wept."

"Watson, did you not experience similar symptoms recently? Watery eyes, coughing, gasping . . . Do those sound familiar?"

"Yes," I answered slowly, "I experienced all of those when you were experimenting with hydrofluoric acid. Breathing the fumes caused those reactions."

"I spared you from those symptoms yesterday, Watson, when I urged you to take the afternoon to yourself. I was testing the cotton in the strongbox, you see. Would it surprise you to learn that I found hydrofluoric acid in that cotton? Especially considering the wax seal, the box sealed tightly enough to contain any fumes that may have been generated inside it."

The cab had come to a stop, and MacDonald and I looked outside. Under a setting sun, we saw that we had been brought to a glazier's shop.

"Do you recall me mentioning that hydrofluoric acid can dissolve glass?" asked Holmes, looking out the window at our destination.

I was beginning to see what he was implying, and I sensed from his the enlightened expression dawning on MacDonald's face that he was, as well, but instead of explaining, Holmes simply added, "Follow my lead," jumped out of the carriage, and headed into the glazier's shop. We followed closely, trying to look and act inconspicuous.

Inside, amidst several panes of glass of varying sizes, a young woman was seated at a work table with chemistry-related equipment and some tools on it, applying something like sandpaper to the edge of a round windowpane. She was thin, had dirty blonde hair, and wore spectacles. I inferred right away that we were beholding Marjorie Tattersby.

In a Scottish accent that was even thicker than MacDonald's, Holmes announced, "I'm the Mr. Clephane who made an appointment fer today."

"We're closing soon," she said curtly, not looking up.

"Ah, but perhaps ye'll want to speak to us, lass," Holmes retorted. He sat down on a bench near her work desk, pulled out the folded piece of paper from his breast pocket, and opened it to reveal a photograph of the Ardagh emeralds, accompanied by a block of text describing them and their history. Miss Tattersby looked at it warily.

"We'd like ye to make some glass replicas of these – so perfect that the most astute appraiser would be fooled – and fill them with hydrofluoric acid so they'll dissolve in a few days."

Miss Tattersby didn't react. Holmes continued.

"We know ye've got the glassmakin' skill *and* the chemistry skills to pull it off. Creighton told us about yer work making the ruby replica for him. We just wan' ye to do the same for us – and we'll pay ye even better than he did for it." Holmes managed to affect an evil smile under his false beard. I gathered that he was mimicking Murdock.

The woman stared and frowned for what felt like a long time. Finally, she went back to her glass sanding.

"I do not know what you are referring to," she said. "I don't know any Mr. Creighton, and I certainly never did what you have described for him." There was a note of unshakable conviction in her voice, not the quaver or hesitancy one might expect from a liar. "What you are asking

218

me to do sounds very much like involvement in a criminal enterprise. Kindly leave now, or I shall summon the police."

She had called his bluff. Holmes looked surprised, and I suspected it was genuine, rather than part of his disguise. A moment of tense silence hung in the air. With a grunt, Holmes slowly rose from the bench. He seemed genuinely defeated. It seemed we would leave empty-handed.

However, although I knew I was supposed to be unnoticed, I had observed something that I felt compelled to remark upon before we left.

"Young lady," I warned, "it isn't safe to be around chemicals like this, or in air that is filled with glass dust, when one is pregnant."

She started, as did Holmes and MacDonald.

"How – how can you tell I am pregnant?" she stammered, utterly losing the cool poise she had possessed since we had entered. "It's been barely two months!" It was clear she had been trying to conceal this. I noted that she wore no wedding ring.

I couldn't think of a plausible lie, so I simply uttered the truth. "I am a doctor," I answered. "I notice these things."

A deep sadness spread over her face. "When one is in my situation, Doctor," she whispered, looking downwards, "one doesn't always have the luxury of going without work."

Holmes's deflated disposition suddenly vanished. I could tell he had experienced an epiphany.

"You weren't *hired* to make a replica of the Dorrington Ruby," he said to her, no longer using his false accent. "The child's father *had* you make it. That's why you're shielding him."

A light of recognition flashed in the young woman's eyes as she looked up at him. Holmes solemnly removed the beard. They looked upon each other for a moment.

"Hello, Marjorie," Holmes greeted quietly. "How has your reverend father responded to the news of his grandchild?"

"He hasn't learned yet," she answered with a touch of bitterness. "But it won't be with gratitude."

Holmes sat down again on the bench. "When I deduced what had happened," he explained gently, "I knew you had to be involved. Only you would have had the skill in both glasswork, glass staining, and in chemistry to have produced a glass copy of the Dorrington Ruby filled with hydrofluoric acid, especially a forgery which would have so much verisimilitude that it would even fool Lord Dorrington himself. After all, the red of that stained glass window I once saw you admiring isn't far from the red of a ruby. I struggled to conceive why someone like you would be party to a low crime like this – but, if it was done for someone you love, perhaps I can understand."

219

Marjorie fiddled with a wrench on her desk.

"After I was driven out of university," she said, not looking at him directly, "it was . . . affirming, I suppose, to be noticed and appreciated, even if it was by a criminal. He assured me we could make enough money from his . . . work . . . that we'd be fine – that the baby would be taken care of – even without my father's support." She blinked hard and rubbed her eyes.

"We can guarantee the child is provided for, Marjorie," said Holmes. "And, if I may be so bold, perhaps our assurance is more reliable than that of a professional thief."

A long silence followed. Marjorie sniffled. MacDonald offered her a bandana handkerchief. After blowing her nose and wiping her eyes, Marjorie looked at us with a hard expression.

"John Creighton isn't his real name. It's the name he uses among . . . among other crooks. His real name is Reginald Harold Crawshay. He often drinks with other robbers at the Castledown Tavern, and he'd heard testimonies from people who had worked for this man the newspapers call Chester Murdock. Reginald figured out that Murdock found and hired people to play small roles within large, ambitious crimes.

"When Murdock approached Reginald with the blueprints of Dorrington Hall and hired him to scratch up the safe but not steal anything from it, Reginald figured out right away that the plan was to scare Dorrington into bringing his ruby to London so it could be stolen here. That's when Reginald told me his own plan.

"He had the idea of stealing the ruby and putting a false one in its place. If he did that, however, eventually the fact that it was a forgery would be discovered, either by Murdock or by the police, in the event they captured Murdock and recovered all his loot. Either way, they'd turn their attention on Reginald at that point.

"But, he reasoned, what if he stole the ruby and replaced it with a false one *that disappeared*? Imagine: Murdock would steal the forgery. Then it would vanish. The police might eventually track Murdock down, and, when they looked for the ruby, they wouldn't be able to find it. What would they assume? That Murdock had hidden it extremely well. If Murdock insisted to the police that the ruby he stole had simply disappeared, were they likely to believe him? Attention would be permanently deflected away from Reginald.

"Of course, Murdock might figure out that Reginald had swindled him. But by the time the ruby dissolved, we were . . . supposed to be out of the country. He told me he's leaving for Australia tomorrow to prepare a place for us to stay when we move there."

Her voice had grown flat, as if even she realized the obvious falsity of what she was repeating. Perhaps explaining the situation had helped her realize its reality.

"Did you use flashed glass?" Holmes asked softly.

"With copper," she responded automatically, "but I think I've developed a better method for staining with it."

For the first time since we arrived, the two smiled at each other. In that moment, I saw the glimmerings of the great friendship that could have existed. The next moment, her smile faded.

"Reginald lives at 65 Fulham Road," she told us. "But he said he would be out tonight robbing some places for cash to pay for tomorrow's trip to Australia. He may not be in his flat right now, but the ruby should be. You'll find it hidden in a flower vase."

MacDonald thanked her for her help. We quickly but quietly began to move towards the door.

"Do you think God will forgive me?" she asked suddenly.

Holmes looked back at her. "Our only conversation before today was about the colour of the Blood of Christ," he answered. "My understanding is that this vibrant red blood can wash away even the blackest sin."

They smiled at each other again. We exited into the deepening darkness of the night.

"Ye're as good as a clergyman, Mr. Holmes," remarked MacDonald.

"My godfather is a priest," replied Holmes as he gestured for a cab. [3] "There's no time to waste. He may be out now, but who knows when he will return home?"

Crawshay's home on Fulham Road was a small, somewhat shabby small house with no lights on inside. The front door was, predictably, locked. Holmes produced his small metal box and removed a skeleton key from it. He exchanged a look with MacDonald, who nodded, cleared his throat, and turned to look the other way. By the time he looked back, Holmes had picked the lock and returned the tools to his pocket.

"Thank God *you* aren't a thief," I whispered.

It was rather bare inside, and everything seemed to be made of inexpensive wood. A candle sat on a table near the door, and we lit it and left it there, needing the illumination but not wishing to carry the light with us, in case Crawshay happened to see it moving through his window. We walked gingerly through the ill-lit house in search of a flower vase, Holmes and MacDonald checking the bedroom and spare room while I took the kitchen. I soon found a vase in a cupboard. Calling out my discovery in a loud whisper, I fished the ruby out of it.

"Who the hell are you?"

221

The sharp voice came from the door. A red-haired, bullet-headed, floridly-dressed figure with a scarf around his neck, a flat cap on his head, and his pockets bulging with cash stood in the doorway, a pistol in each hand and both pointed directly at us, the nearby candle throwing a flickering curtain of orange light over him. We stiffened, but Holmes and MacDonald showed no fear. I only hoped that I also looked brave.

"We're here to arrest you, Mr. Crawshay," announced MacDonald.

Crawshay sneered. "Come and do it, Copper, or else gi' me back my ruby an' get outta here!"

"Oh, Mr. Crawshay?" asked Holmes haughtily. "If we aren't so obliging, will you shoot and kill all three of us? Gracious, sir, right now all you're guilty of is grand theft. That will certainly put you away for a long time. But triple murder? Why, you're sure to be hanged. Have you ever seen a man hanged? The neck breaks first, you know, and the body – Well, it discharges everything it doesn't need, one may politely say. Sometimes the victim slowly chokes to death. Are we – or this ruby – worth all that to you?"

Crawshay's face darkened at Holmes's monologue, but his pistols stayed pointed at us.

"Let's find out, Mr. Holmes," said MacDonald, looking directly at Crawshay. The inspector took a step forward. I felt my body grow even more tense.

"Stay ri' there, Copper!" snapped Crawshay, raising one of his pistols to be level with MacDonald's chest.

"Or what, Mr. Crawshay?" returned MacDonald, taking another step forward. "You're rather a clever man, from what we can tell. Are you going to make the clever choice now, or is it the gallows for you?" And he stepped forward again. I felt terrified, and even Holmes seemed alarmed, though he also looked impressed.

Crawshay's face contorted with rage, but the pistol in his hand began to waver just a little. He suddenly flung the weapon at MacDonald, who leapt backwards as the gun clattered at his feet. The next moment, Crawshay his now empty hand and knocked the candle to the wooden floor before spinning and darting out the door, still gripping his other pistol. A small inferno instantly sprang up between us and the doorway.

We all instinctively pulled off our jackets and began vigorously beating the fire with them. Fortunately, our collective efforts were enough to extinguish the small blaze before it could cause any true damage, but it was clear by the time we had put it out that Crawshay had escaped into the night beyond our grasp.

"We'll have to check all the ships leaving for Australia," I stated. To my great surprise, MacDonald chuckled. He seemed to be in good spirits.

"We'll do that, Doctor, but I can't imagine we'll catch Crawshay that way. That Australia line was probably a *somnol*-laced biscuit he fed his lady love to keep her calm while he rushed off in another direction. Nah, I'm sure the perpetrator may have escaped – for now – but maybe that's all for the best," he mused. "It would have been difficult for Miss Tattersby to have avoided a harsh sentence as a collaborator in crime if this had gone to trial, even if we had stuck up for her to the judge. But now, we can return the ruby to Lord Dorrington and collect the reward – or, rather, you can, Mr. Holmes, since I see this as largely being your success – and it never needs to see a courthouse."

"The reward will be all yours, Mister Mac," Holmes replied admiringly, using that nickname for the first time. Something had changed in Holmes's attitude towards the Scottish detective, and it would never change back. Holmes produced three cigars from his pocket.

"You recently gave thanks that I am not a thief, Watson, but I confess before an officer of the law that I have also stolen from Lord Dorrington. Now, having just extinguished a fire, perhaps we could ignite some fresh ones?"

And, there, in front of Crawshay's home, with a priceless ruby in my pocket, I laughed and enjoyed lit up a cigar with two of the best detectives in the city and conversed with them late into the night.

Epilogue

Crawshay, who would later be famously described by one who should know as being *"one of the cleverest thieves in London"*, did not go to Australia the following day. This was clearly a lie he had told Marjorie so as to escape from her. Instead, as we were ultimately able to ascertain, he went to New York. Not only did MacDonald alert the local police about this, he also reached out to a private detective in that city named Bedford – "I have come to appreciate the value of skilled amateurs in crimefighting," he explained. – and Bedford was able to apprehend Crawshay for a time, though he eventually escaped. [4] MacDonald's pursuit of Crawshay, as well as of other more famous prey, is now well-documented by a pen other than my own. [5]

Marjorie, meanwhile, delivered her baby and raised him with the financial and personal support of Holmes and MacDonald. The three of us visited as often as we could and, I like to think, served as uncles, if not fathers, to the boy in lieu of the fiend who had sired him, though

MacDonald was often distracted with the rearing of his own son, who now works for the Edinburgh Police Force.

Although MacDonald continued to correspond with Holmes and find cases for him even after his retirement, Holmes and MacDonald never did become terribly close. Holmes never accepted any of MacDonald's invitations to go golfing or fishing. In fact, Holmes never became amenable to friendship.

I have often mused deeply on the strange fact that there was only one man Sherlock Holmes ever seriously considered his friend. Surely only an especially remarkable person could earn such a rare honour. As an old man, I find myself wondering: What does it say about myself that this friend was me? Perhaps that fact is the greatest epitaph I could ask for.

Inspector MacDonald of Scotland Yard was ushered into the room . . .
Twice already in his career had Holmes helped him to attain success.
— Dr. John H. Watson
The Valley of Fear

Appendix

Over the course of 1899 to 1909, Harry "Bunder" Manders published four books chronicling his exploits in burglary with well-known cricketer Arthur J. Raffles: *The Amateur Cracksman, The Black Mask, A Thief in the Night*, and *Mr. Justice Raffles*. Manders' literary agent was E.W. Hornung, brother-in-law to Arthur Conan Doyle, who did not share Doyle's moral qualms about having a criminal as a protagonist. The stories not only chronicled Raffles' adventures, but also showcased how Inspector Alec MacDonald, referred to as "MacKenzie" to avoid legal repercussions, identified Raffles as a thief and forced him into hiding, bringing MacDonald into public fame.

During that same period, a New York-based figure calling himself "Raffles Holmes" (who publicly billed himself as being a consulting detective but secretly worked as an amateur cracksman) claimed to have been the son of Sherlock Holmes and the grandson of A.J. Raffles. To justify his claim, he perpetuated a false account of the 1883 Dorrington Ruby theft, which was published as "The Adventure of the Dorrington Ruby Seal" in John Kendrick Bangs' 1906 book *R. Holmes & Co.* In this telling, the Dorrington Ruby was stolen by Raffles. Holmes had solved the case but, when he went to confront Raffles, he fell in love with Raffles' daughter, Marjorie, and agreed to grant Raffles his freedom in exchange for her hand. "Raffles Holmes" claimed to have been the product of this union.

This story never gained wide acceptance due to its obvious implausibility, as well as its incompatibility with the historical record. (In early 1883, as we know from the story "*Le Premier Pas*", Raffles was a penniless university student who had only committed a single crime, not an accomplished criminal and cricketer.) However, now that we have Watson's accurate account of the case, we can infer the truth about this mystery man known as "Raffles Holmes".

In actuality, he was the son of Reginald Crawshay and Marjorie Tattersby. His real name was Reginald Holmes Tattersby, named for his father and for the man who had ensured he and his mother would be taken care of after his father abandoned them. Holmes was relatively present in the boy's life and did what he could to be a positive influence on him. (Years later, as a grown man, he could cite information about the underworld Holmes had shared with him, as seen in "The Adventure of Room 407".) Reginald Tattersby was so inspired by Holmes that he not only became a detective, but also imitated his appearance and mannerisms, to the point where he was once mistaken for Holmes by a crook the Great Detective had once apprehended ("The Nostalgia of Nervy Jim the Snatcher"), though he also shared his father's penchant for thievery.

After 1883, Inspector MacDonald gained a reputation among the criminal underworld for his role in taking down the behemoth that was Chester Murdock. He also continued to maintain Holmes's trust as a thorough and intelligent investigator. Thus, by the end of the 1880's, when Holmes began suspecting Professor Moriarty as being a criminal mastermind on an even greater scale than Murdock had been – indeed, Murdock's arrest had provided new opportunities for Moriarty's criminal empire to expand – MacDonald was initially the only Yarder Holmes confided his suspicions to, as seen in *The Valley of Fear*. MacDonald was dubious: An obvious lowlife like Murdock might be a ruler of the underworld, but surely a respectable public figure like Moriarty could not be. When Holmes and Moriarty both apparently died in May of 1891 ("The Adventure of the Final Problem"), MacDonald realized that Holmes had been correct all along.

Two months before Holmes's disappearance, Raffles had recruited Manders as his accomplice in crime ("The Ides of March"), and their criminal career began in earnest shortly thereafter. In response to the question posed in *R. Holmes & Co.* as to why Holmes and Raffles never seem to have crossed paths, the answer is that most of Raffles' crimes, which largely occurred in London, occurred during The Great Hiatus, when Holmes was out of England.

Raffles was aware of Inspector MacDonald by reputation. When Raffles wanted to ensure another criminal was arrested in April of 1891, he knew to contact MacDonald at the Yard ("A Costume Piece"). However, his first encounter with MacDonald was in summer of that year.

MacDonald was still in pursuit of Crawshay, who had designs on robbing the same estate that Raffles did. Being a more experienced and "professional" criminal, Crawshay beat Raffles to it, and managed to elude MacDonald again, shooting him in the shoulder as he escaped ("Gentlemen and Players"). This near-death experience left the comparatively young MacDonald looking (as Manders put it) "more than middle-aged" (*Mr. Justice Raffles*). [6]

In November of 1892, MacDonald was still on Crawshay's trail. Crawshay managed to escape MacDonald once again, this time with the help of Raffles. This was when MacDonald first began to suspect that perhaps Raffles was also a burglar ("The Return Match"). His experience with Holmes and Moriarty had taught him that respectable public figures could indeed be accomplished criminal geniuses. Sensing that MacDonald had become aware of his double life, Raffles subsequently laid low and reduced his criminal activity over the next few years ("The Chest of Silver", "The Rest Cure").

When Holmes returned to public life in spring of 1894, MacDonald approached him with his suspicions about Raffles. Holmes confirmed that MacDonald's deductions were likely correct and even supplied him with a disguise, including a beard – the same one which appears in this narrative – that he could use to pursue Raffles and Manders unnoticed onto a ship to Italy. There, MacDonald arrested Manders and nearly arrested Raffles, who jumped overboard and was thought to have drowned ("The Gift of the Emperor"). He was forced to spend the rest of his life *incognito* (*The Black Mask*). For his part in exposing Raffles, MacDonald received national fame that continued for the rest of his professional life.

When Raffles subsequently became notorious for being a thief who was also gentlemanly and debonair, and became known for his association with Crawshay, Reginald Holmes Tattersby decided that he preferred to be associated with the aristocratic Raffles and with the paternal figure of Sherlock Holmes than he did with the lowly Reginald Crawshay. When he moved to New York to apprentice under Curtis Bedford and eventually establish his own practice, he therefore began going by "R. Holmes Tattersby" to minimize the connection to his disreputable father. He eventually dropped his surname and went simply by "R.

Holmes," and, by 1906, he claimed that his real name was Raffles Holmes and that he was descended from both of them, an assertion he justified by telling a heavily revised version of the Dorrington Ruby affair. He would even attribute crimes committed by his actual father to his supposed grandfather ("The Major-General's Pepperpots"). While "R. Holmes" was heavily influenced by both Holmes and Raffles, the connection was not biological, and we can be glad that, more than a century later, the record has finally been set straight, thanks to Watson's diligent documentation.

Notes

1. Holmes was kept apprised of who worked in sensitive government offices by his brother, Mycroft. Arthur Dorrington would later work as a secretary for the Ministry of European Affairs. See "The Adventure of the Downing Street Demise" in *The MX Book of New Sherlock Holmes Stories, Part XXXVII: 2023 Annual (1875-1889)*.
2. Holmes would later meet and work with Inspector Brown's brother, Father John Paul Brown, on several occasions, many of which are recorded in *The Detective and The Clergyman: The Adventures of Sherlock Holmes and Father Brown*. Inspector Sam Brown assisted his brother and Holmes in "The Adventure of the Uncommitted Murder".
3. Holmes' godfather was the Reverend Sabine Baring-Gould, the cleric and scholar who was known as *"the last man who knew everything"*, as documented in Mary Russell's *The Moor* (edited by Laurie R. King).
4. The heavily fictionalized 1903 play *Raffles, the Amateur Cracksman* by E.W. Hornung and E.W. Presbrey was accurate in depicting Curtis Bedford, described by one character as *"The Sherlock Holmes of New York"*, briefly capturing Crawshay. In 1897, Bedford, still operating out of New York, would be instrumental in capturing the Randall family gang, as alluded to in "The Adventure of the Abbey Grange".
5. MacDonald's continued pursuit of Crawshay is seen in the stories "Gentlemen and Players" and "The Return Match".
6. Some seem to have taken this reference to "MacKenzie" looking "more than middle-aged" to mean he is a different person than the youthful but dour MacDonald. However, "The Return Match" makes clear that the inspector's *"hair was grizzled at the temples, and his face still cadaverous, from the wound that had nearly been his death."* This is why he appears *"more than middle-aged"*. As Manders himself puts it in "A Bad Night", *"I have seen old men look half their age, and young men look double theirs."*

The Adventure of the
Old Russian Woman
by Susan Knight

"**W**hatever do you ladies think you're doing?"

It was past twelve noon of a crisp winter's day. I had just returned to Baker Street from an extended constitutional stroll around Regent's Park to work up an appetite for luncheon, only to find Mrs. Hudson and her two maidservants, Clara and Phoebe, far from the kitchen where I had assumed they would be busy preparing a delicious meal, and sitting instead on the stairs leading up to Holmes's and my rooms. This astonishing sight was followed by Mrs. Hudson placing a finger on her lips to hush further conversation. She gave a little jerk of her head, calling my attention to what could be heard from above. It was the most glorious violin music imaginable.

My first thought was that Holmes must have been practising secretly, since never in my experience had he played so melodically. Far from it, indeed. I could understand why our landlady and her maids were entranced. I paused with them to listen.

Brahms, I thought to myself, or perhaps Schumann. When the piece finally came to an end, I bounded up the stairs to congratulate my friend, only to discover that it was not he who had been playing, but rather a small stout individual in his middle years, pale of countenance and with fine light hair that curled down over his collar. Holmes, meanwhile, was seated in his customary chair, his chin resting on his steepled fingers.

"Ah, Watson," he remarked. "Here you are at last. Allow me to introduce Mr. Suvorov."

The man, having laid down Holmes's violin, gave a Continental bow.

The name was instantly familiar to me.

"Not Ruslan Suvorov?" I exclaimed.

The man nodded assent, with a polite smile.

To say I was astonished to see him there in front of me would be a mighty understatement. The London music world had been agog for days with news of the visit of this world-famous violinist, invited to perform at the Royal Albert Hall over two nights, one of them having already passed to great acclaim, critics even comparing Suvorov favourably to the great Joachim. I myself had tried to buy tickets, to no avail. They were completely sold out. And now he had condescended to give an impromptu recital here in our modest rooms. What was the explanation?

"You have a fine instrument here, Mr. Holmes," the man remarked in a soft accent I should have recognised as Russian, even had I not known the nationality of the visitor.

"Thank you," Holmes replied. "It was sold to me cheaply as a fake."

"A fake!" exclaimed Suvorov. "Never! This is undoubtedly the genuine work of Antonio Stradivari! I could not be fooled."

"Indeed," Holmes replied. "The man who sold it to me had no ear for music. In fact, I believe he was deaf."

"I should envy you, did I not possess a fine Stradivarius of my own."

"But I am sure," Holmes continued, "that you didn't come here simply to play a tune on my violin."

Play a tune! I winced, but detected in my friend's tone – could it be? – something approaching envy. He always wished to be the best at everything – in this case an impossibility!

"I shouldn't have bothered you with such a trivial matter, Mr. Holmes, had my wife not urged me to consult you."

"Then how can I assist you?" Holmes asked. "And please be seated."

Suvorov took the armchair facing Holmes – my usual place, which I willingly ceded to the great man – while I sat myself in an upright chair at the table.

"In my youth," our visitor began, "I did some foolish things, as I suppose most of us have."

He paused. Holmes said nothing. I doubted that my friend was guilty of any youthful follies whatsoever, but I certainly was, so gave an assenting murmur, as much to encourage the man to proceed as anything else.

"You must know," he continued, "that in Russia there are groups of mainly young men – idealistic, yes, but sometimes given to extreme acts – who wish to overthrow the existing autocratic order and install a fairer society in its place. I associated myself with such a group for several years, before my musical studies took me away from St Petersburg to Paris, where I was too immersed in work to engage any longer in such activities. In addition, by then I had a wife and child to consider – my son Vanya, you know, just now studying to be a doctor in Moscow." The indulgent smile of a proud father passed quickly over his face, before he added, "Imagine my astonishment, therefore, when I received, but two days since, this message in the post."

He reached into his breast pocket and took out a missive which he handed to Holmes. Before opening it, the latter studied the envelope itself with great care.

"Postmarked Belgravia," he said. "A salubrious area and one that, as I believe it, hosts the embassy of the Russian Empire."

Suvorov nodded. "Indeed. In fact, I have been invited to play there this week at a private function. However," he added, "I hardly think the message came from that establishment."

Holmes removed a card from inside the envelope and looked at it for a moment. He then passed it to me without a word.

"I am afraid," I said, regarding it, "that my grasp of Cyrillic isn't what it was."

Both men looked at me. Of course, I have never even attempted to get to grips with the Russian alphabet, let alone those languages that use it. My attempt at a joke had fallen flat on its face. Mind you, I don't think Holmes, in this instance, was better placed than I to read the thing. Under what seemed to be a single word was a bisected rectangle, half black, half red.

"It simply says '*Remember*'," Suvorov explained. "The symbol beneath it – "

"Represents the anarchist movement," Holmes added. "Yes, I recognise that."

"You were an anarchist?" I asked, shocked. Newspapers frequently report the atrocities committed by such groups.

"As I said, I was young. I was idealistic. Indeed, I stand by those ideals today. However, I cannot condone any violent methods employed to realise them."

"So why, after so long, do you think these people have contacted you again?" Holmes asked.

Suvorov shook his head.

"I have not an idea. It isn't as if I have been difficult to find, having been in the public eye for several decades."

"But not perhaps in London."

"No. It's my first visit."

"Hmm . . . ." Holmes drummed his fingers on the arm of his chair. "Whoever sent this will no doubt follow it up with a further message. Until that time, I fear there is little I can do for you."

"That is what I expected you to say – what I told Tatiana. But you know what wives are like."

I nodded again, while Holmes stayed silent.

"The least I can do," Suvorov continued, "is to invite you to my concert tonight."

"I understood all the tickets were sold," I said.

"There are always places kept back for honoured guests. My wife has a box. Please do not offend me by refusing."

231

Holmes smiled. "We shouldn't dream of it, Mr. Suvorov. It would be both an honour and a delight. Thank you so very much."

With that, our visitor took his leave.

"What a charming man," I said.

Holmes was frowning.

"Yes, but I fear that his troubles are only starting. Whoever sent that message will assuredly follow it up."

The Albert Hall was full to bursting with people keen to hear the playing of the famous violinist. An excited buzz filled that vast auditorium as Holmes and I made our way to the box where we found Madame Suvorova already installed, together with a couple she introduced to us as her brother and his wife.

"Count and Countess Razumov," she told us.

Madame Suvorova was a small plump woman in, as I judged, her early forties. Her jet-black hair was pulled back so tightly from her forehead that it rather made me wince to look upon it, but otherwise she had a sweet, if not pretty, face, her Slavic features rather buried in the flesh of her cheeks, which dimpled when she smiled. Her eyes were the soft grey of an autumn sky.

Her brother, the Count, was a gaunt version of herself, small too, but slight, clean-shaven with cheekbones that stood out cadaverously under grey eyes that on him looked wintry. His sleek black hair lent him something of the look of a predatory animal, but he was all courtesy, apologising, in French for his lack of English.

For some reason I didn't care at all for the appearance of his wife, the Countess, lean as a boy and so long in the body that, without seeing her stand, I felt that she must tower over her husband. Gingery curls over rouged cheeks did nothing to dispel the impression of a hard and cold woman. Perhaps conscious of her status, she bestowed on us the very slightest of acknowledgements – in French – and then turned her back on us to regard the assembled audience through opera glasses.

Madame Suvorova herself spoke English quite charmingly, although, to my ears, with more of a French accent than a Russian one. She said nothing to Holmes about her fears for her husband following the receipt of the enigmatic note. I suppose it was hardly the place. In any case, the concert was about to start.

Holmes, sitting back on his upholstered armchair, long legs stretched out in front of him, eyes closed, listened intently, and entirely without moving. For my part, while I enjoy listening to music, my thoughts tend to wander all over the place. I am afraid, moreover, that I'm very much the dilettante, and can seldom put a composer's name to the piece being played. I know that the first half of the programme featured Peter Tchaikovsky and another Russian, whose name I had never heard before and the which, being barely pronounceable, I have already forgotten. Ruslan Suvorov was accompanied both times by an accomplished pianist, a man whose splendid whiskers made up for the baldness of his pate.

During the interval, a steward appeared with a tray holding little squares of bread covered with black caviar, as well as four glasses and a bottle of champagne on ice. Rapid words in Russian were exchanged, Madame Suvorova looking displeased, apparently embarrassed that there weren't enough glasses to go round. I protested that I didn't care for champagne, it being nothing less than the truth, but this wouldn't do, and the Count sent the poor steward off with a flea in his ear – as if it were his fault – to bring another glass. Meanwhile a little smile played over the thin lips of the Countess, for the which I liked her even less than before.

"My husband and I hope, gentlemen," Madame Suvorova was saying, "that you will be able to join us after the concert for dinner at Romanos."

Despite the Italian-sounding name, I knew that this fabled restaurant, which I had never previously had occasion to visit, was renowned for the excellence of its French cuisine. I looked across at Holmes, who, I was pleased to see, graciously nodded his acceptance of the invitation.

"Whatever has happened to the man?" The waiter having failed as yet to return with another glass, Madame Suvorova rapped her fan impatiently on the velvet edge of the balcony.

It was again impossible to insist that I didn't wish for a drink, so since I knew – or thought I knew – my way around the concert hall, I offered to go in search of the fellow, or at least to collect another glass myself. The way wasn't quite as I remembered, however, and, thinking it might be a short-cut to the bar, I soon found myself on an unfrequented staircase. Descending it, I was most taken aback to observe below me none other than the maestro Ruslan Suvorov himself in intense conversation with a young lady of astonishing beauty, garbed in the very height of fashion – I should amend that. Despite my not being up-to-date on ladies' dress, I could tell that her style wasn't that generally seen in London but rather Continental: French or Italian. The pair didn't notice me and, reluctant to disturb them in what seemed a most impassioned colloquy, I returned the way I had come, somewhat puzzled.

By happy chance, I met the same steward, now heading back to our box with the extra glass, and full of apologies.

"I understood four from the lady," he said, "though her English wasn't of the best."

The Countess then, I thought, wondering if it was a genuine mistake on her part, and if not, whyever should she wish to stir up mischief?

She gave me what I thought was an ironic glance on my return. No, I did not care for her.

The company had kindly left me several little squares of the caviar on bread, and I was vouchsafed another ironic glance, this time from Holmes, whose conservative taste in the matter of food, I reckoned, wouldn't extend to sturgeons' eggs. I, however, am quite partial to the delicacy, especially when the quality was as good as this. Not so much, all the same, that I would pay good money for it, a juicy steak being more in my line. However, I complimented Madame Suvorova on the flavour.

"Beluga," she replied "Pearls of delight exploding on the tongue, do you not agree, Doctor?"

Before I could reply, the Count exclaimed, looking down into the auditorium. *"Tiens! C'est Katya Maslinka! Qu'est ce que cette salope fait ici?"*

I followed his gaze and saw that he was indicating the same beauty I had observed so recently on the stairs with Ruslan Suvorov. Whyever, I wondered, would the Count refer to her so very disparagingly? The girl was now accompanied by an old woman whose dress would suggest rather the steppes of Central Asia than a fashionable concert hall in a metropolis, being all homespun weaves with a scarf, if you please, tied around her head. A strange companion, indeed, for a lovely young lady. As we watched, the old woman, as if sensing our interest, turned to look up at us with one of the most evil and vindictive stares I have ever seen. She then addressed the other with a crocodile smile. I couldn't see the young woman's responding expression for she had her back to us.

"And that witch, old Kuragina!" exclaimed Madame Suvorova. "What are they doing here in London?"

"No good, you can be sure," the Count replied in English.

Just then, the lights went down for the second half of the concert. It was Beethoven, the Kreutzer Sonata, as my programme indicated, but I was so distracted by the previous incident that I couldn't pay proper attention to that intricate and challenging piece – only that it was met with uproarious applause at the end.

"And yet," Holmes whispered to me, "I feel that the maestro didn't respond to the music as whole-heartedly as I should have expected. And see – those mysterious ladies didn't even await the ending of it."

I again looked down into the auditorium. Two seats were empty: Those of the Russian women.

Ruslan Suvorov had left the stage, but the applause continued unabated. His accompanist stood by his piano still, as we awaited the return of the maestro to acknowledge the plaudits of the audience, and perhaps even grace us with an encore.

We waited and waited but there was no sign of him. Soon the audience took up a chant of "Suvorov! Suvorov!" but still nothing. His accompanist looked off into the wings but evidently there was no one there. Eventually, the curtain came down and people started shuffling, somewhat discontentedly, to the exits, but not before Holmes had rushed from the box, myself following after.

"I fear something bad has happened," he told me as we hurried down to the lobby, where he asked a doorman if he had seen Ruslan Suvorov leaving.

"Not him," came the reply, "only two ladies who got into a coach that was waiting for them . . . Mind you, sir, the maestro wouldn't come out this way, but would use the stage door."

"Of course," Holmes said. "Where is it?"

On being informed that it was several doors along, around that circular building, we made haste thither, only to find it already blocked by enthusiasts hoping to catch a glimpse of their hero.

"Some 'ope," an old chestnut vendor remarked, standing by with his barrow of hot roasted nuts to tempt the passers-by. "'E's long gawn."

"What did you see?" Holmes asked.

"Well now," the old man replied with a crafty look. "If only I could remember . . . ."

"Give him something, Watson, and quick," Holmes said.

I fished a half-crown, all the change I had, out of my pocket and gave it to the man, who took it without even a thank-you.

"Let me guess," Holmes went on. "A coach drove up, and he got into it."

The old man laughed, revealing toothless gums.

"If you knowed it, why d'you ask?"

"Two ladies within, I suppose."

"No, not a bit . . . ." The old man paused for effect. "One loverly lady and one 'orrible old crone. They went that way," he offered, without being asked, pointing to the road that led to the city centre, "and that were the last I seed of 'em. Good riddance, too."

"Did you notice anything distinguishing the coach from all the others? A coat-of-arms, for instance?"

The old man shook his head. "The look that old one give me were enough to freeze me blood. Like a curse, it were. I looked away after that."

"Well," Holmes said to me as we made our way back to the front of the concert hall, "at least it seems that the maestro left of his own accord and wasn't forced."

"Do you think Suvorov and the young lady have an understanding? It seems surprising under the circumstances."

Holmes shrugged. "At this stage, who knows?"

It was then I told him of my previous sighting of Suvorov with the lady on the stairs.

"Their conversation didn't strike me as that of lovers. However, I am no expert on Russians, whom I understand to be a passionate race."

"Good Heavens, Watson!" Holmes threw up his hands in exasperation. "You didn't think of mentioning this before?"

"I hardly had a chance," I replied, somewhat peeved. "In any case, it is only in retrospect that the encounter has taken on any significance."

"Tsk," was Holmes's response to that.

By now we had arrived back at the concert hall lobby where Madame Suvorova and the Countess were standing waiting.

"*Bozhe moi*, Mr. Holmes!" Madame exclaimed. "Wherever did you rush off to?"

"Where is the Count?" Holmes countered, presumably not wishing to alarm the ladies too much.

"He has gone to fetch Ruslan . . . Though I am most surprised . . . I hope he is well. It is most unlike my husband not to do an encore."

The Countess, meanwhile was smiling at her feet, though I couldn't imagine what she found amusing there.

Soon enough, the Count returned, unsurprisingly to us, without the violinist but with a bearded man I recognised as the accompanist.

The Count spoke rapidly to Madame Suvorova, who seemed to me to turn pale at his words.

"Mr. Benson says that he was most astonished when Ruslan failed to return for his encore," he explained to us.

"We had rehearsed it," the pianist said. "Fauré's *Berceuse*, you know."

Holmes nodded. "A crowd pleaser."

"I felt most ridiculous standing there on stage waiting for him to come back, I can tell you. He might have let me know what his intentions were."

The man was clearly more concerned for his own dignity than for any fate that might have befallen Suvorov.

"So, where is he?" Madame asked.

Benson shook his head. "Apparently he just rushed off."

It was then that Holmes told of what we knew – of Suvorov mounting a coach whose passengers already comprised the two women we had seen in the concert hall. Madame Suvorova turned away abruptly, and might have fallen but for her brother's supporting arm. The Countess continued to grin at her feet.

"It may be nothing," the Count said in English. "I suggest we go to Romano's as planned in the hope that Ruslan will join us there."

"I should like to know," Holmes interpolated, "who these women are, and what might be their relationship with Suvorov."

The Count shot him a dark look, as if to say not in front of his sister, who assuredly was already worried enough.

"Katya was a student of his in Paris, and the old woman is, I believe, her aunt," Madame Suvorova said in shaky tones.

The Countess suddenly chuckled, as if she had heard something extremely amusing.

"If you are thinking," the Count said, again in English – (His command of the language seeming to increase with every speech he gave.) " – that there was more between them – an *attachment*, my dear – you are quite wrong. Ruslan is devoted to you."

"So you say," Madame replied bleakly. "But you have seen her. How lovely she is."

"*Et jeune aussi,*" added the Countess, eyes glinting spitefully. "*Comme les hommes d'un certain âge aiment les jolies jeunes filles! Tu le sais bien, mon chéri.*"

I could not but wonder if the Countess's reference to the predilection of older men for fresh young women was of a more personal nature. Certainly, if I were her husband, I think my eye might rove as well.

"Her youth is neither here nor there," the Count put in, giving his wife a sharp look. He added something in French but so fast that I could make nothing of it.

It was agreed, then, that we should proceed to the restaurant, in the hope that Suvorov might turn up there as planned. Though Holmes, while insisting I go, said that, with Madame's permission, he would make some inquiries of his own, to try and establish the whereabouts of the maestro. Depending on what he found out, if anything, he might, or might not, join us later.

I am not sure if he was invited as well, but the pianist, Benson, showed every intention of accompanying us to Romano's. Finding myself travelling in a cab with him, it turned out that he was an inveterate gossip and, I am sorry to say, ready to imagine the worst of his musical partner.

"These Continentals, Dr. Watson," he confided gleefully, "are not like us Britishers. I should know. I've accompanied the best – and worst – of them. They have the morals of rabbits. I'm not one whit surprised that old Suvorov's lower instincts, if I might put it that way, got the better of him."

Distasteful though it was to hear this man speak so crudely – this same man, whose sensitive rendition of the classics he had so recently been playing would lead one to imagine that his view of humanity was equally uplifting – I felt it incumbent on me, in the interests of the case, to lead him on to speak even more freely.

"So, had you observed anything untoward between Mr. Suvorov and the young person in question?"

Benson shook his head, regretfully, as it seemed to me.

"No, never set eyes on her. But he's a sly one, Dr. Watson. Great artiste, of course, but very sly. Not one for confidences. Butter, you'd think, wouldn't melt in his mouth . . . That's what you'd think, if you didn't know any better."

By now we had reached the restaurant, possessed of a handsome creamy yellow entrance fronting onto the Strand. Our companions had arrived just before us and were now making their way inside, the Count waving at us to follow. We were greeted effusively by the owner's second-in-command, one Signor Antonelli, who showed us to our table. The place, known for the Bohemian set who frequented it – actors, writers, musicians and so forth – possessed a suitably exotic décor, suggestive of a Moorish interior, arches leading into booths enhanced with a series of seascapes that, to me, recalled the Bosphorus, its deep blue waters set with islands, castles, and mosques. I found it a little strange, seeing that the place was owned, as its name suggested, by an Italian – the "Roman" – and that the menu featured French cuisine of a high order.

Sadly, most of our party, myself included, had little appetite, the exceptions being the Countess and Benson, whose little eyes veritably glinted at the variety of comestibles before him. I ordered the famous shellfish soup, "Crème Pink'un", but found it too rich for that time of night and merely took a few spoonfuls before pushing the dish away.

Madame's eyes strayed constantly to the door. Each time it opened, she sat forward, clearly hoping that it would be her husband who appeared on the threshold. Each time she was disappointed. For my part, I was hoping for Holmes, also in vain.

Conversation hardly existed. And when the "Roman" himself, a dapper little man, with a neat black moustache, appeared at our table, clearly distressed that his food wasn't producing the usual delightful effect (our two exceptions notwithstanding), we could only try to assure him that it wasn't the food that was at fault.

We stayed there for a miserable two hours until the waiters started making all the signs of wishing to clear and close up. But just as we were gathering ourselves together, retrieving our coats and cloaks, Ruslan Suvorov himself burst into the place. To me, he looked as if he had aged by ten years. It was surely hardly an amorous encounter that had detained him.

"I'm so sorry," he said. "Let me explain." And then spoke in Russian.

Whatever he said, it failed to satisfy his wife, who spoke back angrily to him, seized her wrap, and stormed out, followed by the Countess, who paused at the door to look back at us, a smirk on her face.

"Look after the ladies, Sergei," Suvorov urged his brother-in-law, and then sank down at the table, his head in his hands.

The Count hurried off, leaving only Benson and myself staring at each other, and at the man before us.

"Wherever did you disappear to?" the pianist asked at last. "I felt most ridiculous, standing there like a fool."

Suvorov shook his head.

"Of course, she didn't believe me," he said. "Why did I even think my stupid excuses would satisfy her?"

I sat down beside him.

"We are at a disadvantage here," I remarked gently. "Would you care to explain, Maestro?"

He raised his head to me.

"Dr. Watson, believe me. I am not in love with that Katya girl. Everything I do, I do for the sake of my wife and son. Their well-being is all to me. Let no one touch a hair of their heads . . . ." He sighed, evidently deeply troubled.

"Is it," I asked carefully, "anything to do with . . . the matter we discussed before?"

He stared up at me again, a wild look in his eyes. Then, to the astonishment of Benson and myself, he leapt up and raced out of the door.

"Well now . . ." the pianist said at last, absently picking up a *petit four* and popping it into his mouth. "What in Heaven's name was all that about?"

He looked at me as if expecting some explanation of my last words, the which I of course wasn't about to divulge. I just shook my head.

Leaving the restaurant – Signor Antonelli assuring us that the bill was settled, though I left a few coins on the table for the patiently waiting staff – I looked for a cab to take me back to Baker Street. It seemed that Benson was determined to accompany me.

"Yes," he said. "That's my direction too."

I should much have preferred to travel without the gentleman and his probing questions, and was relieved when he alighted at Baker Street Station, without, I might add, offering to pay his share of the fare. I last saw him ambling towards the Underground.

Back home, I was more than relieved to find Holmes, also apparently newly returned, about to light up his infernal pipe. I explained what had happened at the restaurant. He shook his head at the intelligence.

"Something is very amiss here. I fear something bad happened after that concert."

I asked him if he had discovered anything.

"I went back to the doorman to ask if he had recognised any distinguishing marks on the carriage taken by the two ladies, but without any luck. The man's powers of observation are even worse than yours, Watson. However, I am not entirely disheartened. The pair are very conspicuous and someone must surely have seen them. I have put Wiggins and the Irregulars on the case, and am hoping for enlightenment through them. By the way, do you recall that our friend, Suvorov, has been requested to play at a private function at the Russian Embassy?"

"Oh yes. He mentioned it when he was here. Is Benson accompanying him, I wonder?"

"I think not. Why do you ask?"

"Excellent pianist he may be, but I must say, I don't like the man. And not just because he is tight-fisted. I shouldn't be at all surprised to find he is up to something."

I was somewhat miffed at Holmes's reference to my supposed short-comings, and wished to show that I too was capable of useful insights.

"Hmm," Holmes said, dismissively. "Meanwhile, another chat with our violinist friend might be in order."

It was easier said than done. The next day, when we visited the hotel where the couple was staying, it transpired that the row between Suvorov and his wife had resulted in him being banished.

"I threw him out, Mr. Holmes," she remarked coldly, "I have no idea where he is now. No doubt with his mistress, Katya Maslinka."

"He assured me that his relations with that person weren't of that nature," I said.

"Ha!"

"I believed him," I continued.

"What other explanation can there be?"

"That, Madame," Holmes said, "is what we hope to find out."

"I pray to God you do."

We bowed and left her, trembling, tears in her eyes, looking out the window.

"Poor woman," I said.

In the hotel foyer, we found Count Razumov, stretched out in a chair, reading a paper and smoking a cigar, a cup of black coffee beside him. He jumped up at the sight of us.

"You have seen Tatiana," he said, in his broken English. "How she is?"

"Upset," Holmes replied abruptly. "We are wondering where her husband might be. Do you have any idea, Count?"

"No." He shrugged his shoulders. "I regret it."

"I understand he is to play for the Russian ambassador."

"Yes, tonight. Great honour."

"And will you be there as well."

"Alas, it is very private concert." He paused. "Someone so important will be visiting."

"From Russia?"

"I suppose. Some brother or cousin of the Tsar, I believe. Some Grand Duke." He waved a beautifully manicured hand in the air dismissively.

"I wonder," Holmes said, sitting down beside the man and lowering his voice, "if you can tell us more about this woman, Katya . . . ."

"Yekaterina Fyodorovna Maslinka! Claims to be daughter of rich Moscow merchant." He shook his sleek head. "I doubt. To me, she is creature of streets."

Surely not, I thought. From my admittedly brief glimpse of her, she seemed elegant, so refined.

"You are surprised, Doctor," Count Razumov remarked, smiling. "I assure you, it is truth. But forget her. It is old woman you must ask for, Mr. Holmes. That witch, Kuragina. Girl is just puppet, in my opinion. Sent to trap." He paused, and leaned forward. "You must know it. I trust my brother-in-law. He loves my sister true. But, well . . . ." That hand in the air again. "Who do people believe?"

"They do this to extort money?"

"Perhaps." He shrugged. "Who knows it?" He rustled the sheets of the newspaper as if to indicate that the interview was over.

"You don't, I suppose, happen to know where they are staying – this witch and her creature?"

"Sergei!" The Countess, silent as a cat, had come up behind us. Her voice was sharp enough, however.

"Ah, *voilà, ma cherie*! At last you are ready . . . My regrets, gentlemen."

We were dismissed, and left, bowing to the lady who barely acknowledged us.

"Did you notice," Holmes said as we exited onto Park Lane, "the man was reading *The Times*? Perhaps our friend's English is rather better than he makes out."

"Or perhaps he is just trying to improve his command of the language," I replied.

Holmes chuckled. "Watson, you are wonderful. Your practical common sense sweeps away my dark suspicions."

Back at Baker Street, Mrs. Hudson, with a shudder, told us "that boy" was waiting for us. Wiggins had returned and was in our landlady's kitchen – "Eating my biscuits like they're going out of fashion, Mr. Holmes!" – and generally getting in the way.

"Send him up to us, if you please, Mrs. Hudson," he told her.

The same Wiggins, biscuit crumbs adorning the front of his grubby jacket, was soon standing before us, very pleased with himself. One of his Irregulars had tracked the Russian women to a shabby hotel in Pimlico.

"The 'Otel Waldon, it is, Mr. 'Olmes. Not the sort o' place a fine lady usually stays in, 'er with all 'er furs and pearls. As for t'other old 'un . . . that figures, awl right."

"Is your man there now?" Holmes asked.

By "man" he meant some raggedy little shrimp, of course, but Wiggins accepted the designation as a right.

"'E is, Tommy is. And 'e won't leave off watchin' til you tells 'im to."

"There's no time to be lost," Holmes said, frowning. "I'll go there now. Wiggins, wait for me to change. And Watson, you stay here to see if there are any further messages from the Suvorovs."

I was a little put out to be assigned such a passive task, but I supposed Holmes had his reasons, and indeed, after he re-emerged from his bedroom, he was no longer recognisable as the eminent detective, but garbed much like an adult version of Wiggins, a labouring man, and somehow even suddenly grizzled. His ability to disappear completely into some guise or other never failed to astonish me: It is a skill I shall never fathom.

He was holding a piece of paper with scribbled writing on it.

"I'll get Mrs. Hudson to send Clara to the telegraph office with this," he told me, "so watch out for any reply. It's of primary importance."

The two of them, then, having bade me farewell, made their way out into the street. From the upstairs window, I watched them walk away, marvelling how Holmes's gait had even changed to a kind of stumbling limp. Assuredly the stage had missed an opportunity with him, consummate actor that he was.

Now all I had to do was wait, and fruitlessly at that because there was neither sight nor sound from the Suvorovs, nor from anyone else involved in the case. Three copies of *The Lancet*, hitherto unread, helped me pass the hours fairly well. I admit, however, that I frequently strayed to the window again, to see if Holmes or anyone else was heading my way.

242

The only person to arrive was the telegraph boy with a missive from Holmes that Clara brought up to me. I was tempted to open it, I admit, but of course did not. In fact, I must have finally dozed off, for I opened my eyes to find my friend standing over me, still in those rags, a quizzical expression on his face.

"I am sorry to disturb your nap," he said.

"Holmes!" I exclaimed. "Any news?"

He sat down and rubbed his dirt-encrusted hands together.

"I believe so." He grinned. "You are looking at the latest member of an anarchist cell operating out of the Hotel Waldon."

I nearly leaped out of my skin.

"Good Lord!"

"Well, maybe I'm getting ahead of myself . . . Knowing in advance the reputation of the place, I approached the reception desk in the person of an angry labourer recently made jobless on account of my radical politics, the sort these people like to recruit, along with disaffected intellectuals. At first, I was fobbed off by the oaf at the desk, but I persisted, and was finally allowed through to a back office, where a heavily bearded individual stared at me for a long time, unnerving me somewhat, I must confess.

"Heavily bearded!" I exclaimed. "Not Benson!"

Holmes sighed. "No, not Benson, however much you want it to be. This man was, I believe, Polish, and I must have convinced him to some extent . . . Oh, Watson," he smiled at the recollection, "you should have heard me rage against the evils of capitalism! My interlocutor, who omitted to introduce himself for obvious reasons, asked a load of questions and said I should call back in a day's time, after which I suppose he will have made full inquiries. No matter that they will lead nowhere. It has been enough to prove to me I am on the right track." He smiled at the memory. "Once outside I approached Wiggins's boy, as if to give him a coin (which in fact I did – he well-deserved it) in order to ask if the Russian women were still within. He told me they were, unless there was a way out the back. I am sure there is, but could see no good reason for them to use it. The women couldn't know, surely, that we are on to them."

"So, what does it all mean?" I asked. "And how does it relate to Ruslan Suvorov?"

"I think I know the answer to that, but confirmation is needed . . . Ah!" He had spotted the telegram. "There's a reply. Excellent! But now I must rid myself of this fancy-dress." And without another word, he disappeared into his bedroom, clutching the message.

How aggravating he was! He must have known how much I was dying to be enlightened. When he eventually emerged, clean, and in his usual "at home" garb of a mouse-coloured dressing-gown over an old pair of trousers, and sat down and reached for his pipe, I hoped at last to hear of his suspicions, as well as the contents of the mysterious telegram. All he told me, however, was that I was to go to the Hotel Waldron that evening, where I should hope to find the old Russian woman and perhaps her young protegée.

"If they aren't there, then one of Wiggins's boys can, I trust, take you to them."

It was hardly a role I relished.

"What then?"

"Stay with them, or at least with her – the witch. Never let her out of your sight. Oh, and take your revolver. Just in case."

"It's that serious?" I gaped at him.

"Who knows? Perhaps. Anyway, in that sort of a den, it's as well to be armed."

"Where will you be?"

"I," he replied, "will be attending a recital at the Russian Embassy. Close your mouth, Watson. You look quite foolish with it hanging open."

"Madame Kuragina, if you please!"

In response, the disreputable-looking individual seated behind what passed for a reception desk at the Hotel Waldron scratched his chin and shook his head.

"Never 'eard of 'er, Guv."

"Come now. That isn't true, is it?" I hoped I knew the sort he was, and slid a shining guinea across the counter to him. If he were part of the anarchist cell, he would surely not rise to the bait. Luckily for me, he was simply the venal creature he appeared to be.

"Oh, you mean the Russky!" he said, slapping his forehead with one dirty hand and sliding the coin off the desk with the other. "Room seven. First floor up them stairs, Guv. Or you can use the lift."

That structure looked decidedly unreliable, so I took the stairs and, without waiting for a reply to my knock, walked inside.

The room was permeated with an evil-smelling bluish fog emanating, as I soon realised, from the pipe the old woman was smoking. She didn't seem surprised or frightened to see me, but fixed me with a basilisk glare that would have turned me to stone if it could. She was not alone, though her companion wasn't young Katya but, to my enormous astonishment, none other than the Countess Razumova. For her part, that lady was considerably put out at the sight of me.

"Dr. Watson," she mumbled. "You here? Why?"

"I might ask the same of you, Countess."

She looked up at me, recovering her *sangfroid* quickly enough, taking on her usual arrogant mien.

"Kuragina . . . How you say it? She reads my fortune. Has gift."

She then said something in Russian to the old woman, who removed the pipe from her mouth, gave me another freezing look, and spat on the floor.

"What future did she see for you, then?" I asked, ignoring the disgusting gesture. "A good one, I trust."

The Countess shrugged. "But you . . . you want fortune read too, perhaps?"

She curled her lip, mocking me.

"No," I replied, laughing (trying to appear more at ease than I really was). "Just a friendly visit, you know."

I sat myself down in a chair between the women and the door.

Kuragina spoke again, quickly.

"But you aren't with friends here," the Countess said, as if translating. "Kuragina says please to go."

"Where is the charming Katya?" I asked.

"Oh, I see now . . . ." The Countess laughed nastily. "You want to be good friends with pretty young miss. Like all men."

I sat back. If that's what they thought, so be it.

"Well, as you see, she isn't here. She is at Russian Embassy. At concert,"

Was she indeed! How ever had she managed that?

"Ruslan insisted she be present!"

I should have liked to wipe that grin off her face, but instead we just stared at each other in silence for a while. Then a timepiece on the wall chimed the hour. Ten o'clock.

The old woman barked a laugh and muttered something.

"How sad," the Countess translated. "You understand, Dr. Watson, I know not what Kuragina means when she says, 'It is too late now.'"

"Too late for what?"

The Countess spoke Russian to the old woman and, listening to the reply, raised a gloved hand to her throat. I could tell she was suddenly frightened by what she heard.

"Tell me," I said.

"I cannot . . . I have not words in English."

"Say it in French then."

She gabbled out something in that tongue.

"More slowly, if you please."

"She says," (I translate) 'The pig is dead now.'"

"Who? Suvorov?"

245

"Perhaps, too. But she means Grand Duke."

The Countess stood up as the old woman babbled some more.

"I think she is mad. She says Ruslan will have stabbed the Grand Duke by now."

Kuragina started nodding and laughing a mocking, gloating laugh. Suddenly, the Countess made a dash for the door. I caught hold of her arm and pushed her back down on to her chair, then drew my revolver.

"You are going nowhere, either of you," I said.

At the sight of my weapon, Kuragina laughed all the more. The Countess, however, started shivering with terror.

"I know nothing of this, Doctor," she bleated, all dignity and arrogance gone from her. "I swear it on lifes of children."

"We'll have to wait and see," I said, wondering at the same time what I would do if the other denizens of the hotel decided to call upon the old woman. I felt myself to be in a horrible predicament but, for Holmes's sake and following his instructions, resolved to remain at my post, come what may.

It seemed an age, but eventually steps were heard on the stairs. I cocked my gun.

Kuragina smiled at me.

"Katya," she whispered. "Katyushka."

But it was not she. I confess, I was never more relieved in my life to see Inspector Lestrade and his constable than at that moment. Even now, the old woman was unmoved. She let herself be led from the room and down the stairs, quite docile. I followed behind, closely guarding the still-trembling Countess. In the lobby, we were confronted by a man wearing what I subsequently discovered to be Tsarist uniform. He addressed a few words to Kuragina, who on the instant fell back, emitting a terrible scream.

What happened next was frightful to witness. The old woman thrust something into her mouth and immediately started writhing in agony, foam boiling from her lips, eyes starting from her head, only to collapse at last in a heap of rags on the floor. I rushed forward to examine her. With her last strength, she bit my finger to the bone, then fell back, quite dead.

Now it was the Countess's turn to start screaming, until, someone – and I think it was Holmes, who had suddenly materialised – slapped her hard on the cheek, and she went silent.

A democratic group, we were all present in Mrs. Hudson's seldom-used front parlour: Holmes, myself, Mrs. Hudson, Clara and Phoebe, Maestro Suvorov, Madame Suvorova, and even Benson, who had somehow managed to tag along, and whom Mrs. Hudson subsequently complained of being as bad as Wiggins, eating all her scones.

246

It was just one day after the events described above. Holmes had returned from Scotland Yard only an hour since, bringing the visitors with him. I was of course most anxious to learn the details of the case, but meanwhile had to be patient and sit quietly with the others, listening entranced to the virtuosic tones of Paganini's *Caprices*, as interpreted by the maestro, now proudly wearing a medal on his coat.

After the improvised concert, we had tea, biscuits, and scones, together with a glass of neat vodka for the gentlemen, brought by our guests to be tossed back, Russian-style, in a toast. After the emotional thanks and farewells of the Russians, all bear hugs, kisses, and tears – even Mrs. Hudson, to that lady's great embarrassment, was subjected to such Continental manners – I could at last retire upstairs to the sitting room with Holmes to learn all.

It seemed that the Hotel Walden had been under scrutiny by The Powers That Be for some time. When the old woman and Katya moved in, interest was heightened, especially because of the forthcoming visit of the Grand Duke, a man distantly related to Queen Victoria, and especially hated by the anarchists. An attempt on his life was likely, but where and how was not evident. The man was always surrounded by guards. It was a lucky chance that we happened to observe a connection between Kuragina and Ruslan Suvorov and, knowing that the latter was to play in front of the Grand Duke at the Embassy, Holmes concluded this was likely to be where the attack was to take place.

True fanatics, of course, hold their own lives to be dispensable for the good of the cause but, from what we knew of him, Suvorov would not willingly agree to complicity in such an action, and not simply because it would prove fatal for him too. Holmes concluded that blackmail must be involved, and, in view of Suvorov's anguished words at the restaurant – "*Everything I do, I do for the sake of my wife and son. Their well-being is all to me. Let no one touch a hair of their heads.*" – as recounted back to him. ("And I thank you for that, Watson. Well noted.") – he suspected they had a hold over Suvorov by threatening his family.

He thereupon consulted (by that telegram) the British Government, already well-informed about the whole sorry business, and with connections ranged to the Russian Empire and, indeed, far beyond. The Government was able at once to pull certain strings. As a result, Ivan, Suvorov's son, was quickly removed from the hospital in Moscow where he was studying to a place of safety, and was even able to send a message to his parents, confirming this.

However, since no one knew where Suvorov had gone, the reassuring note couldn't be delivered immediately. It being too late to cancel the recital, Holmes was thus given a special dispensation to attend the

Embassy recital to convey in person the good news to the violinist. Suvorov fell upon his neck with relief.

"That vile creature, Kuragina, told me my son, darling Vanya, was already in their hands," he told Holmes. "How was I to know this was untrue? She said that he would be tortured and killed if I did not fulfil their wishes. She also threatened my beloved Tatiana, telling me no matter how I tried to protect her, she would never be safe."

The violinist then grasped Holmes's hand in his.

"Please understand that my own life would be as nothing if my beloved family was taken from me. Better I should die, even in disgrace, than that they should suffer."

He had then showed Holmes a stiletto, which had been secreted in his violin case. It was with this weapon, provided by the old woman, that he was to stab the Grand Duke, at the very moment when the latter was presenting him with the high Order of Alexander Nevsky, for his services to music.

"I was most relieved," Holmes told me, "to take charge of the deadly thing."

However, the plot was even then only partly thwarted. When Suvorov failed to execute the deed, Katya Maslinka, poor pawn that she was, jumped up shouting *"Trus! Trus!"* (the word apparently meaning *"Coward"*), and pulled out a pistol which she aimed at the Grand Duke, Luckily the gun misfired, but, in the ensuing fracas, the girl was fatally injured by one of the Grand Duke's entourage. It was that news – the death of her darling, rather than the failure of the plot – that had so overwhelmed Kuragina, driving her to swallow the poisoned pellet she kept hidden about her person.

"Really, Holmes," I said, nursing my throbbing finger. "What a position you put me in! I might have shot the old woman myself. Or the Countess. How was I to know the place was already crawling with Lestrade's men?"

Holmes leaned back, an amused smile playing on his lips.

"I could see how much you wanted to be involved, Watson," he replied. "You did well, my friend. She might still have slipped through our fingers, but for you."

I was only somewhat appeased.

"What of the Razumovs?" I asked.

"The Count is innocent of all involvement. He would hardly hurt his sister, whom he loves dearly. Moreover, his relations with his wife have been strained for a long time. That lady, however, is a different kettle of stinking fish. Entirely without morals or ideals, and in it for the money they gave her. I suspect she would have no qualms about poisoning her

248

sister-in-law, if paid to do so. A quantity of arsenic was found in her boudoir."

"Good gracious." I remarked, "How very Grand Guignol. The whole business, indeed, is like the plot of some preposterous melodrama."

"Russians," Holmes agreed. "Such a passionate people."

He seized his Stradivarius and started to attempt the Paganini, whereupon I made my excuses and set off for another calming stroll round the Regent's Park.

> *"But there are some pretty little problems among them. Here's . . . the adventure of the old Russian woman . . . ."*
>
> – Sherlock Holmes
> "The Musgrave Ritual"

The Adventure of the Silver Snail
by Alan Dimes

Mr. Sherlock Holmes and I were seated at the dining table in our sitting room at 221b Baker Street, smoking an after-breakfast pipe and perusing the morning newspapers, when Holmes gave vent to a short, barking laugh. I looked across at him questioningly. He folded his paper and proffered it to me, tapping the relevant section with the mouthpiece of his pipe.

"As a literary practitioner, dear Doctor, what do you make of that?"

I put down *The Telegraph*, took *The Courier* from him, and looked at the article. It read:

At the Supper Table
A weekly column by
The Daily Courier'*s restaurant critic*
Raymond Arnoux

> *Those of you who are gracious enough to peruse my little essays each week will know that I am not a man to mince my words. I state my conclusions in no uncertain terms. Indeed, how could it be otherwise, when it is my duty to act as a culinary advance guard, braving restaurants where the foot of cultured man has never before trod, and to bring back accurate reports of the wonders, or horrors, that I find there. If, therefore, my conclusions as set out in the following paragraphs seem harsh and acerbic, you may nevertheless rest assured that the establishment in question deserves every iota of the opprobrium I heap upon it.*

> *Like many, I was full of anticipation when I learned that a new French restaurant, L'Auberge de Jehan Cottard, was due to open at 17 Moulton St, Fitzrovia, W. In accordance with my usual policy, I allowed the new enterprise a grace period of two weeks before visiting its premises for the purposes of assessing its value as a venue for the consumption of comestibles worthy of the sophisticated palate. It cannot be gainsaid that the proprietors have made a conspicuous effort*

to ensure that the decor and ambience are redolent of Magny's or Le Grand Vefour. The waiters are modest, efficient, and inconspicuous, the linen spotless, the cutlery and glassware impeccable."

"It seems somewhat verbose and pretentious," I said.

"Two characteristics which are at least conspicuously absent from the modest products of your own pen."

"Thank you. I think. Does he ever get around to mentioning the bill of fare?"

"Read on."

The food, on the other hand, can only be described as execrable. My devoted readers will no doubt recall that it is my custom to always order la specialite d'hote *and the most expensive item on the wine list. The latter, a Chateau Leoville Bordeaux 1864, was excellent, and, indeed, was the only element of the entire experience which prevented me from running screaming into the night.*

"I think the point is made. He doesn't recommend the place. Does anybody pay attention to this pompous windbag?"

"Oh, you'd be surprised," said Holmes. "Apparently, there are quite a few people in polite society who regard his convoluted verbiage as 'good writing' and hang on his every word."

He sighed.

"Well, it provided me with a minute or two of harmless amusement. Anything of interest in *The Telegraph*?"

"Nothing that would concern you, or I would have brought it to your attention."

I glanced across at the clock on the mantelpiece.

"It's only a quarter-to-nine, Holmes. Who knows what the day may bring?"

No sooner were the words out of my mouth than there was a ring at the doorbell, and within minutes we were plunged into a case of paramount importance which, after the passage of a suitable amount of time, may be the subject of one of these narratives. It was, in any event, of sufficient urgency and complexity to drive any remaining thought of Raymond Arnoux completely out of our minds, and it wasn't until several months later that he was thrust once more into our attention, and we found ourselves investigating the murder of the restaurant critic of *The Daily Courier.*

Regular readers of these humble sketches may have noticed that my distinguished friend had a certain affinity with France, and the French. His maternal grandmother had been the sister of the famous French artist, Horace Vernet. His knowledge of French literature far exceeded his acquaintance with that of England, and he could quote freely from Flaubert, Zola, and Georges Sand. And it should be noted that while he refused a knighthood from the English Crown on more than one occasion, he was happy to accept the Order of the *Legion d'Honneur* from the French President, in recognition of his vital part in the arrest of Huret, the infamous boulevard assassin.

One of the ways in which this Gallic connection manifested itself was in a liking for French food. We did not dine out exclusively in French restaurants, but we could usually be found in such establishments two or three times a month. One particular favourite of Holmes was *L'Escargot D'Argent* – in English, *The Silver Snail*. It was small, tucked away in a cul-de-sac in Covent Garden called Little Burbage Street. As well as the attractions of its excellent food, it was a convenient place to dine because of its proximity to the Opera House.

Holmes had had no clients for a week, and I had suggested to him that as a means of occupying himself, he should finish a monograph he had left half-completed on the specialized argots of various professions. He acceded, and spent the next two days researching the subject, riffling through his records of past cases, his own and others', and making copious notes. At last he put pen to paper, and late in the afternoon he stood up from his desk and stretched his long arms.

"You've finished it?" I asked.

"Well, I shall read it through once more tomorrow morning before I send it to the publisher, but I am certainly done for today. How does the idea of an evening out appeal to you?"

"Very much."

Holmes rang the bell, and when Mrs. Hudson appeared, he informed her that we wouldn't be in for dinner, a courtesy which, it has to be said, he didn't always extend to her.

We made our leisurely way on foot to Little Burbage Street, the evening being fresh and clear.

L'Escargot d'Argent was founded, owned, and managed by one Theophile Dumont, who had come to London in 1872. Born in Le Havre, he had fought in the Franco-Prussian War. He survived several of the great battles of that conflict with a few wounds, none of them with any permanent effects other than scars, and after the Battle of Sedan he decided that rather than remain in a country suffering the ill-effects of defeat, he would go to London. He was charmed by the ambience of Covent Garden and its environs and decided to open a restaurant there, which he did with some financial assistance from his parents. Two old friends from his student days, Maurice Leclerc and Alphonse Duvivier, came from Paris to join him as chef and head waiter. Within two years, all had married Englishwomen, assuring their permanent residence in the capital and the continued existence of L'Escargot d'Argent. The place was not, as yet, well known, but had numerous regular patrons, which maintained its success.

It was relatively small for a restaurant, being of enough size to accommodate some twenty diners at one time. The walls were faced with pine and decorated simply with framed photographs of Parisian locales, theatrical posters, and the occasional painting donated by the artist, for, like his fellow-restaurateurs across the Channel, Dumont would often accept a work of art in lieu of payment for a meal. The furniture was of a basic design, and the tablecloths were cotton checkerboards of red and white.

Alphonse Duvivier was a short, slim individual with black hair smoothed to the back of his head and an impressive waxed moustache that ended in two diminutive curls. When Holmes and I entered the restaurant, he came up and greeted us effusively.

"Ah, Monsieur Holmes! And Doctor Watson! Once more you honour us with your presence! It is very pleasant to see you again! Marcel!" he said, clicking his fingers to summon one of the white-uniformed waiters who were gliding efficiently between the tables with their trays of food and wine.

"You remember the famous detective and his colleague?"

"*Bien sur.* Good evening, gentlemen."

Marcel was also somewhat below average height and, like his superior, sported a moustache. His accent was not that of a Parisian, but I couldn't place it.

"Show Mr. Holmes and Doctor Watson to the window table, and take their order."

After we were comfortably seated, and the little waiter had hurried off to fetch a bottle of wine to accompany our meals, Holmes smiled and said, "Marseilles."

"I beg your pardon?"

"Marcel is from Marseilles, in the *departement* of Bouches-du-Rhone As I have said many times, your face is an extremely accurate barometer of your thoughts. Marcel has seen us here before, but has never served us, so you hadn't heard him speak. You know that Alphonse is Parisian, and I could see that you were a little puzzled by the difference in accents."

253

He then gave a brief discourse, to which I listened avidly, on the regions of the French nation and the variations in stress, intonation, and modulation to be found in the accents of each of them.

The waiter returned with our wine and two plates of *vichyssoise*, which we consumed in silence. Then, during the main course, Holmes drew my attention to a new poster on one of the walls, and we embarked on a conversation which began with the career of Jean-Eugène Robert-Houdin and wandered from there to the conquests of the Roman Emperor Aurelian and the likely effects of devaluation on any given currency. I was about to express my own thoughts on the latter subject when the character of the evening was radically changed.

Two men had entered L'Escargot D'Argent while Holmes and I were eating our *vichyssoise*, and I had glanced idly over at them as one of the waiters seated them at a table near the back of the restaurant.

The first was a slim, dapper man of the middle height. The uniform colour and sheen of his thick black hair led one to suspect that they were the result of dye. His features were regular, but his facial expression was one of barely suppressed disdain. His companion appeared to be about ten years older and was about the same height, but rather rotund. His clothes were neither as well-fitting nor of as good quality as that of his companions, and he was carrying a little leather briefcase. His hair was greying, with a distinct bald patch at the back, and I had the impression that for some reason he wasn't comfortable with his surroundings.

After a few minutes, the hum of conversation in the restaurant came to an abrupt end as both men uttered piercing cries. The first slid to the floor and lay prostrate, while the other fell forward onto the table a moment later, his arms outstretched. Heads were turned in curiosity and stayed fixed in horror.

"It seems there is work for us," said Holmes, rising to his feet. "Come, Watson."

Together we hurried to the table where the two men lay inert. I knelt beside the man on the floor and felt his neck for a pulse. There was none. I stood and performed the same action on the other.

"This man is still alive. We must call an ambulance."

"And the police," said Holmes. "Did they have soup?" he asked the white-faced young waiter who had served the pair.

"They both started with *vichyssoise*, and then they had *tournedos Rossini*. And they shared a bottle of Pinot Noir."

Holmes nodded. The bottle of wine stood half-finished on the table, and the two men had clearly just started eating the tournedos.

"The soup plates will have been washed, I suppose."

"Not necessarily, Monsieur Holmes, but there will be a pile of them, and it will be impossible to say which came from this table."

One of the other diners rose and questioned Holmes. "Is it poison?"

"That would seem to be the most likely cause of death," he admitted.

"Food poisoning? Are we all in danger?"

"They had exactly the same meal, but whatever it was is unlikely to have been in the main course, because they had hardly eaten any," said Holmes. He then turned and addressed everyone present "Did anyone else have the *tournedos Rossini*?"

Several diners had, but had eaten them and gone on to their desserts with no ill-effects.

"That leaves the *vichyssoise* and the wine."

"Surely it must have been the wine," I said. "We both had the *vichyssoise*, and we're unharmed, to say nothing of all the others here who must have had it."

"If he has been poisoned," said one of the waiters, gesturing to the unconscious man at the table, "shouldn't we give him something to make him bring it up?"

"No, no," I interjected quickly, "that would be the worst thing to do. We don't know yet what type of poison it was, if it was. When it comes back up it could get into his lungs, or damage his oesophagus. They'll know what to do at the hospital."

A horse-drawn vehicle from the St. John Ambulance Brigade arrived to take the survivor to University College Hospital, followed shortly by the police in the person of one Inspector Lanner, an alert, eager young Scotland Yard Inspector who had called on Holmes for assistance more than once in the recent past. He was accompanied by his sergeant, Ross, a burly ex-military man, and two uniformed constables.

The next to arrive was Theophile Dumont, a tall, imposing man with the traditional ample girth of the successful restaurateur. He hadn't been present at the restaurant but entered now, in an advanced state of agitation, having been summoned by Alphonse. He went from table to table, assuring the customers that under the circumstances they wouldn't be charged for their meal. On reaching the table where we sat, he seized Holmes's hand and cried, "Ah, praise be to *le bon Dieu* that you are here! I confess, I don't trust your English police. But you, Monsieur Holmes, surely you can solve this crime and save my restaurant from shame and ruin?"

Holmes gently disengaged his hand from Dumont's.

"I'm afraid that we must leave the matter to the official force for the time being. If they cannot find the culprit, I promise that I will take up the case. At the moment, however, Monsieur Dumont, I am afraid that Dr. Watson and I are merely witnesses."

Holmes stayed in communication with Lanner for the next week. That was how we learned that the murdered man was restaurant critic Raymond Arnoux. The other man, Charles Morgan, had the same occupation, writing for another newspaper, *The Daily Clarion*. The remaining wine, and the two glasses, had been examined and yielded no trace of poison, although the police autopsy had confirmed that this was the cause of death. The lethal substance was *botulin*, which has the twin advantages, so far as the malefactor is concerned, of being both odourless and tasteless, and easily manufactured, so that unlike arsenic, for example, it need not be purchased at a chemist's, where a record would be made of its sale.

At the end of the week, Lanner called on us, looking rather haggard and woebegone.

"I have my theories, Mr. Holmes," he said, as he took a seat in our living-room, "but no solid evidence to back them up."

Holmes reached for one of his pipes and filled the bowl with tobacco.

"Pray tell me what they are, then," he said, striking a match.

"Well," the inspector began, "French-speaking waiters are a close-knit group. There cannot be more than a hundred of them in the whole of London. Arnoux is at least indirectly responsible for the failure of quite a few restaurants over the last few years. A brother, or a close friend, or the murderer himself, loses a job when one fails, and the killer fixates on the person he holds responsible. The waiter comes to work at L'Escargot d'Argent, and when Arnoux books a table, the murderer sees his time has come."

"Is that feasible?" I asked.

"Oh, yes," said Holmes. "And in terms of motive, waiters who have been employed by the same restaurant for a long time can feel a great sense of loyalty toward the place, and their employers. Ask Alphonse Duvivier. Presumably you have questioned the waiter who served Morgan and Arnoux?"

"Thoroughly, and he would seem to be in the clear. He has only worked there for two weeks, and in fact has only been in London for three. I sent his name and description to the *Sûreté*, and they confirmed his identity. The other person I concentrated on was the chef, Maurice Leclerc, and he most definitely had a motive, of the kind I mentioned earlier. His younger brother had had followed him to London and was employed as the chef at the Auberge de Jehan Cottard, which closed down not long after Arnoux gave it a particularly scathing review, and after that no other restaurateur would employ him."

It was at that point that I recalled the conversation Holmes and had had some months before, and it struck me that to one of a passionate Gallic temperament, that might indeed be motive enough for murder.

"I questioned him long and hard," continued Lanner, "but he didn't break."

"The problem is method, not motive, at least for the moment," said Holmes. "How did the botulin get into the soup, for that is surely where the poison was? If it was done by the chef, or by the waiter, it is difficult to see how it could be carried out without the complicity of the other. The waiter knows to whom he is serving the soup, but how does he get the lethal dose into it without being sure that he will not be seen? True, he is in the middle of the busy kitchen, or the equally busy restaurant, but he is either holding one plate in each hand, or bearing both on a tray. The poison is presumably in a vial or some other small receptacle which he must take from a pocket and pour into the *vichyssoise*. How can he do that without setting down the plates?

"Now let us consider the chef. You will recall that *vichyssoise* is served with a garnish of chopped chives, which is added just before serving the soup. Under cover of this action, it would be easy for him to add the poison. The problem then would be that, unless the waiter were an accomplice, the chef couldn't possibly be sure that the poisoned soup would go to the correct table."

"But why poison both of them," I objected, "if Arnoux was his target?"

"Possibly the killer didn't know him by sight," said Lanner. "He'd have to kill both of them to be sure of Arnoux's death."

"A reasonable assumption," said Holmes.

"Kill an innocent man to ensure the death of a guilty one?" I expostulated.

"It would hardly be without precedent," replied Holmes, "and recent history provides us with several examples. In Adelaide in 1879, Thomas Hawkins killed a pair of twin brothers. He discovered that one of them had seduced his sister, to whom he had an unhealthy attachment. She sought to protect her lover by pretending she didn't know which twin it was, so he murdered both of them. Then there's the case of Sven Jorgenson in Stockholm in '83. He poisoned a dinner party of twelve people by putting strychnine in the dessert. It was revealed at the trial that he only had a motive for killing one of them. And only last year, the case of Wing Fat in San Francisco was along similar lines. But let us not forget, Charles Morgan is still alive, is he not, Lanner?"

"He's still in University College Hospital. They'll be letting him out in a few days, apparently."

The next morning Holmes stood up immediately after breakfast and put on his light summer jacket.

257

"You are going out?" I inquired.

"Yes, to Scotland Yard, and then to L'Escargot D'Argent."

"You have, then, some clue to the solution of this mystery?"

"Like our friend Lanner, I have a theory which must be put to the test. If it rings true, then I will ask you to accompany me to University College Hospital this afternoon. That is, of course, unless you have more pressing business of your own to conduct."

"Holmes, you know full well that I am currently without a practice," I said with not a little irritation.

"So, I can rely on your presence. Until this afternoon, then."

Having lived with Holmes for this long, I was, I presume, more sensitive to his changing moods than any other man alive, but I confess that when he returned to Baker Street at about two o'clock, I found it difficult to discern his frame of mind. As we rattled in a hansom through the crowded streets of London en route to the hospital, it seemed to me that behind his stoic mask there were signs of both triumph and frustration. No doubt, I told myself, there would be answers at our destination. And so it proved.

There was a middle-aged nurse on duty at the hospital reception desk. Holmes gave her his most winning smile and said, "May we see Charles Morgan? We are friends of his, and we have his briefcase."

I had of course noticed what he had been carrying, but as I had seen it only briefly at the restaurant, I hadn't made the connection. Now he held it up so that the nurse could see the little letters "*C.M.*" where they were embossed into the leather surface just below the closed flap.

"He left it at the restaurant that night. Understandably. How is he?"

"He's still a bit weak, but well enough to have visitors. He's in a private room on the second floor. 24-A."

We climbed the stairs and found the room. Morgan lay on his back in bed, dressed in a blue-and-white hospital gown and in a state of half-sleep. He looker older and fatter, and more out of shape than he had in his suit in the restaurant

"Morgan!" Holmes said in a loud, clear voice. The journalist sat up and rubbed his bleary eyes.

"What is it?" he said. "Who are you?"

"You may have heard of us. I am Sherlock Holmes, and this is my friend and colleague Dr. John Watson. You left your briefcase behind at L'Escargot D'Argent. I had to go to Scotland Yard to pick it up. They thought it might be evidence."

"Oh, thank you. But evidence of what?"

"There were a couple of things in it. The police couldn't understand, but to me those two things suggest, although it cannot be proven, that you killed Raymond Arnoux."

Morgan's face twisted into a mask of contempt.

"What on earth are you talking about? Killed him? I nearly died myself."

"Yes, and it seemed odd to me that a man both older and demonstrably less healthy should survive when a younger, fitter man succumbed. You put your own life at risk in order to take his. That indicates a powerful hatred. What was it, Morgan? Professional jealousy of a richer, more successful restaurant critic? A woman, perhaps, whom you wanted and he had? You may as well tell me. I have already told you I can't prove anything."

"I'm telling you nothing." Morgan paused. "There's nothing to tell. And even if there were, I'm not stupid enough to say it in front of two people. That would be tantamount to a confession."

"Very well." Holmes opened the briefcase and reached into it. "Exhibits *A* and *B*."

Morgan gave a false laugh.

"A pair of soup spoons? Are you insane? What does that prove?"

"Let us use the word 'suggest' rather than 'prove'. As you say, two soup spoons, from L'Escargot D'Argent. And, like all the cutlery in that establishment – " Holmes turned them so that Morgan could see the backs of the handles. " – stamped with the letters '*E*' and '*A*'. Now, I went back to the restaurant this morning and, with the kind permission of the manager, examined all the spoons. I found two that had plain backs."

Morgan arched one eyebrow sardonically.

"And what does that 'suggest' to you?"

"It suggests that when you arrived at the restaurant, you had the two plain-handled spoons in your briefcase. You had coated them both with botulin. You had them in separate compartments so that you knew which had the fatal, and which the non-fatal dose. At some point you replaced the restaurant spoons with the poisoned ones, not realising that they weren't identical. Perhaps Arnoux unwittingly made it easier for you by going to the men's room. He ordered first, and you had the same. You knew that by the time the botulin took effect, the spoons would either have been washed or be lying in a pile with many others waiting to be washed, and indistinguishable from them at a casual glance."

"Bravo," said Morgan. "An excellent piece of fiction."

"You are neither as clever nor as original as you may imagine. You are hardly the first murderer by poison who has taken a dose himself to throw the law off the scent. There was Coleraine in Bristol in 1854, and Steiner in Metz in 1873, to cite just two examples. You have escaped punishment on this occasion, but – " Holmes moved a little closer to the bed and lifted an admonitory finger. " – be warned. My eyes are upon you. If you perpetrate any other such crime, I will not hesitate to take the law into my own hands and punish you accordingly."

"Both those eventualities seem unlikely," said Morgan with an unpleasant smile. "And now, I'd like to sleep. Please leave."

I accompanied Holmes out into the cold, antiseptic corridor. I was chilled by the implication of his last words to Morgan, but said nothing. I knew he had spoken the strict truth, for justice was his concern, not the letter of the law.

Holmes informed Lanner of his conclusions, and the inspector agreed that under the circumstances, nothing could be done. Nevertheless, the tale has a sequel. After Arnoux's death, Morgan became the restaurant critic of *The Daily Courier*. Had he known that he would be the likely successor to the dead man's position? Had he feigned friendship and invited Arnoux to L'Escargot D'Argent with that result in mind? Two weeks after starting with his new paper, a fire broke out at a restaurant he had been sent to review. The crowded dining room of Il Piatto d'Oro had suddenly filled with billowing smoke, and although some of the diners had gone to hospital suffering from smoke inhalation, none of them had died. None, that is, except for Charles Morgan.

As for Theophile Dumont, the unsolved murder didn't destroy his restaurant business, as he had expected. In fact, so many people were interested to dine at the establishment where it had taken place that he was obliged to expand L'Escargot D'Argent and bring in more tables. Even after twenty years, Dumont exclaimed, he still didn't understand the English character.

"My collection of M's is a fine one," said he. "Moriarty himself is enough to make any letter illustrious, and here is Morgan the poisoner . . . ."

– Sherlock Holmes
"The Empty House"

The Adventure of the
Invisible Weapon
by Arthur Hall

As I entered our sitting room one bright autumn morning, I was prepared to find my friend, Mr. Sherlock Holmes, engulfed by one of the black moods that I had come to know well. Declining my company and assistance, he had spent the preceding night with Inspector Lestrade in the capture of the notorious Beecham Gang as they attempted to rob the Agricultural and Cattle Farmers Bank by means of a tunnel from a neighbouring shop. Holmes had correctly discerned not only their intentions, but their method and timing of the crime. Consequently, the apprehension of the gang had been effected smoothly by a group of armed constables, and the good inspector had once again added to his formidable record with the approval of my friend.

So it was that I fully expected Holmes to be of a disagreeable state of mind, either as a result of lack of sleep, or because no further case had yet presented itself. I saw that he had consumed his breakfast already and that mine stood awaiting me, a steaming plate upon the table.

"I heard you moving about in your room, and took the liberty of ordering your meal, knowing you would present yourself in a few moments. I hope you have no objection."

"None." I reflected that his tone was lighter than I had anticipated, although he had failed to begin with his usual greeting. The post had evidently arrived, since his eyes had not left the letter he held as he spoke and a small pile of others awaited his attention.

"Interesting," he murmured as he placed the folded sheet aside.

"Did last night's venture proceed well?" I asked him.

His expression lightened. "Exceedingly so. Lestrade was overjoyed, as he has been in pursuit of the gang for a good while. They have eluded him twice within the last six months."

"But no more." I began to eat my bacon and eggs, and then said, "I recall that you mentioned yesterday that you have no other matters on hand, so may I suggest a bracing walk in Regent's Park to begin our day?"

"Had you made that proposal but a minute or two earlier, I would have acquiesced instantly, but I have just read of the problem of Miss Rachel Tarleton of Kirkenfield, near Canterbury. Pray finish your meal and you can then peruse her letter."

I consumed my toast and drank my coffee at a faster rate than I would have otherwise, for I was anxious to see what it was that had captured my friend's interest so quickly. As I pushed my cup away, he handed me the sheet of good-quality notepaper that, I had already noticed, was slightly perfumed. I straightened my posture and observed that, for a woman's hand, the script was boldly formed.

Deacon Hall, Kirkenfield

My Dear Mr. Sherlock Holmes,

Please, I need your help desperately. I am going mad with fear.

My father was murdered on his birthday, six months ago, within this house.

My mother was murdered, on her birthday, three months ago, also within this house.

A week from now is my own birthday, so you will see why I am concerned.

I know of no reason for these tragic events, and our local police force seems to have made no progress from the first. I apologise for this intrusion but, truly, I have nowhere else to turn.

I have heard much about your remarkable powers, so if there is anything you can do, or any advice you can give me that might relieve me of the shadow that hangs over me, then I entreat you to act now, while I still live.

Yours in sincerity and hope,

Miss Rachel Tarleton

"Well, Watson, what do you make of it?" He had rested his chin on steepled fingers, and his eyes glinted.

"The girl, if she is young enough to be called that, is clearly in a state of panic. If her account is true, that is hardly surprising." I saw in his gaunt features, that he had already decided the matter. "I assume you would like me to accompany you to Kent?"

"If you would be so kind, and have nothing better to do." .

"I am at your service, of course."

He rose from his chair, his half-empty cup abandoned. "Excellent. Perhaps then you would care to pack a bag for two or three nights, while I prepare a telegram to inform Miss Tarleton of our impending arrival. I overheard Mrs. Hudson speaking to the page earlier, so there should be no delay in its dispatch."

Less than an hour later, we stood on a busy platform in Victoria Station. Holmes had procured the tickets on arrival.

"I have reserved a compartment in a smoker. It's a short journey, and we should be comfortable."

I heard the train approach, and we moved further back as it appeared with billows of smoke and a screech of brakes. When the passengers had alighted, there was a great surge towards the coaches by the crowd that surrounded us. We settled into a compartment that smelled faintly of cigar smoke, the worn leather seats creaking under our weight. The train began to move almost immediately, our surroundings changing from the built-up capital to the leafy suburbs by the time we lit our pipes.

"This sounds like a bad business," I said. "A curious affair."

Holmes adjusted his thin body to a position where he could more-easily see the ever-changing view. "The culprit, of course, is someone close to Miss Tarleton's family."

"Because the murderer is familiar with the birthdays of her and her parents?"

"Precisely. Also, as far as we can tell right now, it must be someone living in the same house, since there is no mention of intruders. But we shall see."

Little else passed between us during the journey to Canterbury. From there we caught the local train after a wait of no more than fifteen minutes, to arrive at the tiny Kirkenfield Station just before mid-day. A trap awaited us, driven by a cheerful and stout fellow who announced himself rather grandly as Ricketts, formerly coachman and groom serving Mr. Godfrey Tarleton and his wife, and now in the service of Miss Tarleton.

"Has the purpose of our visit been disclosed to you?" Holmes asked him as we passed the small cluster of shops that surrounded the station.

"Yes sir, yes indeed. There have been terrible things happening at Deacon Hall of late, and now Miss Rachel is in fear of her life as her birthday approaches."

"Your local inspector, I understand, could make nothing of the killings."

"Inspector Willis, between you and me, sir, is no longer the man he once was. He is very close to retiring, which is why we were relieved when he requested that Scotland Yard send a man here. Not that much light was shed upon the matter, I'm sorry to say. The fellow was shortly summoned back to London with nothing achieved."

"Do you recall his name?" I enquired.

"He announced himself as Inspector Denning. From the little he said, I gather that he has recently attained that rank, and was sent to us until a more experienced officer becomes available. This we are still expecting."

"Until then," Holmes said dryly, "we will see what progress can be made."

By now, we had left behind the green lanes and open fields to come upon a wide stony coastal path. The crashing of the sea against the cliff and the squawk of swooping seabirds were clearly audible as our talkative driver turned the trap into a sharp curve, passing weathered animal heads that were no longer recognisable atop tall gate-posts. I saw that sheep were abundant, dotting the distant landscape.

The approach was a short climb, with low-hanging oaks and willows intruding from both sides. Deacon Hall was not as I had imagined it to be, my expectation being a former manor house or grand residence such as Holmes and I had been summoned to on many past occasions. In fact, the building was best described as the remains of a Norman castle, doubtless originally intended to act as a seaward watchtower against invading fleets. Some of the battlements and outer quarters were missing, but the tall keep stood solidly before us. Ricketts brought the trap to a halt and unloaded our bags as we alighted, before leading the horse away to be watered. At the same moment, the great iron-studded door swung open, and an elderly butler appeared briefly, before a young woman in riding clothes strode past him and approached us.

"Mr. Holmes." She looked first at my friend, then myself, and back again. "I'm so relieved that you answered my call for help. I cannot begin to thank you both."

"That is quite unnecessary," he replied. "Allow me to introduce my friend and colleague, Doctor John Watson, whose assistance has been invaluable on many such occasions."

The enjoyment that I felt at his description was quickly replaced by mild amazement as Miss Rachel Tarleton acknowledged me. I saw at once that she was not the frightened, wilting woman that I had imagined on reading her letter, but in her face was strength and determination.

"Welcome to Deacon Hall, gentlemen," she said then. "Pray follow Brookes, who will show you to your rooms, where I'm sure you will wish to spend half-an-hour recovering from your journey. Luncheon will be served immediately after."

She strode away abruptly, leaving Holmes and myself somewhat surprised, despite her words of thanks. Brookes proved to be surprisingly sprightly for his age, and he guided us to two pleasant rooms on the first floor that overlooked the sea. Within the stated half-hour, we assembled in the dining room that had been apparent to us from the reception chamber earlier. Miss Tarleton, still in riding apparel, was already seated at the long table.

I will not go into detail regarding the most pleasant luncheon. Suffice it to say, Holmes excelled himself in its consumption, though he refused dessert. The conversation was limited to the history of the house, with Miss Tarleton's response to my enquiry.

"Finally," she concluded, "the original family who had owned the castle since the Norman Conquest became extinct. The man who eventually bought the estate was a churchman, Deacon Berrywell, after whom it was renamed. At his death, during the fourteenth century, my ancestor, Gilbert Tarleton, became the owner, and it has been our family home to this day."

Holmes returned his coffee cup to its saucer. "A most interesting and informative account, and I thank you for it. Perhaps you would now explain more fully to Watson and myself the circumstances that caused you to summon us? You have our assurance that we will assist you in any way that we can."

"A moment, and I will explain." She called for Brookes who, accompanied by a kitchen maid who appeared to be approaching middle-age, quickly cleared the table. Wine was brought, but only Miss Tarleton partook.

She took a long draught and set down her glass. "I realise that your impression of me from my letter, and from what you must perceive as my lack of grief at the loss of my parents, is likely to meet with your disapproval, gentlemen." She looked to our faces for response and, finding none, continued. "I should perhaps mention that we have never been what might be described as a 'close family', and that we have always produced strong women." She paused. "Nevertheless, I wrote to you with words of truth. For the first time in my life, I confess to being terrified."

"I have already stated that we will do all in our power to put things right," Holmes said with a trace of impatience. "Pray tell us from the beginning of the events here, leaving out not the smallest detail."

She nodded and spoke quietly after a moment's hesitation. "As I've indicated, we aren't a family to be trifled with. Past generations have enjoyed connections to the highest quarters, and many were prominent in their day. My mother once hunted tigers in India, while her sister, Esther, bravely led an expedition across the African continent which, to our great regret, never returned."

Holmes held up a hand, surprising me, as I had expected him to advise her to confine herself to the facts of the case, "Can you recall your age at the time of this venture?"

265

"My age?" she repeated. "Why, I expect that I was no more than eight years old. Aunt Esther herself had yet to reach her twentieth birthday, but I remember her as a formidable woman. My parents would often argue with her over her allowance, and sometimes concerning the silliest things."

"Thank you. Pray continue when you are ready."

"Ah yes," she said, as if suddenly aware of wandering from the point of discussion, "The murders. Six months ago, Brookes took my father his customary glass of sherry, as he did before luncheon on every birthday, and found him dead in his sitting room chair. His eyes were wild, as if he had witnessed a horrible and unexpected truth, and it was apparent that he had been stabbed through the heart. Three months later, on the occasion of my mother's birthday, she died in exactly the same circumstances, except that she was engaged in embroidery in the same room."

"When you specify identical circumstances," I said, "are we to understand that the chair was the same, and even the time of day?"

"Excellent, Watson," Holmes murmured.

"That is what I meant," she confirmed. "Except for Brookes' purpose in attending her, which was to bring coffee, the event was repeated. She also was stabbed through the heart as my father had been. The police were summoned at once, on *both* occasions. Our local inspector seemed baffled and sent to Scotland Yard for assistance, but the officer who arrived was recalled after a short while, having reached no conclusions that I know of." At this point, I noticed that a slight tremor had entered her voice for the first time. "You will see then, gentlemen, with my own birthday no more than a week away, why I fear for my life. The murderer of my parents was never seen, nor is his purpose clear."

Holmes's eyes, which had been half-closed as he listened, opened fully and glistened. "You actually saw the bodies of your unfortunate parents, yourself?"

"I did. I am not one to shrink from such things."

"They were both sitting in the same chair, in a similar position?"

"I have said so."

"Did your mother have a fearful expression, as your father did?"

"She looked . . . confused, as well as terrified."

Holmes nodded thoughtfully. "Pray take us to the room where the deaths took place."

"Certainly." Miss Tarleton rose to her feet, and we did likewise.

We followed her from the dining room and across a corridor to a chamber directly opposite. The sounds emanating from further along the passage, and the aromas, caused me to conclude that the kitchen was situated nearby. Ideal, I recognised, since its close proximity to the dining room would ensure that food was served promptly with little time to cool.

The sitting room was large and high-ceilinged, tastefully decorated, and dominated by a huge fireplace with several armchairs at either side. A long sideboard, laden with bottles and a water carafe, took up almost the length of one wall.

Miss Tarleton indicated the chair in which her parents had spent their last moments, and my friend examined it from every angle, pressing and poking the upholstery here and there.

"Can you remember anything else that was common to both tragedies?" he enquired.

She considered, briefly. "Only the streaks of blood."

Holmes inclined his head. "Pray elaborate."

"There were bloody stripes on both my father and mother's right shoulder. As if they had been marked for some purpose. That's all."

"One 'stripe' on each?"

"Yes, I'm sure of that. Is it significant?"

"It is an example of the necessity of including even the slightest detail when reconstructing a crime."

"You have said that no sign whatsoever was seen of the murderer," I reminded her.

"That is so. It could have been a ghost."

I saw a quick smile flit across Holmes's face as I continued.

"Was the weapon ever discovered?"

She shook her head. "Never. That is as much of a mystery as the murders themselves."

"Very well," Holmes said presently. "Miss Tarleton, you may leave us to begin our enquiry, if you would be so kind. It would be helpful to interview your butler, Brookes, if he is available."

"You wish to conduct the exchange here in this room?"

"It would be convenient, I think."

"Then I'll send him to you."

The elderly retainer joined us shortly and was bade to sit, which he did reluctantly.

"May I ask how long you've served the Tarleton family?" Holmes enquired, standing beside me near the fireplace.

"To tell the truth sir, I have quite forgotten. I was little more than a lad when I came to Deacon Hall."

"Quite so. I take it that there is no other manservant."

"That has always been so, sir."

Holmes nodded. "Kindly tell us how many others are employed here at this time."

Brookes reflected. "In recent years, their numbers have been reduced. Apart from myself there is the cook, Rowena, Miss Tarleton's maid,

Kathleen, the kitchen maid, Elizabeth, and various outside staff such as the groom, Ricketts, and the stable boys." His expression became nostalgic. "We are a small household these days, sir."

"How long has Miss Tarleton's maid held her position?"

"Since shortly after Mr. Tarleton died. Her predecessor had served here almost as long as I have, and retired because of failing eyesight."

"And the cook?"

"Seven years, sir. I recommended her myself, as she is a distant cousin."

"Was that before or after Elizabeth took up her duties?"

"Elizabeth has lived and worked here for five years. A matter of weeks before Ricketts arrived, as I recall."

"Thank you. Pray tell us – Have you, yourself, any explanation as to why Mr. Tarleton and his wife should have met such tragic ends?"

The butler shook his head. "I cannot imagine. They were the kindest of people and the most considerate of employers. To the best of my knowledge, there was no one who wished them ill."

"Is that true also, of Miss Tarleton?"

"Most definitely, sir."

I was about to speak, but restrained myself at a gesture from Holmes. He allowed a short silence before his next question.

"It is true, is it not, that the deaths of both Mr. and Mrs. Tarleton were discovered by you, in this room?"

Brookes appeared suddenly uncomfortable. "It is, sir."

"Then pray cast your mind back. Can you recall anything that struck you as odd, at either time, or on both occasions?"

Again, he shook his head. "I don't think so." Then, "Of course, the door. But that was such a small thing."

"Nevertheless, kindly explain."

"It was just that, as I entered the room each time, I found the door ajar. It was unusual for either Mr. or Mrs. Tarleton to leave it so."

"As if someone had left the room hurriedly?" I suggested.

"Exactly that, sir"

The remainder of the afternoon was spent interviewing the rest of the staff in their places of work. The stable boys and Kathleen, Miss Tarleton's maid, were dismissed quickly since, as Holmes pointed out, they entered service after Mr. Tarleton's death. The cook he reserved for possible later enquiries, together with Ricketts. Finally, Elizabeth the kitchen maid returned from an errand to a local farm to join us in the sitting room.

"Mr. Brookes told me you wished to see me, sir," she said pleasantly.

"That is correct," my friend confirmed. "Please be seated."

When she had settled herself, Holmes regarded her with a faint smile. "I understand that you have worked here for some considerable time – well before Mr. Tarleton's death, would you say?"

"Much before that, sir. It must be five years or more, by now."

"Has your time here been to your liking? That is, are you content?"

"Oh yes, sir, as much as a serving girl can be. I have my meals and a roof over my head."

"Quite. Tell us, please, of your situations before coming to Deacon Hall."

She appeared momentarily confused, as if looking back over her life was difficult.

"Well, gentlemen," she explained, "I was in a workhouse in Canterbury for most of my early years. When I entered service at Lord Dornington's estate, I was still a slip of a girl. When he passed on, I was lucky enough to find a situation here."

"You were fortunate indeed," Holmes remarked, "but can you remember anything from the time of the tragic killings here which might aid our investigation? It looks as if progress will be lamentably slow, but we will stick at it until all is known."

Again she seemed to consider deeply. I concluded that she was probably slow-witted.

"No, sir," she answered eventually, "I can bring nothing to mind. I am sorry."

Holmes shrugged. "It is of little consequence. I'm confident that we will shed some light on the events quite soon, regardless." He interrupted to peer at the mantel-shelf near where Elizabeth sat. "What an extraordinary design has been worked into the leather strap of that horse-brass. Pray hand it to me, so that I may examine it."

"Certainly, sir." She rose and complied. Holmes took it from her.

"You may go now, but if anything should occur to you, I would be grateful for your assistance."

"Thank you, gentlemen."

She curtsied, and left us.

"What do you make of her?" my friend asked after the door had closed.

"Elizabeth is no longer young, but seems to possess the disposition of a girl. She doesn't appear to be a quick thinker."

"So it would seem. Well, unless I'm much mistaken, it's almost time for dinner."

The meal was no less satisfying than that which came before. Again, Miss Tarleton took the lead in pleasant conversation, replying to Holmes's questions about the neighbouring estates. At its conclusion, she gave

269

permission for us to smoke, and we filled our pipes as she finished her glass of an exquisite burgundy that we had already sampled.

"I trust you haven't forgotten that Mr. Rodney Knox will be with us for luncheon tomorrow," she reminded Brookes as he took away her glass and the empty bottle.

"No, Miss Rachel. I have informed Cook, as you ordered."

As he left, I saw Holmes's questioning expression, as she apparently did, since she explained before he spoke.

"Mr. Knox is a regular caller, and has been for some time. From his conversation, I imagine he will propose to me sooner or later, but I am undecided."

"I am sure that it will be our pleasure to meet this gentleman." I replied.

Shortly afterwards, Holmes asked permission to remain in the library for the evening, which was granted. I spent the time in conversation with Miss Tarleton, who impressed me greatly as an interesting, if rather excessively forceful, woman. I discovered that the relatives she had mentioned previously weren't alone in their memorable experiences. In return, I related some of the adventures in which I had been privileged to accompany my friend, and sometimes assist him, in the early days of our association. I was pleased to see that she appeared to be fascinated.

It was quite late when I left the lady, and I saw that Holmes had already retired. I slept soundly and woke to see sunlight streaming through the curtains. I could hear movements indicating that he had already risen, and so it was no surprise to find both he and our hostess awaiting me at the breakfast table.

"Did you find our library sufficiently entertaining, Mr. Holmes?" she enquired when all but the coffee cups had been removed.

"Very much so. In particular, the detailed account of your family history maintained by your late father was most enlightening."

I was surprised to see her expression change to one of incomprehension.

"I knew of no such work." Then she visibly collected herself. "Of course, the affairs of the estate, as well as my parents' deaths, have prevented me of late from giving my usual attention to our books."

"It would have surprised me had it been otherwise."

"Have you, as yet, made any progress?"

"I have indeed. In fact, I've been able to form four different theories to explain the most regrettable past events here. I can confidently tell you that my enquiries will soon be at an end."

She was about to reply, doubtless with a question, when Holmes straightened in his chair and peered towards the window on the opposite side of the room.

"What is it?" I asked him.

Miss Tarleton followed his gaze and replied. "If you're concerned about the men you glimpsed from the window, Mr. Holmes, I should tell you that they are here quite often. As you know, Deacon Hall is an ancient building. Several times every year, their services are required for minor, and occasionally substantial, repairs."

"They must be conversant with the basic structure, then?"

She laughed shortly. "By now, they are more familiar with it than I."

"In which case, I must interview them." He rose immediately. "If you will excuse me."

With that he left the room, leaving our hostess exchanging a puzzled glance with me. Moments later, we saw him conversing with two workmen who were passing the window. This didn't surprise me, for I had learned that he could quickly establish a rapport with all classes. Satisfaction was written on his face as he returned, although he didn't explain what he had learned.

About two hours later, the promised Mr. Rodney Knox arrived.

It was about then that I had requested for Holmes enlighten me as to several confusing aspects of this affair, and he was about to explain. We were standing in the reception chamber, near the sitting room where the front door was visible to us and we were unlikely to be overheard, when the insistent ringing of the bell brought Brookes at a run. He had the door half-open when it was roughly pushed the rest of the way. The butler hurriedly stepped aside to allow a tall young man with an arrogant manner to enter, regarding him contemptuously.

"Take these." He forced his hat and stick into Brookes' hands. "Where is she?"

"In the sitting room I believe, sir."

The visitor strode towards us, looking around.

"Who are you?" he asked impertinently.

"They are visitors, here at my invitation," said Miss Tarleton as she descended the stairs.

"I assume there is a good reason for their presence."

"You may assume what you will sir, but as you appear to have forgotten to await the courtesy of formal introductions, I will inform you that I am Mr. Sherlock Holmes, and this is my associate, Doctor John Watson. As for your second question, we are to assist Miss Tarleton with some unpleasant difficulties."

"Holmes, did you say? I have heard of your busy-bodying in the capital before now." He turned to our hostess. "What can you possibly want with these men? Do not pay them a penny – that I must impress upon you. When Scotland Yard decide to send a new man to you, he'll tell you what frauds they are."

An angry outburst, but I noticed that the colour had drained from his face.

I think Holmes would have replied with some force, but before anything else could be said, Miss Tarleton spoke sternly.

"That is enough, Rodney. If you are here for no other reason than to insult my visitors, you should leave immediately."

"No, I want to talk to you." He gave us another furious look. "In private."

"Very well." She led him into the sitting room, with an apologetic glance to us that was almost a plea.

"Charming fellow!" I remarked sarcastically.

"If his intention is to marry Miss Rachel Tarleton, he will be disappointed. She will already have appraised him and found him much wanting."

Holmes was about to continue our previous conversation when raised voices from the sitting room became clearly audible. We both listened in silence.

"I am asking you for no more than a hundred pounds!" Knox stated angrily. "I know that you are well-able to afford it."

"So that you can gamble away more?" Miss Tarleton retorted. "In addition to the sum you already owe?"

"That is none of your affair!"

"Oh, but it is, as long as you are in my debt. It is the extent of my means that is none of your affair."

After a moment of silence, Knox appeared to change his tactics.

"Have you given any thought to my question of the last time we met?" His voice had become smooth, even warm, yet I detected an urgent desperation.

"It was unnecessary to do so. As I have already indicated, I'm not contemplating marriage to you or anyone else. I have my life here and the estate to run. Really, Rodney, now that my father is gone, I can no longer allow you to shoot on my property, so there is no reason for any future calls. When you are able to repay your debt, do so by means of my bank manager or solicitor. I don't expect to hear from you otherwise."

There was another silence, longer this time. Then we heard an exclamation of such forceful anger that we feared for Miss Tarleton and were about to enter the room when the door was slammed open and Mr.

272

Rodney Knox strode out with frustrated fury written on his face. He passed us without a glance or a word. After snatching his hat and stick from Brookes, he left at once, wrenching the door from the butler's hands and closing it with a force that produced a report like a pistol shot.

"Gentlemen," our hostess said in a subdued tone, "I cannot apologise sufficiently for Mr. Knox's behaviour."

"It is quite unnecessary for you to do so," Holmes replied.

An ironic smile flittered across her lips. "I cannot express regret that we shall not have his company at luncheon."

At that moment, the gong was struck to indicate that it was indeed that time. As we entered the dining room, I heard faintly a shouting of oaths and the sudden thunder of the hooves of Knox's mount as he took an undignified leave. I pitied the animal, for it was certain to feel the whip undeservedly.

"It wouldn't surprise me," I whispered to Holmes, "if that gentlemen were found to be the cause of Miss Tarleton's distress."

"An understandable assumption," he replied. "Until you consider that to create such difficulties would be against his interests. From the exchange that we heard, it seems that Mr. Tarleton approved of Knox, even lending him funds and allowing him to shoot grouse or whatever they have here on the estate. Doubtless, he was also in favour of marriage between Knox and his daughter, which also suggests that he had a wrong perception of the fellow. To murder him would have done nothing but harm to our disappointed suitor and made the obtaining of further funds difficult, as we have seen."

I didn't reply, as Miss Tarleton was returning from across the room where she had been instructing Brookes. We rose respectfully as she sat down at the table, her recent embarrassment apparently dispensed with. Shortly afterwards, as a delicious mushroom soup was served, Brookes leaned towards his mistress to speak softly.

"Are the usual arrangements to be observed for the Pagan Parade this evening, Miss Tarleton?"

She appeared totally astonished, covering her open mouth with her hand. "Good Heavens! With the recent happenings here, I had quite forgotten! Yes, Brookes, we must proceed as we always have. The villagers will expect it, and I have no desire to forget such an old tradition."

"Thank you, Miss Rachel, I will inform the others."

As he retreated, she saw our puzzled expressions at once. "A very old ritual hereabouts, gentlemen. I'll explain at the conclusion of our meal."

We consumed our roast chicken, gooseberries and cream, and coffee, with Holmes doubtless wondering, as I was, about this new and unexpected turn of events. When Brookes and Elizabeth had done their work and the table was cleared, our hostess related to us what was intended.

"The Pagan Parade, gentlemen, is a very old local tradition," she explained. "Fuel for a large bonfire will by now have been piled high on the common. The folk from miles around usually attend, bringing roasted potatoes, chestnuts, and beer. Despite the name, it isn't a parade as such, but a frenzied dance by villagers around the flames in ragged costumes. Music is provided by local drummers and flautists."

"These celebrations usually have their origin in historical events," Holmes said then. "Is that the case here?"

"So it is said. According to a fifteenth-century reference in the day-book of our local church, it was an annual happening for the poor to gather and dance after dark on this day. I imagine it was a sort of premature thanksgiving ritual for the coming harvest. The priest of the time decided that this was worship of the Devil and prohibited any further assembly. As far as I know, there is no truth in this supposition, and the parishioners decided to ignore the order."

"That must have resulted in much dispute, in those days," I remarked.

She nodded. "Indeed, but the response was anticipated and easily avoided, by the simple means of changing the appearance of the participants. It became usual for the dancers to be masked, and to wear rags instead of their normal apparel. It is said that even some of the local landowners joined the throng in defiance, for the church was a hard and unyielding influence on the lives of everyone."

"Are we to understand, then," Holmes enquired, "that it is your intention to attend the celebration this evening?"

"If I failed to, it would be the first time in centuries that the owner of Deacon Hall was absent. I appeal to you gentlemen to accompany me, for I see that you are concerned for my welfare still, although it isn't yet my birthday."

"Please bear in mind," I reminded her, "that whoever is responsible for the deaths of your parents may not adhere to a pattern. Were he to strike earlier, it would be far from the first time that Holmes and I had experienced such cunning."

Resentment flashed in her eyes, as she again demonstrated that she was unaccustomed to argument. I thought that she would certainly attend alone if we failed to comply with her wishes, and I saw in my friend's expression that he realised this too, so it was with no surprise that I heard his response.

"Very well. I assume that we'll be sitting apart from the other observers."

"Such a tradition has always been maintained. A sort of rough throne is always constructed for the owner of Deacon Hall and companions or family, quite apart from the activity, so that a better view of the entire scene is obtained."

"It is against my better judgement, but I see that you will not be moved."

"My thanks to you both. Darkness falls just after dinner at this time of year, so we can set off when we've eaten."

She left us shortly after, and Holmes suggested a walk through the garden in order to benefit from the fresh air. The first autumn chill was already present, but the sky was a cloudless blue and I readily agreed, as this struck me as an opportunity to continue my hoped-for explanation of his conclusions.

"If we must attend this fearful charade," he said as we passed beneath an arch laden with wisteria, "we must take care not to let Miss Tarleton out of our sight. To take such a risk is foolishness and I'm much against it, but she's that kind of woman who is determined and will not budge from her intentions. We will both be armed."

"My weapon is ready, as always. Now, will you enlighten me as to what you have learned so far? There are several aspects of this affair that I find puzzling."

"My case is almost complete, but I lack purpose and proof. However, I've reached certain conclusions that you may wish to hear."

We were well away from the house now, close to a splendid array of colour. Nevertheless, Holmes ascertained that there was no gardener or stable boy in sight before he spoke.

"I'll relate to you that which of which I am certain," he began when he was sure that we were quite alone. "For example, what did you understand from the fact that the blood streaks were on the right shoulders of both victims?"

"I . . . ." For a moment I was at a loss for words, then it came to me. "Of course! The murderer is left-handed."

"Bravo, Watson! Now, what purpose do the marks have?"

I considered, but unsuccessfully. "Some sort of signature? A calling-card?"

"Not in this instance. I believe that the murderer simply wiped his weapon free of blood, so that it could be more easily concealed."

"The instrument was never found," I agreed.

"Doesn't it also strike you as strange that on both occasions the door was left ajar after the killings?"

"It does, but although the murderer fled in that way each time, he was never seen elsewhere in the house."

"Quite so. That's because he didn't leave the sitting room by the door."

"Then how? The chamber has no other exit."

"That's what I asked myself. My earlier conversation with the workmen supplied the answer."

"Pray enlighten me."

Holmes paused to inhale the fragrance of a late-blooming blossom before we continued along the path. "We know, by Miss Tarleton's assurance, that those fellows are familiar with the design and condition of Deacon Hall. It therefore occurred to me that they might be aware of a forgotten additional entrance. The elder workman mentioned a concealed passage, once used during the Civil War to effect the escape of supporters of King Charles II during a raid by Cromwell's troops. My informant didn't know of a sitting room entrance to this corridor, and was unsure of its continued existence, but he was quite certain of its place of exit."

"Somewhere away from the house. In this garden, perhaps?"

"No. The kitchen."

"I would have thought it too small to accommodate a sliding panel, in addition to all the hanging pots, pans, and culinary tools adorning its walls."

"You'll recall the large recess behind a narrow door, where food and drink are kept cool on occasion by means of marble shelves, and the fact that it extends underground. I saw that it was sufficiently spacious to contain a person of normal proportions, if uncomfortably."

I nodded. "Then the murderer waited there until the house was deserted, probably until the early hours, before making his escape?"

"That is a possibility," Holmes answered with a faint smile.

He retired again to the library for the remainder of the afternoon. I imagined that this was to acquaint himself further with the strange local custom of the Pagan Parade. A further stroll among the colourful displays of the garden struck me as a pleasant way to pass the next hour or two, but on returning to my room to regain my pocket watch which I had accidentally left there, I succumbed to temptation and lay atop the bed for a few minutes. I awoke with dinner less than a half-hour away, and hurriedly prepared myself.

"Before we embark upon this," Holmes said to Miss Tarleton when all but the wine glasses had been cleared away, "there is one thing I must know."

She smiled and put down her glass. "I am at your service, of course."

"Kindly tell me how many of your staff are to attend with us this evening."

276

"The answer to that is simple, Mr. Holmes. It is customary for two to remain at Deacon Hall during the evening of the Pagan Parade. This is normally achieved by rotation, and this year it will be Brookes and the kitchen maid, Elizabeth. The others will make their way to the common on foot to join those in service from other nearby houses, while Ricketts will drive our coach before joining them also."

"Thank you. That is most helpful."

Holmes's expression gave away nothing as he drained his glass.

Later, Miss Tarleton, Holmes, and I found ourselves upon the common under a full autumn moon. Ricketts had left us to enjoy the company of the other coachmen, servants, and the like, after ensuring that our conveyance remained at a safe distance, and near a water trough for the horse.

Already we could see the blaze ahead and hear the crackling of burning sap from the piled branches. Sparks flew up to the darkness above in an unending stream.

The heat became increasingly apparent as we drew nearer, and some of the throng that sat on blankets or various improvised objects cheered and waved as Miss Tarleton became visible to them. She returned the gesture as we approached an ancient tall-backed chair that I suspected was kept especially for this purpose, with a rough wooden stool at either side and a gnarled table within arm's reach.

Holmes and I each took a stool and our hostess settled into her place. More cheers erupted from sources now unseen beyond the glare of the flames. A fellow who might have been a local innkeeper laid food and drink before us. At once a rhythmic drumming began, mounting in intensity and accompanied by the frantic tones of several flutes. From the far side of the flames, a solitary figure appeared, writhing and spinning in a grotesque parody of dance. Then another appeared beside it, jumping often as if trying to snatch the moon from above. A moment later, yet more came into our view, and then there were more still in a confused tangle that made counting them an impossibility. The drum-beat grew louder and the movements quicker as the dancers drew close enough for us to discern that the clothing of each hung in tatters, and that every face was hidden by a grotesque mask. Some of them cried out, but their words were lost among the music and the roar of the fire. I glanced at my companions and saw a sort of pride in Miss Tarleton's face while Holmes remained expressionless.

Shadows flickered continually across our faces as we ate and drank, Holmes sparingly as was his custom. The scene began to take on the appearance of the tribal rituals that I had witnessed in Afghanistan, and it crossed my mind to wonder at the similarities of the customs of men everywhere.

After a while, someone threw a heavy log into the flames and a great shower of sparks briefly obscured our view. The procession before us was momentarily halted by the increased heat until a lone figure emerged. It threw its body about like an acrobat, bending and stretching between somersaults and turning this way and that. I sensed that Holmes had risen to his feet at the same instant that Miss Tarleton screamed, and I instinctively reached for her and pulled her towards me. Something smashed into the tall chair, and I saw that the masked dancer held a pistol. Holmes's return fire was muted by the surrounding noise, and his aim obscured by the emergence of the other participants, as the assailant disappeared among them. I steadied Miss Tarleton and enquired as to her condition.

"I am unhurt. Thank you, Doctor."

"Holmes, were you hit?"

"Not at all."

"You see, Mr. Holmes?" Miss Tarleton said with a tremor in her voice. "The attack on my life has begun."

"Not so. I'm quite certain that *I* was the intended victim. Our murderer adheres still to his pattern. We were sitting close together, and Henley is no marksman."

We looked at him in astonishment.

"The stable boy?" I said incredulously.

"How could you tell, in the darkness," Miss Tarleton queried nervously.

"Didn't you observe that he limped as he fled? During my interview with him, I noticed his awkwardness. Nevertheless, I would speculate that his former occupation was that of an acrobat or contortionist, during which he sustained an injury."

"Then it was he who killed my parents?"

"Of that I have gravest of doubts. However, the incident seems to have passed unnoticed, since the procession continues unabated. The glare of the fire will have prevented those beyond it from seeing the attempt. I suggest that we now withdraw without communicating our intentions." His glance briefly settled on me. "We have some work to do before we retire."

It surprised me that our hostess offered no resistance. She suggested that we retrieve Ricketts from the crowd that had sat apart from us, now vocally competing with the music, but Holmes wouldn't hear of it. I drove the coach to Deacon Hall, while he conversed inside with Miss Tarleton. Ricketts would doubtless find his way home with the others.

278

There were few lighted windows as we arrived. I saw the lady into the house before she insisted that I join my friend. Holmes and I then led the horse to the stables, where it was given into the care of a young lad who, I learned later, would be there all night in anticipation of the forthcoming birth of a foal. I expected Holmes to immediately approach the outdoor staff living quarters, or to lie in wait, but after inspecting the area, he gave a sigh of resignation.

"What are we searching for?" I asked.

"Henley's body, of course."

"You believe that you fatally wounded him?"

"Not at all. He is, or was, not the murderer. You will recall that he favoured his right hand as he fired."

"Then why did he make the attempt?"

"I suspect that he was somehow compelled. That being so, he could identify the killer, and has therefore silenced. In the morning, we'll inform the local force."

Nor was that the end of the night's events.

We entered Deacon Hall to find no one in sight. Holmes strained his ears to listen, holding up a hand as a signal that I should hesitate also. At first, I heard no sound, but his sharp ears led him towards a faint murmuring from the sitting room. I followed with my hand still resting upon my revolver.

The chamber was lit by candles placed at each end of the mantel. In their flickering light, Brookes and Elizabeth lay as if dead, each sprawled in an armchair. Their appearance was deceptive, since Miss Tarleton had already perceived signs of life and was endeavouring to shake Brookes awake.

His red-rimmed eyes flickered open, and consciousness returned in a moment, although his expression suggested that he hadn't recognised us or his surroundings. He mumbled something unintelligible as his glance took in all three of us. Then he proceeded to speak in the uncertain tone of one who has committed a grave error.

"Oh, good Heavens! I must have fallen asleep. I have never before rested while engaged upon my duties. How can I apologise, Miss Tarleton?"

The harsh response that I expected wasn't forthcoming.

"Apart from this room," she asked him, "have you closed up the house for the night?"

"I have, Miss Tarleton."

"Then it's time you retired. We'll attend to Elizabeth."

Brookes bowed his head in thanks and quickly left us. I turned to Elizabeth, noticing that Holmes was already scrutinizing her and listening to her breathing. I gently pulled up an eyelid and she awoke at once, emerging from her slumber a little more quickly than Brookes, no doubt because of her comparative youth.

"What has occurred in our absence?" my friend enquired.

She gave us a bewildered look, striving to remember. "Brookes and I each consumed a glass of warm milk in the kitchen, I washed the glasses, along with the remainder of the dinner things, and we came in here because he wished to show me where the cleaning has proven inadequate. Since then, I can remember nothing, sir."

"Are you feeling ill now?" I asked her.

"No, Doctor, I'm quite recovered." She turned a wavering glance towards Miss Tarleton. "I am so sorry. I will see that this doesn't recur. I beg you not to dismiss me."

"I will consider the matter," our hostess replied. "Now it's best that you sleep, since you will be required early in the morning."

With mumbled thanks, Elizabeth repaired to her quarters.

Holmes regarded Miss Tarleton and myself thoughtfully.

"Tomorrow morning, I must visit Canterbury," he said. "There, I hope to clear up the remaining questions surrounding this affair. I would be grateful if you would allow Ricketts to convey me to the station, before summoning a local inspector to search the estate."

"Of course, Mr. Holmes. Will Doctor Watson accompany you?"

"I think not." His voice became almost a whisper and his expression grim. "Until my return, you must remain in his company at all times. It isn't yet your birthday, but the threat to your life has never been greater. Ensure that the door of your bed-chamber is locked before you sleep."

With that, I escorted the lady to her bedroom door. When I returned, Holmes spoke to me once more before we parted.

"I am as deadly serious as you have ever seen me, Watson, when I implore you: Do not leave her tomorrow, even for an instant. Keep your revolver near your hand at all times."

I was downstairs the next morning before Miss Tarleton arose, and was surprised to find the dining room empty. Brookes informed me that Holmes and Ricketts had set off earlier. Miss Tarleton appeared a few minutes later. We enjoyed a hearty breakfast, conversing about mundane and unimportant topics, until I brought her down to earth with a reminder of Holmes's warning. I had come to feel that, in order to instill upon herself a state of calm, she had consigned her predicament to the back of her mind, regardless of the attack during the Pagan Parade, but I insisted that she face the situation. Henley's absence continued, and word had been left at the stables that he must report to her immediately should he reappear, but without result. I used this fact to underline my intention to stay by her side until Holmes's return and, reluctantly because of her forceful nature, she agreed.

Miss Tarleton was quiet during luncheon, and it seemed to me that her defiant disposition was increasingly at odds with the growing fear that the passing days brought. Sometime later, Inspector Willis of the local force arrived to supervise a search of the outbuildings and near area with two constables, in response to Ricketts' earlier visit to Kirkenfield Police Station. They found nothing, and the inspector led his men away with an affronted air at the mention of Holmes's name.

In the early afternoon unexpected visitors arrived. Miss Tarleton explained that Mr. and Mrs. Crowther, an elderly couple, were her nearest neighbours who often came by unannounced to drink tea and discuss local events. When the conversation turned to the Pagan Parade, nothing unusual was mentioned and so, I concluded, Holmes had been correct in his supposition that the shootings had gone unnoticed. Several times Miss Tarleton gave me a wary look, as if wondering how much to disclose. I shook my head slowly.

The Crowthers' trap had hardly left when Holmes returned in a hired cart. Its driver touched his cap, indicating that my friend had added a generous tip to the fare, and then he was gone in an instant. Through a leaded window, I saw Holmes stride towards Deacon Hall, his expression of satisfaction evident. I met him at the door, and we shook hands.

"Has anything further occurred?" he asked at once.

"Nothing," I assured him gladly.

Not long after we sat with Miss Tarleton in the sitting room, the door locked and our coffee cups emptied.

"Well, Mr. Holmes," she began, "Doctor Watson and I have anticipated your return anxiously. I trust your efforts have been rewarded."

She was feigning a brave face, I thought, but the fear in her voice was unmistakable.

My friend leaned forward in his chair. "They have indeed. I see that there are almost two hours separating us from one of your excellent dinners, so we have ample time to conclude this case and remove your anxieties. Watson has explained that your local inspector has found nothing amiss here – but no matter. While in Canterbury, I took the precaution of telegraphing Scotland Yard, and a response should soon be forthcoming."

"Thank you," she said. "Any further assistance is most welcome. Please continue."

"Very well." I wondered if she read his expression, as I did. "As I've already confided to Watson, the first thing that struck me as strange was that the sitting room door was left ajar in both instances, and I was able to establish that this was to give the false impression that the murderer had left the room in this way. The exit was actually accomplished by means of a concealed passage which connects with the kitchen. I considered at first that the cool room there was used as a hiding place until conditions were right for escape, but as there is no outside access, I was forced to the conclusion that the murderer works there. Now we come to the bloody streaks on the right side of both bodies." He paused and adopted a more-gentle tone. "Forgive me for my lack of sensitivity."

Miss Tarleton said nothing, but shook her head to indicate that he shouldn't spare her feelings. After a moment, he resumed.

"Those marks were neither a signature nor a signal. They were left by the wiping of the weapon to clean the blade so that it could be hidden in plain sight, but they indicate that the killer is left-handed. By observation and various simple tests, I have ascertained that two people only, beside yourself, are so disposed. They are the kitchen maid, Elizabeth, and Kathleen, your personal maid of whom we've seen so little."

Our hostess sat up straight, her eyes bright. "But Kathleen was employed here since the death of my father, so his murderer was – "

"The woman you know as Elizabeth," Holmes finished.

"But for what purpose?" I asked my friend.

"That will become clear in a moment. I fear that my enquiries have revealed further facts that may shock you."

She collected herself with difficulty. "Kindly proceed, nevertheless."

"One of my calls in Canterbury was to the office of Mr. Sinclair Lomax who, as you have mentioned to me, is now the head of the firm of solicitors who have been concerned with the affairs of your family for years. He is, as you know, quite elderly, and when I had explained that I represent your interests, was willing to disclose to me a portion of your family history. You will recall relating the doings of your Aunt Esther, who as a young woman led an expedition to Africa."

Miss Tarleton showed surprise, but he didn't wait for her reply before continuing. "It seems that you failed to tell us, probably because you were unaware, that the expedition was financed with money stolen from her father – your grandfather – Mr. William Burnside. Esther Burnside had taken up with a certain Byron Jacques, known locally as a notorious thief and kidnapper, and at his instigation, and because the police were closing in, stole the money and fled with him abroad. Jacques is said to have been bitten by a cobra and died in the Transvaal, but your aunt eventually returned to England."

Miss Tarleton looked at him coldly. "Mr. Holmes, are you saying that my kitchen maid is in truth my aunt, who I believed to be long dead?"

"I regret that the conclusion is inescapable. Her resemblance to yourself is thinly disguised, but it is there, once you are aware of it. All of her history that she presented is fictitious. The Canterbury workhouse where she claims to have been brought up burned in a fire, years ago, and no one in the late Lord Dornington's employ has any knowledge of her existence. She arrived here five years ago with forged references which, for some reason, weren't checked."

"My father tended to take too much on trust. I often warned him of the dangers."

"The significance of birthdays is now also apparent. It was on Esther's nineteenth birthday that she left her family home under a cloud. For that reason, it seems likely that she considered it in some way appropriate that every step taken towards gaining mastery of Deacon Hall should be on the birthday of the victim."

Our hostess fixed her eyes on the carpet, her expression one of gloomy disbelief. "This cannot be," she murmured repeatedly.

"What of Henley?" I asked Holmes.

"According to one of the stable boys who I questioned early this morning, Henley confided that he was being blackmailed by Elizabeth. Apparently, there was some trouble with a married lady in Kirkenfield, and the resulting scandal would certainly have meant his dismissal."

Miss Tarleton stood up suddenly. "Excuse me, gentlemen."

She strode to the door, unlocked it, and called for Brookes. Moments later she resumed her seat and spoke quietly, grim-faced. "Now we'll get to the end of this. I have summoned Elizabeth."

The woman, who I now realised appeared much younger than her true age, entered and stood before us, seemingly puzzled as to who to address.

"Mr. Holmes wishes to question you, Elizabeth," Miss Tarleton said in a strangely calm voice.

The kitchen maid turned her innocent gaze on Holmes and myself. "Yes, sir? What is it that you wish to know?"

"You will recall that I explained the purpose of my enquiries to you previously," my friend began.

"Of course."

"I have now completed those enquiries to the extent that but one question remains, and none but yourself can provide the answer."

She took this impassively, but when she spoke, I fancied that wariness had entered her voice. "But whatever could that be?"

"Simply tell us where you have hidden the body of Henley, the stable boy."

Her expression remained unaltered, so that for an instant I believed that Holmes had made a terrible mistake. His eyes were locked on hers in an unflinching stare.

"I don't understand, sir. How would I know such a thing?" But she was moving, slowly and deliberately, towards the sideboard that held the drinks tray.

"Watson!" Holmes exclaimed sharply.

She ran to seize the water carafe and withdrew the glass stopper so that it seemed she was about to drink without permission. Then I saw that a long and cruel-looking blade was attached and realised that Holmes had warned me against the weapon that had killed twice before in this room. But now its hiding place was revealed – hardened, transparent glass, perfectly hidden when submerged in water. I assumed it had been replaced recently in preparation for Miss Tarleton's birthday, as to have otherwise let it remain in the carafe since the last murder would have invited discovery.

"If you fail to drop that knife immediately, I will fire without further warning," I assured her.

Her eyes met mine, and I fancied I saw a trace of madness there. She took a pace towards me and I raised my revolver to point at her heart. She saw the resolve in my expression and shifted her gaze to Holmes, and finally to Miss Tarleton. Hopelessness crept into her face, and the knife fell to the carpet.

"How did you know of the blade?" she asked Holmes as he secured her hands with police handcuffs.

"I interviewed the merchant who made it for you, not three hours ago in Canterbury. He was the fourth tradesman I approached. Apparently, the fellow was confused as to your purpose in requiring it. The reason you gave him was unconvincing."

When she was seated, I stood guard over her, returning to Holmes's previous question. "It is all up with you now. It can be to no advantage to keep poor Henley's whereabouts secret."

She stared into my face with an eerie calmness, looking quite different. It seemed that some of her youthfulness had fallen away, revealing a face much fashioned by years of wrongdoing and a nature turned always towards self.

"Very well," she said in a voice quite unlike that she had used until now. "He lies in a shallow grave quite close, near the edge of the forest to the east of the estate. I had prepared his resting place before I caused him to attempt to rid me of you at the Pagan Parade. You will have realised that I gave opium to Brookes to ensure that he would be unaware of my absence when I left to dispose of Henley afterwards."

Holmes nodded. "I saw that there was a marked difference between his condition and yours on awakening. Watson later confirmed this."

At that instant, Miss Tarleton rose and strode across the room to confront the prisoner. Her face had darkened with rage, and I sensed that she was exercising great restraint.

"Are you truly Esther Burnside?"

The kitchen maid looked up, unruffled. "Can you not see it?"

"And you are the murderer of my parents?"

"They were obstacles – a barrier to my rightful life."

"What do you mean? You chose to spend your life as an adventurer, having no connection with us."

"When I took the money to enable my escape with Byron, I discovered that my father had, for reasons of his own, settled a great deal of money upon yours. I returned to England alone and destitute to find you living as I should be had that money been my inheritance. I entered your house, hoping that my credentials wouldn't be closely scrutinized, and waited. The time came when the urge to regain my rightful place became too strong to delay my actions further. It was time to begin my reappearance by removing those who would have prevented it, one by one."

"So you intended to claim Deacon Hall on some future occasion?" I speculated. "How was your sudden reappearance to be explained?"

An artful and remorseless glint appeared in her eyes. "I was to leave as Elizabeth and return after an appropriate interval as myself, having recently arrived from Africa and read in the newspapers that Deacon Hall now had no claimant. I can prove my lineage. I would have had little difficulty, for to change one's appearance somewhat is a simple matter."

"You have murdered my parents," Miss Tarleton repeated in a voice that hardly contained her anger, "and others. Also, I cannot see the end to the shame you have inflicted upon our family. You would be an outcast for the remainder of your life, were it not that the hangman will take you." The strength of her family's womenfolk filled her voice. "God knows that I would like nothing better than to undertake the task myself."

I believe that Holmes was about to retort that the law would act sufficiently, and that our hostess should do nothing more than set her mind on her recovery from the dreadful events of the last few months, but his whispered words were cut short as Brookes entered the room with a tall man, indistinct in the shadows of the corridor, standing a few feet behind him.

"Our expected visitor, Miss Rachel," he announced. "Inspector Gregson of Scotland Yard."

Miss Tarleton continued to maintain a malevolent stare at our prisoner as if she had failed to hear, but Holmes and I turned to see the official detective enter.

"Ah, Gregson," my friend said with surprising lightness. "Do come in. We have just heard an extraordinary story that will prove your case, and will doubtless do wonders for your reputation."

"But there are some pretty little problems among them. Here's the record of the Tarleton murders . . . ."

– Sherlock Holmes
"The Musgrave Ritual"

The Backwater Affair
by Paula Hammond

Glancing over my records of all the cases in which I have assisted my great friend, Sherlock Holmes, I am struck by the number of times that we have been faced with events which, at first, seem to have no natural explanation. I have said before that Holmes worked not for wealth or prestige, but for the sheer thrill of exercising that singular mind of his. Perhaps this is why he especially sought out the bizarre and the fantastical. Or perhaps it was Holmes himself who acted as a magnet for such things? My friend would, of course, dismiss such a concept, but when I look back at my notes from October 1885, the oddness of the events which were to unfold still strikes me.

Winter already had its grip on our little corner of Baker Street. Snow had fallen overnight – a rare sight in London – and a genuine curiosity so early in the year. I awoke to find ice clinging to the inside of the sash windows and the smell of mildew hanging in the air.

I had only just lit the fire when the door to Holmes's bedroom opened. My surprise at seeing my friend awake so early was doubled at the sight of him already dressed.

"Ah, Watson! As reliable as a metronome," he intoned, clearly in good humor. "I hope you will not object to making a speedy toilet this morning. It seems we are to expect visitors." He pulled a crumpled telegram from his jacket pocket and held it out for me to peruse. "It arrived some hours ago. I should warn you that Mrs. Hudson was not best pleased to be awakened before dawn. I wouldn't wait on breakfast."

The telegram gave no me clues as to what – or who – I should expect. "No name? No hints as to who sent it, then?" I asked.

"Government, naturally" Holmes answered with a familiar smile. "Notice how the message is exactly nine words long – penny-pinching officialdom if ever I saw it. Sent from Whitehall, which tells us nothing in itself, but given that only the military mind would willingly rouse itself at such an ungodly hour, and the fact that the Navy Office is situated on The Mall, I'd say we are to expect a visit from The Right Honorable the Lord Backwater, First Lord of the Admiralty."

"Know the man?" I asked.

"I've heard of him. In the best traditions of British bureaucracy, he has never set foot on a ship, boat, or punt. Highly strung. Considered to be the type to 'get things done' – which, between the two of us, is likely

Admiralty code for someone who makes a lot of unnecessary work for others!"

Holmes was proved entirely correct. At exactly seven a.m., the spare and skittish figure of Phillip George Lorling, 1st Earl of Backwater, Liberal statesman and head of Her Majesty's Navy, entered our sitting room and was ushered towards the battered sofa upon which Holmes habitually lay when in the grip of a particularly knotty problem.

From his wild, untamed hair to his cross-buttoned overcoat, Backwater seemed like a man in a hurry. It was only when I had drawn shut the curtains on the windows and checked that the door to the apartment was securely locked that he could be compelled to sit down at all. "Security," he said in a high, timorous whine. "One can never be too careful."

As I lit the lamp, Holmes made himself comfortable in his easy chair and said, in the soothing tones that he employed so well, "Please start at the beginning. And leave out no detail, no matter how strange it should appear."

At this, our visitor visibly started and looked at Holmes inquiringly.

"No magic I assure you. It's rare for people to consult with me on mundane matters. In fact, Watson believes that I have a knack for attracting the uncanny . . . ." He let his sentence trail off and, with a wave of his hand, motioned our visitor to begin.

Backwater spoke quickly with a tense edge to his voice which was reflected in his body language.

"You will know that I am but newly appointed to the Admiralty. I'm a modern man, Mr. Holmes, and am determined to bring much needed order to the department. Paper – or rather velum I should say – lines the very corridors, and much of my time, thus far, has been spent following paper trails. It was one such trail that led me to a discovery that I believe may imperil the Empire herself."

He paused to glance around the room, then continued in the same oddly strained tone. "In 1850, a private gentlemen – his name is not recorded – saw a paragraph in a newspaper which, although couched in a very guarded manner, attracted his observation. After making enquiries at the newspaper office, he was introduced to someone who called himself 'Captain Werner'. Of particular note was that, during the last war, he had been in the employ of the Government. He is said to have used a small submersible to destroy a French gunship. As an aside here, Mr. Holmes, a gunship was destroyed under – shall we say – strange circumstances during this time, but we have no records of any Captain Werner on our pay books.

"This same gentleman now asserted to have invented a device which was capable of destroying any ship, from a distance, on command. Well, Mr. Holmes, it seems that Werner had friends in Parliament, and they raised a request with the House to fund a trial of this remarkable invention."

"Did such a trial take place?" Holmes asked.

"It seems so. At least there are records of a hulk, called the *John O' Gaunt*, moored in deep waters off Gladwyn Sands, which was destroyed by means unknown. After the demonstration, Werner apparently demanded £200,000 for the secret."

"An incredible sum!" I interjected, unable to stifle my surprise.

"His supporters felt it wasn't unreasonable, given that anyone owning such a device could potentially destroy any ship, any harbor, anywhere."

"Was he paid?" Holmes asked quietly.

"I believe so – "

"Believe?" Holmes barked. "That's quite a sum for the Admiralty to lose!"

"Yes," Lord Backwater answered brittlely. "Yes. He was paid the amount requested. You must understand," he added, as though he felt the need to personally justify such a fabulous expense, "that great ideas have always incurred ridicule. After all, the man who introduced gas, from which we all derive so much benefit, died in a debtor's prison."

"Just so," said Holmes, holding up a placating hand. "Pray continue."

"I have ascertained from reading the Parliamentary records in Hansar that negotiations rumbled on. When it became clear that Werner intended to offer his device to the Portuguese, the issue was referred to the Duke – Wellington you understand – who personally appointed two officers to make a detailed report. Their findings were strongly in favor of securing the device for the country."

"Did it not occur to anyone," Holmes hazarded, "that the British Government was being hoodwinked, possibly with the aid of these officers?"

Lord Backwater scowled. "Reports were made in writing, supported by numerous witnesses to both Werner's character and the efficiency of the device. There was seemingly abundant evidence to support their decision. That, and a year's constant intercourse between the Duke and Captain Werner, was considered sufficient proof of his good intentions."

"Well, one can have friends in high places and still be a scoundrel. So a king's ransom was paid for the plans to this miraculous device. Did it live up to expectations?"

"In all honesty, Mr. Holmes, I can find no one who has any knowledge of the thing. Captain Werner died after delivering the plans.

The officers who made the original report were posted overseas and are now long dead, as is the Duke. The plans themselves simply vanished."

The room fell silent. Holmes regarded Backwater thoughtfully then leaned forward. "It is hard to imagine that the Government, having spent such a vast sum, simply dropped the matter. Were no investigations made at the time?"

"Naturally. Clerks were set to scour the archives in case the plans had been misfiled. Mrs. Hannah Chesters – a lady of independent means whose husband financed some of Werner's work – was interviewed. But she claimed that Werner alone held the secret. The matter was raised again in the Lords, then abandoned."

"How very curious." Holmes eventually said, peering at Backwater with those steady grey eyes of his.

"Mr. Holmes," Lord Backwater answered with a wan smile, "I don't believe that this is a case of fraud, if that's what you're implying. But officials have a long and noble history of burying embarrassing mistakes. Payment was made. A document was logged, archived, then 'lost'. An empty file is all that is left to show for two-hundred-thousand of public money."

"So you wish me to recover the plans for device?"

Backwater didn't answer immediately, and when he did it was in a curiously thoughtful tone. "While, of course, the recovery of these plans would be of immense value to the Empire – and a feather in my cap – it is another question that I find vexes and unnerves me.

"I cannot abide mysteries, Mr. Holmes. I must have things ordered and quantified. It is the only way for a modern man to live, don't you agree?"

I could see Holmes, who was by no means an ordered man himself, appraising Backwater with just the hint of a smile, but he said nothing.

"Things that defy reason cause me sleepless nights," the First Lord continued. "Assuming the device is genuine – and I have read enough to convince me that it is – and assuming it was stolen, why have we not seen it used by our enemies? If someone is holding the plans for their own purposes, surely thirty-five years is time enough? And exactly how was it taken? How was someone able to walk into a locked safe, in the basement of Whitehall's most secure and heavily-guarded rooms? What have I missed, Mr. Holmes? That is the real mystery that I wish you to solve for me. Come by tomorrow – you'll doubtless want to see the strong room for yourself – and I will ensure what records we have are put at your disposal."

The street door had barely closed before Holmes was bounding across the room pulling out files and newspaper clippings, and spreading them across the woefully empty breakfast table.

"Come, Watson, don't look so downcast!" he said. "If I'm not mistaken, that's Mrs. Hudson's queenly tread I hear on the stairs. And if can't smell fresh rashers and hot coffee, then you have my permission to call me a humbug if I ever boast of my olfactory prowess again!"

Sure enough, the door opened and in came our redoubtable landlady with not just bacon and coffee, but eggs and toast. "Given the early start," she said, with just the hint of reproach, "I assumed you would be in need a of good breakfast before you head out to Heaven knows where."

I loaded an appreciatively large plate and sat down to eat while Holmes scattered papers over table and floor, in a vigorous imitation of the snowfall outside. Finally, he held up a small manila folder with a triumphant flourish.

"Ah, here we are," he began. "An obituary from 1880 for Hannah Chesters – the woman mentioned by Backwater. She was single at the time of her death, residing at number 10 Wilton Crescent, Belgrave Square. Former housekeeper to John Chesters, with whom she had three children. She had taken Chesters' last name, and upon his death, Hannah – housekeeper and mistress – inherited the bulk of his vast fortune. The inheritance was hotly contested by Chesters' actual wife, who claimed that her husband wasn't of sound mind when he re-wrote his will in favor of Hannah, the mistress. Apparently it was a *cause célèbre* at the time. The judge decided in the mistress' favor, but the lady opted to share the bequest with the wife, on the condition that her own young daughters were well provided for."

"Sounds like an interesting lady," I said between mouthfuls of hot, buttered toast.

"Interesting couple. According to this clipping, Hannah and John were buried in a rather striking pyramid-shaped mausoleum in Brompton. Apparently Mr. Chesters had a passion for Egyptology."

"Academic or amateur?"

"Unknown. In fact, no one seems to know exactly how he made his fortune."

"Chesters' real wife?"

"Dead for some time."

"Any mention of Werner?"

"None."

Holmes handed me the clipping. Alongside a portrait of the late Hannah Chesters was an illustration of the door of an imposing mausoleum, its surround decorated with *ankh*-shapes and hieroglyphics.

291

"Interesting, but it's a bit thin" I said, loathe to dampen Holmes's enthusiasm.

"It is" he replied, with a look of impish pleasure settling onto his features. The game – as he so often said –was afoot.

We arrived at that monument to officialdom and paper-shuffling – the Admiralty – the next morning, just as Big Ben's distinctive quarter-bells sounded the first division of the hour. The building lacks its own entrance on The Mall, meaning that visitors must cross Horse Guard's Parade where, as the name suggests, the Queen's official bodyguards are put through their daily maneuvers.

The First Lord has rooms on the upper floor, but instead of being escorted to his apartments as expected, Holmes and I found ourselves whisked down several flights of worn steps into a basement which must have pre-dated the Neoclassical building above by several centuries. There were flood marks on the walls hinting that at one time the River Tyburn, which ran beneath our feet, hadn't been quite as tame as it is now.

Backwater hadn't been exaggerating. The place was a lined with paper – boxes and folders, from floor to ceiling – and conducting the chaos was the First Lord of the Admiralty himself, stripped to his shirt-sleeves, and not so much supervising his subordinates as chasing them from room to room. From iron-haired lady archivists to young-buck secretaries, there wasn't a man, woman, or rat who didn't squeak and vanish at his approach.

He hailed us, then darted deeper into undercroft, calling for us to follow. We managed well enough, Holmes's long legs making easy work of it while I stumbled after, leaving more of my shin-skin behind than was all-together comfortable.

When we finally caught up with Backwater he was, if possible, even more excitable than before.

"It's happened again, Mr. Holmes!" he exclaimed, red-faced. "About half-an-hour ago. I had instructed my secretary to collect the files on the original investigation and lay them aside for you, but when he opened the safe, they were gone. Yet the strong room is guarded day and night – and nothing else was taken, though there are secrets inside that would fetch a pretty-penny for anyone inclined towards treason." He paused, glanced around in that same way he had at Baker Street, closed the door to our little *oubliette*, and added in a tone terse with excitement, "Not once now, but *twice* – and with such a gap between visits that it seems inconceivable the same person could be involved in both thefts. There's some devilry here!"

Holmes wasted no time in asking to be shown the strong room and Backwater headed off once again, with even Holmes struggling to keep pace.

292

Given the distance we'd walked, one could imagine that we were now under Parliament itself, only it was quite clear that we'd been led in circles. Backwater's security measures were laughable, but given the man's nervous state, Holmes and I were content to exchange exasperated glances.

We finally arrived at a room lined with cabinets and plan-chests, which boasted a vast iron safe in one corner.

Holmes audibly groaned to see the space, filled as it was with clerks who were in the process of examining every deposit box and every filing cabinet. One elderly lady was carrying boxes piled so high that only her tweed skirt and a pair of floral-patterned shoes were visible. It was something to see her navigate herself out of the room, totally blinded by the ziggurat of paperwork she carried.

"The safe door mechanism is a variation on the Webber and Scott model of 1855," Holmes noted, "requiring two keys to be inserted, simultaneously. Yourself and the guard?"

Newbrook nodded pulling out a large brass key, hanging from a sturdy chain around his neck. "Mine never leaves my person. My secretary has one. And the guards pass theirs to their replacement at their end of their shift."

Holmes asked to examine the keys. I knew from experience that if copies had been made, by pressing some putty or clay into the original, then Holmes's keen eye would spot it.

The secretary and guard both confirmed what Backwater had said. The safe was securely locked and, that morning, had been unlocked using their keys. Once open, the secretary had asked one of the archivists to help find the files. It was then that they discovered it was missing."

"You didn't retrieve them yourself?" Holmes queried.

"I wouldn't know where to begin."

"But you know this archivist?"

"Not personally," the secretary said as though the very suggestion was an affront to his honor.

"Maybe then," Backwater injected, in a tone of palpable frustration, "you could go and find this person?"

The secretary looked quite abashed and vanished into the undercroft, promising to return with the lady in question within a few minutes.

While we waited, Backwater sent the remaining clerks for early lunch, allowing Holmes to began his examination of the strong room. I could see my friend's irritation as he surveyed the chaos in front of him, but he set to work with the same thoroughness as usual.

With his trusty tools – tape measure and magnifying glass – in hand, he trotted noiselessly about the room, pacing and measuring, before finally lying flat upon his face. I saw his hand snake out to grasp something lying in front of a row of deposit boxes affixed to the far wall, then, with a grunt, he was back on his feet.

It seemed that the First Lord of the Admiralty hadn't observed Holmes's furtive motion and it seemed, too, that my colleague wasn't ready to share his discovery.

We made small talk until Backwater's secretary returned, ashen-faced at having been unable to find "the d---ed old woman!", as he put it. Backwater promised to track her down and bring her to our rooms as soon as he located her.

So it was that we wished Backwater a good day and returned to Baker Street.

I was feeling rather deflated when Holmes spun around and, looking strangely animated, grasped me firmly by the shoulders.

"Watson," he said after a moment's pause, "it has long been a belief of mine that it's the little things that are often of most importance. Today, one small thing has proved that axiom to be absolutely correct. You know my methods. You know that I am loathe to reveal my thoughts before all the facts are gathered. I promise you, I will not leave you long in the dark but, for now, I beg that you won't speak to me for a full fifty minutes. This is quite a three-pipe problem."

By the time Holmes emerged from his reverie, the lamps had been re-filled and the shelves tidied. He has been true to his word: Less than an hour had passed since he had sat down to ponder the morning's events but, for me, with nothing to do but wait for enlightenment, time crawled. I filled it with a dozen small tasks but, finally, had to content myself with reading the scurrilous scraps of tittle-tattle that passed for news in the pages of the sporting *Pink*.

"First thing's first, Watson," Holmes said without preamble. "What do you make of this?" He held out his hand, and in it, I observed a small, metal *ankh*, about the size of a writing-box key.

"Tantalizing is it not?" Holmes said thoughtfully.

"Egyptian!" I said, remembering Holmes' news clipping. "Coincidence?"

"I refuse to speculate, but I think a telegram to Wilton Crescent may be in order. If there are any family members left in residence, then perhaps they can shed some light on the mysterious Captain Werner."

"Shouldn't we wait on Backwater and the archivist?"

"You know, my dear fellow" Holmes replied mysteriously, "I have a suspicion that they won't have any luck finding that particular 'old woman'."

The weather was cold, but the route pleasant enough for Holmes to suggest we travel on foot. We walked in silence, as men who know each other well often do. It took us half-an-hour at an energetic pace, loitering in Hyde Park long enough to observe the die-hards of the Serpentine Swimming Club break the ice and plunge into London's least-appealing lido.

I know doctors who swear that such things do wonders for all manner of male ailments, but watching all that white flesh turn blue, it seemed that, if we stayed much longer, I'd be required to administer some form of medical assistance.

We walked briskly on until the fifty buildings that form Wilton Crescent came into view. The street curves gently around a tranquil, private garden whose white houses are amongst some of London's most prestigious residences. Number 10 was marked by an imposing black door, and by the time we reached it, we were feeling heavy-footed and ruddy-faced.

Holmes unceremoniously dumped his coat and ear-flapped cap into the butler's outstretched arms. I followed suit.

We were led to a day room furnished with all manner of Egyptian occultism. We were defrosting nicely in front of the fire when an elderly but sprightly lady entered and introduced herself as Susannah Chesters.

The last-surviving daughter of John and Hannah had surely been a handsome young woman. Now in her seventieth year, she looked considerably younger, with flashing green eyes, a winning smile, and an easy manner. She wore a white, ankle-length robe of a type I'd seen sported by Afghani tribesmen. Her hair was covered by green scarf, presumably chosen to accentuate her eyes. She wore, perhaps, a little too much powder and rouge, but then, even mature ladies must be allowed their vanities.

However, what almost took my breath away was the bracelet hanging about her wrist, which was lined with tiny black *ankhs* that she fingered unconsciously as she spoke. Holmes, curiously, seemed more focused on the lady's shoes, whose dainty floral pattern was certainly appealing, but surely not worth his especial notice.

"Your telegram mentioned my parents?" she began without formalities.

"More specifically about their business partner, Captain Werner," Holmes began.

"Your telegram indicated as much," the lady said. "Something to do with the Admiralty? Please be seated." She waved us towards the wing-backed chairs at either side of the fire. "This will not take long, but you

295

may as well be comfortable. You will no doubt be aware," she said, "that my mother never married the man whose name she took. Please," she added, dismissing my attempts at the social niceties before they'd even been uttered, "this needs to be said. My parents cared deeply for each other, and had my father not already been married – and divorce laws what they are – he would have made things legal. For all that, when a rich, old man takes a young woman for a mistress, she is said to have ruined him. For the latter half of his life, my father was painted as a fool and my mother – worse. For my whole life I, too, have been judged for the perceived sins of my parents. So whatever questions you have, Mr. Holmes, please ask them without judgement."

Susannah spoke with passion but without rancor– something which left me with nothing but admiration for the lady.

"Thank you for you openness, Miss Chesters, but I can assure you," Holmes said with surprising passion, "I have no time for gossip, hearsay, or those who indulge it. My interest lies solely in your parent's business dealings."

Susannah looked at Holmes sharply, in much the same way as I had seen Holmes appraise others in the past. What she saw obviously passed muster, as she flashed him a warm smile and added, "Yes, I can see that you are a singular man, Mr. Holmes. Not one to be cowed by society. Well then, where to begin?

"My parents would sit where you are sit now," she said, sweeping an arm across the room as though painting the scene. "Werner was here by the window, maps, charts, and notebooks spread across that low table between them. The lamps were lit, and it was in that magical world of shadows and half-seen things that my sisters and I would sit, spellbound."

"Do you recall any specifics?"

Susanna Chesters lit up and suddenly she wasn't an elderly spinster, but someone made young again by the warmth of past memories. "My father followed the work of Monsieur Champollion, who had made such amazing strides deciphering the Egyptian's ancient scripts. He believed that hieroglyphs were the key to the secrets of the ancients. The place where magic and science met. My father loved to speculate and dream. He always saw the possibilities."

Holmes shook his head. "Possibilities?"

"For his work."

"If you don't mind the presumption," Holmes asked, "what was his work?"

"He was an inventor – of sorts. It wasn't widely known, but in certain circles he was known as 'the Great Pharaoh'!"

Holmes fairly bolted upright. "Stage magic?" he asked.

"He fabricated what he called 'ingenious devices' – crafted to appear as arcane machines, passed down through the ages! Many of the greatest magicians owe their success to my father. They paid him handsomely for his ideas and his discretion."

"And Werner?"

"A small man in body and character. He knew my father through the theatre, I believe – they were, at any rate, old friends. At least, until he betrayed them."

"How so?" I asked, increasingly intrigued by the tale now unfolding.

"Father had a mind to set his skills to work for the benefit of the Empire. He had an idea for what he called a 'wave generating machine' which could destroy ships remotely. He began making overtures to the Admiralty. Werner got greedy . . . ."

"There was a falling out?" I hazarded.

"Falling out! Dr. Watson, when – " And here she paused for a moment to collect herself before continuing in a more measured tone. "When my mother learned what Werner had done, she chased him from the house. But by then, it was too late. He had stolen my father's work. Thank the Lord he hadn't the brains to pursue it!"

Her speech – both its intensity and its fascinating subject matter – stayed with us long after we returned to Baker Street.

"But look," I said, "this is all just hocus-pocus. Surely Chesters and Werner were slight-of-hand men. Nothing else to it."

"Indeed?" And how do you explain the *ankh*?"

"Yes! Why didn't you challenge her about that?"

Holmes refused to be drawn further on the subject. Instead he pulled a cigar from the coal scuttle and, lighting it, spent the rest of the evening smoking and staring into the fire. I wasn't party to his thoughts, but mine involved vanishing documents and impossible machines. Sadly, my own poor brain couldn't fathom how the two things were related.

The next morning, Baker Street was still blanketed in snow and, with it, came a strange muffling of sound as though the world was whispering. We were demolishing a pot of hot cocoa when the postman broke the hush. Holmes opened telegram after telegram and, while he didn't deign to share their contents, cries of "Ha!" and "Excellent!" told me that he'd received the information he was after.

I spent the some time kicking my heels while Holmes followed whatever clues his correspondents had led him to. By the time he had throughly satisfied himself, I was eager to rejoin the chase, which led us, of all places, to a mausoleum.

An English funeral is a strange thing indeed. Clocks stopped at the hour of death, mirrors turned to the wall, curtains closed, trails of sable-clad mourners lining the street – and not a women amongst them, in case the drunkenness of that solemn occasion should upset their delicate sensibilities. And, if we are to believe the advertisements put abroad by the funeral peddlers, then there are different qualities of grief according to the social standing of the deceased and the money available to be spent on such public displays.

One will find death in all its variety in London's great cemeteries, yet the places themselves are more like gardens than places of grief. Indeed, thousands visit them for leisure, touring the lanes, and even bringing picnics to share with lost loves, whose new "homes" proudly boast of their tenant's Earthly accomplishments. *"Here lies George Farthing, late of Cheyenne Mews, business man, magistrate, kind to women, children, and dogs."* And so it goes.

Brompton is perhaps the most beautiful of London's seven formal cemeteries, and it is here that many of the capitol's richest families end their days.

The Chesters' striking mausoleum wasn't hard to find. Though situated in a less fashionable avenue, away from the cemetery's more popular and well-trod paths, it dominated its surroundings.

The structure resembled the doorway of a giant pyramid, if one could imagine that the rest of the monolith had been eroded away by the passage of time. Flat topped, it was adorned with Egyptian hieroglyphs, with apparent entrances at all four compass points, but only one – to the west – was marked with a bronze door and had a keyhole.

"Would you not say that this fellow seems to looking directly at the Chesters' mausoleum?" Holmes pointed to a small grave marker, opposite the pyramid, which carried the head of Anubis.

Our miniature deity did indeed seem to be showing a marked interest in its neighbor's resting place.

"Two occupants," Holmes noted, motioning to a pair of hieroglyphic-covered lozenge-shaped cartouches on that grave before turning to view the Chesters' tomb.

There, he handed me one of the telegrams which had arrived at Baker Street earlier in the day. I could see that it came from the cemetery's Management Office and contained a concise nine-word reply:

Tomb built 1854. STOP We hold no plans or key. STOP

Holmes rounded on the monument and then, to my unutterable horror, knelt down and pulled a small oilskin bundle from his voluminous pockets. His burglar's tools!

"You can't!" I spluttered.

"I *shouldn't*, perhaps" Holmes replied grimly. "But I *can* and I *will*. And, if you object, then you can do me the favor of watching the path. I have no liking for the work, but logic tells me that what we're looking for is behind this door."

I stayed put and Holmes, glancing back, nodded appreciatively and said in a tone tight with tension, "I knew you wouldn't fail me. Now, hold back, and once I step over the threshold, whatever happens, make no attempt to enter. I may be foolhardy when it comes to my own safety, but I should never forgive myself should anything happen to my dear Watson."

The lock opened with a low click and the door swung open, and I was staring into a tomb so dark that it hurt the eyes to look upon.

Holmes moved to step inside and I was filled with a sense of dread so strong I called out. He looked back at me, his face tight with anxiety. Then, taking a deep breath, he threw the little bundle of burglar's tools to me. "Just in case you need them!" he said, ominously, then stepped over the threshold.

I watched as he turned, looking up, squinting, at something – I knew not what. Then I saw him raise one arm, to touch the far wall. Again, another click, this time from deep within the structure. Holmes stepped briskly backwards.

I heard it as clear as day – an ominous growl deep within the structure. Then there was a magnesium flare, so bright I was forced to look away. My eyes were still adjusting when I heard another click and the door began to swing closed. I looked back just in time to see my friend – Sherlock Holmes – shimmer and vanish into the darkness. The bronze door closed in my face and I was left standing on the steps of that monumental tomb, numb with horror.

I lack Holmes's skills for house-breaking, and it took me quite an hour to find the right combination of picks and torque. I was almost frantic by the time the great door swung open again and I was able to peer inside. The darkness was almost total, and I had to gather my courage before I could persuade myself to enter, dreading what I might find.

The tomb itself exuded an odd scent. Not of decay, as one might expect. More like the earthy odor produced by rain on dry soil. I was relieved to find the floor solid, my first fear being that it had collapsed beneath my friend's feet. Using my cane, I tapped my way across the extent of the vault, but the acoustics were so dampened by the heavy walls and heavy air that if there were any hidden apartments, I couldn't discern them. Next, I worked my way around the walls. Although the structure was little more than a claustrophobic square, it took me another hour to reassure myself that Holmes wasn't trapped within, slumped in an unseen nook.

As I worked my heart pounded, expecting with every step to find Holmes gravely injured – or worse. At the entrance, I noted rows of symbols carved around the edge, in imitation of those on the outside. I girded myself and, standing with my back to the wall, I used the tip of my cane to touch each symbol in turn. I almost expected the floor to descend and carry me into a hidden crypt. I had seen coffin lifts which worked that way, but my hopes were quickly dashed. Finally, in a moment of abject despair, I called out Holmes's name. I repeated it over and over, hearing nothing in return but the dead echo of my own voice.

It was as the day began to fade and the first owls began to emerge from their leafy boughs that I abandoned all hope that Holmes would somehow reappear. I was loathe to call on the police, for this concerned a Government secret. What on Earth would I tell them? But in the end I had no choice. I made my way to the little Porter's Lodge feeling more alone than I had in many years.

In a tomb that clearly wasn't a tomb, I had seen Holmes vanish before my very eyes. I didn't expect the Porter to believe me, but the man's incredulity bordered on the asinine.

I couldn't, of course, admit that we had broken into the mausoleum, and my concern for Holmes' welfare quite sapped my inventiveness. In the end, all I could do was repeat my assertion that Holmes was trapped – maybe dying – and that the fault was his for leaving such a dangerous structure open for anyone to stumble into.

Despite my thinly-veiled accusation, he flatly refused to abandon his post and accompany me to the tomb to resume the search. But I did eventually elicit his promise that he would do so as soon as the Night Porter arrived to start his shift, in just a few minutes.

So equipped with a lantern and a blanket, I headed back to the strange pyramid to watch and wait.

The time passed painfully. I examined the tomb two more times before I admitted defeat and settled down to wait for the Porter.

Unexpectedly, I dozed, fitfully, dreaming of Holmes trapped and alone, buried alive in some monstrous sarcophagus, clawing at the inside of his gilded tomb with fingers worn to the bone. The scene shifted and I was faced with a giant jackal-headed god, holding a set of scales. On one side lay a feather, on the other my own beating heart. I woke with a start, clutching my at chest, expecting for all the world to find my ribs splintered and my chest hollow.

It was as I pulled myself to consciousness that I realized I could still hear the clawing and gnawing sounds that had inhabited my nightmare!

I grabbed the lantern, and dashed inside the tomb. Its garish light threw up hideous shadows which seemed to dance their way around the walls and, at first, I despaired of seeing anything clearly.

Finally I spotted it! One wall which seemed out of true.

Yes! As I held up the lantern, I could see a gap at the top and – *There!* – the fingers of a hand, pale and much bloodied.

I jammed my own hands into the gap and began to push downwards.

It seemed to take forever but, eventually, I heard that same click I had all those hours ago, and a section of the wall in front of me seemed to fall away into nothing.

Behind it, Holmes' distinctive silhouette emerged and I leapt towards it just in time to catch my friend as he toppled forwards, his face, ashy pale, beads of perspiration upon his brow.

Once safely outside, I wrapped the blanket around Holmes' shoulder and managed to dig out my trusty hip-flask.

He took a dram, looking greatly exhausted, his hands, almost purple with cold, shook as he took it. He downed it in one, and it wasn't until another had been disposed of in the same way that he felt able to speak.

"Watson, I've been a damnable fool, and you may tell me so whenever I take it upon myself to investigate a case without first letting my dear friend in on the secret. If it hadn't been for you, I would, even now, be trapped in some icy morgue, waiting for cold and exhaustion to do their worst."

"But where did you go?"

"Where indeed?" Holmes laughed shortly. "Were I inclined to hyperbole, I would say to Hell and back. Suffice to say, I have been visiting what's left of John Chesters' repository of ingenious devices and ingenious ideas. Thank goodness for penny church candles and a ready supply of matches!"

"You knew?"

"The telegrams gave me my clues. It started with the *ankh*. First on the bracelet. Then, in the clipping, we saw the design repeated around the door of the tomb. According to the British Museum's Department of Egyptian and Assyrian Antiquities, a common motif in Egyptian art is a pharaoh holding an *ankh*, or passing it on to someone else. The symbolism represents the pharaoh's survival after death. He literally passes his essence into the care of the gods."

301

I started to wonder how a magician, known as the Great Pharaoh, might interpret that.

"Then there was the fact that, according to Somerset House, the mausoleum was built long before both Hannah and John's deaths. Neither of their daughters were buried in Brompton. So what was it for?"

"John Chesters builds a pyramid to ensure that his 'essence' – his life's work – stays safe?" I asked.

"It would makes sense, especially after the whole Werner debacle." Holmes replied.

"But how was it done?"

"The mechanism was simple enough. You no doubt noted that inside the mausoleum was square. Outside it was pyramidal. I was expecting tricks and hidden compartments. Some sequence linked to the hieroglyphs – a name perhaps – but it turned out that all I needed was a key." He held up the tiny *ankh*.

"Once I had found the key hole, a section of wall slid down to reveal a ladder into the vault below. A little smoke and mirrors added to the theatrical nature of the thing.

"Sadly, time and London weather hasn't been kind to the apparatus. I feared I was trapped there for good." He paused, holding up his bruised and gashed hands, before continuing with ghoulish glee. "There was a point when I believed that I would have to claw my way out of the cold stone surrounding me, inch by inch, but I eventually got the key to turn and, with your help, I ended where I began. I've likely given more than a few cemetery visitor's nightmares with my unearthly scrapings and bangings this evening!"

"The Chesters are buried in the small grave opposite?"

"I'm sure that's what the hieroglyphs would tell us, should we go to the effort of translating them."

"The plans!" In all my excitement I had almost lost sight of why we had visited the mausoleum at all. "Were they there?"

Holmes smiled, pulling a mud-smeared bundle of papers from his coat. "Indeed they were!"

We were inching our way towards the North Lodge when the Porter appeared, armed with more blankets, a pick, and a shovel. "Borrowed off-of old Joe, in case push-came-to-shove."

I must admit that my initial impression of the man warmed considerably at his toothy smile and gushing apologies at the sight of my much-abused friend. Doubly so, when he invited us back to the Lodge to share his supper before waving down a cab to take us back to Baker Street.

Once there, I insisted on applying iodine and bandages to Holmes's ragged fingers, but I couldn't compel him to sleep. Instead, he rang for

Mrs. Hudson and we indulged in a breakfast of curried Guinea fowl. It's a curious thing that Holmes will go without food for days when a case consumes him but, at its conclusion, will eat with the capacity of a hungry python. I judged from the evident gusto with which he demolished breakfast that we were reaching the end of the chase.

We arrived at Wilton Crescent early enough to have to ring several times before a maid, looking like she had been disturbed in the process of making up the morning's fire, opened the door.

Holmes requested – rather demanded – an interview with Miss Chesters and, despite the girl's protests, we admitted ourselves to the day room to once again await the lady of the house.

We didn't have to wait long. She entered like a whirlwind. "And just who are you," she said in a voice cold and low, "to force your way into my home at this hour?"

Holmes rose, his sharp, eager face, calm and forceful. "I am the man, Miss Chesters, who will not be reporting the theft of secret Admiralty documents to the police. I am the man who will not be handing the culprit over to the authorities. In fact, Miss Chesters I am the man who, at this very moment, is putting his reputation on the line because I believe – as do you – that the device your father proposed is not something that any sane person wishes to see unleashed on the world. But most of all, Miss Chesters, I am the man, who at this moment is your fondest ally."

For a moment the lady said nothing, and then all the tension evaporated from her face. Smiling, she crossed the room and took Holmes's hands in hers. "God bless you, Mr. Holmes! Now, you must have a hundred questions. Please, ask what you will. I know my secrets are safe with you."

Holmes pulled out the bundle of papers he had retrieved from the tomb. "I had occasion to read through these this morning," he said. "See here, Watson: A copy of John Scott Russell's paper on waves of translation. Until his work, such waves really were the stuff of myth and legend. Gigantic waves, generated who knew how, able to sink ships without trace. Your father was able to create these, Miss Chesters?"

"I believe he intended to solicit funds for further research. A machine of the sort he imagined may not even have been possible, but you will see letters to Mr. Russell within, where they discuss their planned collaboration. However, before he could proceed, my father discovered that Werner had contacted the Admiralty independently. He'd arranged some demonstration to convince them that the device had already been made."

"He did sink the hulk?"

She nodded again. "Pure showmanship. Sink shells in the seabed, anchor them under the water, with a long rope attached . . . and with a small submersible to pull the ropes, you can bring the explosive materials together. The explosives do the real damage, but you still generate a wave impressive enough to convince people that some magical wave machine has done the work!"

I laughed then. "So he really did have a submersible?"

"Some remnant of the French wars, I believe."

"Did you steal the plans?" Holmes asked in a half-whisper.

"The Admiralty replaced all of their safes in 1855. My mother kept a weather-eye on such things – waiting for an appropriate opportunity. She was able to take advantage of the chaos to acquire the plans then, much as I did a few days ago.

"Oh, I know now it was a silly risk – but when I got your telegram, I realized the Admiralty wouldn't stop. I had to make sure that all references to that horrible device were destroyed."

With his finger and thumb, Holmes plucked the small black *ankh* he had found in the Admiralty strong room from his waistcoat pocket and handed it to Mrs. Chesters.

"I had missed it. Thank you!" the lady laughed and I noticed, then, how different she looked to our last meeting, without all the powder and rouge. "When I saw you at the Admiralty," she said in answer to my inquisitive looks, "and then later at my house, I feared you would recognize me immediately. Too much powder?"

Holmes chuckled, genuinely delighted. "It was well done! Especially the misdirection with the boxes. Although in truth, it was the distinctive design of your shoes, and not your powder, that gave the game away!"

"It helped having a father who was in the theatre," she replied. "And honestly, Backwater has the place in such an uproar – and so many extra staff – who would notice one more elderly lady? I slipped in with the crowds in the morning, then waited for lunch and left with everyone else. It was no great task to find where the First Lord was, attach myself to his retinue, and make myself quietly invaluable. But Oh! Mr. Holmes, my heart almost stopped when I saw you!"

"You took the papers?"

"Yes, as simple as that!" she said clapping her hands in delight. She leapt up from the chair, and began gathering books from this cabinet and that. "Now, Doctor – how many did I just pick up?"

"Five. No – wait six. You picked up a red leather one. But I don't see it now." I said.

"Very good!" she replied, producing the missing book from under her gown, like a magician producing a rabbit.

304

"Misdirection. I guessed that someone would be sent to collect the papers. So when Backwater asked his Secretary, all I had to do was follow him to the Vault Room – while making it seem that he was the one following me. Once the safe was open, I palmed the file!"

For a while none of us spoke. Then, without warning, Holmes stood, like a man startled from a deep sleep and turned to Miss Chesters. "Well," he said, "this has been fascinating, but we have already taken up too much of your time. Come Watson."

"But . . . but . . ." I spluttered. "What will you tell the Admiralty?"

"That there's nothing to worry about. That clearly no one would steal such valuable plans and then not use them. That it's all the fault of outmoded bureaucracy. I suspect Backwater will be more than happy not have any more paperwork on the subject."

"Lord Backwater tells me that I may place implicit reliance upon your judgment and discretion."

– Lord St. Simon
"The Noble Bachelor"

Notes

- While Watson is, as ever, discrete about his use of real names and places, the Chesters are undoubtedly Hannah and John Courtoy, whose mausoleum is a notable feature of Brompton Cemetery. Their Egyptian-style mausoleum has been the subject of considerable curiosity and speculation over the years. Some even believe that it is transportation chamber or time machine! The details of Hannah Courtoy's life follow much of what Watson records here. She had three daughters out of wedlock with John Courtoy, who was one of London's wealthiest men. No one is certain how he made his fortune.

- A small gravestone, said to be designed by Courtoy's great friend, the Egyptologist Joseph Bonomi, is nearby. On it is the head of Anubis, who does appear to look towards the Courtoy mausoleum.

- Also buried in Brompton is Samuel Warner, an English inventor of naval weapons, who did indeed demand £200,000 for the plans to "*a kind of psychic torpedo*" said to be able to destroy ships at great distance. Warner is now regarded as a charlatan. Watson clearly chose to rename him "Werner" to save the authorities embarrassment, as the original enjoyed a great deal of support from his friends in Parliament.

- The weapon trial described did happen and did destroy a hulk, the *John O'Gaunt*, by unknown means. Plans for the invention were apparently given to the Admiralty, but they have never been found. During a House of Lords inquiry, the Duke of Wellington suggested that, as the inquiry was one of a scientific nature, it be entrusted to the Ordnance Department. No report was ever forthcoming.

- In 1800, France built a human-powered submarine called the *Nautilus*. When Warner was questioned by parliament, he is reported to have said that his father, William Warner, had owned the *Nautilus*, and used it to bring over spies during the Napoleonic Wars. Warner later claimed that he served with his father and helped to sink two of the enemy's privateers.

- The *Nautilus* was designed to sink ships using mines which would be attached to the hull of an enemy ship with a spike. As the submarine moved away, a line attached to the device, would pull it into contact with the hull, causing it to explode. The description is similar to Werner's "showmanship" described by Susannah Chesters.

- In 1834, John Scott Russell described observing waves of translation in a Scottish canal. These waves had long been the subject of maritime myth, but having seen them for himself, Russell speculated that underwater objects could produce waves of vast size, capable of sinking ships with no trace. He was later able to generate these waves under laboratory conditions. Russell's work gave birth to the modern study of *solitons*. If Courtoy and Russell actually built a machine to generate such waves, it remains lost.

The Adventure of the
Opening Eyes
by Tracy J. Revels

"You must help me, Mr. Holmes! My case is so strange, my problem so baffling, that surely it will be worth your time. And if not . . . then I can only prepare my soul for death, for surely the devil is after me and I cannot escape his clutches!"

My friend, Mr. Sherlock Holmes, mastered his instinctive smirk and gently waved our overly excited guest onto our sofa. The young man was tall and pale, his almost-skeletal face bathed in sweat despite the morning's autumnal chill.

"What aspect of your recent inheritance do you find so distressing?" Holmes asked. The fellow couldn't have been more than twenty-five, but some pronounced mental disturbance had lined his face and carved deep valleys beneath his eyes. He was plainly dressed, yet carried a heavy antique cane topped with a golden griffon. A large silver watch dangled from a somewhat-tarnished chain. These were the only things which I observed to give merit to Holmes's inquiry about an inheritance, though surely more clues were visible to his keen eye.

"You come directly to the point," the gentleman said, pulling out a monogramed handkerchief and mopping it across his brow. "I see your gifts have not been exaggerated. My name is Clarence Pierpont, and I am indeed troubled by my inheritance, for it comes with a curse."

Holmes settled into his chair, nodding toward the window and the dreary October weather just beyond. "A curse? Well, it is the season for such things. Do indulge us with your story."

"My maternal uncle was Victor Lynch. Perhaps you have heard of him? No?" The nervous gentleman shook his head. "I am not surprised, nor am I offended. Very few people know of him, with good reason. He was an artist, but an undistinguished one. It isn't to say that he completely lacked talent – he could produce a reasonably workmanlike landscape, and he had an aptitude for hunting dogs and horses.

"My uncle created most of his paintings for pretentious country squires and their ilk. But back in 1860, when he was just beginning his career, he produced a large canvas that won him a brief season of fame. It is called *Sleeping Venus*. Here is a reproduction of it."

He handed Holmes a hand-tinted sketch. My friend's eyebrows rose, but he said nothing before passing the image along to me.

"Why, I know this work!" I exclaimed. It was a picture of a lovely woman stretched in mid-doze along a riverbank. She was nude, though draped in her golden, flowing hair, which strategically covered her like a magical blanket. There was much to admire in the painting, from the reflection of the woman in the sparkling water to the realistic quality of the birds that curiously observed her slumber and the supple tendrils of weeping willows which formed a bower around her. But it was more than the setting and the coy pink flesh which elevated a rather pedestrian composition to a near masterpiece. It was something about her repose, the delicacy of her closed eyes, the strange aura of lifelike sleep. Studying her face, one felt drawn into the work, as if at any moment the goddess might draw a deep breath and awaken to smile sweetly at the viewer. "Where have I beheld this enchanting figure?" I asked, as much to myself as to my companions.

"Have you frequented some of our seedier drinking establishments?" Pierpont asked. "I am told that copies of her often hang behind the bar. That she sleeps above the bottles of gin."

"She is also much favored in riotous bachelor households," Holmes chuckled. "In my university days, she graced the wall of a boarding house where several young gentlemen – of the type more inclined to the pursuit of pleasure than their studies – resided in a merry company."

"You are correct, Mr. Holmes. She has become something of a garish and questionable bit of décor these days. I have never seen the original, but my uncle assured me that the copies, as splendid as they are, didn't do it justice. He said that the real *Sleeping Venus* is superb, and quite tasteful and pleasing to look upon. She is chaste and holy. It is the men who worship her image in questionable places who are vulgar and degrade her by association! I am certain that it was this quality of both sensuality and purity which attracted her purchaser, who paid my uncle a small fortune for her."

"Who owns the original?" I asked.

"That was the great family secret," Pierpont answered, lowering his voice, as if he feared we might be overheard. "For years, Uncle wouldn't divulge who had purchased the picture. He even claimed he was forbidden to discuss its buyer. But, finally, about five years ago, he revealed the truth to me. *Sleeping Venus* belongs to Her Majesty, the Queen."

I gasped. "Surely not!"

"I assure you this is true. The late Prince Consort was, as you know, a great aficionado of paintings, and he saw it in a Regent Street Gallery. The next afternoon, a royal courtier arrived to inquire about the painting, and the gallery agent was canny enough to negotiate a higher price because he realized the purchaser was the Queen. The painting was destined to be a birthday gift for His Highness." Pierpont shook his head. "I can see you don't believe me."

"The Queen is the soul of propriety!" I snapped. "To imagine her owning such a thing, it is – "

"Elementary," Holmes said, "for in 1860 the Queen wasn't yet a widow, but a wife who was very much in love with her husband. They had their private rooms and their personal collections." He smiled at my scandalized look. "They were certainly not the first married pair to indulge a love of classical images, and they possessed the wealth to own originals, not mere copies. I have it on the best authority that the Osborne House collection is quite *extensive* in this area."

I stared at Holmes, wondering who his confidant was. Who had seen the inside of Her Majesty's most private suites? Holmes signaled for our guest to continue.

"It was the sale of *Sleeping Venus* which allowed my uncle to dedicate himself solely to the pursuit of his art. Unfortunately, lifelong fame eluded him. Oh, he made enough to buy his country house and indulge his pleasures via sales to local gentry, but actual applause and a place in the pantheon of English artists was never his, and when he died, six months ago, it was in misery and obscurity. Uncle never married, and in his later years he took to drink, so that his life was shortened both through his melancholy and his indulgence in spirits.

"I am his late sister's son, and his only heir. Dale House, as it is called, passed to me, along with all of Uncle's unsold paintings. My health has never been good – indeed I have been troubled with a weak heart all my life – and knew that I couldn't afford any demanding career. I make my living by editing books and stories for aspiring writers, so I may work from any location I choose, and it seemed to me that a house in the country might be a far more pleasant home than a flat in the city. But how wrong I was!

"I took possession of Dale House a month after Uncle's burial. The property had but a single old housekeeper, who was eager to retire, and so I hired a new staff – a butler, a housekeeper who is also a cook, a boy to see after the yards and stable, and a pair of maids, twin girls from the nearby village. There was room enough in the East Wing for them all to live in the house, and it seemed that we would suit each other fine, as my needs were few and my only occasional visitors a handful of university friends.

"But a week after we had all settled in, the first strange note arrived. Harris, my butler, found it on the doorstep one morning. It was a single

309

piece of paper, folded over, the message composed via letters clipped from a newspaper. It read: '*I am owed a thousand pounds for Sleeping Venus. Place it in the garden folly or face my wrath.*'

"You can imagine, sir, that this missive greatly shocked and alarmed me. I took it to the village constable, who dismissed it as a prank by my serving boy. Jackie sobbed and pleaded that he knew nothing of it, and he is a good lad in all regards, quite incapable of such mischief. None of the other servants could make anything of it. Baffled, I visited the former housekeeper and presented it to her. She took one look and nodded.

"'Oh, yes, the Master received many like these in the last year that he lived. Never any clue as to where they came from. Always asking for a thousand pounds, always threatening revenge. Drove him to distraction, it did.'

"'And did he know the sender?'

"'He claimed not, but I thought otherwise. Once, I heard him shrieking in a drunken tantrum that, "Venus is mine, you shall not claim her, no matter how you harass me!" But that is all I know.'"

"And have you continued to receive these messages?" Holmes asked.

"Only one more was found, three days after the first. I somehow misplaced the first letter, but I have the second one. You may read it for yourself."

I rose and moved to look over Holmes's shoulder. The letter read: *The eyes will open until my debt is settled.*

"How bizarre!" I said. "Whatever can it mean?"

"Whisky, please," our client murmured. His body had begun to sway, his hands were shaking as if he had been seized with a palsy. Holmes quickly procured a glass, while I took the man's pulse. He was in a state of such nervous excitement he seemed likely to faint.

"You must understand," he whispered, as he allowed the bracing alcohol to take effect, "that my uncle wanted nothing more than to reclaim the success he had known with his *Sleeping Venus*. To this aim, he painted almost a hundred portraits, studies of celebrities, local villagers, and his servants. In each face, the subject's eyes were closed, for that was the aspect most praised in his *Venus*. But he was never satisfied with the effect, and so the portraits remained scattered about the house, most hanging unframed, each a silent rebuke. I saw them at first as a novelty that would amuse my friends, and so I didn't move them. Now . . . I wouldn't touch one for all the money in the world. For, you see, *they are opening their eyes!*"

Holmes and I exchanged a startled glance.

"The portraits?" I asked.

"Yes. The eyes of the people in the pictures are opening, as if awakening from sleep! It began on the morning after I received that note which you hold. I had just settled into the dining room with my breakfast, and I lifted my gaze to the wall across from me, where a portrait of Lord Melbourne hung. The picture had amused me, for the statesman looked as if he had dozed off while listening to some boring speech in Parliament. But now he was staring at me, his eyes ablaze, as if at any moment he might step down from his frame. I freely confess that I screamed and fainted. My butler and cook were terribly alarmed, and then equally frightened. Harris finally worked up the nerve to throw a canvas over the thing, and I paid a local boy a sovereign to haul the monstrosity away and burn it."

"You didn't examine the picture? You didn't note the wet paint?"

"Mr. Holmes – that would have been the action of a sensible man. But to see unreal eyes suddenly boring into me – it was too much, and I gave the order to destroy the thing before I was rational. Finally, late that evening, a friend came by and convinced me it had been a prank. The next day, all was well, and my friend returned to London. But the following morning, as I was passing along the corridor outside the great hall, I felt as if someone was watching me. I turned about and looked at the little shepherdess, who Uncle had portrayed dozing beside her lamb. She was now awake and leveling an unfriendly gaze at me.

"I confess my nerves gave way again, but before I allowed Harris to carry me off to bed, I asked him to inspect the eyes. Surely, if someone in the house was talented enough to pry them open, as you say, the paint would still be fresh. But no – it was all original. Harris even dared to take a knife and scraped about the face, but there was only one layer applied. Somehow the original paint had become flesh, and capable of movement.

"It has been like this, sir, for a week! Every morning, a new individual is found with his or her eyes alive and following me. I can bear it no longer." He leaned forward, his face in his hands. "A thousand pounds would break me, for Uncle left genuine debts to be settled – money that is owed to flesh-and-blood tradesmen, not to spirits! Please, sir, you must come and rid me of this torment."

"I will be happy to do so, for your case is rather unique," Holmes said. "But allow me to pose a few questions to you first. You mentioned that the painting of Lord Melbourne was in your dining hall, and the little girl was in a hallway. Have the other affected pictures been in these rooms as well?"

"No sir. They have been scattered about the house."

"Please try to recall where in the house each was discovered."

311

Pierpont looked grieved, as if such memory caused pain. But he dutifully put his head down and began counting on his bony fingers.

"After the shepherdess . . . the next was the butcher, who hung in the kitchen passageway. After that was an unknown goddess, whose image graced the foyer. I believe the portrait of Sir Walter Scott in the parlor, and after that – my God, this was the worst, this morning, the thing that drove me to throw my predicament before you – a self-portrait of my uncle, which hung above my bedroom mantel. He was now glaring at me, as if to know why I permitted such mischief in his house."

"Were the any of these pictures in frames?"

Pierpont considered. "No, none of them."

"That is intriguing," my friend murmured. "I would assume these diabolical doings are robbing the entire household of sleep."

The man scowled. "I confess to you, sir, that after the first two incidents, I haven't gone to bed without a dollop of laudanum. The servants have been taking shifts – Harris was first, and then the boy, and the maids sit up together. Last night, it was poor Mrs. Ellis who took the watch, though Harris told me that he found her asleep on the sofa this morning. My housekeeper was exhausted. It is fair to say that all of us walk around rubbing our eyes and yawning. We cannot continue such vigils for much longer."

"Nor shall you have any need to do so," Holmes said, rising and assuring Pierpont that we would follow him to Dale House the next morning. As the man prepared to depart, Holmes asked him to send the references that each of his servants had provided as soon as he returned home.

"You suspect the servants of this strange blackmail?" I asked once Pierpont had exited our rooms. I watched from the window as he did a nervous jig to hail a cab.

"You know my maxim, Watson. Once you have eliminated the impossible – "

"Yes, yes, I recall something of the sort."

Holmes grinned around the stem of his pipe as he struck a match. "Shall we give spirits any latitude this time?"

"Of course not."

"Then the deed is most likely being done by someone in the house, someone who can move easily from room to room and replace the paintings with exact replicas."

"What?"

Holmes nodded. "It is the only explanation. Otherwise, there would be evidence of newly applied paint, some retouching of the older masterpieces."

312

"But to copy such unusual works of art would require great talent."

"Indeed – though seeing as how Mr. Pierpont and all his staff are new residents, it is unlikely that their knowledge of the paintings is exact. A skillful forger could probably recreate one with passable details, especially as our client is so excitable and nervous, and unlikely to have an eye for observation . . . beyond noting the obviously opened ones, of course."

Holmes refused to speculate further. That evening, a small envelope arrived, containing the references that the servants had provided. The maids were only seventeen, and as this was their first employment, there was nothing except a glowing letter from the local vicar, testifying to their good character. Likewise, the stable boy had a letter from his schoolmaster, and the butler came with stellar recommendations from two former employers.

"Nothing for the housekeeper, I see," Holmes muttered. "But Harris, the butler, interests me."

"Why?"

"Because he was previously in service as a footman for Lord Hensley, and as a butler for Sir Edward Ayers. Both gentlemen are noted patrons of the arts – Sir Edward is a rather prolific, if supremely untalented, portrait painter. What might Harris have learned from them, hmm? I fear, Watson, that this will not be one of your more intriguing adventures."

But in that regard, my friend couldn't have been in greater error.

When we arrived at Dale House at exactly nine on the following morning, we found the household in turmoil. A physician's carriage was waiting at the door, and the stable lad was walking around with a tear-stained face. Harris – tall, solemn, and black-bearded – answered our knock. He was the essence of respectability, but he was clearly suppressing a strong emotion. As we stepped inside, I heard feminine weeping from deeper in the house.

"Yes, Mr. Holmes, Doctor Watson, my Master told me to expect you this morning. But I fear there was a tragedy in the nighttime. Mr. Pierpont isn't long for the world – he is grievously injured."

"May I be of assistance to him?" I asked, feeling immediately drawn to the case in my medical capacity. Harris motioned for us to follow him toward the large central staircase.

"What has happened?" Holmes asked. His keen eyes were taking in the bizarre décor on every wall. It was all so strange that for a moment I was frozen in my tracks. Then – embarrassed by my reaction – I hurried to catch up with my friend.

313

Everywhere around us were painted sleepers. My blood ran cold as we passed picture upon picture, of all shapes and sizes, having nothing in common except the closed eyes of their subjects.

"Very early in the morning – I would say about one – the entire household was awakened by a bloodcurdling scream. I rose immediately and, by the time I had thrown on my dressing gown and slippers, the maids and Mrs. Ellis were standing at the doors of their rooms, the girls holding each other in terror. Mrs. Ellis had the good sense to bring a lamp, and together we hurried here, to the landing." Harris paused, pointing downward as we reached the top of the stairs. "At first, I saw nothing, and was about to go on to the west wing, and my Master's bedroom, when Mrs. Ellis gave a cry. I looked where she pointed, and saw Mr. Pierpont. He had fallen down the stairs and struck the bottom of the bannister. Upon reaching him, I thought he was dead, but then I realized he was still breathing. Jackie had run down in his nightshirt, and I sent him at once for the doctor, who is with him now. If you will come this way?"

We followed Harris down a dark, rather dismal hallway lined with even more macabre pictures. He pushed open a doorway, admitting us to a cavernous bedroom. The doctor, a brusque, red-faced man, quickly informed us that Pierpont's prognosis was grim.

"A cracked skull, perhaps bleeding in the brain, and a broken right arm. Only time will tell, and we can but wait and pray."

I feared I had nothing to add after a brief examination of the patient, though I was grateful that the man's breathing wasn't labored, and his pulse was strong. Holmes gave the sufferer only the briefest glance before stalking about the room, gesturing to the discolorations and empty nails on the walls.

"I take it once Mr. Pierpont woke up to his relative's visage, he had the rest of the paintings in the room removed."

"Yes, sir," Harris answered.

"Yet the other paintings in the house remained."

"He felt it best to leave them in place until you were consulted. He told me last evening, as Mrs. Ellis and I were laying out his dinner, that once you were finished, he would have all the paintings destroyed."

"Exactly the course I would have encouraged," Holmes said. "I will have a look around and then I will wish to speak to the staff. Perhaps you can assemble them in the kitchen?"

"At once, sir."

Holmes hummed softly to himself as he stepped into the hall. It was a raw, dreary day, and rain had begun to patter on the roof and rattle at the windows. The house was so old that gas hadn't been laid in it, and we were guided solely by sputtering candles. Holmes moved slowly, examining

314

each picture along the wall. A cold chill crept over my skin. While many of the subjects were portrayed in attitudes of repose – a student slumped on his desk, and baby in a cradle – other posed as if for traditional portraits, sitting or standing upright, but with their eyelids firmly pressed shut. Holmes scowled.

"I will need much better illumination if I am to study the brushwork. However – My word, *this* is a striking composition!"

I almost leapt backward as a sudden bolt of lightning threw an erratic illumination on a nearly life-sized picture that hung on the wall at the top of the grand staircase. I barely noticed it coming up, for my mind had been consumed with concern for the patient. Now I was nearly paralyzed by the emotion the painting provoked.

It was a devil, complete with a stark white face, a pointed black beard, and a red robe. He held a pitchfork above his head, poised as if to lash out and pierce a victim's soul. His ruby lips were pulled back, exposing sharp teeth and a forked tongue. Black horns grew from his brow, and a tail snaked around his waist, seeming to flick and dance with evil vitality.

It was the eyes, however, that pinned me down. Never had I seen such malice and diabolical intent expressed with such realism.

Holmes caught my arm.

"Steady, Watson!"

I realized that I had almost mimicked the Master of the house and plunged backward over the well-worn stairs. Harris was coming up from below and noted my agitation.

"Sir, are you . . . *My God!*"

Holmes lifted an eyebrow. "Has this picture always been in this place?"

"Yes, sir. We called him the *Sleeping Satan*. And now he is *awake!*"

"Did you notice what condition he was in this morning, when you came to your Master's aid?"

"No, sir. I fear we were far more worried about getting Mr. Pierpont to his room to notice the picture. And it was very dark last night – cloudy with no moon."

Lightning flashed again. Holmes reached out and tapped the devil's eyes.

"Dry. Intriguing. You have gathered the staff? Excellent. Would you object to me seeing the interior of their rooms? No? Splendid. Watson, if you will handle the interviews?"

Sometimes Holmes placed me in rather uncomfortable positions. I was uncertain what questions he wished me to pose, or whom he suspected. It dawned on me, as I followed the directions to the kitchen, that perhaps Holmes wished to be alone with the butler to accuse him of

315

the crime. I worried, for Holmes hadn't requested to borrow my revolver, nor had he brought one himself, and Harris was a large, muscular man. While Holmes's abilities in physical confrontations were excellent, I didn't like to leave him with such a fearsome opponent. But what could I say in protest that wouldn't give my friend's game away? I mentally pledged that I would listen intently, and that so much as a squeak would bring me up the stairs in a flash, my gun at the ready.

The household servants had gathered around the table where they took their communal meals. Clearly the home had once required a much larger staff, for there were many more chairs and empty places. I noticed a rather splendidly decorated cake resting in the center of the table. It was a lovely bit of work, covered in pink icing with flowers so intricately shaped that for an instant I thought they were real roses, though of course such quaint spring flowers wouldn't be in bloom in the gloomy autumn season.

"Oh, sir, it is our birthday," one of the little maids said, upon my inquiry. "Mrs. Ellis was so kind to make it for us. Of course, we hardly feel like celebrating now."

"Naturally," I said, asking them their names. Ellen and Abigail answered my questions quickly, with only a slight and natural show of girlish nervousness.

"Mr. Pierpont is such a nice man. It has been a pleasure to work here," Abigail said. "He is so very neat and tidy, it hardly feels like work at all, except on those weekends when his friends from London come to visit."

"They tracked in a lot of mud last time," her quieter sister agreed.

"Have the pictures frightened you?" I asked.

The girls looked to each other, then clasped hands. A tear slipped down Abigail's face.

"They are horrid, sir! We almost gave notice when their eyes started to open. We felt like we might turn a corner and find some painted man staring at us! We wondered . . . Can they really see us? Might they see us when we are asleep, or while we are dressing? I was all for running back home to Mother."

"And I told her how silly that would be," Ellen countered, with a show of sudden spirit. "Papa needs us to work, for the doctor says he will never be well enough to go to the mill again. No ghost or painted ghoul will ever stop us from taking care of Papa."

"And what of you?" I asked the stable lad. "Were you alarmed?"

"Only by that scream last night," he said. "I heard it all the way up in the attic, where I sleep. I'm not afraid of any silly paintings, but that scream – they said it was the Master, but it sounded like a banshee, coming for our souls."

"It woke me from a very deep sleep," Mrs. Ellis volunteered. Even as we had talked, she had been minding her pots. The savory smell emanating from them was almost enough to make me forget that I needed to focus on my questions and take careful notes for Holmes. "I was dreaming I was with my late husband, and we were going to take ship to America and . . . Well, I was ripped away from that lovely dream. I had fallen asleep with my book. It only took me a moment to light a lamp and scurry to my door, but I believe the girls were ahead of me. And Mr. Harris wasn't a second behind them. Sir, would you mind if I set the table? No one had a bite of breakfast earlier, with all the worry about the Master . . . ."

"Of course!" I answered, and in a twinkling the plates were pulled down and napkins folded. I looked through the doorway but there was no sign of Holmes. The ladies insisted that I join them, and soon I understood why Pierpont had been so satisfied with his servants. They were clearly dedicated to him, making constant inquiries as to whether I felt Mr. Holmes could solve the mystery. They seemed to think that should Holmes unveil the secret behind the opening eyes in the paintings, their Master would recover.

"Watson – not missing a meal, I see!"

I turned with some embarrassment to find Holmes standing just behind me. I stammered out quick introductions, noting as I did that Harris was hanging back in the doorway. His face had gone ghastly pale, and I feared that perhaps Pierpont had expired moments before.

"Is there something wrong, sir?" Ellen asked. I realized that Holmes was making an intense study of the cake on the table.

"I am merely admiring the lovely confection," he said. "If it is as tasty as it is charming, it should be the most delicious cake ever cooked." Holmes turned and nodded to Harris. "I see no reason to detain the staff further. I am certain that the physician could use some further towels and bolsters for Mr. Pierpont's comfort, and the doctor's horse also requires attention."

Harris wasted no time in barking orders to his underlings. He followed them out of the kitchen with a quick snap of his heels, leaving us alone with Mrs. Ellis, the cook. She stood stiffly, regarding my friend, whose gaze remained fixed upon the ornate dessert.

"Is there something I can do, sir?" she asked.

"Yes, I believe there is. You can tell me the truth." Holmes lifted his head, meeting the woman's steely gaze. "Are you merely the creator or – as I suspect – both the creator and subject of *Sleeping Venus*?"

I must have made a sound of utter astonishment. The lady sighed and gathered up her apron, wiping her hands upon it.

"Is it so difficult to believe that I was once that beautiful?"

317

Holmes pulled out a chair and, with a gracious motion, guided Mrs. Ellis into it. I leaned closer, and now I saw what Holmes had deduced. Though age had taken its toll and added heaviness to her frame, the lady's skin was as fair and as pure as the sleeping goddess's flesh. Her hands, roughened by domestic labors, still folded into the elegant lines of the painting.

"I will tell you all. There is no use to hide any longer, and I swear upon my soul that I never meant any harm to come to Mr. Pierpont. You cannot imagine the horror I felt when he screamed and tumbled backward down the staircase. Had it been his wicked uncle, Victor Lynch, I would have exulted in it, or given him the fatal push myself. But the young man was good and kind, and I only hoped to frighten him into giving me what I was owed."

Holmes settled across from the lady. "Victor Lynch stole your painting."

"Yes. I was a village girl from the Lake District. In my youth, I was a good sketch artist, and came to London to make my name – a decision which cost me the love of my parents, who disapproved of women's independence. My ambition quickly outstripped my funds, however, and I was soon desperate for employment. The artist Eugene Delarosa – There is a name the world should remember! – hired me as his model. He was a kind and good man, almost thirty years my senior, and he never allowed me to be exploited. My heart was soon given to him despite the great difference in our ages, and we developed an understanding between ourselves, so that I was his both his muse and his protégé. He helped me hone my skills, and I became a skilled painter. It was in his studio that I met Victor Lynch, an only moderately talented student who was paying for lessons. I foolishly allowed Lynch to see my masterpiece, my self-portrait as the goddess. He became obsessed with it and offered to buy it from me. I refused, even though the money would have been welcome.

"Not long afterward, my beloved Eugene fell ill. We journeyed to Bath for him to take the waters, but much to my despair he suddenly weakened and died there, in a lodging house. By the time I was able to return to our London flat, I found that our careless landlady had admitted Lynch when he claimed to have left a canvas in the studio. My *Venus* was missing, and I knew immediately that he had stolen it. I went to him, demanding its return, but it was too late. He had submitted the painting to a gallery as his own work, and it had almost immediately been purchased by the Queen's agent. I was incensed – I threatened prosecution! – but he in turn argued that without my protector, my word was nothing. I was an artist's model – A woman who shamelessly disrobed for men! – and no one would believe my claim that he had painted over my name and signed

318

his own. He gave me a mere ten pounds and promised that if I swore a complaint against him, he would accuse me of being a common harlot. Though my heart was broken, I felt I had no choice, for I had no friends or advocates, and no good reputation of my own.

"I moved away. I became a cook and a housekeeper, instead of the artist I had dreamed of being. I was married for a time, but my husband died young. With each passing year, I grew angrier at the injustice that had been done to me. From time to time, I pondered how I might get revenge. By a stroke of luck, one of my friends, Mrs. Jane Moore, gained employment with Lynch as his housekeeper. It was she who told me of his obsession with painting sleeping figures, hoping to recreate the most magical aspect of my work. She told me also of his descent into melancholy and drunkenness. I saw my opportunity. With her help, I sent the notes, which drove him almost to madness and shortened his life. When he died, I thought my work was done, but the more I considered, the more I felt I was still owed for the theft of my work. Jane told me about the new Master of Dale House, how he was frail and nervous. In that I saw my chance.

"Jane recommended me to replace her. I came to Dale House ahead of the others, which gave me time to observe the paintings. I worked fast and created a dozen duplicates, for if I had waited to merely modify the existing pictures, the deception would be easily discovered. I was fortunate that almost every picture was unframed. Once the time was right, I placed the two notes, and then I began to replace the pictures."

Holmes, who had listened to this recitation with an expression of admiration, rather than condemnation, now gave a brisk nod.

"It was obvious that the instigator was inside the home. The delivery of the notes could hardly have been accomplished otherwise, and certainly the images couldn't have been exchanged unless managed from within."

"I never meant to harm Mr. Pierpont – only to see if I could frighten him into giving me the money."

"Tell us what happened last night."

"I had been saving the Satan for a dramatic moment. When the young Master returned, he told us that you would arrive the next morning. He also said that if you couldn't solve the mystery during your visit, he would order all his uncle's paintings to be burned. I felt this was my final opportunity to manipulate his emotions. His confidence in you was such that he relieved us of any duty to watch during the night, which was helpful to my plan.

"I waited until I was certain the Master and every other member of the staff was asleep. It was almost one when I slipped from my room, bearing the canvas, which had been hidden – as they all were – inside my mattress. I carried a candle with me and worked as quickly and quietly as possible. But then, just as I had completed the exchange, I heard footsteps coming down the hallway from the Master's room. I had no time to flee, but I flung myself behind the curtains to the left of the picture and blew out my candle.

"Mr. Pierpont was clad in his nightshirt and dressing gown and carrying a single candle of his own. He stood on the landing, looking all about, clearly confused by the noise he had heard. He sniffed, and I heard him mutter, 'I smell smoke.' Then he turned, and at that moment lightning flashed close by. He spun around and looked up at the picture. Another flash followed hard, less than a heartbeat after the first. He threw up his hands, his eyes went wide, his mouth opened in a silent scream. To my horror, he dropped his candle and toddled backwards, and then fell and went bounding down the stairs.

"I stepped out. By some miracle, no one had awakened or heard the fall. I retrieved the candle and stamped out the place where it had begun to smolder upon the rug. God forgive me – I seized the painting with the closed eyes, as well as the two candles, and thrust them all into the closet in my room. Then I stepped just far enough into the hallway so that my voice would carry and gave the loudest scream I could manage. I was back inside my room before anyone could arise. Then I pretended to be awakened and followed Mr. Harris in his investigation."

Tears slowly drifted down the elderly lady's cheeks. "I swear I didn't push the Master, nor had I any intention of causing such a hideous shock to him. I only hoped he might restore what was mine. But now I am sorry, and would give anything for him to recover, so that I could beg his forgiveness."

Holmes reached out and gently patted her hand, then signaled for me to rise and follow. We retired to a small library, where a half-dozen portraits, all with their eyes closed, hung on the walls.

"How did you know?" I asked.

Holmes settled into a red leather chair by the fireplace. His expression was unusually troubled, though he answered my question with a quick wave of his hand. "It was elementary. Paintings don't open their eyes. The fact that the paintings were duplicates, rather than merely 'retouched' originals, confirmed that they were the work of a true artist. The fact that they seemed to 'awaken' at odd hours confirmed that the switch was occurring from within the house. Therefore, the artist and culprit must be a member of the household. Only a talented artist could have created the replicas of the paintings, and only an artist could have crafted such an amazing dessert. Surely you noticed how realistic the roses were upon that cake. Art in the blood takes *many* forms. Therefore, the cook was also the artist and culprit. The cake caused me to look more closely at the lady, and when I did, I immediately saw the reflection of the sleeping Venus." Holmes shook his head. "What I didn't note was the burned spot on the carpet, where the Master dropped his candle. But I shall blame that on the abysmal lighting of this ancient home."

I settled opposite to Holmes. "What an amazing story the lady provided."

"One which may be impossible to confirm," Holmes said, "as all the participants are deceased except for the lady. Perhaps a discreet inquiry to Her Majesty's closest confidants would enable us to learn whether there is another signature beneath the paint on the *Sleeping Venus*."

"But who would have the privilege to ask such a thing?"

My friend smiled coyly. "I may know a certain individual whose previous services to Her Majesty's government are legion. But as for now . . . ." He shook his head. "I am loathe to give Mrs. Ellis over to the authorities."

"You believe her? That she didn't push Pierpont?"

"What purpose would murder have served? A dead man couldn't reimburse her, and clearly, she bore him no personal ill-will."

A sharp rap on the door interrupted our discussion. Harris stepped inside, his face ruddy, his eyes wet.

"Sirs! My Master has awakened!"

Of the many strange and bizarre cases my friend handled in his long and distinguished career, this one had a resolution which brought joy to all concerned. Mr. Pierpont made a full recovery, and once he was on the mend and assured that there was no devilment in his home or occult influences in the artwork, Holmes mediated a confession. Mrs. Ellis fell to her knees before her Master and told him everything she had related to us. The young man's jaw dropped. His eyes went wide.

"It is like a novel!" he gasped. "A fair maiden, so cruelly wronged. I always knew Uncle Victor was a wicked, sinful man. How mean and dirty of him to have forged his name upon your art!"

"I wish I had never frightened you, sir. It was wrong to abuse you for another's crimes. I should go to jail."

"And then what would I have to eat?" the young man laughed. "No, dear Mrs. Ellis, please stay. We will say no more about it, and as soon as I can, I will make things right. Is that possible, Mr. Holmes? Is there some way that Mrs. Ellis may receive the proper credit for her beautiful painting?"

I am happy to say that Holmes made a visit to the "certain individual" who could make inquires of Her Majesty's Curator of Pictures, who in turn was able to examine the painting and determine that the name signed to it was indeed the wrong one, and one layer beneath was the signature of the lady as she had been at the time – *Eliza Martin*. Mr. Pierpont in turned helped his housekeeper craft a memoir, which became a best-seller, so that the lady was more than repaid for the theft of her work.

Perhaps most satisfying, one year after the event, Holmes and I attended a celebratory bonfire at Dale House, where the entire collection of sleeping pictures was destroyed, so that no future haunting of master, staff, or home should ever occur.

I leaned back and took down the great index volume to which he referred. Holmes balanced it on his knee and his eyes moved slowly and lovingly over the record of old cases, mixed with the accumulated information of a lifetime. ". . . Victor Lynch, forger . . . ."

– Dr. Watson and Sherlock Holmes
"The Sussex Vampire"

The Man in the Rain
with a Dog
by Brenda Seabrooke

"I'll wager you were out late last night." Sherlock Holmes was at the table in the sitting room, finishing his breakfast, while I hurried to take my place and pour a cup of much-needed coffee to start my day.

"How did you know? The damp coat or my wet shoes? I purposefully didn't put them close to the fire to dry, given how you complained of their aroma last time. 'Wet horse', as I believe you described my overcoat."

"No, not at all.'Wet horse blanket' was the term."

"If my damp garments didn't give me away then what, pray tell, was it?"

"You really cannot deduce it? Come, Watson, how long have you been sharing my cases with me? Can you not even guess?"

Mrs. Hudson's arrival with a plate she'd kept warm saved me from having to admit I didn't know. After several gulps of hot aromatic coffee, I fell on my breakfast like a man who had just climbed the Matterhorn while Holmes concentrated on the morning newspaper.

When I finished, I asked him again how he knew I'd gone out late the previous night.

"Your book – one of those yellow-backed mysteries to which you seem to be addicted."

"Those stories are merely escape from my medical cases," I said, though truth to tell, they were quite enjoyable. "I don't see how my reading material told you I had gone out last night."

"You left it turned over, opened to your place. When I left, you were halfway through the book. If you'd stayed in, you would've finished it, because you can't put down a good yarn."

"Yes, I did go out late for about two hours."

"An urgent call?"

"It was, as are all calls in the night. Illness tends to magnify in the dark, to both the patient and the family members. In this case, the only one I saw was the patient, Colonel Thomas F. Soames. The butler, Beckley, told me the Colonel was wounded in the Crimean War and again in the Bhutan War of 1864.

"The Colonel seemed to be suffering a stroke. He appeared in a great deal of pain as he flailed his arms and legs about. I couldn't understand what he was mumbling as he rolled around on the floor after falling from his bed. The bedclothes were askew as he tossed in his agony. Often strokes are silent attacks, but this one was singularly violent. The butler was concerned for him and, failing to find his regular physician, sent a boy to locate another.

"I calmed him with an injection of salicin and opiate, and as his sunken eyes began to close, he looked at me and said, 'Free Emerald!' I assumed he was remembering something from one of his army campaigns, and he fell silent as we lifted him back into his now-straightened bed. I sat with him and watched his breathing until he seemed to be in a comfortable sleep. I instructed Beckley to have someone stay with him and send for me if his condition worsened.

"Beckley said that the Colonel was in his eightieth year, though he looked older to me, perhaps due to his earlier wounds. His body was thin and almost emaciated, his gaunt face a web of wrinkles that extended into his long neck. If he survived the night, I determined I would institute a healthier regimen to improve his overall health."

"Most commendable. One cannot say that you live an ordinary life."

I raised my eyebrows. Not ordinary, but not exciting either, not like working on Holmes's extraordinary cases. "The strange part of my night's venture came after I left the house. I exited into the mews, as I would have a better chance of finding a cab on the corner since most of the Grosvenor inhabitants kept their own coaches and cabbies seldom drive around the Square at that hour. It was now well past two. A thin misty rain fell, blurring everything in sight. As I turned up my collar, a man walking a dog on a leash, some sort of hunting breed, I surmised, spoke out of the mist. 'I trust your patient is sleeping peacefully now,' he said as the dog attended to the corner of a wall.

"'He is that,' I said. He was a tall, thin man with a woolen hat, its brim pulled low to shield his face from the rain or from onlookers. His coat was dark, as were his trousers, and he blended with the mist and shadows, as did his dog's dark coat.

"'Miss Esmeralda is well then?'

"'I can't say. I do not know her.'

"'I often return late, and Rambler here wants to live up to his name, but I walk him in the daytime as well. I live in the area, but don't know the members of this household. I often saw Miss Esmeralda from time to time – a lovely young lady – and she always spoke to Rambler and gave him a pat, but I haven't seen her in some weeks. Months perhaps. I wondered if she were ill." He nodded at the corner of the back of the house. "Her room

324

is on the second floor. I've seen her looking out of the window in the past. Seeing a doctor emerge from the house – Wll, naturally I worried that she was unwell.'

"'I didn't see her. Just the elderly colonel.'

"Just then I heard the clopping of a horse and, not wanting to walk all the way in rain that might worsen before I got here, I excused myself and hurried to hail the cab – but not before hearing him call after me that he'd seen some suspicious characters observing the house, and a furniture van making deliveries at odd times even at night. I almost called back to him that some might think *he* is a suspicious character, but I was intent I catching the hansom.

"Sometime in the middle of the night, I awoke with the thought that the Colonel might have been saying 'Free Emeralda' or 'Esmeralda'."

"Indeed," Holmes replied. "That was my first thought. When do you return?"

"Return?"

Holmes put down his paper. "You know you will be checking on your patient today, and also trying to find out who this 'Esmeralda' is."

"I thought this afternoon."

"Make it morning. As soon as possible. I'll go with you as a consultant."

"I don't think – "

"Those who live in Grosvenor Square expect such treatment. They'll think nothing if you bring along a colleague for a second opinion."

"What do you suspect?"

"Nothing as yet, but a few details of your story piqued my interest. Let's just say that my curiosity needs to be satisfied on several accounts."

"Oh, very well. Let's go then." I fetched my black medical bag and grabbed my coat on the way.

"I would rather go late tonight and see the man with a dog, but that would be too difficult to explain if we had to."

I couldn't imagine to whom we might have to answer, but I let it go. All would be explained in time – Holmes's time.

The previous night's rain had left the day humid, and I was uncomfortable in my woolen coat. I opened the buttons in an effort to cool myself as the hansom wheels took us to the Square. I paid the driver and stepped up to the door, bracketed by classic style pilasters. Holmes lifted an eyebrow at the terraced house in a long row of them. "Lofty digs here. A former prime minister, some cabinet ministers, and several Lords call this Square home."

"Indeed. I can't be bothered with them unless they fall ill. Sick is sick, whether it be a cabinet minister or a chimney sweep."

I raised the knocker, a brass gauntlet, and let it fall. The butler opened the door a moment later. "Good day, Beckley, I've brought a colleague to see the Colonel – a specialist."

"Indeed, sir." He divested us of our hats and coats and Holmes's stick, and led us up the stairs.

"How was his night?" I inquired.

"Daisy, one of the kitchen maids, sat all night with him. He didn't awaken. She's off duty now, but he was still sleeping when I looked in before you came."

The patient still slept, but appeared to be in no discomfort. His breathing was regular, and his color was improved. Some of the wrinkles had smoothed out of his face. His thin hair had been brushed into place. Holmes immediately became an efficient doctor, taking out my thermometer and slipping it under the Colonel's arm. While Holmes waited, he lifted the patient's eyelids and looked at his sleeping eyes and listened to his heart. He read the thermometer. "So far everything seems to be in order here. Now, if he will awaken soon, all will be as before. Could we have a cup of warm broth here?" he asked Beckley.

"Certainly, sir. I'll see to it."

As soon as he had left the room, I gently shook the Colonel's shoulder. "Sir, we are alone here. I'm Dr. Watson who saw you last night. This is my colleague, Dr. Holmes. You told me about someone last night, but I didn't know to whom you were referring. Is Esmerelda your niece?"

The pale eyelashes fluttered when I said the name. They snapped open. "Granddaughter. Free. Free." He sighed and his eyes closed again.

"He is progressing as to be expected," Holmes said as Beckley entered with a tray containing the broth. "I recommend continuing with the treatment. Allow him to sleep as long as he wishes. When he awakens, try to get him to drink spoonfuls of the broth."

"Thank you, Doctor. I couldn't have said it better." I turned to Beckley as he set the tray on a table. "Do you wish to engage nurses for the night, and perhaps the day as well?"

"We have sufficient staff for that."

"How about family?"

"His Lordship, Lord Rocklandel, will return late today."

I nodded. "Well then, I shall return tomorrow to see how he is progressing."

"Very good, sir." Beckley saw us to the door.

Outside, the Square was busier than previously. Children walked with their nannies in the park square. Ladies chatted in twos or threes on benches, or walked near nannies pushing prams. Two gentlemen enjoyed cigars as they ambled and conversed. A young man with longish hair sat under a tree reading a book, no doubt a volume of poetry, judging by his flowing soft, pale-blue tie. A group of older boys bowled hoops. Carriages passed – indeed, a hansom turned into the street. I started to hail it, but Holmes deterred me. "Not yet, Watson." He lifted his hat to a passing matron.

"I should like to talk to the people in the Square, but we are visible from the house's windows – and in any case, I doubt the Grosvenor Square denizens would talk to a pair of unknown men. But someone in the mews might. Let's walk around the corner and try our luck there."

Holmes hailed a passing hansom and we climbed aboard. "Where to, Guv?"

"Just around the corner," Holmes said. "Watchers," he said to me softly.

As the cab steered into the street, a furniture van from the opposite direction passed us. "I wonder," I murmured, "if that's the one the man with the dog mentioned."

The van was painted a dark green with bright red trim, with *Flourney's Movers* written on the side in bright yellow letters. The driver wore a dark cap pulled low over his forehead that seemed to mirror his black beard. His companion seemed too thin to offer much assistance with furniture delivery.

Around the corner, Holmes directed the driver to pull past the entrance to the mews and wait there. I gave him a coin to ensure he did. He shook his head, but parked the cab.

Holmes and I walked along the mews row. The previous night's misty rain left the cobblestones and bricks refreshed. A bay horse was getting a thorough scrubbing by a stable boy, while another fetched more water from a pump for the job. A pair of coachmen, seated on a mounting block, smoked their pipes while waiting to be called into service. Somewhere in the stables, a horse's neigh received a reply.

We'd passed two stables when Holmes spoke up. "Where did you meet the man with the dog?"

"Up there." I started to point.

Holmes took my arm and turned it so I was pointing at a horse, waiting patiently to be harnessed. "Yes, I agree with you. That is a fine horse. I wonder if he works well in tandem." Under his breath he said, "Just give me the directions to Colonel's room."

"It's on this side of the house in the back, second floor."

Holmes nodded. "You were exiting the house and he was facing it."

"Yes."

He glanced over his shoulder as if something had caught his attention from the house we were directly behind. "Hmm. He had an excellent view

327

of the back of the house. "If there is a Miss Esmerelda, that might indeed be the area of her room. Let's go before we're noticed."

"Do you think something is amiss then?"

"We shall find out. Take your bag and go back to the Square. See if you can find some young lady who might know Esmeralda."

"I'll try."

"When you're finished, take the hansom back while I reconnoiter and see if anyone knows the man from last night. I'll speak to the cabbie first."

The strollers and nannies in the Square earlier were fewer now and I didn't see the poet. As I walked up to the gate, a young lady was on her way out. I didn't like speaking to an unknown woman, but we needed to know if the man with the dog had been correct. I lifted my hat. "Excuse me, Mademoiselle." I tried to imbue my speech with a touch of French. Holmes would have thought it laughable, but I have noticed people will often try to help those who are from far away. "I am Dr. Watteau." It was the only name I could think of that was French and sounded something like my own.

She paused and looked at me. She was dressed in a blue walking suit of the same shade as her eyes. Her hair was light brown and carefully coiffed. A pleasant and pretty young lady.

"Do you know a Mademoiselle Esmeralda Soames?"

"Yes, I do."

"Have you, *peut-etre*, seen her lately?"

Two lines appeared on her forehead as she thought for a minute. "No, I don't believe I have. Not since Easter, I think."

"She hasn't been in the Square this *printemps* – or summer?"

"No. I'm sure I would've seen her. We like to go for ices in a group."

I nodded. "I was afraid of such. *Merci*, Mademoiselle. You 'ave been most helpful." I touched my hat and made my exit.

I returned alone to Baker Street. Holmes wasn't there, but that didn't surprise me. He had people to speak with, information to gather. He'd said he needed to see a man about a dog.

Mrs. Hudson was delighted that I was back, but she was also fretting about Holmes. "He misses too many lunches."

"Not as many as you think. He often has lunch out when he can't make it back here."

"I don't see any results of those lunches," she said with a snort.

I spent the afternoon visiting patients, and managed to sleep a bit to make up for the previous night, and to prepare for whatever Holmes might have in mind for later.

I heard his key as I finished my dinner. He ran up the stairs and opened the door, but instead of his usual attire, the man who entered looked like he'd never been in a house or had a meal or a bath. It was Holmes, of course, at his most disreputable.

"Your afternoon must've been fruitful," I said.

He glanced at me before disappearing into his room. In less time than I expected, he joined me as himself.

"What did you find out from the mews?" I asked as he helped himself to the dishes on the table.

"Later. We have work to do tonight. I hope you were able to nap."

"I didn't need a nap, but I did sleep a few minutes." Or longer. I knew how intense Holmes could be when on an investigation. That reminded me of something. "Why this effort? You aren't on a case."

He continued to chew as he quirked an eyebrow.

"No one has hired you to find Miss Esmeralda."

"You're right." He gulped coffee.

"Actually, it's *my* case."

"No, it isn't. You're only on the Colonel's medical case."

"True, I suppose. Then why are we looking into this Esmeralda matter?"

"Sometimes one does the things one has to. However, these events will merge. I'll explain later. Let's go."

He was out of the door before I stood up. I looked longingly at the sponge cake as I hurried after him, grabbing my bag and pulling on my coat.

Holmes was in a hansom by the time I reached the front door. "Hurry, Watson – We've no time to lose!"

"What are we doing?" I climbed in beside him and the cab moved along Baker Street.

"Have you read my monograph on the possibilities of coincidences?"

I searched my brain. "No, I don't recall that one."

He smiled. "That's because I haven't written it. Possibilities are endless. Writing such would be an infinite task not worth wasting my time. However, coincidences do sometimes slap us in the face."

"Have we been slapped? Are we about to be?"

"Not yet."

"Is this a warning?"

Holmes didn't answer until we'd exited the cab and paid the driver. Dusk was upon us now. Thick shadows fell onto the cobbles from the buildings and the Square's trees. A little wind sprang up, pushing us along the street, rustling leaves somewhere to let us know the weather was turning. At the gate to the Square, Holmes ushered me through.

329

Along the paths, one or two glowing cigar tips signaled the presence of gentlemen who liked to smoke out-of-doors. Perhaps their wives didn't allow it inside. "What are we looking for?"

"Men who don't belong here. A poet."

We'd just enough light to see the faces of those in the park, but none looked like the poet we'd seen earlier. We traversed the length of the inner park on one side, and then started up the far side, checking on connecting paths and benches as we hurried.

We found the man we sought, enjoying the last bite of an eel pie and a bottle of cider. He still wore his soft tie, but had removed his plumed cap, and with it his brown hair. The hair atop his head now was dark, and I saw no sign of the cap. His features, however, were the same, even more pronounced with the dark hair. His eyes were dark blue and penetrating and his mouth generous, but set in a firm line as he tried to determine the situation in which he found himself.

"Who are you?" he rasped. "What do you want? I have no money."

Holmes permitted himself a small laugh. "We don't want your money, or care for your lack of it, except where it concerns Miss Esmeralda Soames."

He dropped the cider bottle and leapt up ready to defend himself – or Miss Esmeralda. His hands folded into fists. "What about her? Who are you? What do you want from her?"

Holmes held up a hand. "We are trying to help her, and we need your assistance to do that."

"How? What do you want from me?"

"How long have you been watching the house?" I asked.

He noticed me for the first time. "A doctor? What's wrong? Is she ill? Have you seen her?"

"No," I said. "At least we don't think so."

"When was the last time you saw her?" Holmes queried.

"It was at Easter. I called at the house to speak to her guardian, Lord Rocklandel. He refused me permission to marry his ward and had me escorted out of the house. I was refused entry the next day, and every day after. I was even told not to come near the door, or I would be arrested." He dropped his gaze, but not before I saw a tear slide out of the corner of one eye.

"So, you found other ways to enter the Square," I said. "Never mind. We understand, and we're here to help both of you."

"You are disguised as a poet," Holmes stated. "How are you able to spend so much time in the Square watching for her?"

"I dress this way in case she looks out the window. She will see me because I'm dressed differently. But yes, I am a poet."

330

"What is your name?" I asked wondering if I had heard of him.

"Edward St. John."

"Is that how you support yourself?" Holmes asked. "Writing poems?"

"I wish it were. No, I'm a writer at *Spectify*. It's a monthly publication. I mostly write little fillers when there isn't enough to fill a page. And odd jobs. It leaves me with time to write my poems. And I'm allowed to live in the garret of the building."

I hoped our skepticism didn't show, but some must have because he added, "I'm hoping to publish my first volume of poems this month. Esmeralda was to illustrate them with pen-and-ink sketches."

"We'll help you see your Esmeralda," said Holmes, "to ascertain she is healthy and under no duress – Tonight, if all goes as I've planned." He lifted his head as if listening for something.

"Ah – I hear it now. Come, Mr. St. John. The game is afoot."

He took off in the direction of the sound of the horse's hooves. St. John stood staring at his back as he was swallowed up in solid darkness.

"Come, man. We've work to do." I had no idea what Holmes's plan was, but when he was in movement, there was no time to lose.

We followed Holmes out of the park and down to the end of the street. Around the corner stood a pair of horses hitched to a furniture moving van – Flournoy's van. A policeman held the horses' reins.

"I hope you're right about this, Mr. Holmes," said a familiar voice. Inspector Lestrade stood there in his brown suit, his ferrety face illuminated by the light of the gas jet.

"Good evening, Inspector. I'm more than right about this situation. Gentlemen, shall we prepare ourselves?"

The inspector handed Holmes a box from which emerged disreputable jackets, caps, and other accoutrements that shortly turned him and the poet into workmen on a job. I began to dread what Holmes might have in store for me. "I shall take the reins. St. John here will be my helper. Watson. You'll be the furniture."

"I'll be the what?"

"Up you go." He reached a hand down from the driver's seat and pulled me up as I scrambled to climb. "Careful there. Don't damage that leg. St. John, help him in."

I appreciated his concern for my war wound, but as I gained the inside of the van, I saw a wooden chest not unlike the kind one might pack clothing into, but also not unlike a coffin except for the rectangular shape.

St. John climbed in behind me and opened the lid. "In you go, Doctor."

I stared down at the rectangle. I didn't want to do this. "Why can't St. John go in?"

"He has to help me carry it into the house," replied Holmes.

I stepped in and lay down with my knees drawn up a bit. St. John closed the lid and all was darkness. "I don't like this," I said in a loud voice. I don't know if they heard me because just then the van began to move. It turned the corner and started up to the Rocklandel house. *"It will only be another minute,"* I told myself, but it seemed more like a month or two before the van drew to a halt. I felt the chest being lifted and carried to the front door.

We stopped and I heard blurred voices. The chest lifted and again was on the move before being set down again. I heard voices again. Holmes saying forcefully, "Then ask Lord Rocklandel!"

Before I could take another breath, the lid was raised. "Quick, Watson! Go up the stairs and find Esmeralda. St. John, go with him. Remember where her room is located, and if you have to break the door down, do it.

St. John and I sprinted up the stairs and to the back of the house. The door was latched on the outside. St. John opened it and there stood his Esmeralda, in her nightclothes and slippers. "Edward! What is happening?"

"No time now for explanations. We must hurry."

"No!" She shrank back. "Stay away! You mustn't catch this wasting disease!"

"You don't look ill to me."

"I look terrible! And I have a dreadful infectious disease. The doctor said so."

I looked around and saw no mirrors. Possibly she didn't know how she looked. "I am a doctor, and you look like a normal person in perfect health. You're a prisoner of your kinsman, Lord Rocklandel. We came to rescue you."

She looked at St. John, who nodded. "Yes, this is Dr. Watson. There's a detective downstairs. We mustn't waste any more time." He put his arm around her and I pushed them ahead of me. We went back down the stairs. though for a fleeting minute I wished I knew where the servants' stairs were.

We reached the foyer just as the butler returned with Rocklandel, a large man with heavy limbs, florid features, and a thunderous scowl. "What is the meaning of this?"

Esmeralda cringed, but held onto St. Johns' hands.

"We are taking charge of your prisoner," Holmes said.

"Sir," the butler said, "the young lady is very ill. The night air could hasten her end."

'Nonsense. I'm a doctor and I wager nothing at all is wrong with her that fresh air and her freedom couldn't cure. You have kept her locked in her room without mirrors for nigh on six months. No doubt you have confined her to bed and fed her only broth and toast. That would sicken anybody."

"How dare you insinuate my ward is a prisoner!" His Lordship bellowed. His face reddened more.

"This is true," Esmeralda spoke up. "I could smell the delicious aromas from the kitchen and so longed for roast chicken, gammon, and pastries."

"She is my ward," Rocklandel said, "and I will not have the sick girl dragged from her home. Now take yourselves from my house before I resort to violence!"

Holmes looked like he would enjoy violence with this unpleasant man, but a thin shaky voice said from the stairs said, "*My* house. *My* ward."

It was the colonel, wrapped in a voluminous dressing gown, slippers on his thin white feet. .

"Grandfather, please go back to your bed. You really are ill."

"I suspect I have received the same treatment as you, my dear granddaughter, but under Dr. Watson's care, I have regained some of my strength."

"Get from my house!" Lord Rocklandel ordered.

St. John thrust Esmeralda behind him as Rocklandel advanced on them. Rocklandel pulled a pistol from the pocket of his smoking jacket.

I slid my Adams from my own pocket. "Drop that gun."

"An Adams! You a soldier! That's ridiculous." He cocked the pistol as Holmes raised his own Webley.

Shots cracked the night. I didn't know who fired besides me, but only one bullet found its mark. Rocklandel dropped his gun and clutched his upper right arm. I snatched his firearm off the floor where it fell, keeping the Adams trained on him as Holmes hastened to open the front door. Lestrade, followed by four of his men, rushed in. Holmes hurriedly told him the gist of what happened.

But from whose gun had the bullet come that was in Rocklandel?

"All right," said Lestrade. "I understand what happened, but not why."

"This man needed a doctor," I said to Lestrade. "I don't have my bag."

"It's in the wagon. I'll have it brought up."

"I'd rather you bring up a police surgeon," I said, "but I realize one might not be available on short notice at this hour."

"Let's retire to the morning room," Esmeralda said, leading the way with her grandfather between her and St. John. "Beckley: Candles, please, and some refreshments."

Beckley hurried ahead of us and lit candles until the room glowed like a ballroom. He then betook himself off to the kitchen,

Two policemen stood by Rocklandel's chair while I attended to his superficial wound, tearing open his sleeve. Another one stood at the door and helped the butler when he returned with a tea cart laden with pastries, while a fourth officer went for my bag. I wondered if Beckley were trying to make up for those months of deprivation.

If I expected Esmeralda to fall on the food like the starving young woman she undoubtedly was, I was mistaken. She poured tea and coffee and made certain everyone had been served before she allowed herself a biscuit to nibble and a cup of fragrant oolong with lemon.

Holmes stood up. "I need to ask you both a question." He addressed Esmeralda and St. John. "Is it your wish to marry? I know this is sudden, but there is a reason."

His Lordship shifted in his chair. Did he think Holmes didn't know the cause of everything that happened in this house?

"Yes," St. John said. He slid down on one knee and took something out of his pocket. "It was my mother's," he said, opening the little box. The diamond on the ring caught the candlelight and flashed a dancing rainbow around the room. "I intended to ask you the day I was barred from this house. I came to ask His Lordship for permission to marry you. He became enraged and showed me the door. Esmeralda, I love you. Will you marry me?"

For a poet he was plain-spoken, but he was also in a hurry. They'd already lost six months. To lovers, that is a lifetime.

"Oh yes! Yes, I will!"

He slid the ring on her finger.

"Excellent!" Holmes said. "There will be a special license waiting for you tomorrow, but you must be married immediately after. This is the reason for all that has gone on in this house since April when Edward St. John came to ask Lord Rocklandel for permission to marry his ward – which everyone mistakenly thought she was. To keep the colonel from interfering in his business, Rocklandel brought in a phony doctor and invalided the colonel. He applied the same measures to his first cousin once removed. That is the correct relationship, is it not, Colonel?"

"It is. He is the son of my older brother and his wife Caroline killed in a carriage accident. Esmeralda is my granddaughter, daughter of my son, Frederick and Jane, his beloved wife.

"This house was built by my grandfather. The reason behind what happened to my granddaughter and me is because of the entail put on the house by the original Lord Rocklandel, my grandfather, that a daughter can inherit this house after she reaches the age of twenty-two, but she must be married. If I die after Esmeralda is twenty-two, the house goes to next of kin – in this case the son of my late brother, *this scoundrel*, who is the *third* Lord Rocklandel." His voice drifted off. He was improving since I stopped the tinctures they were giving him, but still weak.

The constable returned with my bag. I opened it and took out what I needed. I mopped up the blood and poured alcohol into the wound. I could have used hydrogen peroxide, which wouldn't be as painful as alcohol, but I took satisfaction in the patient's groans and grimaces. I found the bullet and slipped it into my handkerchief and pocketed it. I bound his arm with a clean bandage. "That will hold him until the police surgeon can see him," I told the constables.

The colonel sat comfortably tucked into a soft blanket on a large cushioned chair. Esmeralda sat beside him and held his hand. St. John sat on the other side, holding her other hand. "My mother was named Jane," Esmeralda was saying. "She read a story about a heroine named Esmeralda Aragon, and gave me that name so I wouldn't be a plain Jane. Esmeralda is a mouthful. I prefer to be called '*Esme*'."

Holmes nodded. "The present Lord Rocklandel's parents were killed in a carriage accident. Miss Esme's parents contracted a deadly fever. She came to live with her grandfather, though the present Lord Rocklandel put it about that he is her guardian. He'd found out this house was entailed to her unless she was unmarried at age twenty-two. That was when he locked Miss Esme in her room and began giving the colonel drugs to weaken him.

"He had matters under control, but the colonel had a small stroke while he was away from home. Concerned, Beckley sent a boy to fetch a doctor, and he went to Baker Street because he'd heard of Dr. Watson, who told me about his visit to this house, and something he mentioned about a man in the rain with a dog leaped out at me. He said a furniture van and strange men called at this house at odd hours. Did such a van call here this morning?" Holmes asked Beckley.

"Yes sir, it did."

"Will you show me the piece of furniture the van delivered?" Holmes asked.

"This is *my* house!" Rocklandel snarled, attempting to stand. "I will not have you stomping all over the costly carpets with your filthy boots!" The constables pushed him down.

Lestrade and the constables searched the house until they found a dark-haired man hiding behind a bookcase in the library. They brought

335

him to the morning room. Rocklandel turned white when he saw the assassin.

"Take him in," Lestrade instructed several burly men who weren't in uniform who had remained near the door. They hustled the assassin out.

"This is the real reason Lord Rocklandel needed to keep the house under his control. It is a conduit for assassins and saboteurs. He is connected with a network that is deployed all over Europe to keep it in a constant state of fear and unrest in order to enrich these perpetrators. Some men were brought in the same way that Dr. Watson entered – hidden in a chest. Some walked in at night, which is why the man was standing in the mews in the rain with a dog. It was he who let me know that more was going on here than the separation of two young people in love.

"I paid a visit this afternoon to certain quarters and found out a shipment of furniture was expected here tonight. Lestrade and his men waylaid the van, and its inhabitants now are locked up."

"We brought Dr. Watson in, hidden in the chest, to gain entry to the house. Our purpose was to free Miss Esme and her grandfather and clear out this nest of spies. Our work is done. I suggest, Mr. St. John, that you remain here to see that the household runs smoothly. Tomorrow you will present yourself and your fiancée at the registry office and proceed with the marriage immediately by special license. Lestrade, do you have anything to ask?"

Lestrade stood up. "I do. Who shot His Lordship?"

"Does it really matter?" St. John said.

"I rather think it does," Lestrade said. "For my report, if nothing else."

No one admitted to firing the bullet that brought down Lord Rocklandel. Lestrade turned to me. "Well, Dr. Watson, you must've found the bullet. Maybe that will tell me which gun fired it."

"No. It apparently went straight through."

Lestrade scowled. He seemed sure that I had found the bullet, but was hiding it. Still, he bade his men to crawl all over the floor and examine the wall where Rocklandel had been standing, and even the chair in which he sat while I'd attended to his wound, but no bullet appeared. His Lordship laughed as the constables ushered him out to the waiting police wagon.

A tall case clock clanged eleven times. I felt tired after all the excitement. Holmes and I were driven home in a police carriage. Upstairs, we sat in front of the fire and had a spot of brandy.

"I told you this was a singular case," Holmes said.

"You were right, but how did you know? What was it about the man with the dog that informed you, as you said?"

"I've seen the man with the dog before."

"It could've been another man with a dog. Thousands of men have dogs."

"All right. The man, the dog, the furniture van, the dark-haired men at all hours. Her Majesty has been concerned for some time with attempts on herself, on officials, bombs placed at crucial spots, that sort of thing. I knew a man with a dog was watching this house. When you told me where it was and what you saw, I immediately made the connection. It was too much of a coincidence.

"Now tell me, Watson: What did you do with the bullet you took out of Rocklandel?"

I laughed and reached in my pocket for it. "Our two bullets missed their mark. I think we may need to do some practice shooting. This small one, from a Derringer perhaps, was all I found. The bullet did go through, but it hit a piece of metal decoration on a chair. Our ears were ringing with the sound of the explosion, which masked the ping against the metal. I scooped it up in this in the confusion. Thought you might want it – but don't ever tell Lestrade."

I unfolded the handkerchief square and handed him the misshapen lead bullet. "It was the colonel on the stairs, shooting downward," I said. "Should we tell Lestrade?"

"Someday, perhaps," Holmes replied, and we toasted the colonel.

". . . I knew that you had an inquiry on hand and that you disliked the intrusion of other matters."

"Oh, you mean the little problem of the Grosvenor Square furniture van. That is quite cleared up now – though, indeed, it was obvious from the first."

– Dr. John H. Watson and Sherlock Holmes
"The Noble Bachelor"

The Problem of the
Grosvenor Square Moving Van
by Tim Newton Anderson

I have become accustomed over the years of my friendship with Sherlock Holmes to his unusual classification of cases. Those which have baffled the police are often called *trivial* or *simple*, while others which are equally confusing may somehow be classed as *complex*. His assessment does not seem to depend on how dangerous or time consuming they are, or the ingenuity (or lack of it) of the culprits. The Jerusalem Cross affair involved investigations in seven countries, but was classed as simple, while the blackmail of the Viscount of Wymondham didn't need him to leave his seat at 221b Baker Street to solve, but was deemed a vexing puzzle.

A case I found baffling, but which Holmes dismissed as simple, was the theft of William Manderville's home. Please note I do not say *from* his home.

I had joined Holmes at Baker Street for lunch after taking a brief constitutional in Regent's Park. Mrs. Hudson had prepared a cold collation of beef and ham, accompanied by a chilled ale which was most welcome after a brisk walk in the pleasant sunshine.

"How did your meeting with the young lady proceed?" Holmes asked as I settled down in my chair.

"To what meeting do you refer to?" I asked.

"Come now, Watson," he said. "You know you are unable to hide anything from me. Your face is slightly more flushed than can be accounted for purely because of the sun and the exercise. If that weren't enough to suggest you had been talking to a woman who you find attractive, you're wearing your best suit, despite it being rather heavy for the weather. In addition, you brought in the faint aroma of roses, which indicates you spent some time sitting amongst flowers, which is unlike you."

I blushed slightly.

"I admit I hoped to meet a young lady there, a governess, but although I sat there for an hour, she didn't appear."

"I'm sure her absence wasn't to avoid meeting you," Holmes said. "There is an event in Hyde Park, and I suspect she took her young charges to attend that. If you wish to make her acquaintance, you would do well to return to Regent's Park later in the week."

I smiled at my friend and started to eat my lunch, only to be halted by Holmes after the first mouthful.

"Mrs. Hudson's splendid repast must wait, Watson," he said. "We are about to be visited by a client."

"Do you have an appointment?" I asked.

"No, but I can hear a carriage pulling up on the street," he said. "It's large enough to need two horses, which suggests it is the private vehicle of someone who considers him- or herself important, rather than a simple hansom."

As I listened for myself, I heard a knock at our door and the bustle on the stairs of Mrs. Hudson escorting someone up to the sitting room

"Mr. Manderville insisted you would wish to see him," said Mrs. Hudson.

"The gentleman is absolutely correct," said Holmes. "Please join Dr. Watson and me. Mrs. Hudson will be happy to provide us with some refreshment. Your journey from Grosvenor Square must have been uncomfortably warm."

Manderville was a stocky man with thinning sandy hair, dressed in an expensive double-breasted grey suit and shoes that had been shone to perfection. Despite the weather, his jacket was fully buttoned, and his face was glowing with perspiration. His expression indicated he was uncomfortable from more than the heat. This was clearly a man who didn't like to be in unfamiliar situations which he could not control or predict.

"I assume you have come about something of some urgency which is worrying you, but which you aren't comfortable discussing in your own home," said Holmes. "Rest assured that anything you say in this room will remain in confidence, and I can vouch for the discretion of Watson, as well as myself."

"My home has been burgled," Manderville said. "More than that, the entire contents – furniture and all – have been taken!"

"That isn't the reason you have come to me," said Holmes. "There is something you about the crime you have been unable to tell the police, who would otherwise prove adequate to its solution."

Manderville's head dropped.

"I suppose I'll have to tell you the whole story," he said. "I have reason to believe that someone I care for is involved, and I don't wish this person's name to be associated with this."

"I presume this person is a lady," said Holmes.

"That is correct," said Manderville. "A secretary in my diamond business to whom I had entrusted a key to my home when my wife and I travelled to Amsterdam, combining a business trip with a holiday. I had given my domestic staff a holiday at the same time, and I was anxious that there was someone who could unlock the building if there were any issues during our absence."

"I presume you have questioned this young woman, even if the police haven't," Holmes said.

"Of course," said Manderville. "She assured me that she hadn't used the key, and hadn't given it to anyone else. It was in the safe at my Bond Street office the entire time. Miss Ransom has been in my employ for five years, and during that time she has performed her duties in an exemplary way without the least submission attaching to her name. She lives with her elderly mother and, as far as I can ascertain, has no associations with anyone of dubious character."

Holmes smiled. "You should relate to us the events of the theft."

Manderville seemed to have relaxed now that he had detailed the actions of his assistant. He seemed happy that he had unburdened himself.

"Our visit to Amsterdam was to endure a week, while I held negotiations with several dealers in precious stones and my wife enjoyed the sights of the city. My business is a specialist one. I create unique jewellery for some of the most important families across the Continent, and it's important that I source only the best stones for the pieces."

"I have come across some of your creations in previous cases," said Holmes, "Your clients, I believe, include some of the Crowned Heads of Europe. Indeed, you have supplied some of those crowns."

"I'm proud to agree that is the case," said Manderville. "My business was started by my father, but I have expanded it enormously by attracting some of the richest clients in the world. I cannot, of course, mention their names because of confidentiality, but you are correct in your belief they are people of influence. That is one of the reasons this affair is so concerning. I must be seen to be a safe person to carry out their commissions.

"It was on the second day of my trip that my neighbours saw a removal van pull up at my home at 26 Grosvenor Square. During the course of the next two days, it made several trips to and fro, filling up with furniture. My wife has exquisite taste in decor and regularly buys new pieces for our home, so at first this didn't attract suspicion. However on the fifth visit, my neighbour at Number 27 became concerned and contacted the police, not having a way of reaching me. They duly arrived and found the front door unlocked. On entering, they discovered that the house had been completely stripped of furnishings. Even the carpets had been rolled up and removed. They had stolen my entire home!"

"Were they able to trace the removal wagon?" asked Holmes.

"The wagon," said Manderville, "but unfortunately not its drivers. It had the name of a well-known firm painted on its side, but they denied all knowledge of the vehicle, and could account for the movement of all their wagons. There are dozens criss-crossing the capital on any day, so it was impossible to track the route of the imposters. The empty vehicle itself was discovered on Hampstead Heath several days later and had been set on fire. The police were unable to retrieve any clues from its shell."

"Was any jewellery taken?" I asked. "If I were a thief breaking into the home of a diamond merchant, I would be looking for that rather than furniture."

"That is the most baffling thing," said Manderville. "I rarely keep items from my work at home, as they are far safer under lock and key at my business. However, there were some expensive items belonging to my wife in the safe at Grosvenor Square, yet there had been no attempt to open it and everything was still in place. There is considerable value in the furniture, as some are rare pieces acquired at auctions at Sotheby's and other places, but selling them would be a specialist and problematic endeavour. Many of the items are well known, and just a month ago a journalist from *The London Illustrated News* wrote a detailed description of our home as an exemplar of exquisite taste. The police believe this is what alerted the thieves to their value."

"Surely the number of criminals specialising in such thefts is small," I said, "and tracking them down should be a comparatively simple job."

"I'm sure they're engaged in that process as we speak, Watson," said Holmes. "However, I don't believe they will be successful in that line of inquiry. If the criminals had only taken the most expensive items, that would be a logical conclusion. But why take everything including the carpets? I believe this case has sufficient points of interest to warrant my participation in its solution."

"I would be extremely grateful, Mr. Holmes," said Manderville. "But I hope you will handle the matter with the utmost discretion."

"If you're concerned that I will expose the full nature of your relationship with Miss Ransom, you need have no misgivings," said Holmes. "I'm satisfied she had nothing to do with this matter, although if you could ask her to provide me with your business diary for the coming weeks and a list of current clients, that would be most useful."

Manderville flushed a deep red at Holmes's suggestion.

"My relationship with Miss Ransom is entirely professional!" he said with some heat.

"That is a matter between you and your conscience," said Holmes. "Actually, I must inform you that Inspector Lestrade had already informed me of the crime, and earlier today I went to Miss Ransom's home and made some discreet inquiries with her mother. She confirmed Miss Ransom is a creature of fixed habits, returning promptly from work and spending most of her evenings at home, which would leave little time to confer with criminal associates. However, she also said her daughter had been on a number of business trips with her employer and frequently works late – each time having a messenger sent by Mr. Manderville to inform her mother that the lady will not be home at her usual time. Her mother is an extremely observant woman and has drawn conclusions from that behaviour, and also from the gifts which her daughter often receives, suggesting that the relationship between employer and employee iss suspiciously close."

"Any suggestion of that outside of this room would be libellous, as well as ruining two reputations!" asserted Manderville forcefully. "And as for your request for my business records – as I said, Mr. Holmes, my clients are very protective of their identity."

"I will, of course, not share the information beyond Dr. Watson and myself, but I believe it will be essential in the effort to bring this matter to a satisfactory conclusion."

Manderville nodded reluctantly, and then agreed to have what Holmes requested brought to Baker Street later that afternoon. He bustled off to make the arrangements.

"A puzzling matter indeed," I said. "One of your most mysterious cases."

"An unusual matter, I agree, but I believe the solution will be a simple one," he said. "Indeed, I don't need to leave my chair to bring the issue to an end."

"Are you not even going to visit Manderville's home to look for clues?" I asked.

"I'm content to leave you to carry out that task," Holmes said. "You know my methods. Please travel to Grosvenor Square and examine the scene. Be sure to observe every detail, no matter how small, and report back to me when you have finished."

I couldn't blame Holmes for not wishing to venture out in the heat, and I regretted my choice of attire, especially as it hadn't achieved the desired outcome. Even with a slight breeze coming through the open windows of the hansom, it was uncomfortably warm and muggy. I was thankful the route didn't go near the river, as several days of heat had caused a miasma to creep ashore from the sewage that slowly crept down the Thames towards the sea. It was nowhere near as pungent since the extensive sewerage system had been installed, but the East End in particular had an aroma that made the eyes water as the river smell mixed with the stench of tanneries and other industry.

26 Grosvenor Square was a grand building some one-hundred years old. The Square itself was one of the most fashionable in London, and held

a number of embassies as well as private dwellings. Manderville's business must indeed be profitable if he was able to afford an address here. Number 26 was one of those designed by Sir Robert Adam, but had been rebuilt twenty years before. A number of other premises were also in the process of being restored, and dust from the construction hung on the warm air and caught in my throat.

I was greeted by Manderville's butler, who was expecting a visit but seemed disappointed it wasn't Sherlock Holmes in person. Nevertheless, he politely showed me around the empty building. He explained that his employer and his wife were staying in a hotel until the police had finished their investigation, in the hope that at least some of their furniture would be found and remove the necessity to purchase new items. He confirmed that he and the other staff had been away visiting relatives when the theft took place, and also that the police had found no sign of forced entry. I looked out of the window in the grand drawing room and saw the large garden at the centre of the Square. Although it had been designed to emulate a country park, there wasn't much foliage to obscure the view of the houses, and any activity undertaken in daylight would be clearly visible.

I travelled from room to room, as I believe Holmes would have in my place. As Manderville had said, every piece of furniture and the carpets had been removed from the main house. Only the kitchen and servants' quarters were untouched. While the butler – a Charles Smith – had moved back into his room, the other servants were still staying with their families.

"Has the furniture been removed carefully, do you think?" I asked him.

"Most professionally, in my opinion," he said. "This wasn't a hurried theft. The miscreants must have been quite confident they wouldn't be disturbed. Many of the pieces would have had their value diminished had they been damaged."

"Was everything that was taken valuable?"

"That depends on what you consider of value," said Smith. "Everything was in good taste and was quite expensive when purchased, However the resale value at auction would have been far less, apart from the many antique pieces – although, of course, the less expensive items would be easier to sell."

I checked all of the floors and windows in the empty rooms. They had been thoroughly cleaned before Manderville had embarked on his trip, and the thieves had clearly been careful to leave little trace of their presence. There was the odd scuff mark on the paintwork of the doors where it had been scratched by furniture, but no discarded cigarettes or muddy footprints that could be of use to Holmes. This meant I had little to report when I returned to Baker Street.

"On the contrary, Watson," he said. "Your observations confirm my own conclusions. My scrutiny of Manderville's appointment diary has provided enough information to provide a fitting *denouement* to this small puzzle. I have notified Lestrade at the Yard, and he was happy to provide some officers to be on the scene tomorrow evening. I believe that you'll enjoy accompanying me to see the finale."

The following evening, I was there at five p.m. Holmes immediately bustled me into a waiting cab and we proceeded to Grosvenor Square.

"Do you think the thieves will return to break into the safe?" I asked. "Perhaps they were disturbed before they were able to tackle it."

"The safe was never their objective," Holmes said. "It was always the furniture they were after."

We arrived in the Square, but instead of going to Manderville's house, Holmes disembarked the cab and walked over to the gardens, inviting me to sit next to him on a bench.

"This should provide us with a first-row view of events," he said. He looked at his pocket watch. "We are just in time."

I could see little of interest in the normal comings and goings of the Square. Nannies were propelling their charges around the gardens in push-chairs, and there was even a policeman slowly patrolling the pavement. I stared at Number 26 and saw no movement within or without Manderville's home.

"You are looking at the wrong place," said Holmes. "Direct your attention a few doors to the left."

A hansom cab was pulling into the kerb a few doors away, and I watched as a man disembarked. He looked perfectly in place with an expensively cut black suit, top hat, and small valise. As I watched, he walked over to one of the house doors and was admitted as soon as he had knocked.

"I'm not sure what I'm supposed to be observing," I said to Holmes.

"All will become clear in a moment."

As he spoke, a number of policemen appeared in the Square and marched quickly to the house the gentleman had entered. One shouldered the door and they quickly entered *en masse*. There were shouts from the premises that cut across the quiet of the Square, drowning the bird song. Within seconds, they came back out, each holding a man in captivity, their hands clearly shackled in handcuffs. A police wagon had arrived, and the men were bundled in the back.

"And that brings the affair to an end," Holmes said.

"I'm still not sure what I have just witnessed."

"It is quite elementary," he said. "What number house have the police just entered?"

I counted the number of doors from the Manderville home.

"Number 29, I believe," I said.

"Correct," said Holmes. "A number that can easily be altered to *26*, which is what the gang did. If you enter No. 29, you will find all of Mr. Mandeville's furniture laid out exactly as it was in his home. Quite an ingenious plan, although one I found easy to unravel."

"I'm still in the dark," I said. Holmes smiled – a tad condescendingly I thought.

"Consider the unusual nature of the burglary," he said. "Along with some admittedly expensive pieces of furniture, everything else that was taken was hardly worth the considerable effort the thieves went to in order to remove it. One of the main clues I encountered in reading the neighbours' statements was the short period between visits of the moving van, which suggested that wherever the furniture was taken couldn't be far away. Then I discovered something that would make the thieves' efforts worthwhile: Manderville's diary revealed that he was due to have a visit from a diamond dealer from South Africa who was bringing a considerable amount of valuable gems for a number of high-quality commissions that Manderville had received – a value of no less than half-a-million pounds worth of uncut diamonds, which could be easily sold once prepared by an expert."

"That was the man who just arrived in the cab."

"Correct," said Holmes. "Because of the incident at his home, Manderville was about to re-route this man to a different meeting place when I sent him a message yesterday evening and told him to confirm he would meet the man at his home, as originally planned. In the meantime, the gang had also already cabled the dealer with the same message, and arranged for him to be met at the rail station and brought to the house – but they would bring him to No. *29*, now filled with Manderville's furniture, and with the address changed to No. *26*. They believed they would there be safe to rob him there, and then leave him bound and gagged there until they made good their escape. No. 29 has been standing empty because builders are due to start work in a few weeks to remodel it, so it was easy to take the furniture a short distance from No. 26, go around, and gain access at the rear to take the furniture inside and install it."

"But how did they know of the diamond merchant's visit in the first place?" I asked. "Was it the secretary who informed them after all?"

"I don't believe so," said Holmes. "We may find out for certain once Lestrade has interrogated the men, but I believe they have been planning their heist for many months – since discovering the South African dealer was due to bring a consignment to London. It's well known that Manderville meets with dealers at his home, so they safely assumed such would be the case this time, and they took the opportunity to create a duplicate of his house. They may have even been behind persuading the journalist to write his story on Mrs. Manderville's expensive furniture, in order to a copy sent to the South African dealer so he knew what to expect. It would seem that a considerable amount of planning was involved, but an even more considerable reward if it came off."

Lestrade's later interrogations of the suspects confirmed that Holmes's conjectures were correct, including the non-involvement of Miss Ransom.

As Holmes and I sat continued to sit on the bench, some of the neighbours' servants had been sent out into the street to investigate the police presence, but they were now returning to their normal duties, and Grosvenor Square was returning to its previous calm state. I could clearly hear the birds singing in the trees again, and felt the warm sun on my face.

"You told me you were considering submitting your description of our first case together to *Beeton's Annual*," Holmes said. "I'm not sure this case would be of any special fascination, so if you wish to continue detailing our adventures, I can suggest others that might be of more interest."

I wasn't sure that I agreed, but decided to keep my own counsel.

The Dark Tavern
by Robert V. Stapleton

As a result of the professional and personal demands being made upon my life during those darkening days of October, I was relieved that I could find nothing in the national or local press to add to my concerns. On the other hand, neither could I see anything that was likely to bring Sherlock Holmes out of his current gloomy shell. I thought that perhaps he ought to be allowed to browse the dearth of interesting news for himself. Perhaps he might find some mindless article to amuse him. It was for this reason that I passed the morning newspaper over to my friend, with a comment to that effect.

A few moments later, he tossed the journal back to me, with renewed urgency in his voice, and a corrective comment. "Look at the '*Stop Press*', Watson."

I looked. The brief article at the foot of the back page mentioned that a couple of mud larks, while scouring the briefly revealed banks of the low-tide Thames in search of items that they could sell, had discovered the body of a man. The police had not yet managed to identify the corpse.

"That is hardly a novelty," commented Holmes, "but I suppose that is the reason why Lestrade is at this moment climbing the stairs to the landing outside our rooms."

I had failed to hear the tell-tale sound of the inspector's familiar footfall upon the stairs, so I was alerted by the sound of a knock upon the door and the turning of the door-handle. I looked up just in time to watch the inspector enter the room.

"Ah, Lestrade!" said Holmes. "What a refreshing surprise it is to see you this morning. It seems this is becoming something of a habit of yours. Kindly take a seat here beside the fire. You look as if you need warming up."

"Thank you, I'm sure, Mr. Holmes," said Lestrade. "The weather certainly has taken a turn for the colder."

"Now," said Holmes, sitting back in his chair and observing the policeman over his steepled fingers, "what can we do this morning in order to assist the crime-fighting efforts of Scotland Yard?"

"Have you seen the latest in the local newspapers?"

"Reports of the unidentified corpse, you mean? We have indeed seen the article – brief as it is. However, I have usually considered the

347

identification of such victims to be the province of the police. In which case, how do you imagine I may be of assistance?"

"I have to admit, Mr. Holmes, that you have proven to be of some help to us in the past. And it was for that reason that our thoughts turned to you on this occasion."

"Please carry on."

"We are entirely without a lead in this case. We can find no one who recognizes the man. And we can find no means of identification upon his person."

"In that case, how do you suppose I might be able to help?"

"You have your methods, and I merely thought you might be willing to use them to assist us on this occasion."

Holmes smiled. "To help identify the dead man?"

"The circumstances are somewhat perplexing, I have to admit. He was discovered on the mud banks of the Thames at low water. That is all we have to go on."

"Is this matter of any particular importance?"

"Without identifying the man, it is of course impossible to tell. However, I know that you enjoy unscrambling a conundrum, so before consigning the poor victim to a pauper's grave, we thought that perhaps this one might appeal to your turn of mind."

Holmes thought for a moment. Then he pushed himself to his feet. "You have transport for us, I presume."

"Indeed. A cab is waiting for us outside."

"Splendid. Very well, Inspector. Lead on. Watson, are you joining us? This might prove to be in your line of work."

"My appointments diary does appear to be rather full at the moment," I said, "but I suppose I could call upon one of my colleagues to cover my immediate obligations." I stood up reluctantly, grasped my hat, coat, and cane, and followed.

I found the morgue at Scotland Yard to be as cold and clinical as I ever remembered it. The scent of death pervaded every brick and tile of the place. I might be a medical professional, used to dealing with the realities of life and death, but I have to admit that I often feel a slight shudder pass through me on such occasions.

At Lestrade's instruction, the clinician wheeled out the corpse, placed the trolley it in the middle of the room, and removed the shroud to reveal the mortal remains of this unfortunate individual.

Holmes commenced his examination of the body.

"He was a young man, perhaps still in his twenties. The cause of death is obvious."

"Indeed," said Lestrade. "His throat has been cut."

Holmes examined the injury through his magnifying glass. "With the use of a knife which possessed a singular blade – one with a serrated edge, from which a number of teeth are missing. Distinctive. I am sure I would recognize the instrument if I ever saw it."

Lestrade raised an eyebrow in wonder, and perhaps some doubt, at such a confident statement.

Holmes continued his examination of the body. "He looks to be physically fit. Although clearly not a working seaman, his hands show that he has been involved in some kind of manual work, but only in recent days. He has been in the habit of paying particular attention to his own appearance, and his personal care. What do you think, Watson?"

I took off my coat, rolled up my sleeves, and examined the body. "I can add nothing further to what you have said," I told him. "I can only describe this crime as cold-blooded murder."

"Without a doubt."

I stepped back again and retrieved my coat.

"As you say, Inspector," said Holmes, "there is nothing on the body to assist us with identification."

The policeman nodded, relieved that his own conclusion had now been confirmed.

"Now we must turn our attention to whatever the man was wearing when he was discovered," said Holmes, glancing at Lestrade. "Can you show us his clothing?"

"Come. I'll show you." Lestrade led us through a plain green door into the next room. The clothes lay upon a steel table. "As you can see, these would suggest that he was a working seaman, but you have already dismissed that idea."

"Hmm." Holmes carefully sorted through the garments one by one. "Wool underwear. Linen shirt. Cotton trousers. Heavy cotton jacket. Leather sea boots. And a leather cap which might or might not have accompanied the rest." Holmes looked up. "Anything else?"

"That was everything," Lestrade confirmed. "Except that he had been weighed down by having an iron bar strapped across the torso."

"Then why isn't he now at the bottom of the Thames?"

"It seems that the body was dropped over the side of a ship while it was in port, possibly during the gathering darkness, but the pressure of the ebbing tide forced the corpse up against a series of wooden pilings. A group of mud larks found him while they were searching along the foreshore late last night."

Holmes nodded and began to sort through the young man's trouser pockets.

"We've already looked through those," said Lestrade.

Holmes nodded. "It is always worth gaining a second opinion."

We all watched as Holmes pulled out a small and tightly pressed fragment of paper.

"Must have missed that," grouched Lestrade.

"It was pressed well down."

"But I don't see much hope of finding any useful information from it."

"That is to be seen," returned Holmes as he searched through the trouser turn-ups. From these, he poured out a small quantity of clumped white powder, still there after submersion in the river.

Holmes tasted the powder, and examined it more closely through his magnifying glass. "Alum."

"Is that significant?"

"That also remains to be seen. But together with the crumpled paper, it might provide an indication. May I take this paper fragment and see what I can make of it?"

"Certainly, Mr. Holmes. If you can find out anything about this man, then it might be of the greatest help in our search for what happened to him, and why."

"And another thing."

"Yes?"

"I need a list of all the vessels that have visited the docks here in London during the past few days. Where they came from, where they were bound for, and what cargoes they were carrying."

"Do you have any idea how many hundreds of ships and boats pass along the Thames every single day?"

"Certainly I do. But you may confine your search to those which have been trading in both alum and scrap iron. I need that information. I need it quickly, and you are the only organization capable of acquiring it for me in short order."

"Very well, Mr. Holmes," said Lestrade with a sigh. "I'll get every man I have onto the job for you."

Back at 221b Baker Street, Holmes settled himself down to examine the small wad of paper he had discovered. He began by gently teasing the bundle out to its full extent. After several minutes, a small and ragged fragment lay flat upon the table.

He stood back and studied it thoughtfully. Then he examined it at closer range and in greater detail, first using his magnifying lens, and then progressing to placing the paper beneath his microscope.

"Hmm."

"What have you found?" I inquired.

"It appears to be a receipt from a shop in Newcastle-Upon-Tyne. A gentleman's outfitters. The name of the establishment has faded away, but a number appears at the top right-hand corner."

"The number from a receipt pad, perhaps?"

"Precisely. That is the clue we must follow. And we must do it as quickly as possible."

"I wonder how many such businesses there must be in Newcastle," I mused.

"And how many have issued numbered receipts in the recent past?"

A hurried visit to the local Reference Library produced a list of such gentlemen's establishments and their addresses. Holmes sent telegrams to each of these shops, mentioning the receipt number and asking for the name of the client and, if possible, a description of the man concerned.

Holmes received a single positive reply within the hour.

"Now," he declared as he stood before the fire, "at the very least, it seems we have a name."

"Will it be of any help to us?" I asked.

"Possibly. The receipt was given to a man called Richard Cadmus, upon the purchase of a pea-jacket."

"That sounds unusual," I replied. "Was he a military man?"

"Perhaps. But that name – *Cadmus* – rings a bell in my memory."

"The letter you received a few days ago," I said, recalling that Holmes had set it aside after initially dismissing it. "Wasn't that from a man called Cadmus?"

"You mean, the fish-monger?"

"That's the one."

"Whatever became of the letter?"

"It probably became lost among your chaotic filing system," I suggested. "I can only imagine that you put it to one side for future reference, but I have noticed that you often hide such correspondence in the pocket of your purple dressing gown."

"Was I wearing it that day?"

"In all probability. It will take only a few seconds to check the contents."

After a search through the said pockets, Holmes emerged triumphant, clutching several letters, including the one from the fish-monger. This he set about reading with much greater interest than on the previous occasion.

"Here we are. It seems that the writer's name is Joshua Cadmus, and he asks for my help in locating his son, with whom he has lost contact in recent days. He sounds worried. I was busy at the time, but perhaps now is the right moment to respond to his call for help. Ah, now I remember him. Cadmus owns one or two of the stalls down at the Billingsgate Fish Market."

"A businessman," I concluded, "rather than a mere street-corner shopkeeper."

Joshua Cadmus was nearing the conclusion of a particularly busy day when we arrived at the Fish Market in Lower Thames Street. The streets around the market were busy, and at this time of day the traffic consisted of horse-drawn wagons carrying barrels and wooden boxes, emptied and washed, for conveyance to the various railway stations, and thence returned to their home fishing ports. Cadmus was supervising the loading of the final cart leaving for Paddington Station.

On hearing that his son might have been found dead, Cadmus dropped everything he was doing, handed his work over to a subordinate, and insisted on accompanying Holmes and myself back to Scotland Yard in order to make the official identification.

In the gloom of the early evening, the morgue felt even more oppressive than it had on our previous visit earlier in the day. This heavy atmosphere clearly added to the weight of Joshua Cadmus' despair, as he positively identified the body on the trolley as that of his son, Richard. A mixture of emotions crowded through the man's heart and mind, and these showed upon his face until they burst out in a cry of anger which could be heard throughout the building.

"Who did this?" he demanded.

"We have no idea," said Lestrade, his face displaying its usual downcast aspect.

"We thought you might be able to throw some light onto the matter," said Holmes. "After all, you did send me a letter saying that you were concerned for the safety of your missing son."

"And I was right to be concerned, wasn't I?" shot back the fish-monger, as his red and angry eyes riveting Holmes. "But you were too late in offering to help me. The least you can do now is to investigate the matter and help bring the villain who killed my son to justice. Or do I have to do it all by myself?"

"It wouldn't be wise to take the law into your own hands, Mr. Cadmus," said Lestrade. "Now that we have the man's name, we can begin to investigate the matter in earnest."

"Begin? Have you done nothing at all so far?"

"We have these," said Lestrade as he placed a pile of papers on the desk in front of us. "Mr. Holmes, you asked for a list of all the vessels to have passed along the Thames during the past day or two. Here they are. Even down to the smallest barge."

"Thank you, Lestrade," said Holmes.

"And we have noted especially those vessels which have been transporting alum or scrap iron."

Holmes collected the bundle of papers and, as the police morgue attendant tidied away young Cadmus' body, he took them into an adjoining room in order to study them without interruptions from the rest of us.

I joined Lestrade and Mr. Cadmus in another side-office, where the inspector interviewed the grieving father in greater detail. Joshua Cadmus told us that his son had been working with the Coast Guard and law-enforcement officers along the northeast coast of England, keeping an eye open for any illegal smuggling activities.

Lestrade leapt into action, sending out a couple of runners. One he sent to the Admiralty in search of someone who could give further information about the work of the Coast Guard. The other was instructed to deliver a call for an individual from the Foreign Office.

Both officials arrived in short order, in time for Lestrade to outline his case to them. This he finished just as Sherlock Holmes arrived once more upon the scene.

"Well, Mr. Holmes," said Lestrade. "Have you found anything of interest?"

"A schooner, called the *Craster Bay*, arrived from the northeast the day before yesterday, with a cargo of alum."

"Alum? You mentioned that before."

"A salt of potassium sulphate, used in the dyeing industry, paper manufacture, and waterproofing of fabric, amongst other uses."

"And when did she leave?"

"Earlier today."

"Where was she going?"

"If this is indeed the right vessel," said Holmes, "the documents mention Holland. Vaguely."

"That is very interesting," said the official from the Foreign Office.

Holmes turned to the Admiralty official. "Since the Coast Guard are under the authority of the Admiralty, what can you tell us about the young man Cadmus, and the work he was involved in?"

"He was investigating a renewed activity amongst the smuggling community of northeast England," said the official.

"But I thought large-scale smuggling was a thing of the past," I stated.

"True enough," said the Admiralty Official. "Spirits and tobacco no longer bring the financial returns they once did. So these people must be dealing in something else. Something more lucrative."

"That's what we are afraid of," said the man from the Foreign Office.

"What sort of commodity might be attracting them?" Holmes shot back.

"That is the question that Richard Cadmus was investigating He gave us little in the way of feedback, but he felt sure he knew exactly what they were doing. And it all had to do with a certain man living in Northumberland, by the name of Gorgoson."

I had heard of that individual before, so I watched Holmes for some sign that he also recognized the name. His face remained a masterpiece of impassivity. "Whatever they're involved in smuggling," said Holmes thoughtfully, "it seems to be under the cover of a small boat, bringing alum down from the northeast coast, and transporting scrap iron across to the Netherlands."

"Or somewhere else along that coast of the German Ocean," added the Foreign Office man.

"And where might this schooner be at this precise moment?" asked Holmes.

All eyes turned to the man from the Admiralty.

"With the way the tides are running at the moment, and with a contrary wind blowing in from the sea, she is probably at this moment no farther downriver than Gravesend."

"Very well," declared Holmes. "Lestrade, send word down river to hold the schooner for examination, possibly on the pretext of studying her manifest. Meanwhile, get us down there in time to board her before she sails again. If this is indeed the vessel we're looking for, then I might be able to discover exactly what is going on here by posing as a member of her crew."

"You will have to take great care, Mr. Holmes," said Lestrade.

"I have every intention of doing so."

Sherlock Holmes instructed both myself and Joshua Cadmus to pack our bags for a few days away from home, and to meet each other again at King's Cross railway station at our earliest convenience.

Back at our rooms, Holmes gave me his clear instructions. "I want you, Watson, to take Cadmus with you – he may prove to be useful – and travel up to the coast of Northumberland. Wait for me there. Although, as we have already agreed, large-scale smuggling is very much a thing of the past, there is still one place which retains a particularly dubious reputation from those old days: A coastal tavern called The Wheelhouse Inn. Also in that area resides a man who is known to me through a family connection. He's the man we've already heard about: Harold Gorgoson. I suspect him of being at the very heart of this business. Be wary, and be sure to take your service revolver with you whenever you make contact."

"And are you really going to join the crew of that ship?"

"I shall attempt to board the vessel and inform the captain that I'm acting on instructions from Gorgoson, sent to replace the unfortunate Cadmus. If he accepts me, then it will confirm for us three important and significant facts, which will determine the course of this investigation: First, Gorgoson really is the man at the middle of this intrigue. Second, young Cadmus was indeed murdered by one of the crew, most probably by the captain himself. And third, the murder had been planned in advance. That it was cold-blooded and premeditated. Whatever happens, Watson, I want you to wait for me at that tavern. Our paths will surely cross again there."

"And we still have no idea what exactly these people are smuggling."

"None whatsoever, although a number of possibilities come to mind."

Holmes had already left by the time I had packed my traveling bag, pulled on my heavy overcoat, and hurried down the stairs once more.

As planned, I met Joshua Cadmus at King's Cross. There he revealed himself to be dressed and prepared much as I was, and yet he was in a state of mind somewhat different from my own. His face appeared clearly set with the determination of a man intent upon justice at any price.

We took seats on the late-night service on the East Coast line to Edinburgh, although we were due to leave this leg of our journey earlier, at Newcastle-upon-Tyne.

We journeyed north.

Through the darkest hours of that October night, I listened as rain occasionally rattled against the windows, making me glad that at the very least I was under cover. Lights occasionally flashed past us, places which were impossible to identify. Cadmus proved to be a poor traveling companion with little to say, although much seemed to be going on inside his mind.

We stepped down onto the dark platform at Newcastle-upon-Tyne in the early morning of the following day, and I had a painful crick in my neck. I looked around for the connecting train which would take me on to my next stop. Cadmus suddenly announced that he was going to leave me at this point and make contact with a representative from the Coast Guard.

"It was with them that my son was working when he died," said Joshua Cadmus. "At least that's what I understood from what Richard had told me."

"Very well," said I. "In that case, I shall make my own way to The Wheelhouse Inn, exactly as planned. Perhaps we shall meet up again later."

"I am sure we shall, Dr. Watson," he said as he turned his back on me and made his way toward the exit.

From this point, my own route was clear. I was obliged to take the mail train north along the main line, stopping at almost every junction, until we reached the historic market town of Alnwick. I had visited this place on a previous occasion and had been deeply impressed by the magnificent castle which dominates the town. This time, however, a study of that fortress would have to wait – at least until we had successfully dealt with the present crisis.

Standing on the railway platform at Alnwick, just visible in the half-light, I discovered a tall figure in a gray overcoat. My acquaintance with policemen meant that I was able to identify him readily as an officer of the law – not that there were many other people on the platform, apart from several employees of the railway company.

"Dr. Watson?" he inquired.

"Indeed," I replied, grasping his proffered hand. "I am Dr. John Watson."

"I am Inspector Nathaniel Bewick of the Northumberland County Constabulary. I wish you to be assured, Doctor, that we are prepared to provide you with all the support that we have available. Scotland Yard made that matter abundantly clear."

"I am indeed most grateful, Inspector."

"Were there not supposed to be two of you?"

"Two of us did indeed set off from London, but my companion, Mr. Cadmus, has decided to continue with his own inquiries at Newcastle. It is the death of his son that we're investigating."

"Of course."

"My instructions are to check in at The Wheelhouse Inn until Sherlock Holmes makes his appearance there."

"In that case, I have a horse-and-trap waiting to take you to your destination. It isn't very far away."

"Thank you. But one more thing – "

"Yes, Doctor?"

"Does the name 'Gorgoson' mean anything to you, Inspector?"

"Gorgoson? Indeed it does. He used to be high on the list of suspects involved in the smuggling trade. We could never catch the man, but we're sure that he still has his hand in questionable activities, even to this day."

We parted, and I stepped onto the vehicle he had procured for me, headed in the direction of the coast. We passed cold gray fields on both sides, where men, women, and animals were already beginning to emerge and take up their daily work. At that time of the year, the wind was biting as it blew in from the gray and cold waters of the German Ocean. I was tired after a night of failing to find much sleep on the train, and my mind was turning to my friend, Sherlock Holmes. Had he managed to board the

356

schooner? Had he started to unravel this mystery? I thought also of Joshua Cadmus. What were his plans, having left me alone in order to pursue his own investigations? I felt annoyed at being left in the lurch like this.

I was so tired that I was nodding off as we trundled along, but a jolt roused me from a shallow slumber. I felt decidedly unsettled as I realized that we were approaching my final destination.

The prospect on every side had hardly improved. I could see the ocean, but no jetty or quayside. Rather, I could see a line of small, clinker-built fishing boats, or *cobles*, that had been dragged up onto the shingled foreshore. A row of fishermen's cottages overlooked the cold and depressing sea. Here was undoubtedly one of the bleakest places I had ever had cause to visit. Or was that merely a reflection generated by my own grim state of mind?

Our horse-and-trap drew up at the far end of the village road, in front of a solid-looking building which displayed a sign proclaiming it to be *The Wheelhouse Inn*. The building appeared to be constructed of the same gray stone as both the adjacent fishermen's cottages and the other village buildings. Not that there were many of those. On the other hand, this tavern seemed to be the largest building in the village, and sported a roof of red terracotta pantiles – the only color I could make out. In need of some warmth and a decent meal, I hoisted my bag out of the vehicle, paid the driver, and walked toward the front door of the inn. I could see nothing welcoming about the place. Not yet at any rate. The place appeared to be enveloped in a gloomy darkness as I entered.

A man seated at the reception desk looked up at me as I made my way inside. His look of bored disinterest turned to sullen hostility when he noticed that I was a stranger there.

"Yes?" he challenged me.

"My name is Doctor Watson, and I should like a room for the night. Or possibly for more than the one night."

Without looking down at his visitors' book, he sniffed. "All the rooms are full."

I looked around at the barren lounge with its empty chairs and tables. "At this time of the year?"

"At any time of the year."

"In that case, how do you manage to make a living?"

"That's my concern, Dr. Watson. What business do you have here, anyway?"

My mind went back to the instructions Sherlock Holmes had given me. "I am hoping to meet a friend. Harold Gorgoson."

At the mention of this name, an auburn-haired young woman who had been cleaning behind the bar looked up at me and frowned. The attitude of the man also altered considerably.

"Well," he said, "any friend of Mr. Gogoson is welcome here." He consulted his book. "Ah, now that I look more closely, I see that we do indeed have a room for you, Doctor."

He handed me a key.

"The most prestigious room in the place," he added. "With a sea-view prospect. And luncheon will be served in here at noon."

I acknowledged his welcoming comment with a smile. "That would be ideal."

After I had rested for a while, catching up on a couple of hours' lost sleep, I consumed a veritable feast of a midday meal and decided to explore outside. Not that there was much out there to see.

With my coat buttoned up against the cutting east wind, I wandered along the seafront. The only thing I could discover was a great deal of mud, a number of rocks, and the smell of ozone.

Not wanting to risk dampening the turn-ups of my trousers, I returned to the road and decided to continue my explorations on the following day.

I found that The Wheelhouse Inn tended to come alive every evening. It was then, at the end of an arduous working day, that the place would fill up with fishermen and local farm workers in search of companionship and liquid refreshment. Having a fresh audience to hear their tales, namely myself, these people were quick to include me in their conversations, and so I learned a great deal about the local situation and people. I heard of many things: About the legend of a man, one of several, who had been known as "The King of the Gypsies", and who had been involved in smuggling goods into southern Scotland not so many years before.

"But nothing like that is going on at the moment!" declared one man.

"Rubbish," said another, with a look of warning. "Something is going on here – but the truth is that we aren't involved in it."

"It's that fellow Gorgoson," said another, in hushed tones. "And we all know it!"

The atmosphere turned colder, as though some dark truth was being revealed. All eyes turned to the doorway, where a man had just come in. Here was a tough-looking fellow whose appearance brought a look of fear to the eyes of my companions. One man in our company rubbed his face, heavily bruised by some encounter with a weighty object. The message to me was clear: A heavy hand was taking charge of events in this community.

The morning following my first evening at the tavern, when I was much refreshed by another decent meal and a good night's rest, I continued to explore the village and the seafront. I watched the ebb tide. Before long it revealed a truly horrific sight: With the sea having retreated, I could see whole stretches of shoals and reefs of sharp limestone, littered with huge boulders, which had previously been hidden by the water. Here was danger sufficient to rip the bottom out of any ship which struck these underwater hazards.

Farther along, this death trap gave way to a kind of lagoon, or haven, which was protected by yet another obstacle which stretched like a finger out into the ocean, almost entirely surrounding the haven with a promontory of hard, vicious rock. I watched as a gang of men set about unloading a moored fishing boat of its catch of crabs and lobsters, and then hauling the vessel up above the high water line.

I heard a voice behind me. "Dr. Watson, I presume."

I turned, and immediately noticed a man standing a few feet away, watching me intently. His face displayed a disarming smile. He was tall, dark, with graying side-whiskers, and dressed in a smart suit. I failed to recognize him.

"Indeed."

"Allow me to introduce myself. My name is Harold Gorgoson. I understand we have a friend in common."

"Sherlock Holmes?"

He nodded.

"Certainly," I replied.

"In that case, I should like to invite you to visit me, to join me for dinner. I shall send a carriage to collect you at seven. Would that be convenient?"

I had been caught out with a lie, since I wasn't yet acquainted with this man. I felt obliged to remedy that error. I couldn't think at that moment of any convincing reason why I shouldn't be able to attend the appointment. "Seven, you say?" I nodded. "Thank you. I shall be ready."

"Splendid," said Gorgoson, before turning and heading back in the direction of the inn.

Everything and everybody seemed to be quite innocent. Was more going on than appeared on the surface? Perhaps Holmes had been right about shady activities occurring here. But there was no sign of this just yet. The only way I was to discover the truth was to join the man for dinner.

Harold Gorgoson's house was something quite amazing. And yet chilling. It gave the impression of being a small but well-formed country house, a manor house perhaps. Situated only a couple of miles from the ocean, and it stood out on a rise above the small fishing village. Beside the main front door I noticed a nameplate, with the name of the place carved into a slab of white limestone: "*The Furze*". The interior of the building was splendidly furnished and fitted out. The dining table carried silver cutlery and best quality crockery. A series of oil-lamps lined the walls. I wondered how much of this had been paid for from the ill-gotten gains of the smuggling trade.

"Food from the sea which lies not far away," Gorgoson explained as the first course appeared. "Lobster and herring."

"Perfect," I replied, wondering why it was that Holmes had warned me against this man – and why the men of the village seemed to fear him. To me he appeared harmless enough.

"I live here alone," Gorgoson explained. "I have no wife and family. Never have had. So my housekeeper has brought in a few helpers from the village."

In the shadows, I immediately recognized the young woman I had first seen behind the bar at The Wheelhouse Inn. I tried to smile at her, but she remained grim-faced.

After these initial pleasantries, and after the first course of our meal had been cleared away, Gorgoson came to the point of our gathering. "What exactly are you doing here, Dr. Watson? What brings you to this wind-swept place so late in the year?"

"Me? I am waiting for somebody."

"Mr. Holmes, I imagine."

"How perceptive of you. Yes. He told me to stay here until he arrived."

"And when will that be?"

"I suppose that depends upon the tides and the winds."

"He is at sea, then?"

"I really don't know where he is at this precise moment."

"And what exactly is his business?"

"You'll have to ask him about that when he comes. But it has something to do with a body being discovered in the River Thames."

"London? Many miles from here. What would that have to do with me?"

"I'm not sure it has anything at all to do with you, Mr. Gorgoson."

He appeared to be relieved by this statement. And gave a benign smile.

"Sherlock Holmes has a mind," I told him, "which is sometimes difficult to comprehend."

Gorgoson nodded. "He and I have long been acquainted, so I'm well aware of his unfathomable turn of mind."

We sparred with each other for the rest of the evening, he trying to extract from me any further information I possessed about this case, which wasn't a great deal, while in turn, I tried to learn from him anything I could about his involvement in whatever it was that was going on here. And, in passing, I asked about the smuggling trade.

"Be assured, Doctor," he said as I prepared to take my leave, "large-scale smuggling of valuable goods has all but finished now along this coast. It's no longer worth our while to run such risks with the prospect of so little financial gain."

I declined the offer of a carriage back to the inn, and opted instead to walk the couple of miles down toward the coast. I had things to think about. What was he hiding?

Outside, I stood for a while in silence, looking back at the house. What was really going on here? Gorgoson might not be married, but he was clearly devoted to some enterprise in which he was presently involved. But what exactly that was, I still didn't have any idea.

As I stood in the darkness, I noticed figures moving about – men and women walking away from the back of the house. Trudging. The very set of their bodies told me that something was wrong.

Then I became aware of somebody standing close beside me.

"Who's there?" I whispered.

"It's only me," came a young female voice. "Annie. From the inn."

"Oh, hello. You shouldn't be out here alone at this time of night."

"Have no fear for me. I can look after myself, thank you."

I nodded toward the people moving in the darkness. "Who are those people? Where are they going?"

"Those are the latest consignment that Gorgoson and his men are smuggling."

I suddenly felt confused. "People? Is he dealing in illegal immigrants?"

"Illegal, yes. But not willing immigrants. This is a business which is very different from helping migrants. Something really terrible is happening here. Something extremely evil. Something that has to be stopped."

"But aren't you working for these people?"

"I thought *you* were working for them. You said you were Mr. Gorgoson's friend."

"Not me," I told her.

"Yes, I've been working here, but I'm not one of them. Somebody has to find out what's going on in this place."

"What have you done about it so far?"

"I was the one who told Richard Cadmus about what they're doing."

"Cadmus? That makes sense. And now he is dead," I added thoughtlessly.

361

"Is he?" she gasped in horror.

I realized how shocking my careless revelation had been. "And that is why I am here," I added quickly. "Waiting for my friend, Sherlock Holmes, to arrive and help solve this problem. He'll know what to do."

"Richard was such a nice young man. I got to know him quite well. I didn't know he was dead. I'm extremely sorry about that, but that makes it all the more important for *you* to do something. You're the only person here who can do anything now. You'll find that the entire village is on your side."

"Me? What do you imagine I can do?"

"When does your friend Mr. Sherlock Holmes get here?"

"When the schooner that he's on arrives."

"So, he's on board that accursed boat."

"Yes. When does it return?"

"Tomorrow night. It will be dark and moonless – ideal for moving contraband . . . and people. The vessel will anchor off-shore during the darkest hours of the night, and a small boat will bring their consignment ashore."

"You say these rogues are smuggling people. But why?"

"It's a way of making money, of course."

"The notion of slavery is somewhat out of date," I suggested. "The American states fought a war over it not very long ago, and it is outlawed throughout the British Empire.

"It would be naïve to suggest that there is no slavery today, Dr. Watson," said Annie. "There are many things that enslave people: Poverty, illness, disabilities. Heartless crooks like these."

"Could you not tell the whole village about what you've discovered and organize them to put a stop to it?"

"The men of the village are convinced that something is going on here, but they aren't sure what it is. These criminals are ruthless people. If the village rose up against them, there would be a bloodbath. One or two of us have already suffered physical attacks for even suggesting it. Far better to let the police and law enforcement people deal with the matter rather than taking the law into our own hands."

The following day, the village appeared to be going about its daily routine, unhindered by thoughts of what might be going on in their midst. Fishing boats went out to their work, and came back again loaded with crab creels and lobster pots.

I turned away from the coast and back toward Gorgoson's house. I wanted to find out a little more about those people I had seen leaving from the rear of the building. Had they been legitimate workers or slaves?

362

Acting as though I were taking a casual saunter through the countryside, I went along the footpath I had shared with Annie the night before. Gradually, the house came into view. Even in the light of day, the place retained a forbidding appearance.

Not seeing anyone else, I worked around to the other side of the building. There I discovered an entrance, closed by double doors made of stout wood, and fastened with an iron bar across them. I decided to explore, so I lifted the iron bar and pushed open one of the doors, revealing a storage room of some kind.

I stepped across the filthy threshold.

The stale air from inside struck me with what felt almost like a physical blow. The stench of unwashed and uncared-for humanity pervaded the entire place. Iron chains hung from the walls, and the evidence of recent human occupation was unmistakeable. But I found that the place was empty.

"This is a stable," came a voice from behind me.

I turned, to find myself confronted by the owner of the house himself. Harold Gorgoson.

"Stable?"

"Certainly. That smell is a combination of horses, together with various other contributors. We sometimes have vagrants calling at the house here. We even had some call upon us here last night, so we provide this place as a kind of refuge for these unfortunate gentlemen of the road."

I began to doubt myself. Was this explanation enough to account for the existence of this place? And sufficient to explain the people that I'd seen moving about in the darkness on the previous evening? No, I concluded. He was clearly lying.

"I came here to say thank you once again for the excellent dinner you provided me with last night," I told him.

He gave me an innocent smile. "But when you arrived here just now, you were diverted by the sight of this building. Of course you were. Any companion of Sherlock Holmes could be expected to do nothing less."

"With my curiosity now satisfied," said I, "perhaps it's time that I left."

"Quite so, Dr. Watson."

Feeling ashamed at having been caught out, and with plenty more to think about, I realized that I would be pushing my luck if I stayed any longer, so I doffed my hat, returned to the door, and departed.

Back at the inn, I took to studying a couple of the books I had brought with me from home. My attention wasn't fully upon what I was reading, so I resigned myself to waiting for the inevitable events to unfold. For someone to arrive. For the truth to be revealed.

363

For the rest of that day, I remained the only person at the inn, which was hardly surprising given the time of the year. The cold wind was still blowing in from the German Ocean. The sky was overcast, and it mattered little that the night would be dark, windswept and moonless.

At mealtime, I noticed Annie give me a smile. It lit up her face. Had she learned about my morning exploit? Was I now forgiven for visiting Gorgoson?

As a clouded darkness fell, I looked out toward the ocean, but could see no sign of the anticipated vessel.

The usual drinkers and gossipers gathered that evening, and they lost ourselves in storytelling. Perhaps many of these tales had been augmented over the years by vivid imaginations, but my mind was also fixed upon other matters. Finally, when it was time for the others to leave, I retired to my bedroom, with its window looking out over the sea. I could see no sign of the schooner. Of course not. Why was I expecting it to appear so early in the evening? The darkness made it impossible to see anything or anybody out there with any clarity. These were just the right conditions for landing smuggled goods – or smuggled people.

The landlord unexpectedly brought me a mug of mulled wine and advised me to drink it all down. A good night's sleep would do me a world of good, he told me. I was delighted at his thoughtfulness.

But when he had left, I wondered about the man's motive. I suspected that the wine might be drugged. It would certainly suit the purposes of the present operation if I slept through the night, with no chance of interfering with their plans. I poured it out.

I remained in my day clothes, extinguished the lantern, and waited. As far as I could tell, the rest of the inn was enveloped in darkness. Then, at nearly two o'clock in the morning, I heard movement farther along the landing on which my room was situated. I moved quietly to the door, but found that it had been locked. Just then, before I could try to pick it, I heard footsteps. I heard somebody coming along the landing toward my own room. The light from a lantern spilled beneath the door.

I hurriedly climbed back into my bed, pulled up the counterpane, and feigned sleep.

The lock turned, the door opened, and a figure walked in – Careful. Silent.

The figure placed the lighted lantern onto the floor, and unfastened the wooden shutter, and placed the lantern on the windowsill. The darkness of the night appeared even more intense.

In the light of the lantern, I saw a face – no one that I recognized. I wondered about the staff of this tavern, and how deeply they were involved in this conspiracy. Or whether they all, as it appeared to me, being kept in order by Gorgoson's thugs

The man finished his task, returned to the doorway, slipped out onto the landing, and turned the lock closed again, before his footsteps disappeared along the wooden floorboards.

The light, still shining out from the window, was clearly intended to be a signal, a sign to somebody outside, perhaps at sea. It seemed that the arrival of the schooner was certainly now in the offing. Or was it already here?

I crept to the window and peered outside. Against the near blackness of the night, I noticed the dim outline of masts and spars, obviously belonging to some kind of ship, standing out in the ocean. Beyond those cruel and vicious rocks. I also saw movement. Even in the blackness, I could see a couple of small boats going and coming.

Several minutes passed, with people moving about downstairs. Then I heard a noise – footsteps – once again approaching my bedroom door. I dived back into bed.

I heard the lock click open, and the handle turn.

A figure entered. Not the landlord. Not the man who had last visited my room.

"Watson? Are you awake?"

"Holmes? Thank Heavens you're here!"

In the dim light of the lantern, I would never have recognized my friend if not for his voice. He was dressed in the manner of a sailor – and a tough one at that. But I was glad to see him all the same.

"We must be busy," he told me. "This entire business is about to be exposed."

"And about time too."

"Are you dressed?"

"I am."

"Then follow me."

So saying, he grasped hold of the lantern in the window and led the way back out and along the landing.

Holmes stopped at the next doorway and used a bent wire to turn the lock. The door opened, and inside we discovered the entire staff of The Wheelhouse Inn, cowering in the darkness. Annie threw herself at me, and held on tightly to my arm. Then she looked up. "Is this the Mr. Holmes you were telling me about?"

"It is."

"Then we must hurry."

The landlord bustled out onto the landing. "I'm glad you decided not to drink that mulled wine I gave you, Doctor," he told me. "It was Gorgoson's idea. It was drugged with a sleeping potion."

"Naturally."

"His people are taking over the place," he said, "but now we must alert the entire village. With the cat now well-and-truly out of the bag, we must mobilize the fishermen to take action. Quickly now – there is a back staircase we can use that will take us safely outside."

No one else seemed to be around so, as the others went about rousing the village, I followed Holmes toward the entrance hallway.

"This old building must be full of hidey-holes, used in the past for storing contraband," said Holmes. "But the present consignment of smuggled goods is being held down in the basement."

We descended into the depths of the building, where Holmes once more opened a locked door.

There, in the light of the lantern, I saw a sea of eyes, all looking up at me. None made a sound. I recognized the expressions of despair on the faces of the people huddled there in the darkness. Men, woman, and a few children.

"This is Gorgoson's cargo, Watson."

"Slaves," I replied.

Holmes nodded. "Homeless people. Stateless. Hopeless. People from across Europe, unable to afford their passage to a new life across the Atlantic. Swept up, like dregs, to be exploited by these evil people for their own selfish ends."

"The poorest of the poor," I concluded.

"Quite. Now, do you have your revolver with you?"

"I have it in my pocket."

"Capital. Now let us go up and meet these rogues. They will no doubt be waiting for us when we emerge."

He turned toward the staircase, leaving the door open. I followed.

At the top of the flight of stone steps, we emerged once more into the front passageway of the inn. There, as Holmes had predicted, we found that we weren't alone.

Half-a-dozen heavily built seamen stood around us. I noticed a couple of black eyes amongst them, and supposed this to be the work of Holmes in defending himself at some time during the voyage. A couple of lanterns lit up the faces of the two other men who were waiting for us there – one in particular.

"Good evening, Mr. Sherlock Holmes."

"Ah, Harold," said Holmes, standing to his full height, no longer the stooping seaman he had at first appeared. "I am ashamed to admit it, Watson, but this man is an acquaintance of my family."

"This fellow told me his name was Sigerson," said one of the sailors.

"A name he also uses when convenience requires it," said Gorgoson.

"Ah, Sutherland," said Holmes, addressing the man standing beside Gorgoson. "The captain of the schooner, and the man who murdered Richard Cadmus. He threatened me with that knife of his, Watson – the one he had used to kill the young man. And, as I predicted, I recognized it immediately as the murder weapon."

"Gorgoson is the man at the center of this web of intrigue," I noted.

"That was quickly confirmed when Sutherland allowed me to join the crew of the schooner. I rapidly learned the full story from the other members of the crew."

"When you reached Holland," said Gorgoson, "Sutherland sent me a wire to let me know that you were aboard, Holmes. You see, he never really trusted you. I knew immediately what was going on."

"And at the same time," said Holmes, "I sent a communication to Scotland Yard, who are about to descend upon this village in order to dismantle your evil schemes. It's time for you to surrender to the law-enforcement authorities."

Gorgoson raised a small but deadly-looking handgun, and pointed it at Holmes.

"I really have no wish to kill you," he said, "but you are in my way."

"And you are trading in human beings," said Holmes. "People who have been made vulnerable by their poverty, and now enslaved by you and your thugs here. Why?"

"I'm not as inhuman as you might think," said Gorgoson. "England has been made rich through trade, and the use of an industrial workforce provided by the poor working people of our land. Now that the trade unions are gaining power and demanding fair treatment and an increase in wages for their workers, we need a supply of people for our factories who will bring a smaller drain on the profits of our industrialists. These people are vital to the future prosperity of our country. We're merely supplying where there is a need."

"Nonsense!" snarled Holmes. "You're merely exploiting the poor, and being well paid for it by your corrupt cronies. You must surrender yourselves to the authorities and accept the consequences of your crimes. The hangman's rope is awaiting all of you."

A door opened, and we all turned to see Annie standing in the doorway. "There is a man here to see you, Mr. Gorgoson," she said.

Joshua Cadmus walked into the room and stood facing our two main opponents. "Which one of you two is responsible for killing my son?"

The captain looked up and gave a nasty grin. "And any moment now, you will end up as dead as he!" cried the man. "He was poking his nose into our affairs, and was about to go to Scotland Yard, so we had to deal with him. It was just everyone's misfortune that his body was discovered so quickly. Otherwise, we could have continued our business in peace."

"I think not," returned Cadmus. "The men of this village have finally discovered what you've been doing here, and they're coming together at this very moment to stop you. This building is currently surrounded by them, waiting to watch you leave – one way or another."

Gorgoson looked around at the thugs who were standing close behind Sutherland. "Go outside and check."

"Right you are," said one of them.

We waited in silence. Shortly afterwards the sound of shouts and scuffling reached us.

One of the thugs stumbled back inside the inn.

"You'd better think about leaving," he said to Gorgoson. "The fishermen we can deal with, but the village is at this moment filling up with armed men. Too many for us. We're going back to the ship."

Gorgoson looked around at the rest of us. In the confusion, I had taken the opportunity of removing my service revolver from my pocket, and was now pointing it at his head.

"I see we've reached an impasse," he declared. "I can barely say I'm surprised. I'm prepared to offer a solution. As I said, I have no wish to kill a family friend, nor do I relish having my head own blown off. I certainly don't wish to have my neck stretched by the law. If I swear to leave and never return to this village, will you let me go? Otherwise, there will be a bloodbath."

I was prepared to take the villain into custody regardless, but to my surprise, Holmes said nothing in reply.

"You can use your schooner," interrupted Cadmus.

"Go," added Holmes. "And never return."

Without a word, Gorgoson turned, and he and the ship's captain followed their crew, leaving the building quickly and heading for the seafront. From there they took a small boat out across the mounting seas to their vessel, where it was lying beyond the rocks.

As we all watched them go, catching whatever view we could of them in the near pitch blackness, I turned to Holmes. "How can you just let him escape?"

Without answering me, Holmes turned to Cadmus. "Did you accomplish your task?"

"That ship is definitely not seaworthy," said Cadmus, nodding.

This was a different aspect to the situation. "How can you be so certain?" I asked.

"Some of the locals helped me open the sea-cocks on that ship, and to make it impossible to close them. In this rough sea, the schooner will ship water and not be able to pump it out again."

"I estimate that they'll probably sink within the hour," added Holmes.

The police soon descended in number upon that small Northumberland village, where they spent the rest of the night interviewing, asking questions, and taking statements from almost everybody in the village.

Coast Guard vessels and locally owned fishing boats scoured the inshore and offshore waters for any sign of the escaping criminals. Police in the Netherlands closed down that end of the smuggling stream, and set free those unfortunate people who had been the victims of this cruel activity.

Scotland Yard still has an open book on the criminal activities of Gorgoson and his cronies, as the ship and crew were never seen again, but there is little chance of them ever finding the final resting place of the crew of the *Craster Bay*. The official opinion remains that the ship foundered somewhere in the middle of the German Ocean.

By the time daylight broke, we were all exhausted, and I was ready to return home to London.

I was standing on the shoreline with Sherlock Holmes at my side. We were both watching the village emerge out of the darkness of night. The gray skies had rolled back, allowing the first rays of the sun to rise out of the ocean and shine fully upon The Wheelhouse Inn. This gave a magical, almost innocent appearance to the place. And, as I was about to turn away and follow my luggage aboard the horse-and-trap that would take us back to the railway station at Alnwick, I noticed a figure standing on the balcony of the tavern. I recognized the figure that of as Annie, the young woman who had risked her life to inform me of the smuggling activities taking place around her.

She waved, and I waved back.

"Always an eye for the ladies, eh, Watson?" asked Sherlock Holmes.

I gave a chuckle. "It seems to me that perhaps that Inn is not quite such a dark place after all."

"Your morning letters, if I remember right, were from a fish-monger and a tidewaiter."

– Dr. John Watson
"The Noble Bachelor"

Appendix:
The Untold Cases

The following has been assembled from several sources, including lists compiled by Phil Jones and Randall Stock, as well as some internet resources and my own research. I cannot promise that it's complete – some Untold Cases may be missing – after all, there's a great deal of Sherlockian Scholarship that involves interpretation and rationalizing – and there are some listed here that certain readers may believe shouldn't be listed at all.

As a fanatical supporter and collector of pastiches since I was a ten-year-old boy in 1975, reading Nicholas Meyer's *The Seven-Per-Cent Solution* and *The West End Horror* before I'd even read all of The Canon, I can attest that serious and legitimate versions of all of these Untold Cases exist out there – some of them occurring with much greater frequency than others – and I hope to collect, read, and chronologicize them all.

There's so much more to The Adventures of Sherlock Holmes than the pitifully few sixty stories that were fixed up by the First Literary Agent. I highly recommend that you find and read all of the rest of them as well, including those relating these Untold Cases. You won't regret it.

David Marcum

A Study in Scarlet

- Mr. Lestrade . . . got himself in a fog recently over a forgery case
- A young girl called, fashionably dressed
- A gray-headed, seedy visitor, looking like a Jew pedlar who appeared to be very much excited
- A slipshod elderly woman
- An old, white-haired gentleman had an interview
- A railway porter in his velveteen uniform

The Sign of Four

- The consultation last week by Francois le Villard
- The most winning woman Holmes ever knew was hanged for poisoning three little children for their insurance money

- The most repellent man of Holmes's acquaintance was a philanthropist who has spent nearly a quarter of a million upon the London poor
- Holmes once enabled Mrs. Cecil Forrester to unravel a little domestic complication. She was much impressed by his kindness and skill
- Holmes lectured the police on causes and inferences and effects in the Bishopgate jewel case

The Adventures of Sherlock Holmes

"A Scandal in Bohemia"
- The summons to Odessa in the case of the Trepoff murder
- The singular tragedy of the Atkinson brothers at Trincomalee
- The mission which Holmes had accomplished so delicately and successfully for the reigning family of Holland. (He also received a remarkably brilliant ring)
- The Darlington substitution scandal, and . . .
- The Arnsworth castle business. (When a woman thinks that her house is on fire, her instinct is at once to rush to the thing which she values most. It is a perfectly overpowering impulse, and Holmes has more than once taken advantage of it

"The Red-Headed League"
- The previous skirmishes with John Clay

"A Case of Identity"
- The Dundas separation case, where Holmes was engaged in clearing up some small points in connection with it. The husband was a teetotaler, there was no other woman, and the conduct complained of was that he had drifted into the habit of winding up every meal by taking out his false teeth and hurling them at his wife, which is not an action likely to occur to the imagination of the average story-teller.
- The rather intricate matter from Marseilles
- Mrs. Etherege, whose husband Holmes found so easy when the police and everyone had given him up for dead
- Windibank, who will rise from crime to crime until he does something very bad, and ends on a gallows. *(An Untold Case previously unlisted and newly identified for this volume by David Marcum.)*

"The Boscombe Valley Mystery"
NONE LISTED

"The Five Orange Pips"
- The adventure of the Paradol Chamber
- The Amateur Mendicant Society, who held a luxurious club in the lower vault of a furniture warehouse
- The facts connected with the disappearance of the British barque *Sophy Anderson*
- The singular adventures of the Grice-Patersons in the island of Uffa
- The Camberwell poisoning case, in which, as may be remembered, Holmes was able, by winding up the dead man's watch, to prove that it had been wound up two hours before, and that therefore the deceased had gone to bed within that time – a deduction which was of the greatest importance in clearing up the case
- Holmes saved Major Prendergast in the Tankerville Club scandal. He was wrongfully accused of cheating at cards
- Holmes has been beaten four times – three times by men and once by a woman

"The Man with the Twisted Lip"
- The rascally Lascar who runs The Bar of Gold in Upper Swandam Lane has sworn to have vengeance upon Holmes

"The Adventure of the Blue Carbuncle"
NONE LISTED

"The Adventure of the Speckled Band"
- Mrs. Farintosh and an opal tiara. (It was before Watson's time)

"The Adventure of the Engineer's Thumb"
- Colonel Warburton's madness

"The Adventure of the Noble Bachelor"
- The letter from a fishmonger
- The letter a tide-waiter
- The service for Lord Backwater

373

- The little problem of the Grosvenor Square furniture van
- The service for the King of Scandinavia

"The Adventure of the Beryl Coronet"
NONE LISTED

"The Adventure of the Copper Beeches"
NONE LISTED

The Memoirs of Sherlock Holmes

"Silver Blaze"
NONE LISTED

"The Cardboard Box"
- Aldridge, who helped in the bogus laundry affair

"The Yellow Face"
- The (First) Adventure of the Second Stain was a failure which present[s] the strongest features of interest

'The Stockbroker's Clerk"
NONE LISTED

"The "Gloria Scott"
NONE LISTED

"The Musgrave Ritual"
- The Tarleton murders
- The case of Vamberry, the wine merchant
- The adventure of the old Russian woman
- The singular affair of the aluminum crutch
- A full account of Ricoletti of the club foot and his abominable wife
- The two cases before the Musgrave Ritual from Holmes's fellow students

"The Reigate Squires"
- The whole question of the Netherland-Sumatra Company and of the colossal schemes of Baron Maupertuis

The Crooked Man"
NONE LISTED

The Resident Patient"
* [Catalepsy] is a very easy complaint to imitate. Holmes has done it himself.

"The Greek Interpreter"
* Mycroft expected to see Holmes round last week to consult me over that Manor House case. It was Adams, of course
* Some of Holmes's most interesting cases have come to him through Mycroft

"The Naval Treaty"
* The (Second) adventure of the Second Stain, which dealt with interest of such importance and implicated so many of the first families in the kingdom that for many years it would be impossible to make it public. No case, however, in which Holmes was engaged had ever illustrated the value of his analytical methods so clearly or had impressed those who were associated with him so deeply. Watson still retained an almost verbatim report of the interview in which Holmes demonstrated the true facts of the case to Monsieur Dubugue of the Paris police, and Fritz von Waldbaum, the well-known specialist of Dantzig, both of whom had wasted their energies upon what proved to be side-issues. The new century will have come, however, before the story could be safely told.
* The Adventure of the Tired Captain
* A very commonplace little murder. If it [this paper] turns red, it means a man's life . . . .

"The Final Problem"
* The engagement for the French Government upon a matter of supreme importance
* The assistance to the Royal Family of Scandinavia

The Return of Sherlock Holmes

"The Adventure of the Empty House"

- Holmes traveled for two years in Tibet (as) a Norwegian named Sigerson, amusing himself by visiting Lhassa [*sic*] and spending some days with the head Llama [*sic*]
- Holmes traveled in Persia
- . . . looked in at Mecca . . .
- . . . and paid a short but interesting visit to the Khalifa at Khartoum
- Returning to France, Holmes spent some months in a research into the coal-tar derivatives, which he conducted in a laboratory at Montpelier [*sic*], in the South of France
- Mathews, who knocked out Holmes's left canine in the waiting room at Charing Cross
- The death of Mrs. Stewart, of Lauder, in 1887
- Morgan the poisoner
- Merridew of abominable memory
- The Molesey Mystery (Inspector Lestrade's Case. He handled it fairly well.)
- Three undetected murders in one year. Lestrade wants want a little unofficial help. *(An Untold Case previously unlisted and newly identified for this volume by Alan Dimes.)*

"The Adventure of the Norwood Builder"
- The case of the papers of ex-President Murillo
- The shocking affair of the Dutch steamship, *Friesland*, which so nearly cost both Holmes and Watson their lives
- That terrible murderer, Bert Stevens, who wanted Holmes and Watson to get him off in '87

"The Adventure of the Dancing Men"
  NONE LISTED

"The Adventure of the Solitary Cyclist"
- The peculiar persecution of John Vincent Harden, the well-known tobacco millionaire
- It was near Farnham that Holmes and Watson took Archie Stamford, the forger

"The Adventure of the Priory School"
- Holmes was retained in the case of the Ferrers Documents
- The Abergavenny murder, which is coming up for trial

"The Adventure of Black Peter"
- The sudden death of Cardinal Tosca – an inquiry which was carried out by him at the express desire of His Holiness the Pope
- The arrest of Wilson, the notorious canary-trainer, which removed a plague-spot from the East-End of London.

"The Adventure of Charles Augustus Milverton"
- Milverton paid seven hundred pounds to a footman for a note two lines in length, and that the ruin of a noble family was the result. *(An Untold Case previously unlisted and newly identified for this volume by Chris Chan.)*

"The Adventure of the Six Napoleons"
- The dreadful business of the Abernetty family, which was first brought to Holmes's attention by the depth which the parsley had sunk into the butter upon a hot day
- The Conk-Singleton forgery case
- Holmes was consulted upon the case of the disappearance of the black pearl of the Borgias, but was unable to throw any light upon it

"The Adventure of the Three Students"
- Some laborious researches in Early English charters

"The Adventure of the Golden Pince-Nez"
- The repulsive story of the red leech
- . . . and the terrible death of Crosby, the banker
- The Addleton tragedy
- . . . and the singular contents of the ancient British barrow
- The famous Smith-Mortimer succession case
- The tracking and arrest of Huret, the boulevard assassin

"The Adventure of the Missing Three-Quarter"
- Henry Staunton, whom Holmes helped to hang
- Arthur H. Staunton, the rising young forger

"The Adventure of the Abbey Grange"
- Hopkins called Holmes in seven times, and on each occasion his summons was entirely justified

"The Adventure of the Second Stain"

- The woman at Margate. No powder on her nose – that proved to be the correct solution. How can one build on such a quicksand? A woman's most trivial action may mean volumes, or their most extraordinary conduct may depend upon a hairpin or a curling-tong

The Hound of the Baskervilles

- That little affair of the Vatican cameos, in which Holmes obliged the Pope
- The little case in which Holmes had the good fortune to help Messenger Manager Wilson
- One of the most revered names in England is being besmirched by a blackmailer, and only Holmes can stop a disastrous scandal
- The atrocious conduct of Colonel Upwood in connection with the famous card scandal at the Nonpareil Club
- Holmes defended the unfortunate Mme. Montpensier from the charge of murder that hung over her in connection with the death of her stepdaughter Mlle. Carere, the young lady who, as it will be remembered, was found six months later alive and married in New York

The Valley of Fear

- Twice already Holmes had helped Inspector Macdonald

His Last Bow

"The Adventure of Wisteria Lodge"
- The locking-up Colonel Carruthers

"The Adventure of the Red Circle"
- The affair last year for Mr. Fairdale Hobbs
- The Long Island cave mystery

"The Adventure of the Bruce-Partington Plans"
- Brooks . . .

378

- ... or Woodhouse, or any of the fifty men who have good reason for taking Holmes's life

"The Adventure of the Dying Detective"
NONE LISTED

"The Disappearance of Lady Frances Carfax"
- Holmes cannot possibly leave London while old Abrahams is in such mortal terror of his life

"The Adventure of the Devil's Foot"
- Holmes's dramatic introduction to Dr. Moore Agar, of Harley Street

"His Last Bow"
- Holmes started his pilgrimage at Chicago . . .
- . . . graduated in an Irish secret society at Buffalo
- . . . gave serious trouble to the constabulary at Skibbareen
- Holmes saves Count Von und Zu Grafenstein from murder by the Nihilist Klopman

The Case-Book of Sherlock Holmes

"The Adventure of the Illustrious Client"
- Negotiations with Sir George Lewis over the Hammerford Will case

"The Adventure of the Blanched Soldier"
- The Abbey School in which the Duke of Greyminster was so deeply involved
- The commission from the Sultan of Turkey which required immediate action
- The professional service for Sir James Saunders

"The Adventure of the Mazarin Stone"
- Old Baron Dowson said the night before he was hanged that in Holmes's case what the law had gained the stage had lost
- The death of old Mrs. Harold, who left Count Sylvius the Blymer estate
- The compete life history of Miss Minnie Warrender

379

- The robbery in the train de-luxe to the Riviera on February 13, 1892

"The Adventure of the Three Gables"
- The killing of young Perkins outside the Holborn Bar
- Mortimer Maberly, was one of Holmes's early clients

"The Adventure of the Sussex Vampire"
- *Matilda Briggs*, a ship which is associated with the giant rat of Sumatra, a story for which the world is not yet prepared
- Victor Lynch, the forger
- Venomous lizard, or Gila. Remarkable case, that!
- Vittoria the circus belle
- Vanderbilt and the Yeggman
- Vigor, the Hammersmith wonder

"The Adventure of the Three Garridebs"
- Holmes refused a knighthood for services which may, someday, be described

"The Problem of Thor Bridge"
- Mr. James Phillimore who, stepping back into his own house to get his umbrella, was never more seen in this world
- The cutter *Alicia*, which sailed one spring morning into a patch of mist from where she never again emerged, nor was anything further ever heard of herself and her crew.
- Isadora Persano, the well-known journalist and duelist who was found stark staring mad with a match box in front of him which contained a remarkable worm said to be unknown to science

"The Adventure of the Creeping Man"
NONE LISTED

"The Adventure of the Lion's Mane"
NONE LISTED

"The Adventure of the Veiled Lodger"
- The whole story concerning the politician, the lighthouse, and the trained cormorant

380

"The Adventure of Shoscombe Old Place"
- Holmes ran down that coiner by the zinc and copper filings in the seam of his cuff
- The St. Pancras case, where a cap was found beside the dead policeman. The accused man denied that it is his. But he was a picture-frame maker who habitually handled glue.
  - "Is it one of your cases?" Merivale of the Yard asked Holmes to look into it

"The Adventure of the Retired Colourman"
- The case of the two Coptic Patriarchs

About the Contributors

The following contributors appear in this volume:
The MX Book of New Sherlock Holmes Stories
Part XL – Further Untold Cases (1879-1886)

Mike Adamson holds a Doctoral degree from Flinders University of South Australia. After early aspirations in art and writing, Mike secured qualifications in both marine biology and archaeology. Mike has been a university educator since 2006, has worked in the replication of convincing ancient fossils, is a passionate photographer, master-level hobbyist, and journalist for international magazines. Short fiction sales include to *Metastellar, Strand Magazine, Little Blue Marble, Abyss*, and *Apex, Daily Science Fiction, Compelling Science Fiction*, and *Nature Futures*. Mike has placed some two-hundred stories to date, totaling over a million words. Mike has completed his first Sherlock Holmes novel with Belanger Books, and will be appearing in translation in European magazines. You can catch up with his journey at his blog "The View From the Keyboard" *http://mike-adamson.blogspot.com*

Tim Newton Anderson is a former senior daily newspaper journalist and PR manager who has recently started writing fiction. In the past six months, he has placed fourteen stories in publications including *Parsec Magazine, Tales of the Shadowmen, SF Writers Guild, Zoetic Press, Dark Lane Books, Dark Horses Magazine, Emanations*, and *Planet Bizarro*.

Hugh Ashton was born in the U.K., and moved to Japan in 1988, where he remained until 2016, living with his wife Yoshiko in the historic city of Kamakura, a little to the south of Yokohama. He and Yoshiko have now moved to Lichfield, a small cathedral city in the Midlands of the U.K., the birthplace of Samuel Johnson, and one-time home of Erasmus Darwin. In the past, he has worked in the technology and financial services industries, which have provided him with material for some of his books set in the 21st century. He currently works as a writer: Novelist, freelance editor, and copywriter, (his work for large Japanese corporations has appeared in international business journals), and journalist, as well as producing industry reports on various aspects of the financial services industry. However, his lifelong interest in Sherlock Holmes has developed into an acclaimed series of adventures
featuring the world's most famous detective, written in the style of the originals. In addition to these, he has also published historical and alternate historical novels, short stories, and thrillers. Together with artist Andy Boerger, he has produced the *Sherlock Ferret* series of stories for children, featuring the world's cutest detective.

Brian Belanger, PSI, is a publisher, illustrator, graphic designer, editor, and author. In 2015, he co-founded Belanger Books publishing company along with his brother, author Derrick Belanger. His illustrations have appeared in *The Essential Sherlock Holmes* and *Sherlock Holmes: A Three-Pipe Christmas*, and in children's books such as *The MacDougall Twins with Sherlock Holmes* series, *Dragonella*, and *Scones and Bones on Baker Street*. Brian has published a number of Sherlock Holmes anthologies and novels through Belanger Books, as well as new editions of August Derleth's classic Solar Pons mysteries. Brian continues to design all of the covers for Belanger Books, and since 2016 he has designed the majority of book covers for MX Publishing. In 2019, Brian received his investiture in the PSI as "Sir Ronald Duveen." More recently, he illustrated a comic

book featuring the band The Moonlight Initiative, created the logo for the Arthur Conan Doyle Society and designed *The Great Game of Sherlock Holmes* card game. Find him online at:
www.belangerbooks.com and
www.redbubble.com/people/zhahadun and
zhahadun.wixsite.com/221b

Alan Dimes was born in Northwest London and graduated from Sussex University with a BA in English Literature. He has spent most of his working life teaching English. Living in the Czech Republic since 2003, he is now semi-retired and divides his time between Prague and his country cottage. He has also written some fifty stories of horror and fantasy and thirty stories about his husband-and-wife detectives, Peter and Deirdre Creighton, set in the 1930's.

Sir Arthur Conan Doyle (1859-1930) *Holmes Chronicler Emeritus.* If not for him, this anthology would not exist. Author, physician, patriot, sportsman, spiritualist, husband and father, and advocate for the oppressed. He is remembered and honored for the purposes of this collection by being the man who introduced Sherlock Holmes to the world. Through fifty-six Holmes short stories, four novels, and additional Apocryphal entries, Doyle revolutionized mystery stories and also greatly influenced and improved police forensic methods and techniques for the betterment of all. *Steel True Blade Straight.*

Steve Emecz's main field is technology, in which he has been working for about twenty-five years. Steve is a regular speaker at trade shows and his tech career has taken him to more than fifty countries – so he's no stranger to planes and airports. In 2008, MX published its first Sherlock Holmes book, and MX has gone on to become the largest specialist Holmes publisher in the world with over 500 books. MX is a social enterprise and supports three main causes. The first is Happy Life, a children's rescue project in Nairobi, Kenya, where he and his wife, Sharon, spend every Christmas at the rescue centre in Kasarani. They have written two editions of a short book about the project, *The Happy Life Story.* The second is Undershaw, Sir Arthur Conan Doyle's former home, which is a school for children with learning disabilities for which Steve is a patron. Steve has been a mentor for the World Food Programme for several years, and was part of the Nobel Peace Prize winning team in 2020.

Brett Fawcett is a humanities and Latin teacher at the Chesterton Academy of St. Isidore in Sherwood Park, Alberta. He lives with his wife and son in Edmonton, where he is a member of The Wisteria Lodgers (The Sherlock Holmes Society of Edmonton). He vividly remembers the first time he finished reading the Sherlock Holmes stories in Grade 6, and has been a student of Holmesian literature and scholarship since then. He is also a frequent author of columns and articles on topics like theology, education, and mental health, as well as the occasional mystery story.

Mark A. Gagen BSI is co-founder of Wessex Press, sponsor of the popular *From Gillette to Brett* conferences, and publisher of *The Sherlock Holmes Reference Library* and many other fine Sherlockian titles. A life-long Holmes enthusiast, he is a member of *The Baker Street Irregulars* and *The Illustrious Clients of Indianapolis.* A graphic artist by profession, his work is often seen on the covers of *The Baker Street Journal* and various BSI books.

John Atkinson Grimshaw (1836-1893) was born in Leeds, England. His amazing paintings, usually featuring twilight or night scenes illuminated by gas-lamps or moonlight, are easily recognizable, and are often used on the covers of books about The Great Detective to set the mood, as shadowy figures move in the distance through misty mysterious settings and over rain-slicked streets.

Arthur Hall was born in Aston, Birmingham, UK, in 1944. He discovered his interest in writing during his schooldays, along with a love of fictional adventure and suspense. His first novel, *Sole Contact*, was an espionage story about an ultra-secret government department known as "Sector Three", and was followed, to date, by three sequels. Other works include seven Sherlock Holmes novels, *The Demon of the Dusk*, *The One Hundred Percent Society*, *The Secret Assassin*, *The Phantom Killer*, *In Pursuit of the Dead*, *The Justice Master*, and *The Experience Club* as well as three collections of Holmes *Further Little-Known Cases of Sherlock* Holmes, *Tales from the Annals of Sherlock* Holmes, and *The Additional Investigations of Sherlock Holmes.* He has also written other short stories and a modern detective novel. He lives in the West Midlands, United Kingdom.

Paula Hammond has written over sixty fiction and non-fiction books, as well as short stories, comics, poetry, and scripts for educational DVD's. When not glued to the keyboard, she can usually be found prowling round second-hand books shops or hunkered down in a hide, soaking up the joys of the natural world.

Roger Johnson, BSI, ASH, PSI, etc, is a member of more Holmesian societies than he can remember, thanks to his (so far) 16 years as editor of *The Sherlock Holmes Journal*, and thirty-two years as editor of *The District Messenger*. The latter, the newsletter of *The Sherlock Holmes Society of London*, is now in the safe hands of Jean Upton, with whom he collaborated on the well-received book, *The Sherlock Holmes Miscellany*. Roger is resigned to the fact that he will never match the Du
ke of Holdernesse, whose name was followed by "*half the alphabet*".

Susan Knight's newest novel, *Death in the Garden of England* (2023) from MX publishing, is the latest in a series which began with her collection of stories, *Mrs. Hudson Investigates* (2019), the novel *Mrs. Hudson goes to Ireland* (2020), and *Mrs. Hudson Goes to Paris* (2022). She has contributed to many recent MX anthologies of new Sherlock Holmes short stories and enjoys writing as Dr. Watson as much as she does Mrs. Hudson. Nine of these stories comprise a new collection of hers, *The Strange Case of the Pale Boy and Other Mysteries* (2023). Susan is the author of two other non-Sherlockian story collections, as well as three novels, a book of non-fiction, and several plays, and has won several prizes for her writing. Susan lives in Dublin.

Gordon Linzner is founder and former editor of *Space and Time Magazine*, and author of four published novels and dozens of short stories in *F&SF*, *Twilight Zone*, *Sherlock Holmes Mystery Magazine*, and numerous other magazines and anthologies. He is a full member of the *Horror Writers Association* and a lifetime member of *Science Fiction and Fantasy Writers Association*.

David Marcum plays *The Game* with deadly seriousness. He first discovered Sherlock Holmes in 1975 at the age of ten, and since that time, he has collected, read, and chronologicized literally thousands of traditional Holmes pastiches in the form of novels, short stories, radio and television episodes, movies and scripts, comics, fan-fiction, and unpublished manuscripts. He is the author of over one-hundred Sherlockian pastiches, some published in anthologies and magazines such as *The Best Mystery Stories of the Year 2021* and *The Strand*, and others collected in his own books, *The Papers of Sherlock*

Holmes, Sherlock Holmes and A Quantity of Debt, Sherlock Holmes – Tangled Skeins, Sherlock Holmes and The Eye of Heka, and *The Collected Papers of Sherlock Holmes.* He has won first place fiction awards from *The Arthur Conan Doyle Society* and the Nero Wolfe *Wolfe Pack.* He has edited over eighty books, including several dozen traditional Sherlockian anthologies, such as the ongoing series *The MX Book of New Sherlock Holmes Stories*, which he created in 2015. This collection is now at forty-two volumes, with more in preparation. He was responsible for bringing back August Derleth's Solar Pons for a new generation with his collection of authorized Pons stories, *The Papers of Solar Pons* and *The Further Papers of Solar Pons.* Pons's return was further assisted by his editing of the reissued authorized versions of the original Pons books, and then several volumes of new Pons adventures. He has done the same for the adventures of Dr. Thorndyke, and has plans for similar projects in the future. He has contributed numerous essays to various publications, and is a member of a number of Sherlockian groups and Scions, as well as *The Mystery Writers of America.* His irregular Sherlockian blog, *A Seventeen Step Program*, addresses various topics related to his favorite book friends (as his son used to call them when he was small), and can be found at *http://17stepprogram.blogspot.com/* He is a licensed Civil Engineer, living in Tennessee with his wife and son. Since the age of nineteen, he has worn a deerstalker as his regular-and-only hat. In 2013, he and his deerstalker were finally able make his first trip-of-a-lifetime Holmes Pilgrimage to England, with return Pilgrimages in 2015 and 2016, where you may have spotted him. If you ever run into him and his deerstalker out and about, feel free to say hello!

Tom Mead is a UK-based author and Golden Age Mystery aficionado. His debut novel, *Death and the Conjuror*, was an international bestseller, and named one of the best mysteries of 2022 by *Publishers Weekly.* The sequel, *The Murder Wheel*, was published in July 2023, and described as "compelling" by *Crimereads* and "pure nostalgic pleasure" by the *Wall Street Journal.* His short fiction has appeared in *Ellery Queen's Mystery Magazine, Alfred Hitchcock Mystery Magazine*, and *The Best Mystery Stories of the Year*, edited by Lee Child.

Sidney Paget (1860-1908), a few of whose illustrations are used within this anthology, was born in London, and like his two older brothers, became a famed illustrator and painter. He completed over three-hundred-and-fifty drawings for the Sherlock Holmes stories that were first published in *The Strand* magazine, defining Holmes's image forever after in the public mind.

Tracy J. Revels, a Sherlockian from the age of eleven, is a professor of history at Wofford College in Spartanburg, South Carolina. She is a member of *The Survivors of the Gloria Scott* and *The Studious Scarlets Society*, and is a past recipient of the Beacon Society Award. Almost every semester, she teaches a class that covers The Canon, either to college students or to senior citizens. She is also the author of three supernatural Sherlockian pastiches with MX (*Shadowfall, Shadowblood*, and *Shadowwraith*), and a regular contributor to her scion's newsletter. She also has some notoriety as an author of very silly skits: For proof, see "The Adventure of the Adversarial Adventuress" and "Occupy Baker Street" on YouTube. When not studying Sherlock, she can be found researching the history of her native state, and has written books on Florida in the Civil War and on the development of Florida's tourism industry.

Roger Riccard's family history has Scottish roots, which trace his lineage back to Highland Scotland. This British Isles ancestry encouraged his interest in the writings of Sir Arthur Conan Doyle at an early age. He has authored the novels, *Sherlock Holmes & The*

Case of the Poisoned Lilly, and *Sherlock Holmes & The Case of the Twain Papers*. In addition he has produced several short stories in *Sherlock Holmes Adventures for the Twelve Days of Christmas* and the series *A Sherlock Holmes Alphabet of Cases*. A new series will begin publishing in the Autumn of 2022, and his has another novel in the works. All of his books have been published by Baker Street Studios. His Bachelor of Arts Degrees in both Journalism and History from California State University, Northridge, have proven valuable to his writing historical fiction, as well as the encouragement of his wife/editor/inspiration and Sherlock Holmes fan, Rosilyn. She passed in 2021, and it is in her memory that he continues to contribute to the legacy of the *"man who never lived and will never die"*.

Jane Rubino is the author of *A Jersey Shore* mystery series, featuring a Jane Austen-loving amateur sleuth and a Sherlock Holmes-quoting detective, *Knight Errant, Lady Vernon and Her Daughter*, (a novel-length adaptation of Jane Austen's novella *Lady Susan*, co-authored with her daughter Caitlen Rubino-Bradway, *What Would Austen Do?*, also co-authored with her daughter, a short story in the anthology *Jane Austen Made Me Do It*, *The Rucastles' Pawn, The Copper Beeches from Violet Turner's POV*, and, of course, there's the Sherlockian novel in the drawer – who doesn't have one? Jane lives on a barrier island at the New Jersey shore.

Fifteen of **Brenda Seabrooke**'s Sherlock Holmes pastiches have been anthologized in MX Publishing and Belanger Books, six in *Best Crime Stories of New England*, one in *Destination: Mystery* and *Mystery Tribune*, and twelve in literary reviews such as *Yemassee, Confrontation*, and one in *Redbook*. Twenty-two of her books for young readers have been published at Penguin, Clarion, etc., and won awards such as a Notable from the National Council of Social Studies, Junior Literary Guild, Hornbook Honor, an Edgar finalist, etc. She received a grant from the National Endowment for the Arts, and The Robie Macauley Award from Emerson College. In 2022, MX published her collection, *Sherlock Holmes: The Persian Slipper and Other Stories*.

Liese Sherwood-Fabre knew she was destined to write when she got an A+ in the second grade for her story about Dick, Jane, and Sally's ruined picnic. After obtaining her PhD, she joined the federal government and worked and lived internationally for more than fifteen years. Returning to the states, she seriously pursued her writing career, garnering such awards as a finalist in the Romance Writers of America's Golden Heart contest and a Pushcart Prize nomination. A recognized Sherlockian scholar, her essays have appeared in newsletters, *The Baker Street Journal*, and *Canadian Holmes*. She has recently turned to a childhood passion: Sherlock Holmes. *The Adventure of the Murdered Midwife*, the first book in *The Early Case Files of Sherlock Holmes* series, was the CIBA Mystery and Mayhem 2020 first-place winner. *Her latest book is a young adult fantasy Wilhelmina Quigley: Magic School Dropout*, which is available through all major booksellers. More about her writing can be found at *www.liesesherwoodfabre.com*.

Robert V. Stapleton was born and brought up in Leeds, Yorkshire, England, and studied at Durham University. After working in various parts of the country as an Anglican parish priest, he is now retired and lives with his wife in North Yorkshire. As a member of his local writing group, he now has time to develop his other life as a writer of adventure stories. He has published a number of short stories, and he is hoping to have a couple of completed novels published at some time in the future.

Award winning poet and author **Joseph W. Svec III** enjoys writing, poetry, and stories, and creating new adventures for Holmes and Watson that take them into the worlds of famous literary authors and scientists. His *Missing Authors* trilogy introduced Holmes to Lewis Carroll, Jules Verne, H.G. Wells, and Alfred Lord Tennyson, as well as many of their characters. His transitional story *Sherlock Holmes and the Mystery of the First Unicorn* involved several historical figures, besides a Unicorn or two. He has also written the rhymed and metered Sherlock Holmes Christmas adventure, *The Night Before Christmas in 221b*, sure to be a delight for Sherlock Holmes enthusiasts of all ages. Joseph won the Amador Arts Council 2021 Original Poetry Contest, with his Rhymed and metered story poem, "The Homecoming". Joseph has presented a literary paper on Sherlock Holmes/Alice in Wonderland crossover literature to the Lewis Carroll Society of North America, as well as given several presentations to the Amador County Holmes Hounds, Sherlockian Society. He is currently working on his first book in the *Missing Scientist Trilogy, Sherlock Holmes and the Adventure of the Demonstrative Dinosaur*, in which Sherlock meets Professor George Edward Challenger. Joseph has Masters Degrees in Systems Engineering and Human Organization Management, and has written numerous technical papers on Aerospace Testing. In addition to writing, Joseph enjoys creating miniature dioramas based on music, literature, and history from many different eras. His dioramas have been featured in magazine articles and many different blogs, including the North American Jules Verne society newsletter. He currently has 57 dioramas set up in his display area, and has written a reference book on toy castles and knights from around the world. An avid tea enthusiast, his tea cabinet contains over five-hundred different varieties, and he delights in sharing afternoon tea with his childhood sweetheart and wonderful wife, who has inspired and coauthored several books with him.

Emma West joined Undershaw in April 2021 as the Director of Education with a brief to ensure that qualifications formed the bedrock of our provision, whilst facilitating a positive balance between academia, pastoral care, and well-being. She quickly took on the role of Acting Headteacher from early summer 2021. Under her leadership, Undershaw has embraced its new name, new vision, and consequently we have seen an exponential increase in demand for places. There is a buzz in the air as we invite prospective students and families through the doors. Emma has overseen a strategic review, re-cemented relationships with Local Authorities, and positioned Undershaw at the helm of SEND education in Surrey and beyond. Undershaw has a wide appeal: Our students present to us with mild to moderate learning needs and therefore may have some very recent memories of poor experiences in their previous schools. Emma's background as a senior leader within the independent school sector has meant she is well-versed in brokering relationships between the key stakeholders, our many interdependences, local businesses, families, and staff, and all this while ensuring Undershaw remains relentlessly child-centric in its approach. Emma's energetic smile and boundless enthusiasm for Undershaw is inspiring.

*The following contributors appear
in the companion volumes:*
The MX Book of New Sherlock Holmes Stories
Part XLI – Further Untold Cases (1887-1892)
Part XLII – Further Untold Cases (1894-1922)

Tim Newton Anderson *also has stories in Parts XLI and XLII*

Deanna Baran lives in a remote part of Texas where cowboys may still be seen in their natural habitat. A librarian and former museum curator, she writes in between cups of tea, playing *Go*, and trading postcards with people around the world.

Donald I. Baxter has practiced medicine for over forty years. He resides in Erie Pennsylvania with his wife and their dog. His family and his friends are for the most part lawyers who have given him the ability to make stuff up just as they do.

Thomas A. Burns Jr. writes *The Natalie McMasters Mysteries* from the small town of Wendell, North Carolina, where he lives with his wife and son, four cats, and a Cardigan Welsh Corgi. He was born and grew up in New Jersey, attended Xavier High School in Manhattan, earned B.S degrees in Zoology and Microbiology at Michigan State University, and a M.S. in Microbiology at North Carolina State University. As a kid, Tom started reading mysteries with The Hardy Boys, Ken Holt, and Rick Brant, then graduated to the classic stories by authors such as A. Conan Doyle, Dorothy Sayers, John Dickson Carr, Erle Stanley Gardner, and Rex Stout, to name a few. Tom has written fiction as a hobby all of his life, starting with *The Man from U.N.C.L.E.* stories in marble-backed copybooks in grade school. He built a career as technical, science, and medical writer and editor for nearly thirty years in industry and government. Now that he's a full-time novelist, he's excited to publish his own mystery series, as well as to write stories about his second most favorite detective, Sherlock Holmes. His Holmes story, "The Camberwell Poisoner", appeared in the March-June 2021 issue of *The Strand Magazine*. Tom has also written a Lovecraftian horror novel, *The Legacy of the Unborn*, under the pen name of Silas K. Henderson – a sequel to H.P. Lovecraft's masterpiece *At the Mountains of Madness*. His Natalie McMasters novel *Killers!* won the Killer Nashville Silver Falchion Award for Best Book of 2021.

Chris Chan is a writer, educator, and historian. He works as a researcher and "International Goodwill Ambassador" for Agatha Christie Ltd. His true crime articles, reviews, and short fiction have appeared (or will soon appear) in *The Strand, The Wisconsin Magazine of History, Mystery Weekly, Gilbert!, Nerd HQ,* Akashic Books' *Mondays are Murder* web series, *The Baker Street Journal, The MX Book of New Sherlock Holmes Stories, Masthead: The Best New England Crime Stories, Sherlock Holmes Mystery Magazine,* and multiple Belanger Books anthologies. He is the creator of the Funderburke mysteries, a series featuring a private investigator who works for a school and helps students during times of crisis. The Funderburke short story "The Six-Year-Old Serial Killer" was nominated for a Derringer Award. His first book, *Sherlock & Irene: The Secret Truth Behind "A Scandal in Bohemia"*, was published in 2020 by MX Publishing. His second book, *Murder Most Grotesque: The Comedic Crime Fiction of Joyce Porter* will be released by Level Best Books in 2021, and his first novel, *Sherlock's Secretary*, was published by MX Publishing in 2021. *Murder Most Grotesque* was nominated for the Agatha and Silver Falchion Awards for Nonfiction Writing, and *Sherlock's Secretary* was nominated for the Silver

Falchion for Best Comedy. He is also the author of the anthology of Sherlock Holmes stories *Of Course He Pushed Him*.

Mike Chinn's first-ever Sherlock Holmes fiction was a steampunk mashup of *The Valley of Fear*, entitled *Vallis Timoris* (Fringeworks 2015). Since then he has written about Holmes's archenemy in *The Mammoth Book of the Adventures of Moriarty* (Robinson 2015), appeared in three volumes of *The MX Book of New Sherlock Holmes Stories*, and faced the retired detective with cross-dimensional magic in the second volume of *Sherlock Holmes and the Occult Detectives* (Belanger Books 2020).

Barry Clay is a graduate of Shippensburg University with a BA in English. He's dug ditches, stocked grocery shelves, tutored for room and board, cleaned restrooms, mopped floors, taught cartooning, worked in a bank, asked if you'd like fries with that (and cooked the fries to boot), ordered carpet for cars, and worked commission sales at Sears, and most recently a long-time veteran of the Federal employee workforce. He has been writing all his life, in different genres, and he has written thirteen books ranging from Christian theology, anthologies, speculative fiction, horror, science fiction, and humor. He volunteers as conductor of a local student orchestra and has been commissioned to write music. His first two musicals were locally produced. He is the husband of one wife, father of four children, and "Opa" to one granddaughter.

Martin Daley was born in Carlisle, Cumbria in 1964. His thirty-year writing career has seen over twenty books and numerous short stories published. Inevitably, Holmes and Watson remain his favourite literary characters, and they continue to inspire his own detective writing. In 2010, Martin created Inspector Cornelius Armstrong, who carries out his police work against the backdrop of Edwardian Carlisle. With the publication of the first Inspector Armstrong Casebook (published by MX Publishing), Martin became a member of the Crime Writers' Association. He lives with his wife Wendy, in Kirkcudbrightshire, in Southwest.

Alan Dimes *also has stories in Part XLII*

Paul D. Gilbert was born in 1954 and has lived in and around London all of his life. His wife Jackie is a Holmes expert who keeps him on the straight and narrow! He has two sons, one of whom now lives in Spain. His interests include literature, ancient history, all religions, most sports, and movies. He is currently employed full-time as a funeral director. His books so far include *The Lost Files of Sherlock Holmes* (2007), *The Chronicles of Sherlock Holmes* (2008), *Sherlock Holmes and the Giant Rat of Sumatra* (2010), *The Annals of Sherlock Holmes* (2012), *Sherlock Holmes and the Unholy Trinity* (2015), *Sherlock Holmes: The Four Handed Game* (2017), *The Illumination of Sherlock Holmes* (2019), and *The Treasure of the Poison King* (2021).

Arthur Hall *also has stories in Parts XL and XLII*

Stephen Herczeg is an IT Geek, writer, actor, and film-maker based in Canberra Australia. He has been writing for over twenty years and has completed a couple of dodgy novels, sixteen feature-length screenplays, and numerous short stories and scripts. Stephen was very successful in 2017's International Horror Hotel screenplay competition, with his scripts *TITAN* winning the Sci-Fi category and *Dark are the Woods* placing second in the horror category. His three-volume short story collection, *The Curious Cases of Sherlock Holmes*, will be published in 2021. His work has featured in *Sproutlings – A Compendium* *of Little Fictions* from Hunter Anthologies, the *Hells Bells* Christmas horror anthology published by the Australasian Horror Writers Association, and the *Below the Stairs, Trickster's Treats, Shades of Santa, Behind the Mask,* and *Beyond the Infinite* anthologies from OzHorror.Con, *The Body Horror Book, Anemone Enemy,* and *Petrified Punks* from Oscillate Wildly Press, and *Sherlock Holmes In the Realms of H.G. Wells* and *Sherlock Holmes: Adventures Beyond the Canon* from Belanger Books.

Paul Hiscock is an author of crime, fantasy, horror, and science fiction tales. His short stories have appeared in a variety of anthologies, and include a seventeenth-century whodunnit, a science fiction western, a clockpunk fairytale, and numerous Sherlock Holmes pastiches. He lives with his family in Kent (England) and spends his days taking care of his two children. He mainly does his writing in coffee shops with members of the local NaNoWriMo group, or in the middle of the night when his family has gone to sleep. Consequently, his stories tend to be fuelled by large amounts of black coffee. You can find out more about Paul's writing at *www.detectivesanddragons.uk*.

Kelvin I. Jones is the author of six books about Sherlock Holmes and the definitive biography of Conan Doyle as a spiritualist, *Conan Doyle and The Spirits*. A member of *The Sherlock Holmes Society of London*, he has published numerous short occult and ghost stories in British anthologies over the last thirty years. His work has appeared on BBC Radio, and in 1984 he won the Mason Hall Literary Award for his poem cycle about the survivors of Hiroshima and Nagasaki, recently reprinted as "Omega". (Oakmagic Publications) A one-time teacher of creative writing at the University of East Anglia, he is also the author of four crime novels featuring his ex-met sleuth John Bottrell, who first appeared in *Stone Dead*. He has over fifty titles on Kindle, and is also the author of several novellas and short story collections featuring a Norwich based detective, DCI Ketch, an intrepid sleuth who investigates East Anglian murder cases. He also published a series of short stories about an Edwardian psychic detective, Dr. John Carter (*Carter's Occult Casebook*). Ramsey Campbell, the British horror writer, and Francis King, the renowned novelist, have both compared his supernatural stories to those of M. R. James. He has also published children's fiction, namely *Odin's Eye*, and, in collaboration with his wife Debbie, *The Dark Entry*. Since 1995, he has been the proprietor of Oakmagic Publications, publishers of British folklore and of his fiction titles.

Naching T. Kassa is a wife, mother, and writer. She's created short stories, novellas, poems, and co-created three children. She resides in Eastern Washington State with her husband, Dan Kassa. Naching is a member of *The Horror Writers Association, Mystery Writers of America, The Sound of the Baskervilles, The ACD Society, The Crew of the Barque Lone Star,* and *The Sherlock Holmes Society of London.* She works in Talent Relations at Crystal Lake Publishing and was a recipient of the 2022 HWA Diversity Grant. You can find her work on Amazon.
https://www.amazon.com/Naching-T-Kassa/e/B005ZGHTI0

Susan Knight *also has a story in Part XLII*

David MacGregor is a playwright, screenwriter, novelist, and nonfiction writer. He is a resident artist at The Purple Rose Theatre in Michigan, where a number of his plays have been produced. His plays have been performed from New York to Tasmania, and his work has been published by Dramatic Publishing, Playscripts, Smith & Kraus, Applause, Heuer Publishing, and Theatrical Rights Worldwide (TRW). He adapted his dark comedy, *Vino Veritas*, for the silver screen, and it stars Carrie Preston (Emmy-winner for *The Good Wife*).

Several of his short plays have also been adapted into films. He is the author of three Sherlock Holmes plays: *Sherlock Holmes and the Adventure of the Elusive Ear*, *Sherlock Holmes and the Adventure of the Fallen Soufflé*, and *Sherlock Holmes and the Adventure of the Ghost Machine*. He adapted all three plays into novels for Orange Pip Books, and also wrote the two-volume nonfiction *Sherlock Holmes: The Hero with a Thousand Faces* for MX Publishing. He teaches writing at Wayne State University in Detroit and is inordinately fond of cheese and terriers.

David Marcum *also has stories in Parts XLI and XLII*

Kevin Patrick McCann has published eight collections of poems for adults, one for children (*Diary of a Shapeshifter*, Beul Aithris), a book of ghost stories (*It's Gone Dark*, The Otherside Books), *Teach Yourself Self-Publishing* (Hodder) co-written with the playwright Tom Green, and *Ov* (Beul Aithris Publications) a fantasy novel for children.

Adrian Middleton is a Staffordshire-born independent publisher. The son of a real-world detective, he is a former civil servant and policy adviser who now writes and edits science fiction, fantasy, and a popular series of steampunked Sherlock Holmes stories.

Will Murray is the author of some 75 novels, including some 20 posthumous Doc Savage collaborations with Lester Dent, and 40 books in the long-running Destroyer series. Other Murray novels star the Executioner, Tarzan of the Apes, The Spider, Pat Savage and the Mars Attacks characters. His book, *Nick Fury, Agent of S.H.I.E.L.D.: Empyre* (2000) foreshadowed the 9/11 terrorist attacks. Murray has penned more than 45 Sherlock Holmes short stories. Twenty of Murray's Holmes short stories have been collected as *The Wild Adventures of Sherlock Holmes*, Vols 1 and 2. His novelette, "The Adventure of the Vengeful Viscount", in which Tarzan of the Apes, otherwise Lord Greystoke, hires Sherlock Holmes to solve a mystery, was approved by both the Estate of Sir Arthur Conan Doyle and Edgar Rice Burroughs, Inc. Murray is the author of the non-fiction book, *Master of Mystery: The Rise of The Shadow*, which is an exploration of the famous radio and magazine character, and a sequel, *Dark Avenger: The Strange Saga of The Shadow*. *The Wild Adventures of Cthulhu* Vols 1 & 2 collect Murray's Lovecraftian short stories. For Marvel Comics, Murray created the Unbeatable Squirrel Girl with legendary artist Steve Ditko. Website: *www.adventuresinbronze.com*

Tracy J. Revels *also has a story in Part XLII*

Dan Rowley practiced law for over forty years in private practice and with a large international corporation. He is retired and lives in Erie, Pennsylvania, with his wife Judy, who puts her artistic eye to his transcription of Watson's manuscripts. He inherited his writing ability and creativity from his children, Jim and Katy, and his love of mysteries from his parents, Jim and Ruth.

Brenda Seabrooke *also has a story in Part XLII*

Kevin P. Thornton was shortlisted six times for the Crime Writers of Canada best unpublished novel. He never won – they are all still unpublished, and now he writes short stories. He lives in Canada, north enough that ringing Santa Claus is a local call and winter is a way of life. He has contributed numerous short stories to The MX Book of New

Sherlock Holmes Stories. By the time you next hear from him, he hopes to have written more.

DJ Tyrer is the person behind Atlantean Publishing and has had fiction featuring Sherlock Holmes published in volumes from MX Publishing and Belanger Books, and an issue of *Awesome Tales*, and has a forthcoming story in *Sherlock Holmes Mystery Magazine*. DJ's non-Sherlockian mysteries can be found in anthologies such as *Mardi Gras Mysteries* (Mystery and Horror LLC) and *The Trench Coat Chronicles* (Celestial Echo Press), and on *Mystery Tribune*.
DJ Tyrer's website is at *https://djtyrer.blogspot.co.uk/*
DJ's Facebook page is at *https://www.facebook.com/DJTyrerwriter/*
The Atlantean Publishing website is at *https://atlanteanpublishing.wordpress.com/*

Margaret Walsh was born Auckland, New Zealand and now lives in Melbourne, Australia. She is the author of *Sherlock Holmes and the Molly-Boy Murders*, *Sherlock Holmes and the Case of the Perplexed Politician*, *Sherlock Holmes and the Case of the London Dock Deaths*, *The Adventure of the Bloody Duck and Other Tales of Sherlock Holmes*, *Sherlock Holmes and the Curse of Neb-Heka-Ra*, and *Sherlock Holmes and the Hellfire Heirs*, all published by MX Publishing. She is currently working on her seventh book, *Sherlock Holmes and the Deathly Clairvoyant*. Margaret has been a devotee of Sherlock Holmes since childhood and has had several Holmesian related essays printed in anthologies, and is a member of the online society *Doyle's Rotary Coffin*, as well as being *a member of Sisters of Crime Australia*. She has an ongoing love affair with the city of London. When she's not working or planning trips to London. Margaret can be found frequenting the many and varied bookshops of Melbourne.

I.A. Watson great-grand-nephew of Dr. John H. Watson, has been intrigued by the notorious "black sheep" of the family since childhood, and was fascinated to inherit from his grandmother a number of unedited manuscripts removed circa 1956 from a rather larger collection reposing at Lloyds Bank Ltd (which acquired Cox & Co Bank in 1923). Upon discovering the published corpus of accounts regarding the detective Sherlock Holmes from which a censorious upbringing had shielded him, he felt obliged to allow an interested public access to these additional memoranda, and is gradually undertaking the task of transcribing them for admirers of Mr. Holmes and Dr. Watson's works. In the meantime, I.A. Watson continues to pen other books, the latest of which is *The Incunabulum of Sherlock Holmes*. A full list of his seventy or so published works are available at: *http://www.chillwater.org.uk/writing/iawatsonhome.htm*

The MX Book of New Sherlock Holmes Stories
Edited by David Marcum
((MX Publishing, 2015-)

"This is the finest volume of Sherlockian fiction I have ever read, and I have read, literally, thousands." – Philip K. Jones

"Beyond Impressive . . . This is a splendid venture for a great cause!"
– Roger Johnson, Editor, *The Sherlock Holmes Journal,*
The Sherlock Holmes Society of London

Part I: 1881-1889; Part II: 1890-1895; Part III: 1896-1929

Part IV: 2016 Annual

Part V: Christmas Adventures

Part VI: 2017 Annual

Eliminate the Impossible
Part VII: (1880-1891); Part VIII: (1892-1905)

2018 Annual
Part IX: (1879-1895); Part X: (1896-1916)

Some Untold Cases
Part XI: (1880-1891); Part XII: (1894-1902)

2019 Annual
Part XIII: (1881-1890); Part XIV: (1891-1897); Part XV: (1898-1917)

Whatever Remains . . . Must be the Truth
Part XVI: (1881-1890); Part XVII: (1891-1898); Part XVIII: (1898-1925)

2020 Annual
Part XIX: (1882-1890); Part XX: (1891-1897); Part XXI: (1898-1923).

Some More Untold Cases
Part XXII: (1877-1887); Part XXIII: (1888-1894); Part XXIV: (1895-1903)

2021 Annual
Part XXV: (1881-1888); Part XXVI: (1889-1897); Part XXVII: (1898-1928)

More Christmas Adventures
Part XXVIII: (1869-1888); Part XXIX: (1889-1896); Part XXX: (1897-1928)

2022 Annual
Part XXXI: (1875-1887); Part XXXII: (1888-1895); Part XXXIII: (1896-1919)

"However Improbable . . . ."
Part XXXIV: (1878-1888); Part XXXV: (1889-1896); Part XXXVI: (1897-1919)

2023 Annual
Parts XXXVII (1875-1889), XXXVIII (1889-1896), and XXXIX (1897-1923)

Further Untold Cases
Part XL: (1879-1886), Part XLI: (1887-1892) and Part XLII: (1894-1922)

<u>**In Preparation**</u> *. . . Part XLIII (and XLIV and XLV as well?)*
and more to come!

The MX Book of New Sherlock Holmes Stories
Edited by David Marcum
(MX Publishing, 2015-   )

Publishers Weekly says:

Part VI: *The traditional pastiche is alive and well . . . .*

Part VII: *Sherlockians eager for faithful-to-the-canon plots and characters will be delighted.*

Part VIII: *The imagination of the contributors in coming up with variations on the volume's theme is matched by their ingenious resolutions.*

Part IX: *The 18 stories . . . will satisfy fans of Conan Doyle's originals. Sherlockians will rejoice that more volumes are on the way.*

Part X: *. . . new Sherlock Holmes adventures of consistently high quality.*

Part XI: *. . . an essential volume for Sherlock Holmes fans.*

Part XII: *. . . continues to amaze with the number of high-quality pastiches.*

Part XIII: *. . . Amazingly, Marcum has found 22 superb pastiches . . . his is more catnip for fans of stories faithful to Conan Doyle's original*

Part XIV: *. . . this standout anthology of 21 short stories written in the spirit of Conan Doyle's originals.*

Part XV: *Stories pitting Sherlock Holmes against seemingly supernatural phenomena highlight Marcum's 15th anthology of superior short pastiches.*

Part XVI: *Marcum has once again done fans of Conan Doyle's originals a service.*

Part XVII: *This is yet another impressive array of new but traditional Holmes stories.*

Part XVIII: *Sherlockians will again be grateful to Marcum and MX for high-quality new Holmes tales.*

Part XIX: *Inventive plots and intriguing explorations of aspects of Dr. Watson's life and beliefs lift the 24 pastiches in Marcum's impressive 19th Sherlock Holmes anthology*

Part XX: *Marcum's reserve of high-quality new Holmes exploits seems endless.*

Part XXI: *This is another must-have for Sherlockians.*

Part XXII: *Marcum's superlative 22nd Sherlock Holmes pastiche anthology features 21 short stories that successfully emulate the spirit of Conan Doyle's originals while expanding on the canon's tantalizing references to mysteries Dr. Watson never got around to chronicling.*

Part XXIII: *Marcum's well of talented authors able to mimic the feel of The Canon seems bottomless.*

Part XXIV: *Marcum's expertise at selecting high-quality pastiches remains impressive.*

Part XXVIII: *All entries adhere to the spirit, language, and characterizations of Conan Doyle's originals, evincing the deep pool of talent Marcum has access to. Against the odds, this series remains strong, hundreds of stories in.*

Part XXXI: *. . . yet another stellar anthology of 21 short pastiches that effectively mimic the originals . . . Marcum's diligent searches for high-quality stories has again paid off for Sherlockians.*

Part XXXIV: *Mind-bending puzzles are the highlight of Marcum's fully satisfying 34th anthology, which again demonstrates that multiple authors are capable of giving Sherlock Holmes and Watson innovative mysteries to tackle while staying in character. Marcum's inventory of canonical pastiches shows no signs of being exhausted any time soon.*

The MX Book of New Sherlock Holmes Stories
Edited by David Marcum
(MX Publishing, 2015-   )

An Investees' Anthology
Edited by David Marcum
(MX Publishing, 2022)

Selected Contributions to
The MX Book of New Sherlock Holmes Stories
by Members of
The Baker Street Irregulars

*All royalties from this collection are being donated
for the benefit of the preservation of Undershaw,
a school for special needs students located at
one of the former homes of Sir Arthur Conan Doyle*

Stories, Forewords, and Poems in this volume
have previously appeared in Parts I – XXXVI of
The MX Book of New Sherlock Holmes Stories

Featuring Contributions by:

Mark Alberstat, Marino C. Alvarez, Peter Calamai, Catherine Cooke, Carla Coupe, David Stuart Davies, John Farrell, Lyndsay Faye, Sonia Fetherston, Jayantika Ganguly, Jeffrey Hatcher, Roger Johnson, Leslie S. Klinger, Ann Margaret Lewis, Bonnie MacBird, Stephen Mason, Julie McKuras Nicholas Meyer, Jacquelynn Morris, Otto Penzler, Christopher Redmond, Tracy J. Revels, Steven Rothman, Nancy Holder, Mark Levy (and Arlene Mantin Levy), Nicholas Utechin, and Sean M. Wright (and DeForeest B. Wright, III)

MX Publishing

MX Publishing is the world's largest specialist Sherlock Holmes publisher, with over five-hundred titles and over two-hundred authors creating the latest in Sherlock Holmes fiction and non-fiction

The catalogue includes several award winning books, and over two-hundred-and-fifty have been converted into audio.

MX Publishing also has one of the largest communities of Holmes fans on Facebook, with regular contributions from dozens of authors.

www.mxpublishing.com

@mxpublishing on Facebook, Twitter, and Instagram

Milton Keynes UK
Ingram Content Group UK Ltd.
UKHW040930160324
439502UK00001B/58